THE WOMAN IN THE VEIL

THE
WOMAN
IN THE
VEIL

A VICTORIAN MYSTERY

Laura Joh Rowland

CROOKED
LANE

NEW YORK

Published in the United States by Crooked Lane Books, an imprint of The Quick Brown Fox & Company LLC.

Crooked Lane Books and its logo are trademarks of The Quick Brown Fox & Company LLC.

Library of Congress Catalog-in-Publication data available upon request.

ISBN (hardcover): 978-1-64385-241-6
ISBN (ebook): 978-1-64385-242-3

Cover design by Melanie Sun
Book design by Jennifer Canzone

Printed in the United States.

www.crookedlanebooks.com

Crooked Lane Books
34 West 27th St., 10th Floor
New York, NY 10001

First Edition: January 2020

10 9 8 7 6 5 4 3 2 1

To Matt Martz, Jenny Chen, and the gang at Crooked Lane, for making this book possible

THE
WOMAN
IN THE
VEIL

London, June 1890

CHAPTER 1

"I just love dark passages that lead to God knows what," Lord Hugh Staunton says.

It's two o'clock in the morning, and we're outside a riverfront tavern whose sign, illuminated by gas lamps, reads, "Prospect of Whitby." The fog is so thick that the world seems to dissolve in its cold vapor. The Thames is so rank with the smell of dead fish and sewage that I can taste it, even though this is early summer and the stench is far from as bad as it gets. A distant foghorn bellows. I glance nervously around the deserted street. Shadwell is only a mile southeast of our home in Whitechapel, but it feels utterly remote, and the Prospect of Whitby is a notorious haunt of smugglers and thieves.

Mick O'Reilly aims his lantern into the narrow space between the tavern and the building next door. "Hurry, or we'll miss everything." Lanky and red-haired, fourteen years old, a former street urchin, Mick knows every inch of London's East End. Confident to a fault, he fears no danger until he's in the thick of it, and maybe not even then. He carries my tripod and flash lamp into the passage.

"After you, Sarah," Hugh says to me with a theatrical sweep of his hand.

I follow Mick, with my leather satchel and my trunk of photographic supplies. Hugh brings up the rear, lugging my heavy camera in its wooden case. An aristocrat from a wealthy family, he once belonged to the class of persons I only encountered when the wheels of their coaches splattered mud on me as I trudged along the street. A former popular man-about-high-society, he'd never worked a day in his life until two years ago, when his circumstances changed drastically for the worse. Now he and Mick are my partners in business, my comrades on late-night expeditions.

The river stench grows stronger. The fog dampens my face, invades my lungs. I shiver as anticipation mingles with dread and speeds up my heartbeat. At the end of the passage is a flight of wooden steps that lead to the water. They're slimy with algae. As we descend them, Hugh slips, stumbles, and curses under his breath.

"We should get hazard pay."

"We're paid quite well," I remind him. And we all enjoy the challenge. I'm as much attracted to danger as frightened by it—a quirk of my personality. But I sometimes yearn for the days when the most hazardous thing I did was taking portraits of fractious children at my photography studio. Now Mick, Hugh, and I are crime photographers, investigators, and reporters for the *Daily World* newspaper. Crime doesn't wait for morning, and scenes don't remain intact for long. The newspaper has informants who loiter around police stations, taverns, and other places where word from the streets comes in. The East End of London is rife with violence. Every day, sometimes more than once a day, I hear the knock at the door—or in the night, the rapping of a cane on my bedroom window—summoning my friends and me to a new scene. I've learned to sleep with one ear cocked and my equipment packed, ready to go.

"We won't keep gettin' paid unless we find somethin' good soon," Mick says. "Another deader from a brawl at a pub ain't gonna cut it."

That kind of crime scene, and many at which the victims were killed in alleys by cutpurses or at home by their relatives, constitutes most of our work. On the rare day without a murder, we photograph accident scenes. The inconvenient hours and hazardous conditions aren't the reason for our high salary. In the past, our photographs and investigations begot sensational stories that helped make the *Daily World* the bestselling paper in London and brought us the favor of its owner, Sir Gerald Mariner. But we've not produced anything lucrative in the six months since we solved the murder of England's top hangman, and our success has raised Sir Gerald's expectations.

"Mick is right," Hugh says. "We need another sensational murder case."

At the bottom of the stairs, we step onto black mud strewn with clamshells, rocks, dead fish, broken wine bottles, and clumps of debris. The low tide has exposed it all, like dirty secrets. I hear water lapping the shore, but the river is invisible under the shroud of fog. Voices and raucous laughter erupt nearby. To my left, some thirty paces distant, flickering lights from lanterns set on the mud illuminate shadowy human figures gathered near the water's edge. By now I have a second sense about crime scenes, and I know that this one is murder and the body hasn't been removed yet. We've a chance for good photographs. I've seen so many corpses that I've become inured, but I have an ever-present fear that the next will be the one I can't take.

"The hyenas have beaten us to the kill." Hugh's black humor doesn't hide how much he dreads the sight of death. His stomach is weaker than mine.

"What are we waiting for?" Mick says.

We trudge through the mud that sucks at our shoes. Buildings rise from a retaining wall that's coated with algae below the high-tide line. Boats sit on the exposed riverbed. Behind the Prospect of Whitby, people on a terrace lean over the railing. The crowd comes into focus as we approach. It's some dozen men and two women. Lewd cackles arise as they gaze at the ground in the center of the circle of lanterns. There I glimpse a pale human shape. We weave through the crowd, which smells of liquor. I take a deep breath, steel myself, and look down at the shape.

It's a woman lying on her back, completely naked. Her white skin gleams; her face is hidden by her long, tangled golden hair, which stirs in the moist wind. Full breasts with pink nipples point skyward. The river laps at her, covering her legs up to her knees with foam. She looks like a mermaid that has washed ashore—a wounded mermaid. Blood stains her hair near the scalp, and bruises mar her torso, arms, and thighs. Her knuckles are scraped, her fingernails ragged. My heart contracts as painfully as if squeezed by a fist. Crime scenes involving female victims are particularly difficult for me because I'm a woman myself and because of my past experiences.

"This could be our big break," Hugh says with a mixture of hope and shame. We've learned that a female victim is more interesting to the public than a male, and nudity is a titillating detail that sells newspapers. "But I'd hate to get it at this poor woman's expense."

"So would I." The spectators aren't the carrion-eaters; we are. We earn our "meat" from other people's misfortunes. I wish that just once I could save a victim, not take photographs for the public's ghoulish delight.

A big, burly fellow with whisker stubble shoves the man beside him and says, "Go on—I dare you." He and his comrade look to be English boatmen or dockworkers. Others among the men are pigtailed Chinese and dark-skinned Indians from the merchant ships or their local enclaves.

"He ain't got the balls," says one of the women. She's young, slim, and pretty, her black hair an upswept mass of ringlets, her dark eyes as sharp, hot, and glittering as fresh cinders. The neckline of her yellow frock is cut low to reveal as much of her bosom as the law permits.

The other woman giggles. She's plainer and plumper, with frizzed, puffed brown hair, and is dressed in blue. Both look akin to women of ill repute I have encountered.

The man accepting the dare swaggers toward the body. Small and long-armed like a monkey, he crouches and squeezes the woman's breast. The crowd guffaws. Appalled by this taking of liberties with the dead, I look around for the police. They're nowhere in sight. I fear the police for reasons that stem from my recent as well as my distant past. Usually, when I arrive at a crime scene before they do, I'm glad, but tonight I wish they would come.

The monkey man calls to someone, "How's this for a picture?" He grins, his hand still holding the woman's breast.

Now I see a man with a camera on a tripod. He wears spectacles, a derby, and a rumpled jacket and trousers. I recognize him as a photographer from the *Telegraph*. The competition has beaten us to the crime scene.

"Put me in the picture too." Another man, clad in a sailor's cap and middy, lumbers over to the woman and thrusts his hand between her legs.

The pretty black-haired woman jeers, "You can't get any action with a live woman, so maybe you'll do better with a deader." She and her friend laugh.

I'm usually shy with strangers, but I say, "Take your hands off her!"

"Have some respect for the deceased," Hugh says, careful not to look at the victim. His complexion is green and sickly, even though her condition is far from the worst we've ever seen.

"Who're you?" The burly, whiskered man's puzzled glance takes in Hugh, who's dressed in an elegant gray summer suit and silk bowler hat, and me, prim in my bonnet, brown jacket, and modest brown frock, my ash-blonde hair braided in a neat crown around my head. Mick always looks scruffy, no matter how new his clothes are or how fresh his haircut, and he fits in with this rough crowd; but Hugh and I look distinctly out of place.

"We're from the *Daily World*," Hugh says, and introduces us with a debonair bow. "Miss Sarah Bain, Mr. Mick O'Reilly, and yours truly, Hugh Staunton."

"Ooh." The pretty woman's glittery eyes fix on Hugh. "I'll take him."

Tall, slender but muscular, with blond hair and noble features, Hugh is among the handsomest men in London.

Her friend pouts. "You take all the good ones, Rose."

Rose curls her arm around Hugh's and bats her eyelashes. "Buy us a drink?"

"I'm sorry, Miss Rose," Hugh says with his usual good manners. He pats her hand before gently detaching himself. "I'm working tonight." He's also not interested in women. His preference for men led to his estrangement from his family and social set, his downfall from his privileged life. He and I are the best of friends, our romantic affections engaged elsewhere.

Rose looks disappointed. "Maybe some other time?"

The whiskered man beholds us in surprise. "Hey, didn't you solve the murder of the hangman? I've heard of you. You're famous."

Our role in the hangman's murder investigation and the newspaper stories about us have made us celebrities—a mixed blessing.

"Hello, Lord Hugh, Mr. O'Reilly, and Miss Bain," says the photographer, whose name is Craig. "Here to get the goods for Sir Gerald Mariner and earn your daily gold-plated roast goose?" He's among many of our counterparts who envy our success and would love to take us down a notch. "Well, I got here first. Piss off."

Mick snorts in derision. "There's no dibs on crime scenes."

"We'll see about that." Mr. Craig moves toward me like a steamroller ready to flatten anything in its path. "This is no job for a woman, even if you do sleep with Sir Gerald Mariner."

It's not the first time I've been accused—wrongly so—of improper relations with my employer. I march toward Mr. Craig, my shoulders squared, my chin high. Under my sedate façade, I have a temper that surfaces on not always convenient occasions—usually when I perceive injustice to myself or other people—with sometimes catastrophic results. Already angry with the men molesting the dead woman, I feel the familiar heat in my blood. Mr. Craig is about to get a tongue-lashing at best or a wallop with my satchel at worst.

Mick reads my intent in my face and steps between Craig and me. "Leave Miss Sarah alone."

Craig laughs. "Or you'll—what?" Almost twenty years older than Mick, but some four inches taller and twenty pounds heavier, he raises his palm. "Get a spanking?"

Mick puts up his fists. I say, "Mick, don't." Concern for his safety cools my temper.

But Mick has a temper too, and it's been short lately. He's in love with Catherine Price, a beautiful young actress who's not in love with him and refuses to see him. Sometimes he takes out his hurt on people who cross him. Now he swings at Mr. Craig. As Craig dodges, he bumps against his camera. It teeters on its tripod, then falls with a thud. The lens pops off and rolls into the river. Foamy, dirty water washes into the round hole on the front of the camera, where the lens had been attached.

"You little bastard!" Craig gropes for the lens. "See what you've done?"

"I didn't even touch it," Mick says with innocent glee.

The crowd laughs while Craig collects his damaged equipment. He points a finger at my friends and me. "You're riding high for a fall. I'll laugh when you crash."

"Good riddance!" Mick calls as Craig stalks off.

Hugh addresses the crowd. "Ladies and gentlemen, this is a crime scene. Would you kindly remove yourselves before you contaminate it?"

Monkey Man pinches the woman's nipple before he rises. "Are you a copper now?"

"No, but I'm an experienced private detective," Hugh says. Before we started working for the *Daily World*, he and Mick and I had our own private detective agency. It was formed out of necessity when Hugh had to earn his own living and I lost my photography studio. Mick joined us after he ran away from an orphanage. "My friends and I solved not only the murder of England's top hangman but also the Robin Mariner kidnapping." We mustn't mention the Jack the Ripper murders, our biggest triumph. Our role in the case is a deep, dark secret.

"That so?" Monkey Man says with a challenging grin, "Well, let's see you solve this one." He points at the corpse.

"I'll certainly try," Hugh says. "Tell you what—you can help me."

"Help you how?"

"You're all witnesses who may know something that could crack the case. If you help me find the villain who killed this poor woman, then I'll get your names printed in the newspaper. With your photographs." Hugh gestures toward my camera and me.

I watch the suspicion on the people's faces turn to pleased surprise and hear murmurs of assent. Hugh's charm is his great strength as a detective.

"First things first," he says. "Who found the body?"

"It were us." The plain woman points to herself and an Indian man. "We were in the pub, and we came out for . . . well, a breath o' fresh air."

Hugh favors the woman with his best smile. "Then you're the most important witnesses of all." She simpers. "When was this?"

"About an hour ago."

"Exactly what did you see?"

She points at the victim. "Her, lyin' there just like that—naked as the day she were born."

"Did you see anyone around? Or hear anything out of the ordinary?" When she and the Indian say no, he asks the crowd, "What about the rest of you?"

Everyone replies in the negative.

I suppose one of these people might be the killer, but I can't believe he would risk staying at the scene instead of fleeing into the night. "Does anyone know the woman?" I ask.

Heads shake. The whiskered man says, "It's hard to tell, 'cause of her face."

The wind lifts the woman's hair, and I see what was hidden underneath. Her face is a mask of blood; her forehead, cheeks, nose, and chin scored by jagged red cuts. Dark, swollen bruises circle her throat; whoever strangled her left fingerprints. My stomach lurches, and vicarious pain stabs my own face. *What monster could have done this?* The savagery seems so vicious, so personal— almost worse than the blows to her head and body that must have caused her death.

"Gorblimey!" Mick says.

Hugh gulps; his face turns even paler. I watch him struggle not to be sick in front of the bystanders and lose their respect. He clears his throat and says, "Terrible, terrible. All the more reason why we must catch her killer." He sidles away from the corpse. "Have you noticed anyone behaving suspiciously in the neighborhood lately?"

The crowd moves with Hugh. I lug my equipment nearer to the body and spread the tripod. As I adjust its height, my gaze wanders to the woman. She commands my attention as if she's calling me in a voice that I perceive with some sense beyond ordinary hearing. I mount the camera on the tripod, and when I peer through the viewfinder and crank the bellows to adjust the focus, I see her more clearly than with my unaided eye. She's slender and well proportioned, with a tiny waist and long, shapely limbs. Her blonde hair appears natural, not darker at the roots. Her skin is smooth; she can't be much older than thirty. She might have been beautiful when alive. I wonder what her name is. Was she the beloved treasure of her mother and father? Although there's no ring on her finger, she could have been married. Did she kiss her husband goodbye when he went to work this morning, and put her children to bed tonight? Someone must have tortured and killed her and dumped her here like garbage. Someone else must be waiting and praying for her safe return. Aching with sorrow for a life stolen in its prime, I fill the flash lamp with powder and open the camera's shutter.

The flash powder ignites with a loud bang. In the momentary white-hot light, the woman's image blazes, the blood on her hair shiny and crimson as enamel, the bruises on her white skin like red tattoos. I remove the exposed glass negative plate, insert a fresh one. I take photographs from various angles and distances, and each time I note some new detail. Her hair isn't wet and stringy, which it would be if she'd just washed up from the river. There's mud on her arms and thighs. Long scuff marks in the muddy ground, trampled over with footprints, lead toward the stairs. I take some shots of the surrounding area. I don't see a knife or other weapon.

Now I have more than enough photographs for the newspaper, but not the most important one. Sir Gerald—and the public—will want to see the worst that the killer has done. I crouch by the woman and wince as I lift the hair away from her face. The golden strands feel like silk floss. I force myself to bear witness to her ravaged features, and inside me swells the urge to know who did the evil, and to see justice done. As I tuck her hair behind her ear, I feel a faint, fleeting, damp warmth on my bare wrist.

My heart jolts.

I freeze.

Then I hear a soft noise like liquid sucked through a whistle. I see mucous bubbles at her nostrils.

"Ma'am?" I say. "Can you hear me?"

She doesn't answer, doesn't move. I touch her shoulder. It's cold. Maybe I only imagined that she breathed; maybe the process of decay pushed air out of her dead lungs. But a wild hope fills me. I put my ear to her bruised chest and listen.

I jump to my feet, looking for Hugh and Mick. They've left the crowd to greet two police constables who are descending the stairs. Dressed in tall helmets and blue uniforms, the constables carry bulls-eye lanterns that cast bright beams of light through the fog. I run toward them, waving frantically, my usual fear of the police all but forgotten.

"Sarah, what is it?" Hugh says.

"She's alive!"

CHAPTER 2

"Help!" I call as Hugh, Mick, and I jump out from the back of the police wagon. The top of the massive, palatial London Hospital is lost in the fog. "We've a seriously injured woman!"

Two orderlies run to the wagon and lift out the woman, whom we've wrapped in the rough, stained blanket used to cover the dead bodies that the wagon usually transports. They place her on a stretcher, and as they wheel her into the hospital, we run alongside her. It's three thirty in the morning, and heaven knows how long she's been unconscious. A few more minutes could mean the difference between life and death. I think of Polly Nichols, Annie Chapman, Kate Eddowes, Liz Stride, and Mary Jane Kelly—Jack the Ripper's victims. Once they were the closest people I had to friends. Their deaths haunt me because I tried to save them but failed. If I can save this woman, then I'm not just a carrion-eater after all.

We enter a large room that smells of bleach and echoes with voices, footsteps on the stone floor, and moans from patients lying on cots. "Oh God," Hugh says, gazing at men with their heads or limbs covered in bloody rags and a girl with open sores all over her bare legs. He sways as if he's about to faint.

Mick hustles him out the door. I stay with the woman. People flock around her, gape at her disfigured face. Some shriek;

others giggle or curse. A doctor in a white coat pushes past them, saying, "Stand back! This is hospital, not a carnival show, for Christ's sake!" He speaks with a Scottish accent. Middle-aged, he has sparse hair and a pudgy, sallow face. I see intelligence and compassion in the eyes behind his spectacles as he frowns at the woman.

"I'm Dr. Enoch," he says to me. "Are you her relative?"

"No." I tell him my name and quickly explain that the woman was found unconscious by the river and that I'm a newspaper photographer. "Nobody knows who she is. I'm here because she doesn't have anyone else."

"Then you'd better come with us, Miss Bain."

The orderlies wheel the stretcher away from the gawkers, down a hall. Dr. Enoch and I follow them to a small examination room. They move the woman to the bed, and a gray-haired nurse joins us. Dr. Enoch holds smelling salts near the woman's nose. She doesn't stir. Her eyes are half open, staring blankly. He takes her head in his hands and turns it to examine the bloody gash. In the harsh glare of the electric lights, she looks worse than ever, like a corpse ravaged by a tiger's fangs.

"She's in a coma. She probably has a concussion." He inspects the cuts on her cheeks and forehead and says to the nurse, "She needs stitches."

The nurse fetches a tray that holds needles, scissors, razor, thread, sticking plaster, gauze pads, and a bottle of alcohol. Dr. Enoch peels back the blanket, revealing the woman's naked body. Mud from the riverbed splotches the red bruises. He speaks in a tone of quiet, controlled outrage. "Who did this?"

"We don't know yet." My urge to find out grows stronger.

"He must have hated her," Dr. Enoch says, voicing my own thought. "To obliterate her face, her individuality, then leave her for dead . . ."

Another idea comes to my mind. "Perhaps he didn't want her to be identified."

The nurse trims, then shaves the blonde hair around the gash on the woman's head. As Dr. Enoch cleans the facial cuts, bruises around her eyes become visible. He says to me, "You can wait outside."

"No, I'll stay." When I'd told the police she was alive, they hadn't believed me. I had to argue with them until they listened to her heartbeat. If I'd taken the photographs and gone home, she might have died in the mortuary. I feel as if my brief, one-sided acquaintance with the woman has formed a connection between us, and I can't help fancying myself a guardian angel.

I grit my teeth and watch while Dr. Enoch sews. I imagine the pain of the needle piercing my own scalp and cheeks, the tug of the thread. Other patients moan in the distance, but she doesn't make a sound, doesn't even flinch. That she's unconscious seems a blessing. By the time Dr. Enoch is done, she looks like the rag dolls that little girls in Whitechapel carry about, her face a patchwork crisscrossed with stitches.

"Will she recover?" I say.

"That's difficult to predict." Dr. Enoch pinches the skin on her hand. It seems loose, and when he lets go, it stays up in a thin peak instead of flattening immediately. "She's dehydrated. If she doesn't regain consciousness soon . . ."

Neither of us wants to complete the sentence.

Dr. Enoch cleans her hands, applies healing ointment on their scraped knuckles and torn fingertips, and bandages them. After he leaves, the nurse bathes her and covers her with a clean blanket. She sponges mud from her hair and plaits it in two loose braids. "Such pretty hair," she says sadly. "You can go home and then visit her later."

I look at the window, surprised to see foggy daylight. I'm exhausted and hungry, longing for a meal and bed, but I say, "I'll stay awhile." Left alone with the woman, seated by her side, I speak because perhaps she can hear, even if she can't respond. "Don't be afraid. You're safe now. The doctor and nurses will take good care of you. You're . . ." I can't promise she's going to be all right. The damage to her face makes that questionable. "You're going to survive." I take her hand.

Her fingers, limp and cold, squeeze mine.

Startled, I say, "Are you awake?"

She doesn't reply. The rest of her body hasn't moved; her mutilated face remains still, her eyes now closed. It must be an involuntary muscle contraction, but it feels like a plea.

"I promise I'm going to find out who you are, and I'll make whoever did this pay." It's a solemn oath that I only hope I can fulfill.

Footsteps approach. Her hand relaxes its grip. I withdraw mine as I behold Detective Sergeant Thomas Barrett, the only policeman I'm always glad to see. Toughly handsome, with unruly dark hair and keen, crystal-clear gray eyes, he smiles at me. Three white chevrons, still new and fresh, brighten each sleeve of his blue uniform. I smile too as my heart leaps, and my exhaustion evaporates like dew in the sun.

"I saw Mick and Hugh outside," Barrett says. "They told me you were here."

I rise from my chair, into his arms. As we embrace, I feel the rush of desire that his nearness always arouses. I savor his warmth as I press my ear against the rough wool of his uniform coat and listen to his strong, steady heartbeat. His aliveness and his love for me are comforting after the night's encounter with mortality. Then I stand back, ashamed of expressing affection in a public place, even though the only other person present is unconscious and Barrett is my fiancé.

"What are you doing here?" I say.

"Is this the woman who was found by the river in Shadwell?" Barrett looks at her and sucks air through his teeth. "My God." After a pause, he says, "She's my new case."

I'm surprised. "How can she be? Isn't Shadwell outside your district?"

"Yes, but Inspector Reid pulled some strings and got the case transferred to us." Barrett doesn't sound happy.

"Oh," I say as comprehension dawns. His superior, Inspector Edmund Reid, has a vicious grudge against him. Reid thinks Barrett is responsible for some trouble he got into during the Ripper investigation in 1888. He can't prove it, but he's right. Since then, he's done everything in his power to get Barrett fired. He opposed Barrett's promotion to detective sergeant six months ago, after Barrett played a major role in solving the hangman's murder. Having failed, he's trying to make Barrett flub his new job and get himself demoted back to constable.

"This makes six murder investigations on my plate," Barrett says, "and my other five are nowhere near solved."

Reid gives Barrett the toughest assignments. "But you've solved other cases," I say, trying to boost his morale.

"Yeah—the fellow whose skull was cracked during a pub fight. The bartender told me the name of the killer. And the woman beaten to death by her husband, who confessed. I can't claim much credit for those."

I glance at the unconscious woman. "Why did Reid give you this case? It doesn't seem hopeless." Then again, the police probably thought that about the first Ripper murder. They've never caught the Ripper. Barrett, Hugh, Mick, and I are among the few people who know why they never will.

"Reid wants me running back and forth between Whitechapel and Shadwell, investigating this case on top of my others. He's hoping that if my bad record doesn't get me demoted, I'll drop dead of exhaustion."

He rubs his eyes, which have dark shadows underneath from late nights spent chasing elusive clues. We haven't seen each other in two weeks, and he's thinner than he was then.

"I'm worried about your health." I don't say that I'm afraid this case will be the straw that breaks his career.

Barrett smiles, grateful for my concern. "It'll take more than hard work to do me in." His smile turns rueful. "But I'm afraid we'll have to postpone our wedding even longer."

We became engaged in January, planned the wedding for April, and canceled it because of Barrett's heavy workload. I feel a terrible disappointment, which is a big switch from my attitude when he first proposed to me more than a year ago. Then, I was ambivalent about marriage. My parents' marriage had been troubled, and I couldn't picture myself happily wed. Other issues related to my past further complicate my feelings. I have a deep, ingrained fear that every man I love will abandon me. But Barrett has proven himself steadfast and loyal, and remained as deeply in love with me as I am with him, despite circumstances that would have sent any other suitor running. I've experienced my most joyous moments with him, and we've overcome difficulties that seemed insurmountable. But now that I'm eager for us to live together, see each other every day, and sleep together every night, practicalities are keeping us apart.

"That's all right," I say, not wanting to make Barrett feel worse than he obviously does.

"I just want to be sure I have a job, so I can support you," he says.

I once suggested that we could live on my salary if we had to, and he was aghast at the idea of my supporting him. The issue of whether I'll keep working after we're married is yet to be resolved. "I can wait as long as necessary." His parents won't mind the delay. They don't like my looks, my job, or my living situation; they wish he would find someone prettier and more conventional.

A male voice outside the door says, "Guv?" Police Constable John Porter joins us. He's taller than Barrett—who is of average height—and fifteen years older, in his forties. Gray strands lace his curly brown hair and beard. His figure is stout, his complexion ruddy. He's Barrett's only assistant. Other sergeants have two or more. Reid has kept Barrett shorthanded.

"Good morning, Miss Bain." PC Porter smiles at me and bows.

I smile too; I like him. "Good morning, Constable Porter." Barrett has told me that Porter isn't very sharp, and that's why he's never been promoted, but he's loyal to Barrett because he used to work with Barrett's father, a now retired constable.

Porter looks at the woman. "So this is the poor lass. Her own ma wouldn't recognize her." Pity darkens his twinkly blue eyes.

"She's our newest tough case to crack," Barrett says. "We'd better get started."

CHAPTER 3

Carrying my photography equipment, Hugh, Mick, and I dodge the pedestrians, carriages, cabs, and wagons that clog Fleet Street. My friends look wilted after our long night, and my own energy flags, but we've come straight from the hospital, instead of going home, because we've more work to do. The sun has burned away the fog, and it would be a beautiful, clear summer day if not for the smoke and steam from the printing presses, whose loud, mechanical clatter vibrates the air.

"We're gonna help Barrett solve the case, aren't we?" Mick shouts over the din. He and Hugh like Barrett and want him to succeed. They also hate Inspector Reid for things he's done to all of us, and they would love for Barrett to get the better of him. I too want to help Barrett, but we don't get to choose which crimes we investigate.

"It depends on Sir Gerald," I remind Mick and Hugh. "He decides what will make good stories for the *Daily World*."

"But you've a special angle," Hugh says.

"Yeah, Sarah, you saved that lady's life," Mick says.

I remember the cold, damp pressure of her fingers on my hand, like the bestowal of an obligation I can't refuse.

"I'll tell Sir Gerald that we should investigate the crime," I say. If he agrees, then perhaps I can identify the woman and reunite her with her family, as well as help Barrett deliver her attacker to justice and save his job.

The headquarters of the *Daily World* occupies one of many tall buildings on Fleet Street, where all the major newspapers are based. Its building reigns over the others, lordly with Greek columns, Moorish arched windows, and Baroque turrets. Above the giant clock on the corner juts the Mariner insignia—a marble sculpture of a ship, symbolic of Sir Gerald's past as a shipping magnate. Outside the main entrance stands one of the muscular, taciturn fellows that Sir Gerald employs as doormen, drivers, bodyguards, and only he knows what else.

"Sir Gerald wants to see you," the fellow says.

A current of anxiety speeds along my nerves. Sir Gerald has the power to make or break virtually anyone. He's done both to us, and we're already on our second or third chance with him. There can't be many more.

"We should have reported in with the photographs hours ago," Hugh says uneasily.

Inside the building, we hasten to the elevator that Sir Gerald recently installed so that he wouldn't have to walk up the stairs to his office on the top floor. Not many buildings have elevators; they're a newfangled, expensive luxury. The operator lets us into the little wood and brass cage. We've ridden in it before, but as it bears us upward with grinding gears and hissing steam, Hugh and Mick laugh like little boys on their first carnival merry-go-round ride. I know people here who won't ride in the elevator for fear that it will drop five stories and crash. When we get out, I sigh with relief.

The racket of machinery is muted up here; the odors of ink, hot metal, and motor oil not as strong. Stopping outside his office, we see Sir Gerald seated behind his desk and the *Daily World*'s chief bookkeeper in a chair opposite him, conversing while they pore over a ledger. Sir Gerald is in his sixties, big and stout; the body under his black suit and double-breasted waistcoat is still robust. His thick, coarse dark hair and beard are streaked with gray, his broad face permanently tanned and toughened by the elements and lined with age, but even while at ease, he radiates confidence and power.

He's a former slave trader who made part of his first fortune dealing in human lives. He made his second fortune in banking, where he ruined many competitors. Rumor says he murdered some of them. I believe it.

While we wait, I glance around the room. I remember the massive wooden desk, leather-backed chair, and lone painting—a ship in a storm at sea—from his office at the Mariner Bank. Other furnishings include shelves neatly stacked with back editions of the newspaper, a globe on a stand, and a telescope on the sill of the window that looks over the rooftops toward the distant river. The room is plainer and barer than one might expect, but I think it suits Sir Gerald, once a cabin boy who started from nothing, who must have stood in the crow's nest on a ship, gazing across distant vistas and imagining his brilliant future. It also suggests an emptiness in the heart of the man.

Sir Gerald doesn't look at us, but I know he's aware of our presence; he seldom misses a thing. He dismisses the bookkeeper and meets our gazes. His eyes are deep brown, opaque, and watchful. He beckons. We drop my equipment in the passage and troop into the office. Sir Gerald stands. Taller than Hugh, who's almost six feet in height, he cuts a formidable figure.

"Where the hell have you been?" He speaks with a rough Liverpool accent. He's proud of his humble origins and doesn't try to hide them. He's also a man who doesn't need to raise his voice to seem menacing. "You missed a call to a crime scene this morning."

He still runs his banking empire, but he takes an active role in the *Daily World*'s operation. I once heard him say, "I didn't get where I am by leaving my business in the hands of people who don't care about it as much as I do." He's aware of everything that goes on, thanks to countless informants and spies. Woe betide anyone who slips up.

Hugh, Mick, and I stand close together, seeking safety in our meager numbers. My feelings toward Sir Gerald are a complicated blend of awe, kinship born of things that he and I have in common, and fear. I don't trust him, but I'm attracted to his strength and ruthlessness.

"Something unusual happened at the crime scene last night," I say. "Please allow us to explain."

"This had better be good. I don't pay you to drag out one assignment to avoid the next." Sir Gerald folds his hands and waits. His black look reminds us that we haven't brought in a good story since the hangman's murder.

Uncomfortably aware that this could be the day we lose our jobs, I tell him that the woman found on the riverbed in Shadwell turned out to be unconscious, not dead. "I think this is a crime we should investigate."

"So there's no corpse. It's hardly worth a story on the back page, let alone an investigation."

I realize I'm going to have to sell him on this story, which is something I've never done before.

"Her face was terribly injured, and she hasn't been identified."

"Just another day in the East End," Sir Gerald says.

"The woman's a blonde," Hugh says.

"And she were naked," Mick says.

"A naked blonde in a coma, eh?" Sir Gerald's eyes glimmer with interest. "Tell me more."

Hugh and Mick look to me. Even though they want to investigate the case, they don't feel as strongly about it as I do. It's up to me to persuade Sir Gerald, and I can't show him the photographs as I haven't developed them yet. I'll have to use speech alone—not my strong point. I project my mind back to the riverbed and visualize the images that my camera captured.

"She looked like a mermaid washed ashore, with her legs in the water, and her long golden hair rippling in the wind." I try to make my manner more dramatic than usual. "When I put my ear to her chest and heard her heartbeat, it was like a miracle. In the hospital, when I spoke to her, she clasped my hand without waking." I extend my hand. "It was as if her soul was begging me for help."

I'm afraid I sounded like a bad actress in a penny dreadful show. But Sir Gerald beholds me with fascination, as though I've conjured up a blonde-haired, naked ghost who's attached herself to me. "You're right—there's a good story in that."

I smile, elated by my victory. Hugh and Mick regard me with admiration.

"We'll put it on the front page, with the headline 'Who Is Sleeping Beauty?'" Sir Gerald says. "We'll ask anyone who thinks they can identify her or her would-be murderer to come forward."

I'm horrified by the sudden turn that events have taken. He means to call her *Sleeping Beauty*!

Hugh clears his throat and says, "With all due respect, Sir Gerald, but she's not exactly beautiful, what with the terrible cuts on her face."

"Yeah," Mick says. "Wait'll you see the photos."

Sir Gerald shrugs. "It's a catchier nickname than 'Jane Doe.' It will attract attention. And if we want to identify her, attention is what we need."

Although I can't disagree with that, I say, "To call her a beauty seems cruel." If I awakened from a coma to find myself disfigured and dubbed 'Sleeping Beauty,' I would think it a mockery piled on top of my misfortune.

"Which is more important—being delicate or identifying her and catching the bastard who carved her up? Not to mention reuniting her with her family." Sir Gerald's eyes take on a distant, haunted look.

I perceive that he's thinking of his kidnapped baby son. He rarely talks about Robin, and it's a tacit rule that no one mentions the kidnapping in his presence. But I think he's interested in crimes not only because they sell newspapers; I believe he wants to catch criminals because of Robin, because of his unsatisfied hunger for vengeance. The man who owns banks, a newspaper company, and everything else money can buy has lost the thing he valued most—his child. He knows what it's like to be desperate for a missing loved one to come back.

That's what he and I have in common despite all our differences. That's why I can sympathize with him despite his evils,
both rumored and those I've witnessed.

Now Sir Gerald points at us and says, "I'm taking you off the
roster for photographing new crime scenes. You'll investigate this
case."

"Just what we wanted to hear," Hugh says.

"Yeah!" Mick grins.

"Thank you." I'm glad too, but we'll have to accept the cruel
angle he's put on the story, the shard of broken glass in the plum
pie. And his pressure to solve the case isn't my only other reason for
misgivings. "We'll have to tread carefully around the police." Our
investigation into the hangman's murder had dire consequences
for the paper as well as my friends and me.

"Don't worry about the police. They'll let you in on their
investigations, and they won't interfere with yours." Sir Gerald
explains, "I've twisted some arms in high places and worked out
a deal."

"Great!" Mick says.

Hugh and I glance at each other in trepidation. "What does
that mean, 'let us in on their investigations'?" I say.

Sir Gerald spreads his hands. "Anything you want, as long as
you bring me the story."

I doubt that his friends agreed to a deal that only benefited
him. "In exchange for what?"

"The *Daily World*'s stories will bring in tips from the public
and help the police solve cases." Sir Gerald sounds pleased to com-
bine crusading for justice with turning a profit. "I'll throw in a
little praise for the boys in blue. That'll polish their reputation."

"Their reputation could use some polishing after the Ripper
murders." Hugh winks at Mick and me, reminding us that they
failed to solve that case, where we succeeded.

I wonder how Barrett will react to Sir Gerald's deal. I think
he'll welcome our help, but the police generally don't like outsiders

meddling in their work and conducting their own investigations. I can predict with great certainty that Inspector Reid will be furious.

Mick, restless with excitement, says, "Let's get started."

"Develop the photographs first," Sir Gerald says. "I want to see them before they go to press." He calls to someone behind us, "Come in."

We turn to see his son Tristan Mariner at the door. Tall, dark of hair and eyes, swarthy of complexion, and arrestingly handsome, Tristan says, "Hello, Father. Excuse me—I didn't know you had company."

"They were just leaving," Sir Gerald says. "You remember Miss Bain, Lord Hugh, and Mr. O'Reilly?"

"Of course." Tristan bows to me, nods at Hugh and Mick.

He quit the Roman Catholic priesthood five months ago, and he wears ordinary business clothes, but his manner is as grave as if he were in clerical garb at mass. Although he and Hugh barely look at each other, the passion between them seems to raise the temperature in the room ten degrees. They met when Sir Gerald hired my friends and me to find Robin, and they've been lovers ever since. That's why Tristan left the Church, which considers homosexual relations a sin. Hugh was delighted that Tristan chose him over his religious vocation, but I know that all is far from well. Homosexual relations are also against civil law, frowned on by society. When Hugh was exposed in the press, his family disowned him, and his aristocratic friends ostracized him. Tristan's homosexuality is still secret, but his exposure would create an even bigger scandal than Hugh's because he's a former priest and the son of Sir Gerald Mariner.

Sir Gerald is among the few people who know about Tristan and Hugh. He tolerates their relationship because he wants to be on friendly terms with his son, but he doesn't like it, and he's warned them to be discreet. In public places they have to pretend they're mere acquaintances. They can't afford one incriminating look, word, or touch.

"Tristan and I often have lunch together now that he works in town." Sir Gerald regards Tristan with proud, possessive satisfaction.

Tristan works at the Mariner Bank, learning the business, preparing to take it over when Sir Gerald retires. It's what Sir Gerald has always wanted—his heir out of the Church, following in his footsteps. But Tristan looks far from happy. Hugh tells me that Tristan is guilt-ridden about his sins and suffers from depression, insomnia, and migraine headaches. The adjustment has taken a severe toll on Hugh too. Sir Gerald has insisted that Tristan live at Mariner House, his estate on Hampstead Heath, in order to settle their stormy relationship and limit his contact with Hugh. He hopes Tristan will change his ways, marry a woman, and perpetuate the Mariner family line. Hugh and Tristan seldom see each other, and I know Hugh fears for their future.

"We'll be on our way, then." Hugh pretends to ignore Tristan as he and Mick and I move toward the door.

"Hugh, I want a word," Sir Gerald says. "Tristan, wait for me downstairs."

Tristan makes a hasty exit so that he won't have to walk with Mick and me. He's uncomfortable around us, although we're friendly toward him. He must be aware that we distrust him more than we like him. We're afraid he'll crumble under the weight of his guilt, leave Hugh, and break his heart.

When we're in the darkroom, as we mix chemical solutions and pour them into trays, Mick says, "I think Hugh's in trouble with Sir G."

So do I, but I say, "Maybe it's nothing."

Mick snorts. "What're they gonna talk about—the weather?"

This could be the day when the fragile accord between Sir Gerald, Tristan, and Hugh ruptures. I turn off the lights, and we develop the negative plates. Two hours later, when we're ready to print the photographs, Hugh joins us, his expression grim.

"What did Sir Gerald want?" I ask.

"I don't want to talk about it."

It must have been bad. "You were with him a long time."

"Not long. I went for a walk afterward."

When Hugh is in a disturbed state of mind, he goes for walks that sometimes last all night. Mick and I exchange worried glances but don't press him. I turn on the safe lamp, which is red because photographic paper isn't sensitive to red light. Red objects come out black in the prints. The lamp allows me to see while it mimics complete darkness. I insert the first negative plate in the enlarger. Hugh leans against the worktop, arms folded, and broods while I make exposures, and Mick transfers the sheets of photographic paper from one tray of solution to the next. As we clip the wet prints onto a string, Hugh musters his usual cheer.

"Excellent pictures, Sarah."

We behold the grisly images of the woman lying naked on the black mud, her blonde hair rendered white by the flash lamp. The bruises are dark smudges on her pale skin. In the close-up shots of her face, the mutilation is starkly detailed, as bad as the memory of my first impression. Most of my pictures of the scene are too dark, blurred by the fog, but in my long exposure of the Prospect of Whitby, the pub looks intriguingly sinister. The bystanders are like ghouls about to feast. The pretty black-haired woman named Rose grins.

"They'll be great in the paper," Mick says.

"The paper can't run photographs of people naked," Hugh says. "That would be illegal as well as scandalous. Sir Gerald will have to use only the close-ups of Sleeping Beauty."

I frown. "*You're* calling her that?"

"For lack of her real name," Hugh says, apologetic.

"By tomorrow, when the paper comes out, everyone'll be callin' her 'Sleepin' Beauty,'" Mick says.

"So we'd better make haste to identify her." I feel responsible for her, and my responsibility includes putting a name to her before she wakes up, shielding her from public mockery. And the fact that Hugh is at odds with Sir Gerald means we can't afford not to solve this case. "Let's go back to Shadwell and look for clues."

CHAPTER 4

I leave the negatives of my photographs with the engravers who will prepare the images for the press. Then my friends and I travel by train to Mark Lane station, and from there in a cab along Wapping Wall Road. The weather has warmed up; the sun filters through the haze of smoke and steam from factories. The afternoon light reveals the brick warehouses that darkness rendered invisible last night. Wagons filled with goods slow our progress. We disembark outside the Prospect of Whitby's three-story wooden building. Inside, the glare from the mullioned windows that overlook the river illuminates the wood paneling and columns, the nautical paraphernalia hung above the hearth, and customers at the bar and tables.

"I'm hungry," Mick says, sniffing the odors of food and ale. He's always hungry. He eats so much, making up for his famished years as a street urchin; he's growing fast.

My stomach growls. "It's lunchtime."

We sit at a table and consume ale and fish pie, which contains succulent cod and oysters in a buttery crust. The other customers eye us with the curiosity of regulars appraising strangers. The proprietor comes over and says, "New to these parts, are you?" He has a rough, genial red face, hair combed over his bald crown, and a pot belly.

Hugh introduces us and says, "We're from the *Daily World*. We were here last night about the woman who was found by the river. We came back to follow up on the story."

The customer at the next table fixes his bright, speculative, blue-eyed gaze on me. "I heard there was a lady photographer. So that was you." He's young, with a bronzy tan and cropped hair bleached white by the sun; a sailor hat sits by his plate.

"Do you know who she is?" I say.

"How would anybody know? Her face were hacked off."

Rumors are already spreading, the details being exaggerated. I reach in my satchel, pull out extra photographs of Sleeping Beauty that I printed, and lay them on the table. I realize that I too have begun to think of her by her nickname.

"Whoa!" the sailor exclaims. "But she ain't as bad as I were led to believe."

Before I left the *Daily World* building, I glued black paper rectangles over certain areas on the photographs of her body. The sailor tries to peel them off. Mick slaps at his hand, and he withdraws it.

"If she was your wife, how'd you like some bloke pawin' her picture?" Mick says.

The sailor grins sheepishly. The proprietor says, "Haven't seen any woman around here with hair like that. She must be from someplace else."

I ask the men if they saw anything suspicious last night. The proprietor shakes his head, and the sailor says, "I weren't here. My ship just got in from Africa this morning."

"Do you know of anyone hereabouts who might attack a woman?" Hugh says.

The proprietor's eyes narrow. "Not offhand."

I suspect he has some violent men among his customers, but tattling on them would be bad for business.

"What are you trying to do," he says, "catch the bastard and beat the coppers at their own game?"

I remember Sir Gerald's ill-fated contest between the *Daily World* and the police, in which we competed to solve the hangman's murder. "We'd like to catch him, but we also want to help the poor woman by locating her family. A story in the newspaper might bring them together."

"If you come by any useful information, would you please let us know?" Hugh gives the proprietor a card that bears his name and the address of the *Daily World*. "In the meantime, we'll have another look at the crime scene."

After paying for our lunch, we walk down the passage beside the pub. I see names and obscenities chalked on the brick walls. The pavement is damp, as though someone sluiced it with water. A moist breeze blows the river's stench toward us. At the end of the passage, we find a scene that's vastly different from last night. Barges move along the wide, gray, glittering water. At the quays along the bank, men unload cargo. The tide is higher; the boats that were grounded behind the buildings are now afloat. The mud on which Sleeping Beauty had lain is covered by at least a foot of water that's so murky, iridescent with oil slicks, and layered with debris that I can't see the bottom.

"Damnation. Any clues will have been washed away," Hugh says.

"We shoulda looked around last night," Mick says.

"Saving the woman's life was more important," I remind him.

"But perhaps not all of the crime scene has been obliterated." Hugh is ever the optimist, no matter how cruelly life has treated him. "I've been wondering how Sleeping Beauty got to the river-bank. My guess is that her would-be killer carried her down the steps. He may have left some evidence there."

We examine the steps. Those near the bottom are wet from the tide. The algae on them are littered with pebbles, clamshell frag-ments, and bird droppings. They look as they might have looked for years, with no obvious clues.

"She was naked while he carried her from the street?" I say. "Wouldn't that have attracted attention?"

"The fog were pretty heavy," Mick says. "No one woulda seen."

Hugh considers, then says, "Maybe he brought her in a carriage."

I picture a carriage stopping, a shadowy figure lifting out the nude, unconscious woman and lugging her down the steps. "But that would mean she was attacked someplace else, and this isn't the real crime scene."

Now we not only don't know who Sleeping Beauty is or who tried to kill her, but the one thing we thought we knew—where the crime occurred—is in question. It's a setback at a bad time. Our jobs hinge on this case. If Sir Gerald fires us, we could revive our private detective agency and my photography studio, but neither ever earned enough to support all of us. And in the hospital lies a woman who's depending on me to solve the riddle of her identity, who may die nameless while her loved ones suffer, not knowing her fate.

"If the real crime scene is someplace else, we'd better find it," I say.

We ascend the steps and walk up and down the road, trying to trace the woman's path to the riverbank. We see broken glass, fish bones, horse manure, tobacco shreds, spit, and dirty, crumpled paper. The fact that we don't know what we're looking for makes our task more difficult, and so many people have trodden and vehicles rolled over the area since last night. We stop passersby, show them Sleeping Beauty's photographs, and question them, to no avail.

"Anyone who was out late enough last night to see anything of interest to us is probably at home asleep now." I rub my tired eyes. "We could use some sleep ourselves."

Mick yawns. "Sir Gerald don't pay us to sleep."

"I'm at the point where I could fall over a big fat clue and not notice it," Hugh says.

"Let's go home," I say. "We'll come back tonight."

★ ★ ★

Our home is one in a row of eighteenth-century buildings on White-chapel High Street, in the sprucest, most prosperous and respectable part of the district. Three stories high, these buildings have attics set in gables, and whitewashed stucco fronts. Ours, located between a watchmaker and a jeweler, has "S. Bain Photographer & Co." painted in gold letters over the display window. My studio is on the ground floor, our residence above. Certainly, there are better loca-tions than Whitechapel, which contains some of London's worst slums and is known as Jack the Ripper's hunting ground. By day, our neighborhood is noisy with traffic and commerce; all night one can hear machinery clang in factories and the thunder of trains. But I love its vitality; Mick knows every inch of the streets he once lived on; and Hugh likes avoiding onetime friends who've shunned him. We moved in together after a series of events that included Hugh being disowned by his family, my eviction from my first studio, and Mick running away from the orphanage. At first, the idea of myself as a single woman living with single men troubled me. Certainly, people—including Barrett's parents—have told me it's improper. But I was once a loner who yearned for companionship, and now Hugh and Mick are my beloved family.

I must keep our family afloat, and I don't see how it will be possible if Sir Gerald cuts us loose.

At nine thirty at night, after a long nap, I join Hugh for a late supper in our dining room. Fitzmorris—the fourth member of our household—serves us fried eggs, sausages, and bread. Offi-cially Hugh's valet, the thin, solemn, gray-haired man is also our accountant, manager, housekeeper, and cook. It's more a casual than a traditional arrangement, with the chores shared, and we consider him one of our family. His own family has been in ser-vice to Hugh's for generations, and after his own parents died while he was a child, the Stauntons gave him and his siblings a home, an education, and affection; hence, Fitzmorris's unstinting devotion to Hugh, whom he loves as a younger brother. Fortu-nately for Mick and me, his devotion extends to us.

"Where is Mick?" I ask.

"At the Working Lads Institute," Fitzmorris says.

The Institute provides education and recreation for youths, and beds for those without homes. Funded by charitable donations, it aims to draw the boys away from the evils of the streets and help them obtain better jobs. Mick attends classes there every night when we don't have a crime scene to photograph. It's a big change. Until a few months ago, he'd resisted my attempts to make him get an education. He thought that because he could read and do arithmetic, his poor grammar, writing skills, and his ignorance about the world outside London didn't matter. He hated school, where he was forced to sit still in a classroom, disciplined by teachers who treated him like a child, and bullied by boys from better backgrounds. But after Catherine shunned him, he decided that education was crucial to transforming himself into an accomplished, wealthy man. He chose the Institute because he can take classes during his spare time, for a modest fee. There, he's among boys of his own kind, and he's made friends.

I'm just not sure that his getting an education will make a difference with Catherine.

While we eat, Hugh is quiet, and I suppose he's thinking about Tristan and Sir Gerald. I'm about to ask him what happened, when the doorbell rings downstairs. We jump up from our seats, conditioned to expect a summons to a crime scene. Then we recall that we don't have to photograph any new scenes while we're investigating the Sleeping Beauty case. Fitzmorris goes to answer the door and returns with Barrett. My heart lifts as we greet each other and smile.

"This is a nice surprise," Hugh says. He loves company, and he and Barrett are good friends. "You hardly ever visit anymore."

Barrett, still in his police uniform, says, "I've been busy on the job." He glances at me.

Although he looks tired, I see desire in his bloodshot eyes. It's been weeks since we've had a chance to be alone together. Between his job and mine, there's little time for those stolen moments when Hugh, Mick, and Fitzmorris aren't home. My cheeks flush at the memory of those moments, and I lower my gaze. When we marry and establish our own home, I'll miss my "family," but I'll be glad for some privacy.

"Would you like something to eat?" Fitzmorris asks Barrett.

"Thanks." Barrett sits at the table, accepts a full plate, and devours food as fast as good manners allow.

"Any progress on the Sleeping Beauty case?" Hugh asks.

Barrett raises his eyebrows as he wipes his mouth on his napkin. "Is that what you're calling it?"

"It was Sir Gerald's idea," I say.

"No witnesses, no suspects yet." Barrett takes a thirsty swallow of tea.

"Same here," Hugh says.

"No progress on my other cases either, unfortunately."

"Does that mean we won't be hearing wedding bells soon?" Hugh sounds disappointed. He has told me that he'll be sorry when I marry and move out of our house, but he wants me to be settled and happy.

"You'll have to wait awhile longer to drink a toast to us," Barrett says, making a brave attempt at humor.

"Well, Sarah, you'll be able to find your father in time for him to walk you down the aisle," Hugh says.

My father, Benjamin Bain, disappeared in 1866, when I was ten. He was a photographer, he taught me his trade, and he was my closest confidante, the person I loved most in the world. A few weeks after his disappearance, my mother told me he'd been killed in a riot during a workers' protest demonstration he'd organized. She died in 1879. In 1888, I discovered that Benjamin Bain was the primary suspect in the murder of a fourteen-year-old neighbor girl named Ellen Casey, and he was a fugitive from the law. Within the past two years, I've discovered evidence that he's still alive.

My mother lied. She was a woman with secrets, some of which I now know, others I fear to learn.

As for my father, I don't know where he is or whether he's innocent or guilty. Hugh is sure that my father is innocent, that I'll find him and we'll have a joyous reunion. I wish I were as sure. Barrett thinks it would be good for me to reunite with my father, and learn the truth about him, before our wedding. I think he's right; the truth would free me from the disturbing spell of the past. But I haven't located my father despite multiple attempts, sightings, and shocking revelations.

"Any new clues to your father's whereabouts?" Barrett asks, hopeful that one impediment to our marriage will soon crumble.

"No." It's ironic that I grew up to solve three major crimes, when I can't solve the central mystery of my own life. I still don't know whether I should invite my father to our wedding or turn him over to the police when I find him. No matter that I still love him, if he murdered Ellen Casey, I couldn't let him go unpunished. "I haven't looked for my father because I've been too busy working." It's true, but it's only half the reason. I've put off the search because I'm afraid of what I'll learn when—*if*—I find him. The possibility that he's guilty of the murder is only one of the reasons for my fear.

"Look for him tomorrow," Hugh urges. "We won't have any calls to new crime scenes."

"But I have to help investigate the Sleeping Beauty case," I say.

"Mick and I can cope by ourselves." Hugh says to Barrett, "We'll pool our clues and catch the culprit."

Barrett smiles and says, "Thanks," then tells me, "Hugh is right. You may not have another chance like this."

"All right. Maybe." Despite my misgivings, I mustn't put off the search. My father is old, and if I let too much time slip by, he'll die before I can see him again and learn the answers to my questions.

"I'd better get back to the barracks for a few hours' sleep," Barrett says. "Thanks for dinner." He lays down his napkin and rises.

Hugh and I follow suit. "We'll walk with you," I say.

"Where are you going?" Barrett says.

"Back to Shadwell, to look for witnesses," Hugh says.

"Don't you know that's a dangerous place to wander around late at night?" Barrett says.

I've already decided not to take my photography equipment and risk losing it to thieves. "That's where the witnesses and clues are."

"Well, then, I won't stop you," Barrett says.

He and I have come to an understanding: He doesn't dispute my need, my desire, or my right to do my job, because six months ago it led to his promotion. He also wants me to be happy. But he's protective of me because he loves me, and he doesn't like me to risk my life. He doesn't understand my most perverse character trait—my attraction to danger.

When I come across a dangerous person or situation, I'm tempted to draw nearer, as if it's a sleeping wolf that I have an urge to poke and wake up, just to see what will happen. That's one reason I keep searching for my father, no matter my ambivalence, no matter what I might discover. And investigating crimes offers me plentiful, welcome opportunities to poke the wolf, no matter that it's almost cost me my life.

There's no exhilaration like facing death and surviving.

On our way downstairs, Hugh stops in the parlor, opens the drawer in the table by the chaise longue, and takes out his pistol. It's new, bought after his first one was lost during our investigation of the hangman's murder.

"Do you really know how to use that?" Barrett says, looking askance at the pistol.

"Oh yes. Sarah and I have been practicing on Hampstead Heath. Sir Gerald's bodyguards were nice enough to give us a few pointers."

Having faced an armed adversary more than once, I thought it wise to learn how to use a gun. "I'm not a bad shot," I say modestly.

We don our coats and leave the house. As Hugh and I part from Barrett at Whitechapel station, he calls, "Be careful."

CHAPTER 5

At the late hour of ten thirty, Hugh and I have the hot, smoky train car to ourselves. The roar of the steam engine and the clatter of iron wheels on the track fill our silence. In the brief intervals of light when we pass gas lamps in the tunnel, Hugh's face is somber, pensive. He speaks during a plunge into darkness between lamps.

"Sir Gerald thinks Tristan is in trouble."

"Is that what he said to you today?" I try not to sound too eager for news.

"More or less."

I wait. After a long pause, Hugh says, "Tristan has been leaving Mariner House at night. He doesn't come home until morning. He refuses to tell Sir Gerald where he goes and what he does. Sir Gerald asked me if he was with me."

"Wasn't he?" I know Hugh and Tristan meet at hotels in parts of town where they're unlikely to run into anyone they know, and I recall several nights when Mick and I photographed crime scenes by ourselves because Hugh wasn't home when the summons came.

"The last few times I went to meet him, I waited for him until dawn. He never showed."

My concern for him ignites a spark of anger toward Tristan. How dare he treat Hugh this way? I fear that my worst premonition about Tristan is coming true—he's cracking under the strain of a relationship that he believes is sinful; he's going to leave Hugh. I bite my tongue, as Hugh hates any criticism of Tristan.

"What did Tristan say about those nights?" I ask as casually as I can.

"Nothing. I haven't asked why he stood me up. I'm afraid"— Hugh's voice cracks—"he's been with someone else."

"No. I can't believe it." No matter how ill I think of Tristan, I defend him, for Hugh's sake. "He's in love with you."

A glum laugh issues from Hugh. "Since when is love a guarantee of faithfulness?"

I want to think Barrett would never betray me, and as far as I know, he hasn't. "I don't think Tristan would consort with another man." I think he feels guilty enough about sinning with one man; I can't imagine him having multiple affairs.

"Thanks for trying to reassure me, Sarah, but men have wild oats to sow—especially when they've kept them pent up for as long as Tristan has." He'd told me that their relationship is the first for Tristan, whose religion and inhibitions had formerly kept him celibate.

Still, I can't picture Tristan roaming London at night, picking up men in alleys, parks, or pubs where men of their kind congregate. "Is that what Sir Gerald thinks Tristan is doing?"

"He accused me of taking Tristan out to parties like the one that was my downfall."

The vice squadron had raided a party attended by homosexuals, and the newspapers printed stories in which Hugh was mentioned as being among those caught. That incident prompted his family to disown him and his high-society friends to ostracize him. Since then, as far as I know, Hugh avoids those parties and would never consider taking Tristan to one.

"I told Sir Gerald that Tristan wasn't with me, and I've no idea where he goes or whom he sees. But the fact that Tristan is keeping us both in the dark can't mean anything good."

I have to agree, but I say, "You shouldn't assume the worst before you investigate."

Hugh laughs, amused yet irate. "This isn't a murder case."

"At least talk to Tristan. See what he has to say for himself."

"That's what Sir Gerald wants me to do. All right, I will. Sometime. Maybe." The train shudders to a halt in the bright lights at Mark Lane station. "Here we are."

The street outside the station is misty, deserted, with no cabs in sight. As we set out on foot, Hugh seems more cheerful now that he's confided in me, but my sense of adventure is tempered by the fact that somewhere there's a would-be killer who slashed a woman's face. The gun is little comfort, because I know what can happen during gunfights.

Lights in taverns along Wapping Wall Road are a welcome sight. Hugh says, "I hope you're thirsty."

We stop at one tavern after another, buying rounds for the few late-night patrons and chatting them up. After three hours we're both tipsy, but no one had seen or heard anything yesterday that pertains to Sleeping Beauty. As we leave the last tavern, I say, "We need to find someone who was outdoors during the time shortly before she was found."

We walk past dark tenements that line the street. I feel as if we're pursuing a naked ghost woman with long blonde hair. I hear clinking noises—a shovel against stone—from a passage between two tenements. An awful odor of excrement deluges us. Flies buzz around a large handcart parked in the street.

"Ugh." Hugh walks faster to get away from the smell.

"Wait." I cover my nose with a handkerchief and step into the passage.

"Sarah, what are you doing? Come on!"

"We're looking for people who were out late last night. I've found some."

The courtyard is enclosed by high brick walls and paved with flagstones. A small wooden shack stands in the corner—a public privy, shared by the residents of the surrounding buildings. Lanterns are placed around a wide, square cesspit some ten feet deep. Three men stand beside the pit and the paving stones they've pried up to uncover it. They're dressed in filthy clothes and rubber galoshes, kerchiefs tied over their heads and the lower halves of their faces. Their comrade is inside the pit, shoveling the foul muck into a tub.

These are jakesmen—workers who empty cesspits throughout London, remove the waste, and cart it away. It's arguably the world's worst job.

The man in the hole ties a rope to the full tub. The men outside haul it up. When I call, "Hello," they're startled; folks tend to give jakesmen a wide berth. As I question them, they swig liquor from pocket flasks.

"Yeah," says the man in the pit, "we saw a woman last night. Noticed her 'cause she were walkin' alone."

I'm nauseated from the odor, but my hope revives. "Where?"

"Over on Church Street."

When I ask what time, the man says it was after midnight. "Can you describe her?"

"No. She were too far away, and it were too foggy."

After eliciting the information that they noticed nothing else remarkable, we head for Church Street, and Hugh sniffs his sleeves. "My clothes stink."

"If Sleeping Beauty was the woman he saw, then she lost her clothes sometime between midnight and two in the morning, when she was found by the river," I say. Her nudity suggests a crime of a carnal nature. "Maybe she was going to meet a man, and he's the one who beat her and cut her face."

"Then he thought she was dead and needed to get rid of her body," Hugh suggests.

"The crime could have happened in any of these buildings." I look around at the tenements.

"Here's another idea: she and her would-be killer were on a boat, and she was dumped from it onto the riverbank. That could be why nobody saw."

I feel bad for Barrett, who can ill afford another hard-to-solve case. "Maybe the story in the *Daily World* will bring in some tips."

"There's the station," Hugh says. "We might as well go home." In the dim, cavernous building, he asks the ticket seller, "Was there a woman passenger at about this time last night?"

"I was off-duty. You'll have to come back tomorrow and ask the man who was on."

"Why spoil a nice run of bad luck?" Hugh says as we descend the staircase to the deserted platform.

A lone figure walks toward us from the far end. "Don't give up hope yet," I say. "Here comes another potential witness."

The short, thin man wears a derby and carries a bundle on his back, a walking stick in one hand, and what looks to be a dome-shaped hatbox in the other. I call, "Excuse me, sir?"

As he draws near, I see the small brown terrier trotting by his side. The bundle is a full burlap sack, the hatbox an iron cage. The man is a ratcatcher, one of many who trap and kill the rats that infest buildings and sewers. He's dressed in a heavy, dirty canvas jacket and trousers and knee-high leather boots. His round face could belong to a merry elf. He holds up the cage.

"Like to buy her, miss?"

The cage contains a large rat such as I've never seen—white with gray patches on its back and over its right eye. It scratches the bars of the cage and sniffs at me.

"I keep the special ones to sell or breed."

"No, thank you." Some people like rats as pets, but they give me the shivers.

Hugh says, "Were you working here last night, Mr. . . .?"

"Indeed I was. Lenny Dawson, at your service." We introduce ourselves, and he offers us his hand. I shake it reluctantly. His dirty hand is rough with scars and scabs that must be from rat bites.

"Looks like you bagged quite a few tonight." Hugh eyes the full burlap sack.

"We're always sure of a good haul at Mark Lane station." Mr. Dawson addresses his dog. "Aren't we, Mr. Black?"

The terrier barks. Ratcatchers employ dogs to kill the rats, and this one is named after Jack Black, who was once Queen Victoria's famous ratcatcher.

Hugh asks Mr. Dawson if he's heard about the woman who was found by the river, and when he nods, I say, "We're trying to figure out who she is and where she came from. Did you see a blonde woman walking by herself last night?"

"Aye." An expression of shame and sadness clouds his elfin face.

"What did she look like?"

"She had on a fancy red dress. It had—" At a loss for descriptive words, he wiggles his fingers around his neck and down his chest.

"Ruffles?" I say.

He nods. "And little shiny beads all over."

"Can you describe her face?" Hugh says.

"Didn't see it. She had on a hat with a black—" Mr. Dawson waves his hand over his face, sketching a veil.

"Where exactly did you see her?" I say.

"Going out of the station. She tripped. She looked drunk."

"Did she speak to anyone?" Hugh says.

"No." The shame and sadness on his face deepen.

Something about the encounter must have troubled him. "What happened?"

"I asked her if she wanted to—if she would—" His awkwardness makes it embarrassingly clear. "I thought she was a streetwalker. What other kind of woman would be out so late alone?" His expression turns wistful. "She didn't answer. She just stumbled away. Even a drunk streetwalker thinks she's too good for the ratcatcher."

The train rumbles into the station, and Hugh and I climb aboard. Our last glimpse of the ratcatcher shows him standing forlorn on the platform with his dog and rat. As we sit side by side in the empty car, the reality of our predicament sinks in.

"The underground trains make dozens of stops," I say.

"And they connect with Victoria, Euston, King's Cross, and other big stations," Hugh says. "If the woman in the red dress came to Shadwell by train . . ."

"*If* she did."

"And if she is Sleeping Beauty . . ."

"That's the bigger 'if.'"

"Then she could be from anywhere in London, or the kingdom," Hugh says.

Which would mean that the scope of our search for Sleeping Beauty's origin and identity has expanded to enormous proportions while her trail has grown colder.

CHAPTER 6

The next morning, the headline in bold type on the front page of the *Daily World* reads "Who Is Sleeping Beauty?"

Underneath are printed two of my photographs. One shows the woman lying on the riverbed, the spectators in the background. The engravers have etched lines across her body to obscure her private parts. The other is a close-up of her mutilated face in sharp, graphic detail. I spread the newspaper on the dining room table amid the breakfast plates and coffee cups. Hugh, Mick, and Fitzmorris look over my shoulders as we read the article, which praises "our own photographer, Sarah Bain," for making the miraculous discovery that the victim was alive.

"'Like a mermaid washed ashore,'" Hugh reads aloud, chuckling, "'as if her soul was begging me for help.' You're in the wrong field, Sarah. You should be a writer."

My words look embarrassingly sentimental. "I'll stick with photography, thank you."

Mick points to a paragraph. "Look, Barrett is in here. 'Anyone who has information that could lead to identifying her or her would-be murderer is asked to report it to Detective Sergeant Thomas Barrett, the officer in charge of the case, at the Whitechapel Police station.'"

"This could help him solve the case," I say. But publicity is a double-edged sword: if Barrett fails, thousands of people will know. I'm more determined than ever to help him succeed.

A sidebar rehashes the Ripper murders and ends with these lines, which Hugh reads aloud: "'Has the Ripper come out of hibernation? Will he attack more women and slash their faces? We warn the public to exercise caution.'"

"Could it really be the Ripper?" Fitzmorris says. He doesn't know the secret that explains why it isn't. "This woman wasn't cut open, and her internal organs weren't stolen."

"Sir Gerald is just trying to pump the story up by connecting the crime to the Ripper murders," I explain.

"Let's see what our competition says." Hugh spreads a copy of the *Telegraph* on the table. "Drat."

Its article about the crime is illustrated with photographs of Hugh, Mick, and myself, our names in the captions. They were taken outside Newgate Prison this past winter. In them, my face wears a grimace of shame; Hugh looks distraught; Mick, pugnacious. The headline reads, *"Daily World* Reporters in the Stew Again?" The text relates our mishaps in the hangman murder case and accuses us of trying to boost our celebrity status with this new case. I smell Mr. Craig avenging the damage to his camera. Worse, it serves up this dirt from our personal backgrounds:

In 1888, the vice squadron caught Lord Hugh Staunton in a compromising position at the Thousand Crowns Club, a notorious haunt of sodomites. Lord Hugh has turned his hand to investigating crimes against citizens in addition to committing crimes against nature.

Mick O'Reilly has a long record of petty larceny. "He stole from our shops," say Whitechapel businessmen. "The dirty little ragamuffin ought to be in jail."

Sarah Bain is living proof that bad character is hereditary. She is the daughter of Benjamin Bain, the primary suspect in the murder of fourteen-year-old Ellen Casey in Clerkenwell in 1866. Mr. Bain is still a fugitive from the law. Anyone with information regarding his whereabouts is instructed to report it to the nearest police station.

"I'm sorry," I say to Hugh and Mick. I'm even more upset on their behalf than mine.

"Don't worry about me; I can handle it," Mick says with less than his usual confidence. This won't improve his stock with Catherine.

"My name's already been dragged through the mud," Hugh says. "A little more dragging won't matter. I'm more concerned about your father."

"This could set everybody in London after him," Mick says.

The publicity that could help identify Sleeping Beauty and her attacker could also help the law flush my father out of hiding. Unless I find him before the police do, I might never see him again. He could be killed while trying to evade arrest or while being tortured in jail. I might never know the truth I desperately need to know.

"You should look for your father today as planned," Hugh says.

The reasons I don't want to find him tear at me like a flock of hungry, sharp-beaked crows. I'm afraid I'll learn that he raped and murdered Ellen Casey, and if I do, I'm not the only one who will suffer from knowing. "But the investigation—"

"I'll keep trying to retrace Sleeping Beauty's footsteps to wherever she came from," Hugh says. "Mick can help me."

"Yeah," Mick says. "You oughta go now, before it's too late."

★   ★   ★

A thin, warm rain falls through the mist and smoke that cloud Whitechapel. Sheltering under my umbrella, I walk to London Hospital to check on Sleeping Beauty. She's been moved to a ward for female patients. Her bed is curtained off from the others, but patients and visitors are gathered around her, staring between the parted curtains, conversing in horror, disgust, or pity. She lies still and silent under a blanket. Her face is now covered with gauze bandages and sticking plaster, except where holes have been left for her eyes, nostrils, and mouth. Dr. Enoch must have put on the bandages to protect the cuts from dirt and her from rude attention. I march up to the gawkers.

"Leave her alone! Go away!"

They beat a hasty retreat. I've never looked at myself in a mirror while losing my temper, but judging from other people's reactions, I'm quite intimidating. A nurse approaches, and I say, "Can't you keep her safe from curiosity seekers?"

"We can't guard her every minute," the nurse says, tart and defensive. "We've other patients to take care of, and when people find out Sleeping Beauty is here, they want a look."

I'm disturbed to learn that word of her location is spreading, even though the *Daily World* didn't print it.

The nurse takes a second look at me, and her manner turns friendlier. "You're Sarah Bain! I read about how you rescued her when the police thought she was dead. I'm sorry I snapped at you."

"That's all right." I gaze at Sleeping Beauty. Her eyes and mouth are closed within the holes in the bandages, and she seems smaller. "Has she awakened?"

The nurse shakes her head regretfully. "But there's no sign of infection. Dr. Enoch says that's probably the best we can expect for now."

★ ★ ★

An hour later, I'm skirting puddles in an alley in Chelsea, behind tall brick townhouses, while the rain pelts my umbrella. I halt outside the servants' entrance to one townhouse and look around to make sure no one is coming down the alley or gazing out the windows. Then I reach in my pocketbook and bring out a set of thin, bent metal shafts on a key ring.

Mick has taught me to pick locks. I've practiced at home, but this is my first time attempting it elsewhere.

I close my umbrella and hook the handle over my arm. The narrow overhang above the plain wooden door is scant shelter from the rain. My hands tremble as I insert one pick after another in the lock before I find one that fits. I jiggle it, sweating with fear that I'll be arrested for housebreaking and serve years of hard labor in a workhouse. It seems like hours before the tumblers shift and click. I ease the door open and peek inside.

The hall is empty. I step in, closing the door quietly behind me. Tiptoeing down the hall, I hear clatters and voices from the kitchen. I press my back against the wall as a woman with gray-streaked brown hair coiled atop her head, dressed in a black frock and white apron, comes out. My heart lurches. It's Mrs. Genevieve Albert, my father's second wife, whom he married after he disappeared on my mother and me. Fortunately, she doesn't notice me as she heads toward the stairs at the far end of the hall. She's the reason I picked the lock, the person who's decreed that I'm not welcome here. She hates me for various reasons, including the fact that I'm a reminder that Benjamin Bain—whom she knew as George Albert, his false name—had a secret past.

After she's out of sight, I peer into the kitchen. The cook and the scullery maid are the only inhabitants. I hurry up the stairs. On the main story, twin parlors open onto a foyer with a green-and-white marble floor and a crystal chandelier. The man of the house usually spends his days at the shipyard he owns; his wife and daughters spend theirs visiting and shopping. There's nobody in the parlors. Determined to search every room, I tiptoe to the library, whose shelves are filled with books and topped with marble busts. At the table sits a young woman clad in the white cap, white apron, and gray frock of a housemaid, a mop and bucket by her side. She hunches over a small notebook, scribbling furiously with a pencil. As I approach and close the door behind me, she gasps and jumps to her feet, crams the notebook and pencil into her apron pocket. Her face, a younger mirror image of mine, is panic-stricken.

"Sarah?" My half-sister—Benjamin Bain's second daughter—clasps her throat, sags with relief, and smiles.

"Hello, Sally. I didn't mean to frighten you."

"Oh God, I thought you were Mother." She casts a guilty look at the mop and bucket. "If she knew I was writing instead of working, she would kill me."

It's Sally's dream to be an authoress. Mrs. Albert is vehemently opposed, even though many authoresses have attained great popularity and high incomes. Here's another reason Mrs. Albert hates me: because I encourage Sally by example and praise her efforts. Sally wants to follow in my footsteps as an independent woman with a professional career. Mrs. Albert disapproves of my unconventional lifestyle and wants Sally to stay safely in her place.

"How is the writing going?" I say.

Sally makes a rueful face. "I sent my latest story to five magazines. They all rejected it."

"Oh, I'm sorry."

"The editors all said the same thing—not enough happens."

"*I* thought it was wonderful."

She sighs. "Thank you, but they're right. I get to a certain point in every story where I don't know where it should go. I suppose it's because I haven't lived enough to tell an exciting story." With a glum laugh, she adds, "How could I, when I've been trapped in this house for eleven years?"

I feel bad for her because although my life has brought me many hardships, at least I'm my own mistress. "I took a lot of bad photographs when I was just starting out. If you keep writing, you're bound to get better."

"Yes, I know." Sally makes a visible effort to cheer up. "How did you get into the house?"

I jingle Mick's picklocks.

She eyes me with admiration; I've set another dubious example. "What brings you here? I thought you were busy photographing crime scenes."

"Something's come up." There's no time to explain before I'm caught trespassing. "I need to look for Father today."

Sally's face lights up. "Oh, splendid!"

She loves our father and longs to be reunited with him as much as I do. That gave us something in common, a basis for an affectionate sisterly relationship despite the fact that neither of us knew the other existed until fourteen months ago, when my search for Benjamin Bain led me to his second family. We like to spend her days off together, but I've had to cancel often because of my job. Sally, kind and forgiving, never holds it against me.

"Let's go now!" she says. "We can investigate Lucas Zehnpfennig."

Lucas is the clue we discovered when we first met and compared childhood memories. He cropped up at my family home shortly before my father disappeared from my life in 1866. Shortly before my father disappeared on Sally and her mother in 1879, he received a letter from Lucas. Sally saw it, although she doesn't know what it said. She and I don't think the coincidence was indeed mere coincidence. Certain that the man is the link between the two disappearances and a clue to our father's present-day whereabouts, we began a search for Lucas.

Inspector Reid doesn't know about him. He's our advantage in the contest to find Benjamin Bain.

A harsh voice interrupts: "You're not going anywhere, my girl."

Mrs. Albert stalks into the library. Her face, still pretty despite the lines that frame her features, is dark with rage. Sally cringes. I'm dismayed because I've been caught and because she's in trouble and it's my fault.

Mrs. Albert points at the door and says to Sally, "Get to work upstairs." When Sally hesitates, she speaks in a quiet, menacing tone. "*Now*, girl, or I'll drag you by your hair."

With an apologetic glance at me, Sally picks up her mop and bucket and departs.

Mrs. Albert faces me and demands, "Who let you in?"

I keep silent rather than admit I picked the lock.

"What a sneaky bitch you are. A chip off your father's old block." She regards me with a loathing that goes far deeper than our few previous clashes can account for. She hates my father for keeping secrets from her, for abandoning her and Sally. She's had eleven years to nurse her bitterness toward him, and it's spilled over onto me.

I bite back a sharp retort. For Sally's sake, I say, "Mrs. Albert, I don't want to be your enemy. I would rather we be friends. Can we start over?"

Mrs. Albert laughs with incredulous contempt. "Friends? After that story about you and your father in the newspaper this morning?"

I'd hoped she hadn't seen it. "I'm sorry."

"A lot of good 'sorry' does. The police already know I was married to Benjamin Bain. Now every busybody in London will be sniffing around his trail, digging up dirt. They'll find out that Sally is his daughter, and her good name will be ruined."

I'm horrified that my notoriety could hurt Sally, but I see a way to turn a potential catastrophe to our advantage. "Then it's more important than ever for us to find our father."

"No!" Mrs. Albert is as vehemently opposed as ever. She prefers to think Benjamin Bain is dead because it's more comfortable than the prospect of seeing him again and opening unhealed wounds.

"If we can prove he's innocent—"

"He's guilty. Why else would he hide from the law?"

I don't give her a chance to remind me that he was the last person to see Ellen Casey alive. Compelled by an intuition that I've experienced on past occasions, I take a stab in the dark. "Do you know something about him that you're not telling?"

"No." She looks me straight in the eye, but emotion flickers behind her stony gaze. Is it fear or guilt?

"Yes, you do," I say, moving closer to her. "Tell me what it is."

She stands her ground, folds her arms across her ample bosom. "Don't be silly. I've not seen or heard from my husband in eleven years." She has herself under control now, all emotions except disdain erased from her face. "How could I know anything?"

But I'm certain that I'm right. "Sally desperately wants to find our father. Whatever you're withholding could be important." Urgency raises my voice. "For her sake, tell me!"

Mrs. Albert's brown eyes spark with anger. "If you care so much about Sally, you'll stop encouraging her foolish notion of being a writer. You'll keep your dirty laundry out of the newspapers." She grabs my arm and marches me out of the library, down the hall. "You'll let sleeping dogs lie and stay away from Sally!"

She opens the front door, shoves me out, yells "Good riddance!" and slams the door.

Chapter 7

Somewhat relieved to have an excuse not to search for my father, I return to Whitechapel in late morning. The rain has diminished to a misty drizzle. I walk down Leman Street, past the new sugar warehouse, a veritable palace whose gigantic white stone and bright red brick structure, complete with a clock tower, dwarfs the adjacent shops. Newsboys waving papers accost pedestrians, yelling, "Read all about Sleeping Beauty!"

Mick was right—the nickname will stick with everyone who hears it.

The Metropolitan Police's H Division headquarters occupies a brown brick building, five stories high, with a triangular pediment over its arched doorway. Barrett tells me that H Division covers one and a quarter square miles and has almost six hundred policemen, and I see them everywhere—walking to and from their barracks; loitering by the station and the local public houses. My longtime fear of the police stems from the year I was ten, when two constables barged into my family's house and threatened my father while my mother and I cowered in the bedroom. My mother said they were after him because he was a troublemaker who tried to help poor people by organizing workers' protest marches. It was one of the many lies she told me. Not until twenty-two years later did I learn the real story: the police were trying to force him to confess to Ellen Casey's rape and murder. Since then, I've experienced my own sometimes violent clashes with the law; but repeated contact with policemen while doing my job, plus my relationship with Barrett, has diminished my fear to a manageable level. Now, as I pass through the door of the station, my heartbeat quickens, but I don't panic.

Inside the reception room, citizens sit on benches and lean against the walls while constables man the reception desk and stand guard. The air is hazy with tobacco smoke, damp from dripping umbrellas and mackintoshes. There are as many women as men, and most seem too respectable to be criminals under arrest.

PC Porter greets me with a smile and says, "Your newspaper photographs are bringing them in droves."

"All these people have come forward with information about . . . Sleeping Beauty?" It feels wrong to call her that, but the nickname has stuck with me too.

"We've had over a hundred tips already."

I'm glad the publicity is serving a purpose. "Where is Barrett?"

Porter points to the doorway behind the desk. "Go on in."

I walk down a hall, past vacant jail cells, and find Barrett in a small chamber furnished with a table and chairs. He sits with his back to the barred window, opposite an old man. Pencil in hand, a notebook open in front of him, Barrett looks up at me, nods in greeting, then says to the old man, "So when did your wife run away?"

"In 1859. Haven't seen her since."

Barrett jots down the information. "I'm sorry, but she's too old to be Sleeping Beauty. But thank you for coming." After the man leaves, he smiles at me and rises. "You saw the crowd out there? Want to watch me do interviews?"

"If that's all right." Despite Sir Gerald's deal with the police, I don't want to trespass on Barrett's territory.

"Sure. Maybe you'll bring me good luck. None of the tips have panned out so far. I've heard about missing wives, daughters, sisters, and neighbors, but they're all too young, too old, or they don't fit Sleeping Beauty's description." Barrett explains, "They're so desperate to find their missing person, they're grasping at straws."

I nod; I know how they feel. For the next hour I sit beside Barrett while he conducts interviews. It's a sobering, educational experience. I never realized how many people are in the same position as Sally and myself. I feel sorry for them. I can't help hoping that the *Telegraph*'s story on Benjamin Bain will elicit tips regarding his whereabouts.

After Barrett dismisses a woman who thought Sleeping Beauty was her sister—who would be fifty now—we hear PC Porter yell, "Hey! Stop!"

"Kindly move out of my way," replies an angry male voice with a cultured French accent.

"You can't go in there," Porter shouts.

As a man bursts in through the door, Barrett and I jump to our feet. My first impression of the intruder is that he resembles a Roman marble bust. His head is large for his average height, with a smooth cap of light brown hair. In his forties, he has a straight, prominent nose and pale eyes, like those on statues that lack pupils. Powerful, broad shoulders and a long torso add to his top-heaviness. He's holding a folded newspaper.

"Are you Detective Sergeant Barrett?" he says.

"Yes," Barrett says, caught off guard.

"Sorry, guv. I tried to explain to this gentleman that there are other people in line ahead of him." Porter grabs the man's arm. "Come along now."

Trying to shake Porter off him, the man demands, "Do you people know who I am?"

"I don't care," Barrett says. "You'll wait your turn."

"I am August Legrand, the artist."

I recognize the name; I saw it in an advertisement for his show at the Dowdeswell and Dowdeswell's Gallery. From the large size of the advertisement, I gather that he's successful and important, but that doesn't give him the right to cut in line. He's wearing a dandyish blue ascot and a silk waistcoat patterned with peacock feathers, and the snug, sleek fit of his light gray suit screams bespoke tailoring. I immediately dislike him. He's the kind of wealthy, upper-class man who steps on my foot without noticing, let alone apologizing.

"Show Mr. Legrand back to the waiting room," Barrett tells Porter.

Mr. Legrand unfolds the newspaper, slaps it onto the table, and points at the photograph of Sleeping Beauty's face. "She is my wife."

"You're the tenth chap to say so," Porter replies. As he starts to drag Legrand out the door, I'm glad to see the belligerent artist put in his place.

Barrett says, "Wait."

Porter and I regard him with surprise. "Guv?" Porter says.

"I'll interview Mr. Legrand now. You may go."

Porter leaves, shaking his head in puzzlement. I look to Barrett for an explanation. He just motions for Mr. Legrand and me to sit down. Mr. Legrand seats himself as if it's no more than his due. He ignores me and brushes off his clothes as if Porter's touch had contaminated them. His shirt collar and cuffs are perfectly starched and snowy white.

"Where are you keeping my wife?" he demands.

"Slow down." Barrett picks up his pencil. "Where do you live?"

"Twenty-three Holland Park, Kensington."

Barrett writes on his notepad. "What is your wife's name?"

"Jenny Legrand. I want to see her."

"How old is she? How tall?"

Mr. Legrand sighs with impatience. "She is thirty-three years old and exactly five feet, four inches."

She's the same age as I am, as tall as Sleeping Beauty appeared to be.

"What color are your wife's eyes?" Barrett says.

"Blue."

I begin to understand why Barrett decided to see Mr. Legrand now. He must be acting on a hunch that Mr. Legrand has a valid tip about Sleeping Beauty.

"Is she French like you?"

If she wakes up and she speaks with a French accent, that could confirm her identity.

"I am Belgian," Mr. Legrand says, proud and irate. "Jenny is English. This is intolerable!"

"I need information," Barrett says in a soothing tone. "This will go faster if you cooperate."

Mr. Legrand exhales in resignation.

"The face of the woman in the picture is badly injured. How do you know she's your wife?"

"Jenny and I have been married for two years. I would know her anywhere, and as an artist, I am trained to see the bone structure beneath the surface of the skin."

"When did you last see Jenny?" Barrett says.

"The day before yesterday. I had dinner at my club and came home at about midnight. She was gone."

"Where do you think she went? How could she have ended up unconscious by the river?"

"I don't know!" Mr. Legrand's Roman face is tense with frustration and shiny with sweat, like polished marble. "She didn't tell me or the servants where she was going." He leans forward. "How is she?"

"The woman is still unconscious," Barrett says.

Mr. Legrand looks as disappointed and worried as should a man who believes his wife is a comatose victim of attempted murder. I caution myself not to distrust him just because I don't like him. While Barrett is writing, I venture a question.

"If your wife disappeared the day before yesterday, what have you been doing about it since then?"

Mr. Legrand glances at me as he might at a fly that buzzed near his ear. "Looking for her, of course." He asks Barrett, "Who is *she*?"

Barrett compresses his lips in a thin smile. "This is Miss Sarah Bain, the newspaper photographer who saved the woman's life."

"Oh." Sheepish, Mr. Legrand bows to me. "I am grateful, Miss Bain."

Maybe he's only rude because he's distraught. I of all people should know how distraught a person with a missing loved one feels. But when a married woman is the victim of a violent crime, her husband is automatically a suspect. If Sleeping Beauty is Jenny Legrand, then perhaps Barrett and I are on the verge of solving the case in one fell swoop—identifying both Sleeping Beauty and her would-be killer. But I would hate to discover that she's married to a husband who slashed her face. My sense of connection with her is clouding my judgment, and so is my past. I want a joyous reunion for her because my search for my father hasn't ended with one and perhaps never will. But my job is to determine and report the facts.

"Is your marriage happy?" I ask Mr. Legrand.

"What?" He frowns, offended.

"Answer her," Barrett says.

"Yes," Mr. Legrand snaps. "Very happy."

"If your wife were asked the same question, would she give the same answer?" I say.

"But of course."

"Have you ever harmed your wife?"

"Never!" Mr. Legrand swells with indignation. "What is this, a court of law? And are we not getting far off the subject?" He reaches into his coat pocket. "I have a photograph of Jenny." He brings out a print and slaps it onto the table. "This is the woman whom the newspapers call Sleeping Beauty."

The picture shows August Legrand and a woman seated on a bench, with sun-dappled foliage behind them. Mr. Legrand, on the right, wears a white suit and a straw boater hat. His face looks the same as now; the photograph is recent. Jenny wears an ornate, long-sleeved black dress with a ruffle around her neck and more ruffles layered down the front and at the wrists. Small white specks on the puffed skirt look to be from defects on the negative plate. Her face is delicately beautiful, with light eyes. Her blonde hair, pulled back from her brow, cascades in loose ringlets. To my dismay, it's not impossible that she could be Sleeping Beauty, whose face is so distorted by her injuries that I couldn't tell what she looked like before she got them. August Legrand wears a smug, lordly expression; he looks straight at the camera. Jenny gazes sideways at him. Her hands, clasped in her lap, are shifted toward the left edge of the picture. Her black dress seems to absorb the sunlight. Barrett positions the photograph side by side with the newspaper, the better to compare. He cups his chin and frowns.

"If I were to see her, I could identify her for certain," Mr. Legrand says. "You must take me to her!"

"Not until I've checked out your story," Barrett says.

I'm relieved that he isn't going to expose Sleeping Beauty to this man before he determines whether the story holds water. Mr. Legrand could be a pervert who wants to take advantage of a helpless stranger.

"Does your wife have any distinctive marks on her body, such as birthmarks, moles, or scars?" Barrett asks Mr. Legrand.

If so, and an examination of Sleeping Beauty shows that she has them too, it would mean she is Jenny Legrand. Now Mr. Legrand's expression turns cunning.

"Take me to her and I'll tell you."

Barrett shakes his head, refusing to be manipulated. "You tell me first."

Mr. Legrand jumps up so quickly that his chair topples and crashes onto the floor. His eyes blaze with anger. "I want to see her now!"

"Sit down, or get out," Barrett says in the stern, authoritative tone he's cultivated while rousting criminals on the streets.

"Damn you!" Mr. Legrand lunges across the table, grabs Barrett by the front of his uniform, and shouts, "Where is she?"

As they tussle, I jump up and lift my chair to bash Mr. Legrand's head. Past experience with fights has taught me to pitch in, not stand idle. Before I can deliver the blow, Porter and two other constables rush into the room; they must have heard the crash and the shouts. Barrett bends Mr. Legrand over the table with his arm twisted behind his back.

"Looks like you didn't need us, guv," Porter says, grinning.

The other constables seize Mr. Legrand, who struggles and curses in French. "Unhand me!" Livid with anger, he looks like a Roman bust painted red—a mad Julius Caesar. As they drag him out the door, he yells, "You have no right to abuse me, and no right to keep me away from my wife. I shall bring a lawsuit against the entire police department!"

I set down my chair. My heart races with lingering fear, excitement, and—I must admit—the bloodlust that comes over me during fights. Barrett glances at me. He knows what I'm capable of, and his expression says he's glad it didn't come to that today.

"Give us a minute before you bring in the next one," he says to Porter. When we're alone, he asks, "What do you think about Mr. Legrand?"

This is the moment when we truly begin working together on this case. The sense of collaboration is thrilling, but Barrett and I haven't always seen eye to eye during past investigations, and our differences of opinion almost tore us apart. So did my lack of honesty, which I considered necessary and he thought unconscionable. I have to be honest with him, and myself, now.

"I don't want Sleeping Beauty to be Jenny Legrand," I say.

Barrett nods, his expression neutral.

"You think she is, don't you?" I say.

He rakes his hand through his hair, his habit when he's riled, worried, or experiencing other uncomfortable emotions. "Call it a hunch."

I raise my eyebrows. "Aren't you the one who's always warning me not to rely on my intuition?"

"So now the shoe is on the other foot. But I've been on the force for eleven years. Experience counts."

"So does evidence—or lack thereof." I'm stung by his words, which imply that my experience solving three major crimes doesn't count. I tap the photograph, which Mr. Legrand left on the table. I study Jenny as if I were taking her picture myself. I notice that her expression is wary, and the position of her hands suggests a desire to move away from her husband. She's afraid of him. It's more reason why I don't want her to be Sleeping Beauty. "This isn't proof."

"You don't need to remind me."

We're not really arguing about hunches versus evidence, or whose experience matters more. We're on edge because we have a difference of opinion already, and we're both under pressure to solve the case.

To smooth troubled waters, I say, "Just because I don't like the idea of Sleeping Beauty as the wife of that odious man, it doesn't mean she isn't. Maybe your hunch is correct."

The tension in Barrett's face relaxes. "I know I shouldn't jump to conclusions. But Mr. Legrand seems so certain that he's right. I think he loves his wife and he's desperate to get her back." His gaze softens. "I know how a man feels when he loses the woman he loves."

I know Barrett is thinking of us, referring to the times when we were estranged and the instance when he thought I'd been killed. I'm not the only one whose personal issues are coming into play during this investigation.

"We both need to be objective," I say.

"You're right." He sounds relieved that we've sidestepped a quarrel.

I'm relieved too. "It's early yet. One of the other tips might identify Sleeping Beauty."

Barrett smiles. "Or maybe she'll wake up and identify herself. I wish she would, even though we'd lose my chance to solve a big case and yours for a big story. Are you ready for the next tip?"

CHAPTER 8

Curious to see how many more people have shown up with tips, I follow Barrett out to the waiting room. We hear a thud, then a woman screaming. We rush in to find a crowd gathered around a lady who lies motionless on the floor. Her eyes are closed, her mouth agape, and her face stark white in contrast to her black frock and black hat trimmed with black silk flowers. Two younger women are kneeling beside her. One screams, "Mother! Oh dear God! Mother!"

I've seen people suddenly fall dead in the street. I wring my hands, helpless while I stare.

"What happened?" Barrett asks PC Porter.

Porter spreads his hands. "I told her she was next in line to see you, and she stood up and then just keeled over."

"She has a bad heart." The woman who screamed holds the lady's hand, pats her cheek, and cries, "Mother, speak to me!"

The lady doesn't respond. Onlookers murmur in concern. Barrett says, "Call a doctor."

"That won't be necessary," the other woman says in a crisp, calm voice. She says to the screamer, "Do be quiet, Faith. You sound like a stuck pig."

Faith puts her hands over her mouth. The other woman reaches into her pocketbook, a small oval bag made of purple satin, encrusted with iridescent beads, with a silver chain for a handle.

She pulls out a small glass vial, opens it, and holds it under the lady's nose. The lady jerks as her nostrils flare. She grimaces, turning her head aside to escape the pungent smelling salts. Her eyes pop open.

"What . . .?" she mutters.

I sigh with relief. Faith bursts into tears. "Mother! Thank God."

"She has dizzy spells, and sometimes she faints," the other woman explains. "She's all right now. Aren't you, Mother?"

The lady pushes herself upright. "I certainly am." She has a plummy, affected voice. Frowning at the spectators, she says, "What are you looking at?" They retreat. "Get me off this filthy floor." She extends her hands to her daughters.

As they help her stand, her black crepe skirts rustle, and she wobbles on her small feet, which are shod in elegant black boots. I make a closer observation of the three women. The mother appears to be in her late forties, the daughters in their twenties. All stout and dark-haired, they share the weakest jawlines I've ever seen. Their faces blend directly into their necks, like those of yarn dolls. By contrast, their noses are sharp protrusions between their small eyes and thin, prim mouths.

Faith brushes dust off her mother's backside. Her own frock is a gray and lavender floral print, her hat made of natural straw adorned with fake lavender sprigs. She seems the younger of the sisters. "Frances, perhaps we should take Mother home."

"Nonsense." Frances is stylish in a frock with a bold pattern of mauve diamonds on black. Purple feathers bristle from her black straw bonnet. "We've been waiting two hours, and it's our turn."

The mother fixes Barrett with her haughty gaze. "Are you Detective Sergeant Barrett?" When he nods, she says, "I am Mrs. Esther Oliphant. I will speak with you now." She sounds like a queen granting a favor.

"Right this way, ma'am," Barrett says with a covert, amused glance at me.

I follow him and the women through the door. Their bustles accentuate large posteriors. Frances wears her brunette hair pinned in a skimpy knot at her nape; Faith's mousier hair is twisted up into a fluff; Mrs. Oliphant's, a flat, uniform dyed brown near her scalp, sprouts shiny coils of a slightly different color—a hairpiece. Whenever I see hairpieces, I wonder if they were purchased from one of the undertakers who rob corpses.

In the interview room, I tuck the photograph of Jenny Legrand inside my pocketbook before Barrett and I resume our seats behind the table. The Oliphant family sits in the chairs facing us. Mrs. Oliphant, in the center, has what seems to be a permanent twist to her lips, as if she's tasting vinegar. Faith, on her left, dabs a handkerchief against her tear-stained face. Her nervous gaze darts from Barrett to her mother and sister. Frances's expression is avid, as though Barrett has food and she's hungry.

Barrett asks the three women to spell their names. After he writes them down, he introduces me. Mrs. Oliphant and Faith nod politely, then ignore me, but Frances studies me with an interest that's more disturbing than flattering. When Barrett asks for their address, Mrs. Oliphant replies in her haughty voice.

"We reside at the Oliphant Convalescent Home on East Hill, Wandsworth. It was founded by my late husband, Dr. Stanley Oliphant." Mrs. Oliphant touches the string of carved jet beads around her neck. "He died in April of 1887. My daughters and I operate the home. We take in patients who aren't sick enough to be in hospitals but are too sick to manage in their own homes or have nobody to care for them." She adds, "I was a widow when I met Dr. Oliphant. He adopted my daughters after we married, nine years ago."

She's still in full mourning for her husband, long past the traditional one-year period. Frances and Faith wear the purple shades of half-mourning.

"What brought you here?" Barrett says.

"My stepdaughter is missing." Mrs. Oliphant explains, "She is my husband's child by his late first wife."

Faith speaks up, as if anxious for attention. "Her name is Peggy—Margaret Oliphant."

Barrett writes down the name. Mrs. Oliphant says, "We think the woman in the newspaper photographs may be Peggy."

Although I would prefer Sleeping Beauty to be their kin rather than August Legrand's wife, there's something unlikeable about them as well, and I think it goes deeper than their looks and manners.

Barrett asks for Peggy's age and height. Mrs. Oliphant looks to Frances. I get the impression that Mrs. Oliphant is the queen of the family, and Frances the smart, capable handmaiden. Frances says, "Peggy is twenty-nine, five feet four inches, with long blonde hair, like the woman in the newspaper."

She matches Sleeping Beauty's description as well as Jenny Legrand does.

"She's so proud of her hair." Faith sounds resentful. "She's always combing it and looking in the mirror. She likes that it's prettier than ours."

And Faith is the jealous stepsister.

"Does Peggy have any distinctive birthmarks, scars, or moles on her body?" Barrett says.

The three women regard him as though offended by the idea that they're vulgar enough to be so intimately familiar with anyone. "We certainly wouldn't know," Frances says.

"When did Peggy go missing?" Barrett says.

"Last Monday," Mrs. Oliphant says.

That's ten days before Sleeping Beauty turned up unconscious by the river. If she's Peggy, where had she been for so long? I wonder if her attacker held her captive. Was he someone she knew?

"Did you report it to the Wandsworth police?" Barrett says.

"Yes," Mrs. Oliphant says. "They don't think Peggy was kidnapped—there was no evidence of a break-in or a struggle. She just seems to have vanished into thin air."

I notice Frances scrutinizing me. Does she think I'm someone to reckon with, or is she merely curious about my relationship with Barrett?

"Have you any idea where Peggy could have gone, or why?" Barrett says.

The three women exchange glances that seem more calculating than his logical question merits. Mrs. Oliphant says, "She probably wandered off and got lost. She's like that."

"Like what?" Barrett's expression says he hasn't missed the glances, and he thinks the answer is as odd as I do.

Mrs. Oliphant hesitates, Faith bites her lip, and they both look to Frances, who says, "Oh, well, I'll be the one to air our dirty laundry. Peggy isn't right in the head. She acts like a child. She plays games and has tantrums."

"I see." Barrett's expression turns grave, sympathetic. "I'm sorry."

Many people think that having a mentally impaired family member is shameful, as if they're at fault or they're tainted by association, and they prefer to keep it secret. The thought that Sleeping Beauty may be abnormal upsets me. It's not that I would think less of her; it's that she seems even more vulnerable, and the injuries to her more egregious.

"Peggy's favorite game is 'Hansel and Gretel,'" Faith chimes in. "She must have been pretending she was lost in the woods, and she couldn't find her way home." Faith giggles. "Maybe the wicked witch got her."

"Faith! This isn't a time for jokes." Mrs. Oliphant gives her daughter a stern look, but a smile hovers around her sour mouth.

Frances says in a sweet voice laced with acid, "We must be nice to poor Peggy."

It troubles me to imagine Sleeping Beauty an outsider in this unpleasant family, ridiculed for her problems and considered a burden. Perhaps Sir Gerald has cast Sleeping Beauty in the wrong fairy tale, and she fell prey to some evil person who took advantage of an innocent, childlike creature pretending she was Gretel.

"I'll start a search for Peggy." Barrett adds in a consoling tone, "Chances are, she's not Sleeping Beauty, and she'll turn up safe and sound."

I hope so. Recalling Hugh's and my talk with the ratcatcher, I ask, "Does Peggy own a fancy red dress?" I wish I'd had time to ask Mr. Legrand the same question about Jenny.

"Certainly not," Mrs. Oliphant says. "She has no use for such a thing."

Perhaps Sleeping Beauty is neither Jenny Legrand nor Peggy Oliphant, and the woman in the red dress is someone totally unrelated to the case. "Have you a picture of Peggy?" I say.

Mrs. Oliphant opens her capacious black handbag, removes a photograph in an oval silver frame, and hands it to Barrett. "This is the most recent. It was taken in 1887, shortly before my husband's death."

Barrett and I examine the picture of five people standing on a porch. At the center is an emaciated man with a beard, sunken eyes, and hollow cheeks. The late Dr. Oliphant is clearly unwell. On his left, Frances and Faith pose on either side of Mrs. Oliphant. They all wear pale, frilly dresses, flower-trimmed hats, and proud expressions, like homely fashion plates. On his right, slender Peggy smiles. Her dark-colored dress is outdated and too loose, as if it had been a castoff from one of her large stepsisters. Blonde ringlets hang under her white bonnet. She's a bit younger than and not as pretty as Jenny Legrand, but I can't tell that she's mentally impaired. She's the beauty of the family, and she's as set apart from it as if she were Cinderella sitting in the ashes by the hearth—another fairy tale.

"She could be the woman in the newspaper." Mrs. Oliphant's manner combines hope and anxiety.

"There is a superficial resemblance." Barrett's tone says that neither the photograph nor the Oliphants' story has dispelled his hunch that Sleeping Beauty is Jenny Legrand.

"Peggy is very trusting," Frances says. "A man could have invited her to go with him to buy sweets at the candy shop, and she wouldn't have suspected he had anything else in mind."

I've heard tales of women abducted and forced to work in houses of ill repute.

"She's so pretty, men buzz around her like flies," Faith says. "It's sickening."

I'm surprised that she can be jealous of a missing stepsister who's mentally abnormal. However, emotions aren't always rational and don't always change when circumstances do. I still love my father since learning that he's the prime suspect in Ellen Casey's murder, and I still love my mother even though she lied to me about so much.

"Now, now, Faith, don't speak ill of poor, dear Peggy." Mrs. Oliphant pats a handkerchief against her perspiring face. "I'm so worried about her, I'm at my wits' end! If Stanley were alive, he would be furious at me for losing her. He doted on Peggy. She was his darling." Resentment creeps into her voice. She adds hastily, "Ours too."

Frances leans toward Barrett. "Can you let us see Sleeping Beauty? So that we can tell if she's Peggy?"

Barrett repeats the answer he gave August Legrand: "After I've checked out your story."

I'm glad he's not buying it at face value, but Mrs. Oliphant sits up straight and demands, "Why must you do that?"

"To verify that the information is accurate."

"When will that be?" Faith says.

"As soon as possible." Barrett must be thinking that it will take him ages to finish hearing all the tips and checking out the most promising ones.

Mrs. Oliphant throws up her hands. "You expect us to wait, all the while poor, dear Peggy may be lying unconscious on her deathbed? This is too much for me." She pulls a black silk fan from her bag, fans herself, and pants.

"I'm sorry, ma'am." Barrett is sympathetic but unyielding.

"Calm down, Mother, or you'll have another spell," Frances says.

A loud clank at the window behind me startles us all. Some-thing hit one of the iron bars that protect the glass. I turn to peer outside, but I don't see anything except the brick wall of the build-ing across the alley.

"What was that?" Faith says.

"Probably just a bird." Frances says to Barrett, "The news-papers didn't say where Sleeping Beauty is, but she must be in a hospital. Who is paying the bill?"

"Charitable donations, I suppose," Barrett says.

"Our convalescent home has all the facilities of the best hos-pitals and the comforts of a fine hotel. We employ an excellent physician and trained nurses." Frances sounds as if she's quoting an advertisement. "If you let us see Sleeping Beauty and we identify her as Peggy, we'll bring her home and see to her care."

"And she won't waste the do-gooders' money," Faith says.

"Hush, dear," Mrs. Oliphant says and then, turning to Barrett, adds, "We're so desperate to have Peggy back with us."

The three women eye Barrett with hopeful smiles. I silently entreat him not to cave in. Even if Sleeping Beauty is Peggy and they have every right to her, they seem suspiciously eager to get custody. I don't think it's because they love Peggy. August Legrand is one suspect in the attack on her; now Barrett and I could be looking at three others.

"I shall have to ask my superior before I can allow her to be moved or anyone to see her," Barrett says.

I sense that he too distrusts the Oliphants, and I'm glad. While it's hard to imagine them inflicting the sort of violence that was done to Sleeping Beauty, I know that women are capable of much worse. And if Mrs. Oliphant and her daughters are the culprits, then Barrett mustn't give them the opportunity to finish Sleeping Beauty off.

"Can you ask your superior now?" Annoyance shows through Frances's wheedling smile.

"After I finish the interviews and check out your story," Barrett says.

"By then it may be too late!" Mrs. Oliphant cries. "The quacks at the hospital may kill Peggy, if she hasn't already passed away while we've been sitting here."

A sudden qualm grips me. If my notions and suspicions about them are wrong, then I'm helping to keep these women separated from a beloved family member. I think of my father, and how my mother's lie in effect kept us apart for twenty-two years, during which I thought he was dead.

Frances stands. Mrs. Oliphant and Faith follow suit. "Mother demands to speak to your superior," Frances says. "Don't you, Mother?"

"I certainly do. Take me to him at once!"

Before Barrett can respond, a crash explodes behind us. A hard object strikes my back, shattered glass from the window flies into the room, and I scream as memory catapults me back to the night a gas explosion almost killed me. Flames consume my vision. I lunge forward and thud against a hard surface.

"Sarah!"

Barrett's voice brings me back to the present. Gasping, I find myself sprawled across the table. A sore spot on my back throbs. Mrs. Oliphant has fainted again; she's slumped in her chair, her daughters trying to revive her.

"You're all right. Stand up and hold still." Barrett raises me to my feet and picks broken glass from my hair and clothes.

"What happened?" I say.

"Someone threw a rock at the window." Barrett holds up a rock as large as my fist. "It wasn't the first time. Remember that sound we heard? It wasn't a bird hitting the bars."

I stare at him. "Who? . . . *Why?*"

Just as Mrs. Oliphant opens her eyes, another rock flies through the hole in the window, sails past Barrett and me, and lands in her lap. "Dear God, we're under attack!" she screams.

PC Porter and the two constables rush into the room. More rocks pelt the window bars. Barrett points at the Oliphants and orders, "Get them to safety."

The constables herd them out. Even as my heart pounds with residual fright, I move to the window, curious to see who dared bombard a police station. Barrett, Porter, and I cautiously peer outside.

CHAPTER 9

Across the alley, some six feet below us and twenty distant, a little girl stands by the brick building opposite the police station. She looks to be about ten years old, her dark hair and pale frock drenched from the rain that's still falling. At her feet is a little heap of rocks. She holds a rock in her hand, poised to throw it. When she sees Barrett, Porter, and me at the window, she lowers the rock and smiles as if she's scored a point in a game.

"Hello. Detective Sergeant Barrett?" Her accent places her among the upper classes.

"Yes?" Barrett says.

"Hey! I thought I told you to get lost," Porter says.

"You did, but I don't care," the girl says.

My breath catches. At her age, I wouldn't have dared talk back to a policeman.

"I have to talk to him." She points at Barrett. "About the lady in the newspaper."

Porter glares. "I oughta arrest you for breaking the window."

"I had to get his attention. I wouldn't have needed to throw rocks if you hadn't thrown me out of the building."

"Why, you little—"

Barrett grabs Porter by his arm before he makes good on his threat. "Did she come in to give a tip?"

"So she said. Thinks she's smart, playing a joke on the coppers, the nasty street urchin."

"I told you I want to hear from everyone who comes." Barrett's tone is quiet, his anger controlled. "You're not to turn away people you think aren't worth the bother. Is that clear?"

Porter's eyes flash with animosity. Then he regains his usual, genial manner. "Yes, guv."

Barrett calls to the girl, "What's your name?"

She moves closer to us. Her pink-and-white-striped frock, white stockings, and white boots are splashed with mud, her hands and face dirty from the rocks. "Venetia Napier."

The elegant name matches her upper-class speech. Porter misidentified her because he didn't look past her bedraggled appearance. He really isn't very bright, as Barrett said.

Venetia Napier cocks her head and scrutinizes me. "You're Sarah Bain. You look better than that picture of you in the newspaper."

"Thank you." I'm not sure it's a compliment, and her forwardness is disconcerting, but I admire her nerve.

"Go apologize to Miss Napier and bring her inside," Barrett says to Porter. "I'll see her in the canteen. Get somebody to clean up this glass and fix the window."

"Yes, guv." Porter's voice has a resentful edge.

★ ★ ★

The canteen is a small room fitted out like a kitchen; it smells of tobacco smoke and coffee, boiled eggs and fish paste. Barrett seats Venetia Napier at the table while I wet a dishcloth at the tap. I reach out to wipe the mud off Venetia.

She takes the cloth from me, saying "Thank you," and wipes her own face and hands.

Barrett crouches in front of her, to give her a face-to-face reprimand for the broken window, then straightens up; he too has clearly realized that she's mature and self-sufficient beyond her years, and it would be silly to treat her as a typical child. As she hands me the muddy cloth, I take a closer look at her. Her damp hair, tied back with a pink ribbon, is drying into glossy auburn waves. She has big violet eyes fringed with long black lashes. Heavy, straight dark eyebrows give her a fierce expression. A patrician nose and wide, delicately carved mouth with a full lower lip complete the picture of remarkable beauty.

When I was a plain, ordinary child, this is how I wished I looked. Now I'm at peace with my appearance, but still I can envy the stunning woman that Venetia Napier will be someday.

Barrett and I take seats opposite her. As he studies her, his eyebrows rise; her beauty isn't lost on him either. His stern expression softens. "Did you come here all by yourself?"

"Yes." Venetia seems unaware of, or indifferent to, her looks. She calmly studies us, taking our measure.

"From where?" Barrett says.

"St. John's Wood."

"That's seven miles away. How did you get here?"

"I took the train."

"Where are your mother and father?" I can't believe they would let her travel around London by herself. All manner of evils can befall an unaccompanied child, especially one as beautiful as Venetia. Then again, this is a girl who threw rocks at a police station.

"My father is dead. I think my mother is the lady in the newspaper. That's why I came."

I read my own thoughts on Barrett's face—how nice for Sleeping Beauty if this remarkable child is her daughter, and she doesn't belong to August Legrand or the Oliphants. But how terrible for Venetia if her mother is in a coma from which she may never awaken.

"What makes you think the lady is your mother?" Barrett says gently.

"My mother went to Egypt. I've waited and waited for her to come back, and she hasn't yet. Something bad must have happened." Venetia delivers this bizarre explanation in a matter-of-fact tone.

Barrett's forehead crinkles. *"Egypt?"*

I'm doubtful, too. Venetia is a child, even though she doesn't act like one, and children have lively imaginations.

"Yes. That's where we lived. Before Father had his accident. He was digging a tunnel, and it caved in, and he was killed." Venetia glances at Barrett's notebook and pencil on the table. "Aren't you going to write this down?"

"Uh, yes." Barrett opens the notebook to a blank page, writes "Venetia Napier," then "Egypt."

My credulity is fading fast, and so is my hope that Sleeping Beauty is kin to Venetia rather than August Legrand, the Oliphants, or some yet unknown party.

"Mother writes books about Father's work," Venetia says. "She was writing one when he died. We came back to England. But she had to finish her book, so she went to Egypt again."

These details strike an unexpected chord in my memory. I like to read during my limited spare time, and since Sally is a zealous reader, we often visit her local public library together on her days off. That's where she sighted our father six months ago. The sighting is another reason for our visits to the library. Although he hasn't returned, we're hoping he will. There, I once saw a display of intriguing books. The latest was titled *In Search of the Pharaohs*, and the cover illustration showed a golden sarcophagus against pyramids in a desert. The introduction said the book described the adventures of an archaeologist who conducted excavations in Egypt. The author was a woman—his wife.

"Is your mother named Maude Napier?" I ask Venetia.

"Yes." She sounds pleased, but not surprised, that I've heard of her mother. "My mother gets paid a lot of money for her books. They're very popular."

"And your father was Cyril Napier, the archaeologist?" I say.

"Yes. He dug up mummies and treasures." Venetia glances at Barrett, who's shaking his head in amazement. "I can show you his things at the British Museum, if you like."

"That won't be necessary." Barrett seems convinced that her parents are who she says they are.

As he writes down the information about the Napiers, I fit it into the puzzle at hand. Living in Egypt might explain Venetia's unconventional personality. I try to imagine Sleeping Beauty as an authoress who rode camels across deserts and peered inside two-thousand-year-old tombs. It's easier to imagine her as an artist's wife or a step-relative in a family that owns a convalescent home.

"When was your mother supposed to arrive back in England?" Barrett asks Venetia.

"I don't know."

"When did she leave Egypt?"

"I don't know." Venetia doesn't seem upset by her lack of these facts.

Barrett visibly musters his patience. "Then how can you be sure that she's not still there?"

"I just am."

When I was her age and my father went missing, I was sure he would come back. If I'd heard of an unidentified man found unconscious, I probably would have jumped to believe he was my father.

Barrett hesitates before he says, "You do understand that it would be better if your mother is still in Egypt? The lady in the newspaper is very badly hurt."

"Yes. But my mother is here in England." Venetia speaks with unshaken certainty.

The passage of twenty-four years has taught me a lesson that Venetia hasn't had time to learn—that wishful thinking and reality aren't the same thing. I'm torn between wanting Maude Napier safe and sound in Egypt and wanting to reunite her with her daughter.

Barrett gives me a glance that says we might as well drop the subject of Egypt because Venetia isn't going to change her mind. He asks her whether her mother has any distinctive birthmarks, moles, or scars.

"Not that I know of. But I don't recall ever seeing her undressed."

"You wouldn't happen to have a photograph of her, would you?"

"Yes, right here." Venetia pulls a small, sepia-toned print out of her skirt pocket and lays it on the table.

A baby girl sits in a high-backed armchair. She's wearing a white dress, bonnet, socks, and booties, and she has Venetia's straight, dark eyebrows and fierce expression. A closer look shows me that the chair is actually a seated figure, completely veiled in opaque black fabric. This is a "hidden mother" photograph—a common relic from the earlier years of photography, before the advent of reliable, inexpensive flash lamps. Exposures were long, and for a picture of a child by itself, the parent had to cover up and hold it still. I find such photographs disturbing because I imagine that the mother, while she was covered up, changed into a different, alien person from the one she'd been while she was visible. I wonder if the children were frightened by their hidden mother and her muffled, eerie voice speaking to them through the veil.

Barrett grimaces, rubbing his forehead, as if he hates to break bad news to Venetia. "You do realize that this photograph doesn't actually show your mother?"

"Yes, but it's the only one." Venetia's lip trembles, and she suddenly looks her age. "She doesn't like having her picture taken."

I've wondered why the hidden mothers wanted to be covered up instead of posing openly for the camera. Did Maude Napier think she looked unattractive in photographs? The camera doesn't always flatter, but I think some women thought the camera could see into them and expose things they wanted to keep under wraps.

A sudden recollection stuns me. My mother never let my father, or me, photograph her. Did she fear that her secrets would be written on her face?

Venetia leans forward, her little hands clasped in entreaty. "Please, can I see the lady? I want to know if she's Mother."

I want Barrett to say yes so that we can clear this up now, but Sleeping Beauty is a sight that no child should have to see.

"I must do some more investigating first," Barrett says in a kinder tone than he used with August Legrand and the Oliphant family.

Venetia nods, stoic, as though she's experienced many disappointments in her short life.

"In case I need to speak with you again, what is your address?" Barrett says.

"Number Seventeen Grove End Road, St. John's Wood."

Barrett, writing, says, "Do you live with someone?"

"My aunt. Miss Caroline Napier. She's Father's sister and my guardian."

"Why didn't she come with you?"

"She said I could come by myself. I'm not a baby." Venetia reminds me of Mick, who's thought himself an adult since he began living on the streets at age eight.

"I'll take you home," I say. "You shouldn't be running around the city alone."

"I ran around Cairo while Father was digging up tombs and Mother was writing. It was fun. I made all sorts of friends."

I shudder to think what friends. "That was then. This is now." I walk to Venetia and hold out my hand. "Come with me."

"All right." Venetia rises and takes my hand. "It was nice meeting you, Detective Sergeant Barrett. Thank you for speaking with me."

However wild she is, she could teach August Legrand and the Oliphants a thing or two about manners.

When we pass through the reception room, there are far fewer people than I saw earlier. Some must have grown tired of waiting

and left. I hope Barrett hasn't missed out on any useful information. PC Porter is absent; I suppose he's still seeing to the broken
window.

Venetia and I walk up Leman Street together, but as soon as we
turn the corner onto the busy, noisy Whitechapel High Street, her
hand slips from my grasp.

"Venetia!" I cry as she darts away through the crowds.

CHAPTER 10

I search up and down the street, but Venetia is gone. Why did she run away? I hope she gets home safely.

When I return to the police station, a constable at the desk reads a name off a list, and a plump woman rises from a bench. I presume he's taking her to Barrett, but instead he leads her up a flight of stairs. Compelled by an intuition that something's not right, I follow them to the second floor. They enter a doorway. I wait a moment, then peer through it to a large room furnished with desks, chairs, cabinets, and coatracks. It exudes the odors of tobacco smoke and male sweat. The constable lounges in a chair, his feet up on a desk. A corner of the room is enclosed by a partition. Black letters on the glass spell out, "Inspector Edmund Reid." My heart thumps. My insides burn as I see the man himself, who has done Barrett, my friends, and me so much evil.

Dressed in plain clothes, he sits behind his desk, facing the plump woman, who occupies a chair. He has iron-gray hair worn in a fringe across his forehead. His fluffy mustache and beard, his pink complexion and crinkled eyes, give him a deceptively jovial aspect. He has yet to notice me. Moving toward him, I hear the woman say, "I think Sleeping Beauty is my lodger. She skipped out last week without payin' the rent."

As Reid writes in a notepad, the constable sees me and says, "Hey! You can't go in there."

I bang on the open door to Reid's office, enter, and say, "Inspector."

Hostility glints in his eyes, which are a pale brown that reminds me of frozen mud. "Sarah Bain. I heard you were here today. Damn Sir Gerald Mariner. He's dropped you on us like a rotten egg."

He's not the only one who's angry. Two years ago, he delivered Hugh, Mick, and me into the hands of the Ripper. If he'd had his way with us, we'd all be dead now. And it seems he's devised a new plot to take Barrett down and us along with him—four birds with one stone.

"Why are you interviewing people who came to report tips about Sleeping Beauty?" I say.

Reid bares his sharp teeth in a nasty smile. His shaving soap smells of harsh, chemical pine. "Not that you've any right to ask, but I thought I'd give Detective Sergeant Barrett a hand."

"Really. I suppose you intend to share the information with Barrett."

"Of course."

Reid thinks Barrett attained his promotion at his own expense, and he's partially right. Reid thought he'd solved the hangman's murder, but Barrett, my friends, and I proved him wrong. He lost much credibility with his fellow police officers and the public, and I'm certain he's seized on the Sleeping Beauty case as his opportunity for revenge.

The plump woman says, "I should be going," and scurries out of the office.

I glance at Reid's notebook. The two visible pages are covered with his thorny handwriting. He's collected a wealth of tips that may help him identify Sleeping Beauty and discover who attacked her, before Barrett can.

"Then you won't mind if I take this to Barrett." I snatch the notebook.

"Hey!" Reid lunges for it.

Thrilled by my own daring, I hasten toward the door. Reid falls across his desk, curses, and yells to the constable, "Stop her!"

I run past the constable. He chases me out to the hall, where I crash into Barrett. "Whoa!" Barrett says, putting his arms around me to steady us. "The constable downstairs said he saw you come up here. Why—?"

Reid, behind me, snatches at the notebook. As we tussle, it falls on the floor. Reid bends to pick it up, but I kick it down the hall.

"You little bitch!"

Barrett pulls me behind himself, shielding me from Reid. "What's going on?"

"She tried to steal police property." Reid points at the notebook.

Although Barrett could get in trouble because of my actions, he looks more concerned for me than for himself. Reid could arrest me and throw me in jail.

"Inspector Reid has been interviewing people who came in with tips about Sleeping Beauty," I say. "He wasn't going to tell you. We need the notes he took."

Comprehension and anger dawn on Barrett's face. "Is that true?" he asks Reid.

"So what if it is? I'm your superior. I don't have to tell you anything unless I choose to."

I dart over to the notebook and pick it up.

"You're trying to solve the case yourself!" Fury heightens Barrett's color.

Reid shrugs. "Why shouldn't I? If I remember correctly, you've got six unsolved cases. You're bringing down H Division's reputation. Somebody has to raise it back up."

"This isn't about H Division's reputation," Barrett says. "The Sleeping Beauty investigation has blown up into a major case, and you want credit for solving it. While sabotaging me—how convenient."

"You're a fine one to talk about sabotage." Reid's disgust includes me. "You threw a wrench into the Ripper investigation.

You were hiding something then. You still are now." He thrusts his sharp nose at us. "I want to know what it is."

He's steered the conversation into dangerous territory. If the truth about our role in the Ripper case ever came out, Hugh, Mick, Barrett, and I would go to the gallows. And now the temptation to tell Reid is written all over Barrett's face.

Reid sees it too. A malevolent smile distorts his mouth as he snaps his fingers at Barrett. "Come on, then. Out with it."

Barrett would love to throw it in Reid's face that we know who the Ripper is, why he'll never be caught, and how badly Reid botched the investigation. As Barrett opens his mouth, I say to Reid, "Don't try to change the subject. The past is over." Barrett looks as if I'd flung my arm across his chest just in time to prevent him from stepping in front of a runaway horse. "There's a poor, injured woman who's in a coma, without a name. Forget the bad blood between us. Work with us to identify her and catch her attacker."

My suggestion is akin to asking a wolf to serve petit fours to sheep. Reid says, "It'll be a cold day in hell. Now I'll take that, thank you." He snatches at the notebook.

When I hold it out of his reach, he swats my jaw. As I shriek with more indignation than pain, Barrett grabs Reid from behind and locks his arm across Reid's throat. Reid bucks, trying to pry Barrett's arm loose, yelling curses. Barrett clenches his teeth as he throttles Reid; his face wears a ruthless, frightening expression. Reid's face turns red as he wheezes. I'm furious at Reid myself, but heaven help us if he's finally pushed Barrett too far.

"Stop!" I tug at Barrett and pound his back with my fists.

He lets go of Reid and stands breathing hard, chastened, as if he's only just realized what he almost did. Reid bends over, hands on his knees, coughing and gasping. He looks up at us, his eyes burning with humiliation. I almost feel sorry for him as I rub my sore jaw.

Then he says, "Attempted murder of your superior." His voice is breathless but exultant. "Grounds for immediate dismissal. Thanks, Barrett. You just handed me your head on a silver platter."

This is the end of Barrett's police career—and of our hopes for the future; he won't marry me unless he can support me, and he may even go to prison. But as I swallow my pride so I can beg Barrett to apologize and Reid to forgive him, Barrett smiles.

"What are you talking about? I never touched you."

"Don't try to deny it. There's a witness . . ." Reid's voice trails off as he looks around; his smile fades because he realizes that he, Barrett, and I are alone.

The constable has vanished rather than get caught between Reid and Barrett.

"It'll be your word against ours, and who are the top brass going to believe?" Barrett says. "We're the ones who caught the hangman's murderer, and you're the one who tried to railroad an innocent man. Not for the first time," he adds, alluding to the Ripper case, rubbing salt into Reid's sorest spot.

Reid scowls. "All right, you win again. Take my notebook, if you want it that badly. Those tips are probably useless." Then his smile returns, and he says to me, "The next time you see Sally, give her my regards."

His words are a more shattering blow than the physical one he dealt to my jaw. *He knows about Sally.* I thought I'd managed to keep her existence a secret from him, but I was wrong.

"Sally who? What are you talking about?" The confusion in my voice sounds artificial to my own ears.

Reid smirks, not fooled. "Sally Albert. Your sister." As if to cap a masterful performance with an encore, he adds, "Benjamin Bain's other daughter."

"I don't have a sister." These are the words I've memorized just in case the subject of Sally ever come up under dangerous circumstances.

"Oh, bollocks. She looks just like you," Reid says, adding with insulting candor, "only younger and prettier."

My gaze involuntarily flies to Barrett. He says, "I didn't tell him."

"He didn't have to tell me," Reid says. "If you wanted to keep your sister a secret, you shouldn't have let her come to your house."

"Do you have someone spying on me?"

"I have constables patrolling Whitechapel High Street. If they see something interesting, they report it to me."

Now I'm angry with myself, for I should have known he was keeping tabs on me. "Leave Sally alone." My voice is breathy, the warning hiss of a snake.

"Ooh." Reid widens his eyes and flaps his hands in mock fright.

I've only made matters worse—I've told him how important Sally is to me.

"Mrs. Albert's not bad-looking for her age," Reid says. "How long have you known that your father has a second wife and daughter?"

"It's none of your business." Although I love Sally, I wish we'd never met, so she would be safe from Reid.

"On the contrary," Reid says. "Everything related to Benjamin Bain is my business. They're potential witnesses in the Ellen Casey murder investigation."

"Mrs. Albert didn't know Benjamin Bain at the time of the murder," Barrett says, "and Sally wasn't born yet."

"They may know his current whereabouts," Reid says.

"They don't!" But I can't deny my own suspicion that Mrs. Albert knows something.

"I should stop by for a little chat with them. They have plum positions at that townhouse in Chelsea. The trusted housekeeper and her daughter, the sweet, lovely maid." Reid is showing off how much he knows about my stepfamily. "But that could change if their master learns the police are questioning them in regards to a murder."

Alarmed because Sally and her mother could lose their positions, I say, "They've never done you any wrong. They don't deserve to be punished!"

"Who said anything about punishing *them*?" Reid isn't above hurting me through Sally and her mother. "I'll drop a word about them to the newspapers. When it comes out that they're kin to Benjamin Bain, the rapist and murderer, they'll never work in a respectable house again."

My temper is like claws inside me, tearing at my self-control. I assail Reid, my fists upraised. "If you hurt them, I'll—"

"That's enough, Sarah!" Barrett grabs my arm.

In the moment before he rushes me down the stairs, I see Reid smile, as if he's storing away my threat as a weapon to turn against me someday.

★   ★   ★

Barrett takes me to the Brown Bear, the public house across the street from the police station. He seats me at a table at the back, distant from the few constables gathered by the bar. While he fetches our drinks, I breathe deeply, trying to calm the emotions that howl like a storm in me. Barrett sets two glasses of ale on the table. As we drink, the glass rattles against my teeth. The cool, sour ale spreads a sedative warmth through my body, and my temper settles like a hibernating bear.

"Is that better?" Barrett asks.

Nodding, I manage a smile. "I'm sorry I lost my temper."

"Yeah. Well. I'm sorry I almost let the cat out of the bag."

We drink in silence, aware of how close we came to putting ourselves in Reid's power. Then Barrett says, "You should go home."

"But I have to watch the interviews. Sir Gerald will expect a report, and he'll want to publish the tips in the paper tomorrow."

"You already have plenty to report—our three likeliest tips on Sleeping Beauty's identity." Barrett says, with an attempt at humor, "You must have brought me good luck. Before you showed up, I was getting nowhere fast."

"But there might be other good tips coming. I don't want to miss them."

"You can't be at the police station." Barrett's voice is gentle but firm.

"Sir Gerald and the police made a deal. Inspector Reid has to abide by it. He can't keep me out."

"Forget Sir Gerald's deal!" Barrett reaches across the table and clutches my shoulders. "Didn't you see the way Reid looked at you? He knows he can push you far enough that you'll snap. Next time, I might not be there to stop you."

"Next time, *I* might not be there to stop *you* when you snap." But I sigh; he's right. "Why must Reid waste so much time and effort thinking up new ways to hurt us?"

"His work is his life. He throws his whole might at everything related to it—not just at you and me."

I hate to imagine how many other people are the brunt of Reid's one-track mind. "If only he could let bygones be bygones."

"Hmm." Barrett ponders a moment. "I think I understand why he can't. The Ripper case is probably the biggest of his career. He must be afraid he'll be remembered for failing to solve it, no matter how hard he works and what else he accomplishes. If I were in his shoes, I would be hard-pressed to let go of my grudge against the people I thought were responsible for my failure."

"You're more charitable than I am." Humbled, and proud of Barrett, I squeeze his hands. "But I can't quit the investigation. Sir Gerald wouldn't like it, and I have to find out who Sleeping Beauty is." I voice the idea that's taken stubborn root in my mind. "I think she's Venetia Napier's mother."

Barrett withdraws his hands; his gaze on me is shrewd. "You mean, you want her to be. *I* think Venetia Napier has an overactive imagination."

I look into my empty glass. He knows my history, and I frown at his not inaccurate implication that my experience has biased me in favor of Venetia Napier.

"Do you really want Sleeping Beauty to be the wife of that obnoxious artist?" I say, challenging his own bias.

"No, but what I *want* doesn't matter," Barrett says. "I just have a hunch that she is. It's not the same thing as trying to match her with someone for my own personal reasons."

My temper resurges. "That's not what I'm doing."

"All right; I didn't mean to say you were," he says. "Who knows? Sleeping Beauty could be Peggy Oliphant or somebody we haven't heard of yet. At any rate, you don't need to hear all of the tips. I'll tell you about them later. By the way, thanks for this." He holds up Reid's notebook. "Without you, I'd never have known I missed anything."

"He won't stop trying to sabotage you."

"I'll have Porter watch out for him. In the meantime, you should warn Sally that Reid is on to her. And step up your search for your father, so Reid doesn't get to him first."

CHAPTER 11

I go to the *Daily World* headquarters, report the tips to the editor at the copy desk, and leave the photographs of Jenny Legrand and Peggy Oliphant, which Barrett let me borrow. Then I go home. In the parlor, I find Hugh and Tristan seated at opposite ends of the sofa. The air between them is as dark and turbulent as a tornado—they've been quarreling. As they jump to their feet, I note Tristan's face. Bruises and raw, red cuts mar his cheeks. His left eye is swollen shut, the skin around it turning purple.

"My God, what happened?" I'm afraid their quarrel was serious enough to come to blows.

"It wasn't me." Hugh's own face is unmarked.

"Then who . . .?"

"He won't tell me." Hugh looks worried sick, exasperated by Tristan's reticence.

"I should go." Tristan picks up his hat from the table and starts toward the door.

"Wait!" Hugh follows Tristan downstairs. I hear him say, "Why won't you talk to me?"

Tristan replies in a voice so low that I can't discern his words. The bell jangles as the door opens and then closes. Rubbing my tired eyes, I brace myself for yet another crisis. Hugh comes back, flops on the chaise longue, and blinks, fighting tears. I go to the kitchen and put on the kettle. When I return with the tea, he takes the cup I hand him, and says, "Thanks."

We drink the hot, strong, sweet tea; I wait. At last Hugh says. "He must have picked up a man who plays rough. Or they were caught in the act by someone who despises men like us."

Both possibilities are terrible. I can't think of anything to say except, "Tristan loves you. He'll come back."

Hugh chuckles glumly, says, "He won't be coming back anytime soon," and points to a newspaper on the table.

It's the *Telegraph*, spread open to the gossip column. I read a paragraph circled in black ink: *Who is the man engaged in a secret love affair with Lord Hugh Staunton, the notorious sodomite? Our source says he is a former priest from a prominent family.*

"Oh no." I try to find some consolation. "They didn't mention Tristan by name."

"Their 'source' knows he's a former priest. I work for Sir Gerald Mariner. Sir Gerald's son is a former priest. Anyone can put two and two together."

What Hugh and Tristan feared has happened: their liaison has been made public, and Tristan will face the same revulsion and ostracism as Hugh.

"We have to put some distance between us. At least that will keep the newspapers from publishing photographs of us together. It's what Tristan wants anyway." Hugh wipes his eyes. "He says he needs time on his own, to think."

To think about how to protect himself, regardless of Hugh's feelings. I don't say it lest I make Hugh feel worse.

"If the story blows up into a huge scandal, Tristan won't be able to take it," Hugh says. "It will destroy him."

Tristan may be Hugh's primary concern, but he's not mine. I think of Hugh's black depressions, his suicide attempt. "I'm sorry" is all I can say.

We sit in helpless silence as the daylight fades. At six thirty, I say, "I should get supper." Fitzmorris and I share the cooking, and he isn't here.

I'm in the kitchen, frying eggs and sausages and bread, when the bell on the front door jangles and Mick bounds up the stairs. He greets Hugh, who doesn't answer, then joins me in the kitchen. He's grimy with soot and sweat, and I remind him to wash his hands.

"What's the matter with Hugh?" Mick whispers.

I whisper the explanation.

At the table, Hugh picks at his food and gulps wine. Mick eats with his usual voracious appetite but is less than cheerful. "I rode around on the underground trains all day and got off at all the stations and asked around the shops. Nobody knew of a woman who might be Sleeping Beauty. Nobody remembers seein' a red dress on anyone neither. I'll have to go back after school, when the people who work at the stations at night are there, and ask them. Maybe I can pick up her trail." Exhausted from his long, strenuous day, he cleans his plate and falls silent.

I know he's thinking about Catherine. Last week, when I was taking out the garbage, I found a crumpled playbill from a West End music theater. Catherine was listed among the performers. Her stage career had faltered as a result of our last murder investigation, but she's managing to build it up again. Surely Mick wishes he could attend her shows and take her to dinner afterward instead of toiling on a fruitless search for clues to Sleeping Beauty's identity.

"I thought it was possible that a woman wearing a fancy red dress in the middle of the night had come from a house of ill repute," Hugh rouses himself to say. "I visited thirty-two around the East End."

"That's a good theory," I say, wanting to boost his spirits. "Any luck?"

"No missing blondes with red dresses. What about you, Sarah?"

I describe my clash with Inspector Reid. It's embarrassing to admit that I lost my temper, but Hugh and Mick need to know that Reid will be even more determined to get us.

"Reid is a scoundrel who ought to be pilloried and stoned," Hugh says.

"I'd pay a guinea to see that!" Mick laughs, then says, "Barrett's right. Steer clear of the police station, or Reid will give you rope to hang yourself."

I describe the tips Barrett and I heard. My friends listen with interest and revived spirits while I describe August Legrand, the Oliphants, and Venetia Napier. "Sir Gerald should be satisfied that we're making progress."

"Thank God for some good news," Hugh says.

I put down my fork and rise. "I have to tell Sally what's happened."

"By the way," Hugh says, "she left a note for you."

★   ★   ★

An hour later, I find Sally inside the vast, noisy, glass-roofed concourse of Liverpool Street station, where her note asked me to meet her. When I tell her that Inspector Reid knows about her, she says, "It's all right, Sarah. I'm not afraid of him."

I'm glad she's not mad at me for bringing her to Reid's attention, but dismayed by her lack of concern. "You should be afraid. He could make you and your mother lose your jobs, or even arrest you and put you in jail."

"But we haven't done anything wrong."

"Reid isn't above hurting you to get revenge on me."

"I see," Sally says, but I can tell that she really doesn't. Despite the fact that she thinks our father has been persecuted for a crime he didn't commit, she still believes fair is fair and good behavior equals protection from punishment. She has an innocence that other people's vices and her own hardships can't corrupt.

"It would be good for you and your mother to leave town," I say.

"But we have to work."

It's an argument I can't refute. Sally says, "Besides, I have to help you find Father. Now that Inspector Reid is so angry at you, it's more important than ever."

I can't disagree, and I'm touched by her steadfastness, but I say, "You can't be running around the city. You should stay home."

"Inspector Reid could come after me there."

"At least your mother would know what had happened to you. So would I. It's better than if he snatched you off the street and nobody knew."

Sally's eyes widen in dismay. "You would think I'd disappeared, just like Father."

The mere thought of reliving my father's disappearance via Sally's terrifies me, and harm to her is the biggest threat that Reid could hold over my head. "Then you understand why you must stay home."

"We have to find Father and clear his name. Then Inspector Reid won't have any power over us." Sally presents this solution as if it's simple, practical, and obvious.

Sometimes her innocence is exasperating. "Even if we find Father, we might not be able to prove he didn't kill Ellen Casey."

"If I'm going to hide at home for days or weeks or months, I should make good use of my last bit of freedom." Sally leads me out of the station, past the cabs lined up along the street. "Tonight we'll see if we can learn more about Lucas Zehnpfennig."

I had already learned, to my great shock, that Lucas is my mother's illegitimate son by someone she knew before she married my father. The circumstances surrounding my father's disappearance weren't the only secret she kept from me. Not until recently did I learn that Lucas molested at least two young girls and was in the vicinity when Ellen Casey was raped and murdered. Sally and I once believed that if we were to find Lucas—a better suspect in the crime—we could clear our father's name. Then we discovered that Lucas died eight years ago. Even if he was guilty, we can't turn him over to the police, and he can't be made to confess and exonerate Benjamin Bain. However, Sally apparently thinks Lucas merits further investigation. I think she's grasping at straws.

Now we walk onto a bridge that spans the train yard on the north side of the station. We peer over the side of the bridge, down a drop of some thirty feet to a long, wide chasm enclosed by high walls. At the bottom, dozens of tracks parallel, cross, and merge. Trains puff out steam as they barrel along the tracks. The night resounds with the roar of their engines, the clatter of their wheels on the iron rails. Their headlamps send glaring rays of light into the fog.

"Down there is where Lucas died," Sally says.

Barrett had discovered the record of Lucas's death and looked up the police report. Lucas had been on the tracks when a train accidentally ran him over. Within the yard, gas lamps illuminate signal posts by the tracks, train cars, and coal wagons parked on sidings, and workers going about their business. On both sides of the bridge, buildings loom above the walls. In the distance, the tall, vast hulk of the station rises in a pall of smoke and fog that veils its gables and turrets. With lights burning in its arched windows, it looks like a cathedral on fire.

"I thought maybe we could learn something from the scene of his death," Sally says.

"That's a good idea." I'm surprised that my little sister is shaping up as a detective.

Sally smiles at my praise, then sighs with disappointment. "But I don't see anything."

"The accident was eight years ago."

"I want a closer look. I'm going down there." Sally trots along the bridge. At the end, mounted on the outside, is a metal ladder. Sally pulls herself up onto the side of the bridge, swings her legs over it, and grasps the ladder with both hands.

"Sally, no!"

"You can stay up here. I'll be right back." She's already climbing down the ladder.

Cursing under my breath, I follow. My legs tangle in my skirts as I clamber onto the side of the bridge. I almost fall off while groping for the ladder, whose rails are cold, damp, and slick. As I descend, my shoes slip on the rungs. The bridge and wall are defaced with obscene words. Several rungs from the bottom, I lose my footing, slide the rest of the way, and land with a thud that twists my ankle.

"Sally!"

She's walking along a track, gazing at the ground as if she expects to find an explanation for Lucas's death written in traces of his blood. Trains roll past us along nearby tracks. Their headlamps seem brighter from down here; the roar of their engines, the racket of their wheels, and the screech of brakes are louder.

"Come back!" I yell to Sally.

"Just a minute."

I glance side to side and behind me, watching for trains, as I hurry after Sally. A round light from a headlamp suddenly looms out of the mist, expanding into a giant white sun as it approaches me. I'm not in the train's path, but Sally is, silhouetted in the light. She tugs her skirt, which is caught on the rail. Screaming her name, I race toward her. A man suddenly appears, grabs her, and pulls her off the track. The train thunders over the spot where she'd stood.

Gasping, I wait for the eternity until it's gone. I see Sally standing beside the man. I hop over the track and enfold her in my arms. "Are you all right?"

"Yes." She's crying, shivering.

I shake her until her head bobbles. "You scared me half to death!"

"I'm sorry, I'm sorry," she wails.

I turn to the man and say with fervent gratitude, "Thank you."

He's dressed in a worker's cap and rough clothes, and he's so covered with black soot that I can't make out any of his features except his eyes, which reflect the light from the gas lamps. "What're you ladies doing here?" he demands. "Don't you know it's dangerous?"

"Yes, and we're sorry to trouble you," I say.

"Sorry wouldn't do much good if you'd been killed." He herds us across the tracks, toward doors set in arches carved into the wall. He leads us through one, then up a stairway. At the top, he unlocks another door, and then we're in a street lined with buildings, the shops on their ground floors closed for the night, their fronts plastered with signs I can't read because of the fog that dims the light from the street lamps.

"You've not answered my first question," the man says.

I bend the truth. "We're reporters from the *Daily World*. We're writing a story about train accidents. We understand that this was the scene of a fatal one."

"Lady reporters, eh?" The man eyes us with new interest. "Well, you understand right. It happened in 1880. I was here."

"Wonderful! I'd like to interview you. May I have your name?"

He smiles. "Gus Jones. I never been in the paper before."

This is one story I hope will never be in the paper. "Did you see the accident, Mr. Jones?"

"No. Neither did anybody else. The fog was thick that night. He'd fallen across the tracks before the train came. His body was crushed from the waist down. He was lying face up, with blood oozing out of his mouth." Mr. Jones shudders. "I'll never forget the look in his eyes."

Sally moans softly. I remind myself that if Lucas murdered Ellen Casey, as Sally and I believe he did, then he deserved his grisly death.

Mr. Jones shakes his head. "Lucas Zehnpfennig, may he rest in peace. I seen lots of accidents, but it's different when it's somebody you know."

"You knew him?" I say, surprised.

"Yeah. I identified his body."

Sally, recovered from her scare, smiles as if to say her close call was worthwhile. "How well did you know Lucas Zehnpfennig?"

"Only to say hello. I used to see him at the King's Arms sometimes." He points down the street. "Just yonder."

Chapter 12

The King's Arms is one in a row of drab brick buildings that back onto the thirty-foot drop to the train yard below street level. Signs on its front advertise Bass Ale and rooms for rent. Entering the dim taproom, Sally and I find tables occupied by men with the sooty clothes and faces of railway workers. They pause in their conversation to stare at us. From behind the bar, a short man with a receding hairline and broad shoulders nods a cordial welcome and gestures toward the lone empty table. Sally stays close to me; she's shy, as I naturally am, but my experience as a detective and a newspaper photographer has emboldened me.

"What should we do?" Sally whispers as we seat ourselves.

The barmaid, carrying a tray, comes toward us. She's less than five feet tall, with the face and the body of an undernourished fourteen-year-old. The sleeves of her brown cotton frock are rolled up as if they're too long for her, and her ash-blonde braids, tied up in two loops under her white cap, emphasize her childishness. But her dark eyes, underscored with puffy lower lids, have a somber, knowing, adult expression.

"I'll have another, Lizzie Zee," calls a man at the next table.

Zee. A hunch jolts me. When the girl walks up to us, I ask, "Are you a relative of Lucas Zehnpfennig?"

"Yeah. Mrs. Elizabeth Zehnpfennig, his widow." Her voice is husky, a woman's; she must be at least ten years older than she looks.

Sally and I gape and blurt, "Lucas was *married*?" It's the last thing we'd expected to learn about him.

"What of it?" Elizabeth's puffy eyes narrow. "Who're you?"

"I'm Sarah Bain. This is Sally Albert, my sister." I wait for a sign of recognition. When she shows none, I take a deep breath, then say, "I am Lucas's half-sister."

This is the first time I've publicly acknowledged my relationship to Lucas. It's as if I've crossed a river; unknown dangers await me on this new shore, and I can't go back. Shame makes me cringe inside, and not only because I'm imaging Lucas exposed as a rapist and murderer and my own reputation damaged. It's also because I've revealed a secret that my parents took pains to keep hidden.

Elizabeth Zehnpfennig drops her tray on the floor; her face goes blank with shock. The publican calls, "Lizzie! Be careful."

"Yeah, Dad."

"Bring us two glasses of ale," I say, "and one for yourself."

She walks on unsteady legs to the bar. When she returns with the drinks, her hands shake as she sets them on the table. She lowers herself into a chair.

"Lucas never told me he had a sister. When I asked him about his family, he said they were all dead." As she scrutinizes me, her pale complexion turns paler. "My God, you look like him! He was tall and thin and blond too."

Until now I've had no information about his physical appearance, and I'm sickened to hear that I resemble him. I realize that I've not wanted to put a face to Lucas because I was afraid the face would be my own.

Struggling to compose myself, I say, "I didn't know I had a brother until recently. My mother died without telling me. She had him before she married my father."

"Then how did you find out?" Elizabeth's expression remains wary.

I don't want to upset her by telling her the whole story, which includes Lucas's sordid past. "An acquaintance of my mother's told me about Lucas."

"How did you find me?"

"Sally and I went to the scene of his accident and met a man who'd known him."

Elizabeth glances toward the bar; her father is watching us. "Keep your voice down. Dad didn't like Lucas." Resentment burns through the tears that fill her eyes. "He wants to pretend we never met Lucas, and everything's like it was before."

I can think of one reason Elizabeth's father had disliked Lucas: he must have been some twenty-five years older than Elizabeth, and she little more than a child, when they married. I can understand his attraction to Elizabeth, and I wonder if her father was aware that Lucas was a pervert.

"But it's hard, pretendin' your husband never existed." Elizabeth sniffles. "I loved him more than anything in the world." She reaches inside her collar and pulls out a thin wedding ring that hangs from a string around her neck. It's tarnished where the gold plate has worn off. "I'll never love anyone else again."

Sally shifts in her chair; she's impatient, but it would be cruel to cut to the chase and ask Elizabeth if Lucas told her anything about Benjamin Bain. I say, "How did you and Lucas meet?"

"He rented a room here," Elizabeth says. "He'd just come from America, and he needed lodging."

"*America?*" It's the first I've heard that Lucas had ever been there.

"Yeah. He was American. Wasn't your mother?"

"No. She was English. And Lucas was born in England."

"Well, I thought he was American. He talked like it. He never said he wasn't."

We both fall silent, I wondering why Lucas had gone to America and stayed long enough to acquire an accent, she perhaps wondering why he'd concealed his real nationality.

"Who was his father?" Elizabeth says.

"I don't know." According to her acquaintance, my mother had refused to name the man.

"Was your mother married to him?"

"No."

"So Lucas was a bastard. That must be why he said his family was dead—he was ashamed."

Sally overcomes her shyness and attempts to hurry the story along. "So Lucas was staying here. He courted you?"

"Yeah. He would talk to me while I was working. I thought he was handsome and nice." Elizabeth smiles, and I see how pretty she must have been before the loss of her husband crushed her. "Well, one thing led to another." A blush turns her pale face a glowing pink. "Dad caught us in bed together. I never seen him so angry! He wanted to kill Lucas, but I begged him not to. I said we were in love. So he made Lucas marry me. He told Lucas that if he didn't, he would turn him over to the police." She fingers her wedding ring and adds in a wistful tone, "I was thirteen."

Sally and I drink our ale to hide our disgust toward both Lucas and the man filling glasses behind the bar. Lucas had preyed upon Elizabeth, and her father had wed her to a monster.

"Dad put Lucas to work helping around the pub. They never got along. He hated Lucas, but I was happy. For a while, at least." Unpleasant recollection darkens Elizabeth's gaze. "Lucas started going out at night. He wouldn't tell me where, or what he was up to."

I think of Tristan Mariner behaving with the same secrecy. Heaven knows what he's up to, but in the case of Lucas Zehnpfennig, I'm sure that as his wife got older, he began seeking out younger girls. How many more did he violate before his death?

"Oh, well, all husbands stray, don't they?" Elizabeth laughs at her own pathetic attempt to excuse Lucas. She looks at Sally and me, and her suspicion returns. "Why are you interested in any of this? What do you want with me?"

I choose my words with care, so as not to offend her or give away too much to a stranger whom I've no reason to trust. "I want to make your acquaintance. We're sisters-in-law."

Her eyebrows lift; she knows it's not the whole answer.

"I lost my father some time ago." I hesitate to mention his name, which she might have seen in the newspaper story; I don't want her to tell anyone I came here looking for the missing fugitive and the news to reach Inspector Reid. "His name is Benjamin Bain."

Elizabeth's face is blank. "Never heard of him."

I'm disappointed that she hasn't any information about my father, yet relieved because there's none she could give Reid. "He and Lucas once knew each other. I just wanted to know if Lucas said anything about him. Any memories he passed on, that you could tell me . . ."

Elizabeth reaches across the table and pats my hand. I'm so startled that I jump. "I know how you feel," she says. "If I'd known about you, I'd have looked you up, hoping you could tell me something about Lucas. I'm sorry he never mentioned your father."

Her sympathy is so unexpected, so moving. "Thank you."

"Did Lucas leave you any papers?" Sally says.

"Just some letters."

My hope revives. "Who were they from? What did they say?"

Elizabeth looks away, as if humiliated. "I don't know. I can't read."

"May I see them?" I say.

"Lizzie! Stop chattering and get back to work." Her father points at customers holding up empty glasses.

"Yeah, just a minute." Elizabeth runs up the stairs and soon returns. She pulls a bundle of letters out of her apron pocket, thrusts it into my hands, and whispers, "Dad's getting suspicious. If he finds out you're kin to Lucas—well, you'd better go."

★   ★   ★

There are five letters with no envelopes or return addresses. Sally and I examine them while sitting on a bench in Liverpool Street station. The date on the first is October 1852. The childish handwriting looks surprisingly familiar. The letter, yellow with age, reads,

My dearest son,

How are you? I miss you so much! Are the people in that terrible school treating you well? It's so lonely here without you. I feel as if my heart was cut out of me. I can't wait to visit you at Christmas. Here are some cookies I baked. I hope you like them, my darling.

With all my love,
Mama

An underground train thunders past below us. I feel as flattened as though it had rolled over me.

"My mother wrote this!"

It's not only the discovery that shocks me, but the sentiments she expressed. The letters she wrote me while I was away at school were dry instructions to obey my teachers and not cause trouble. She'd never sent me cookies, never let me call her "Mama." I can't bear to look at the letter again; I hand it to Sally and read three others. They're all from my mother, dated 1868, 1871, and 1874—after my father disappeared. Her fervent declarations of how much she loved, missed, and longed to be with Lucas are the same as in the earlier letter. They cover most of the pages, leaving scant space for description of her work at the button factory, her own life. She asks if he received the money she sent.

I wore secondhand clothes, and she sent money to Lucas.

She never mentions my father. Even if she knew where he was, the information isn't here. She mentions me only once—in the 1871 letter:

Sarah is fifteen. After she's done with school in three more years, she'll be on her own. Then I can come to you in America, and we can live together just as we've always dreamed of. My darling, I can't wait!

My mother meant to leave me so that she could be with Lucas. I would have been abandoned by her as well as my father. Speechless from the lump of outrage and grief in my throat, I pass the letter to Sally.

She reads it and murmurs, "Sarah, I'm so sorry." She clasps my hand, her own eyes tearful. I draw comfort from the one member of my family who refuses to leave me, no matter that she should for her own sake.

"But she didn't go to America," Sally says. "She stayed with you."

"I know why," I say, and the 1874 letter confirms the sad fact.

My darling Lucas,

I'm sorry to say that I won't be coming to you. I'm very ill. The doctor says it's cancer, and I haven't long to live. I pray that someday we'll be together again. Here is all the money I've saved. Know that I love you, and remember me fondly.

God bless you,
Mama

"She died the year she sent this." My chest hurts as if her hand had reached from beyond the grave to crush my heart. I'm also furious, and not only because she'd given Lucas all her savings and left me nothing except the next month's rent on the flat where we lived. "She could have told me about Lucas while she was on her deathbed. She could have told me the truth about my father, that he was alive. But she didn't." My voice rises in an anguished plea. *"Why?"*

I'll never know. My mother is as much a mystery to me as the hidden mother in Venetia Napier's photograph.

"There's one more letter." Sally unfolds the paper. As she reads, she clutches her throat as if she's choking.

Braced for more alarming discoveries, I take the letter and read aloud,

Dear Mr. Zehnpfennig,

Whoever you are, stop writing to my husband. How many times do I have to say it? LEAVE HIM ALONE!

Mrs. Genevieve Albert

"It's from *my* mother!" Sally says.

CHAPTER 13

"It's clear from her letter that Sally's mother corresponded with Lucas Zehnpfennig more than once." At seven o'clock in the morning, I'm breakfasting with Hugh, Mick, and Fitzmorris, telling them about yesterday's events.

"It's also clear that Mrs. Albert didn't know who Lucas was," Hugh says, "but he knew your father was married to her and using the name 'George Albert.'"

"And he knew where she lived, and he'd been trying to track my father down. Mrs. Albert wrote that letter eight months before Lucas died in January 1880." I tell Hugh and Mick about the deduction that had stunned Sally and me. "The letter that my father received from Lucas—the one that Sally saw in December 1879—wasn't the only one Lucas wrote him. There were others that Mrs. Albert must have intercepted."

"So how did your pa get the one that Sally saw?" Mick says between bites of a crumpet. "The one you think had something to do with why he disappeared?"

"Sally remembered that she brought in the post that day. She gave that one to our father."

"This is wonderful news, Sarah!" Hugh points out the other conclusion that Sally and I had drawn from our discovery. "You were right—Mrs. Albert does know more than she's admitted to you."

For at least eleven years, Mrs. Albert has known of the man that Sally and I think is the key to finding our father. She's as much a woman of mystery as my own mother.

"Sally plans to confront her and ask her what else she knows," I say. "She should have better luck than I would." I'm afraid that the secret of my father's whereabouts is in the sole possession of a woman who hates me and doesn't want him found.

The doorbell rings. Fitzmorris says, "I'll get it." He goes downstairs, then returns with Barrett.

"Good morning." Barrett smiles at us. "I came to see if anyone wants to go check on Sleeping Beauty with me."

★   ★   ★

I sent Mick to school because he's missed so many days recently. Hugh decided to go to Wandsworth, try to pick up the trail of Peggy Oliphant, then go to Holland Park and do the same for Jenny Legrand. As Barrett and I walk along Whitechapel High Street through the morning fog and traffic, I see newsboys hawking copies of the *Daily World*. On the front page are Jenny Legrand's and Peggy Oliphant's photographs, with the headline "Is One of These Women Sleeping Beauty?" The police have seen fit to share them with the press.

I fill Barrett in on the news about Tristan and my search for my father. Barrett tells me that after I left the police station yesterday, there were only a few more tips, all concerning women who didn't fit Sleeping Beauty's description.

"Was there any more trouble from Inspector Reid?" I say.

"None, thank God. I left Constable Porter to collect tips today while I check the archives for reports of missing women and attacks on women."

I don't say that I still think Sleeping Beauty is Maude Napier, and Barrett doesn't say that he still thinks she's Jenny Legrand, although I sense that he does. We haven't any evidence with which to convince each other, and we don't want to quarrel.

"The newspapers are saying the Ripper is back at work," Barrett says. "You and I know it's impossible, but there could be a copycat."

"Heaven help us." I glance into an alley and remember the night I saw Kate Eddowes lying slaughtered in a welter of blood.

"There's talk of restarting the Ripper investigation," Barrett says.

After the murder of Mary Jane Kelly in November 1888, the investigation had waned because of a lack of clues and suspects. Although there have been other women murdered since then, none of the crimes were officially blamed on the Ripper.

"Let's hope it's just talk," I say. The last thing we need is the police reexamining old evidence and discovering our secret involvement in the case.

At the hospital, we find Sleeping Beauty in a private room. She's still unconscious, her breathing shallow; the bandages on her face are like a death mask. Dr. Enoch wheels in a cart that holds large glass flasks of clear liquid, various other articles, and a strange contraption—a metal cylinder about twelve inches long and three inches wide, with a ring on one end and a long, thin, sharp-pointed metal tube on the other, mounted vertically on a stand.

After I introduce Barrett and Dr. Enoch, I say, "What is that?"

"It's an apparatus for injecting fluid into her veins," Dr. Enoch says.

"I've never heard of such a thing," Barrett says.

"Not many people have." Dr. Enoch explains, "The technique was invented in Edinburgh in 1832, during a cholera epidemic. Cholera causes massive diarrhea that kills people by purging the water and salts from their blood. One of my countrymen discovered that if you replace the water and salts, they have a much better chance of surviving."

"But people still die of cholera," I say. "Why isn't the procedure commonly used?"

"Because it's risky and not widely accepted by the medical establishment. In her case, however, I think it's necessary. Her condition is deteriorating. Without fluids, she won't last long enough to wake up."

Barrett and I watch Dr. Enoch pull on the ring on the cylinder, remove a plunger, and pour in liquid from a flask.

"This is a sterile solution of potassium and sodium bicarbonates and chlorides." He gently removes Sleeping Beauty's arm from beneath the blanket and ties a strap around the upper part. A thin blue vein bulges under the white skin above her wrist. He inserts the sharp end of the tube into the vein.

Feeling faint, I sit in the bedside chair and take deep breaths. Dr. Enoch repeatedly fills the syringe with fluid and pumps it into Sleeping Beauty. When he's done, he feels her pulse.

"It's stronger. The procedure sometimes has immediate positive results."

Within an hour, her breathing deepens; her chest rises higher with each inhalation. Faint, pink color seeps into the skin of her arm. Barrett and I regard Dr. Enoch with wonder, as if he's reanimated the dead. Sleeping Beauty stirs under the blanket; her chapped lips move within the gap in the bandages.

"Who's there?" Her voice is a thick, hoarse croak that rises on a note of fear.

My skin ripples as if a ghost had spoken. I turn to Barrett, and I see on his face the same awestruck expression that I feel on mine.

Sleeping Beauty is awake.

Her eyes, framed by holes in the bandages, flutter open. The irises are a bright, crystalline blue, the whites veined with red. Her pupils are black, dilated pools of terror.

"Where am I?" She struggles to sit up, her bandaged hands pushing against the bed, her body straining. She's so weak that she can only lift her head.

I hesitate before I rise from the chair and move close to her. I'm relieved that she's alert and coherent, but I feel shy because she's a stranger despite my sense of connection with her. "You're in London Hospital."

She stares at me, uncomprehending. "Who are you?"

It's a good sign that she's asking the logical questions. Her brain must have escaped damage. I feel awkward because I'm the first person she's seeing at this terrible moment in her life. "My name is Sarah Bain. This is Detective Sergeant Barrett and Dr. Enoch."

Her head drops against the pillow; she gasps from exertion. "Why am I in the hospital?" Her accent is London bred, and she's at about the same place on the social scale as myself. "What's wrong with my voice? What happened to me?"

"Your throat must have been injured." Cold, ominous dismay trickles through my veins, like the fluid from Dr. Enoch's apparatus. "Don't you remember?"

". . . No." She must be confused; she's been unconscious for three days. She raises her hands to her face. *"What . . . ?"* Moaning, she claws at the bandages.

"Don't do that!" I say.

She rips the gauze strips off her face, exposes the raw, red, stitched cuts on swollen, puffy flesh. As her fingers probe the cuts, she wails, "No!"

I grab her wrists. They're thin and fragile—twigs covered with soft, dry, feverish skin. I pull her hands away from her face while she pants. Her breath is sour, decayed. I'm afraid of hurting her, but also afraid she'll tear out the stitches and hurt herself.

"Oh no, oh no." Sobs wrack her body.

Even under the best circumstances, I'm not good at comforting people. I look to Barrett and Dr. Enoch for help, but they seem just as much at a loss as I feel I am. I hold her hand and murmur, "Shh—don't cry. It's all right."

Of course it isn't. Even when her face heals, it will never be the same. But here is a chance to solve the mystery of her identity.

"What is your name?" I'm tense with eagerness to hear *"Maude Napier."*

Her sobs stop with a gulp. "I don't know." The terror in her eyes darkens into horror. "Oh God. I can't remember!"

"She has amnesia." Dr. Enoch says regretfully, "It's not uncommon with head injuries."

Pity for her eclipses the disappointment I feel as I realize that my investigation is far from its conclusion.

Dr. Enoch turns up the flame in the gas lamp. Sleeping Beauty squints and puts up her right hand to shield her eyes. Her other hand clings to mine. As Dr. Enoch leans over her, she cringes in fear.

"Dr. Enoch saved your life," I say.

She relaxes and murmurs, "Thank you." She's polite despite her anguish and confusion. Her personality is emerging despite her mental impairment, and she seems a nice, sweet woman.

Dr. Enoch peers into her eyes. "Your right pupil is larger than the left. You've had a concussion. That means that the blow to your head knocked your brain against the inside of your skull. Do you know what year this is?"

After a moment's hesitation, Sleeping Beauty says, "Eighteen ninety."

Dr. Enoch smiles. "That's correct. Can you tell me who is queen?"

"Victoria." Sleeping Beauty moans. "If I can remember her name, why can't I remember my own?"

"The brain is a mysterious thing," Dr. Enoch says.

"Will I ever remember?"

"Probably. Cases of permanent amnesia are rare."

She turns to me, still clinging to my hand as if it's a rope that I'd tossed her after she'd fallen into the sea. "How did I get here?"

"The police brought you," I say. "You were found lying unconscious by the river, in Shadwell."

"Shadwell?" Incredulity raises her hoarse voice. "What was I doing there?"

"You don't remember that either?"

"No." She whimpers, on the verge of more tears.

"Where do you live?" Barrett says.

She shakes her head. Barrett and I look at each other. We'd had such high hopes for the moment when Sleeping Beauty awakened.

"I want to see myself," she says. "Could you please bring me a mirror?"

Barrett, Dr. Enoch, and I share a glance of mutual alarm. I say, "I don't think that's a good idea."

"If I can see myself, maybe I'll remember who I am." Her body trembles with urgency; I can feel the vibration in my own. *"Please!"*

Dr. Enoch says with marked reluctance, "It might snap her out of the amnesia." He goes to the door and calls a nurse, who brings a round mirror with a wooden back and handle.

The pressure of Sleeping Beauty's fingers around mine is stronger than I'd thought possible. I brace myself as I hold the mirror above her face. She silently contemplates her reflection, the red cuts and stitches on her cheeks, forehead, and nose; the bruises around her eyes and on her neck. The injuries are so disfiguring that even if I had the photographs of Jenny Legrand and Peggy Oliphant at hand, I wouldn't be able to tell if she was one or the other. And there's no photograph of Maude Napier to compare.

Sleeping Beauty frowns, seeming more nonplussed than upset. "I don't know her. I've never seen her before in my life." It's as if she's been shown a stranger's photograph to identify. Then she reaches her hand toward the mirror, sees her reflection do the same thing, and inhales a shuddering gasp. "Oh God." Her voice quavers. She withdraws her hand to trace the cuts with her fingertip. Her eyes spill tears. *"Who did this to me?"*

The nurse takes the mirror away. My heart sinks as I lose my last hope that Sleeping Beauty would recall the events that transpired before she was found by the river.

"We were hoping you could tell us," Barrett says gently.

"I don't know, I don't know."

"Can you remember the names of your family, your friends— anybody who knows you?" Barrett says.

She tosses her head from side to side on the pillow. "I can't. Oh God!"

"You should go," Dr. Enoch says to Barrett and me. "Questioning her will only make her more upset. She needs to calm down, eat, drink, and rest."

I start to pull my hand loose, but Sleeping Beauty clutches it and cries, "Don't leave me!"

I know it's selfish to think that our sense of connection is mutual and to feel flattered. Like a chick just hatched from the egg, she must have latched onto the first person she saw after regaining consciousness.

"Just another minute?" Barrett says. When Dr. Enoch reluctantly nods, he says, "The *Daily World* newspaper published a story about you and asked anyone who thinks they might know you to report it to me at the Whitechapel police station. More than a hundred people have come forward."

Sleeping Beauty goes still and quiet.

"There are three parties that seemed more credible than the others," Barrett says. "If I tell you who they think you are, will you tell me if you recognize your name?"

"Yes." Her wet, reddened eyes shine with cautious hope.

I feel her hand trembling, and my own heart begins to pound as Barrett says, "Jenny Legrand."

Sleeping Beauty's blonde eyebrows draw together with a frown of intense concentration. I hold my breath, afraid she's going to remember that she's Jenny. When she shakes her head, I exhale with tentative relief.

Barrett's expression is deliberately neutral; I can't tell if he's disappointed. "Peggy Oliphant."

Her expression doesn't change.

"Maude Napier," Barrett says.

I avert my gaze from Sleeping Beauty, as if to look at her would bring bad luck. My heart pounds so fast and hard, she must feel it through our joined hands. Even though I know I shouldn't influence her, I silently will her to say that she's Maude.

"None of those names are familiar." Her hoarse, weary voice shreds my hope. Her hand goes limp in mine. When I look at her, I see her ravaged face crumple.

Barrett shakes his head at me, his expression bleak. After all the tips from the public, all the hours devoted to seeking her identity, we're right where we started.

I say, "Perhaps if we compared her handwriting to samples from—"

Before I can finish the sentence, Dr. Enoch shushes me. He whispers in my ear, "Some people with head injuries entirely forget how to write because of brain damage. I strongly advise against asking her to try writing, because if she discovers that she can't, it will make things worse. Even if she can, her injury could change the style of her handwriting. Better wait a few days."

"What am I going to do?" Sleeping Beauty whispers. "I haven't any money. How am I to pay the hospital?"

As bad as things are for Barrett's and my investigation, they're far worse for her. She's nameless, alone in the world, her past a mystery, her future uncertain.

"We'll keep you on as a charity patient," Dr. Enoch says. "We won't discharge you until you're well."

"But then what? Where will I go?"

Footsteps clatter down the hall, and an excited voice says, "There she is!"

Two men burst into the room. One holds a camera and tripod, the other a notebook. Dr. Enoch says, "This is a private treatment room. You can't come in."

The reporter leans over the bed, peers into Sleeping Beauty's startled face, and laughs. "Well, what do you know—Sleeping Beauty is awake! Prince Charming must have kissed her. Hello, little lady."

News that she's conscious must have spread like wildfire through the hospital, via eavesdropping nurses or visitors, and out to the streets. She cringes in fright. The photographer is setting up his camera. I say, "Leave her alone!"

"Get out!" Barrett orders.

"So what's your name?" the reporter asks Sleeping Beauty.

The photographer aims his camera at her, ducks under the black drape to adjust the focus, and holds up his flash lamp. I step between him and Sleeping Beauty, shield her from the white, fiery explosion. Many more people rush into the room. They're nurses chasing other reporters and photographers, trying to protect their patient. The reporters shout questions at Sleeping Beauty while the photographers scuffle for the best camera angles. Barrett yells and shoves at them in vain.

A familiar, angry male voice shouts above the din: "What is this, a beer brawl?"

It's Sir Gerald, accompanied by two of his bodyguards. The bodyguards force the intruders out of the room, and Sleeping Beauty beholds Sir Gerald with awe.

"Thank you," she whispers.

He frowns as he nods. "My pleasure." I think he's repulsed by her cut face, but he gently pats her bandaged hand and says, "I came to see how you're doing. I'm Gerald Mariner."

"It's nice to meet you." Sleeping Beauty doesn't seem to recognize his name. Either she never heard of him before the coma, or it's among the things she's forgotten. When she doesn't introduce herself, Sir Gerald turns a quizzical gaze on me.

"She has amnesia," I say. "She doesn't remember who she is."

If Sir Gerald is displeased because the mystery of her identity isn't solved, he doesn't show it. He addresses Sleeping Beauty with more kindness than I'd thought he had in him. "I'm sorry to hear that. I'll help you in any way I can. First, don't worry about money. I'll pay for your hospital bills and whatever else you need. And I'll put guards by your door to keep out the riffraff."

Sleeping Beauty stares at him as though he's a god who magically descended from on high to bring her good fortune. "Sir, you're too kind."

I wonder if somebody once came to his aid when he was in trouble and he's repaying the favor, balancing the books. Or maybe he does have a heart after all.

"But I can't accept your generosity," Sleeping Beauty says. "I've nothing to give you in return."

"There is something," Sir Gerald says. "I own a newspaper—the *Daily World*. You're a big story. Everybody in London is interested in you. Do an exclusive interview for the *Daily World*, and we'll be even."

That's more like the Sir Gerald I know.

Sleeping Beauty's eyes widen with amazement at the idea that she's famous. Obviously confused and uncertain, she turns to me. My own experience has taught me that deals with Sir Gerald can be dangerous, but she needs his help.

"If you give the *Daily World* an exclusive interview, you won't have to talk to reporters from the other newspapers," I say.

"You don't have to do it right away," Sir Gerald says. "Whenever you're ready."

"It will keep your story in front of the public," Barrett says. "Someone might come forward to identify you."

"Miss Bain works for me," Sir Gerald says. "She'll do the interview."

Sleeping Beauty seems surprised by this new bit of information about me, but not unhappily so. "All right," she says with a weak smile, her hand still holding mine.

"It's a deal, then," Sir Gerald says, as if he'd expected it all along.

I feel more responsible for her than ever.

"Goodbye for now, Miss—" Sir Gerald says, "What shall we call you?" He isn't insensitive enough to use the cruel nickname he gave her to her face.

Again she turns to me. "Can you pick a name for me to use until I remember my real one?"

Touched by her trust, I say, "How about Rosamond?" The name of the enchanted princess in the Sleeping Beauty fairy tale is the first, logical one that occurs to me.

She smiles. "Yes. That's a pretty name. Thank you."

Sir Gerald and his men take their leave. Sleeping Beauty, whom I must now think of as Rosamond, closes her eyes, drained by all that's happened. She winces, her breathing labored. Dr. Enoch tells the nurse to bring warm milk mixed with medicine for pain. I sit by Rosamond while the nurse helps her drink. After she falls asleep and her hand releases mine, I join Barrett and Dr. Enoch in the hall.

"I think she'll make a full recovery from her injuries," Dr. Enoch says.

"What about her memory?" Barrett says.

"It's anyone's guess," Dr. Enoch says. "The next forty-eight hours are crucial."

Barrett's eyes gleam with inspiration. "I have an idea."

Chapter 14

"I don't think I can go through with it," Rosamond says.

It's the day after she awakened, and her face is again covered with bandages. She's seated in a wheelchair in the patients' day room at the hospital, with Barrett, Hugh, Mick, Sir Gerald, Dr. Enoch, and myself gathered around her. She wears new clothes that Sir Gerald bought her—a pale-blue cashmere dressing gown, blue slippers lined with white rabbit fur, a lacy white nightcap, and white silk gloves.

"I can't meet them." Her hoarse voice trembles.

Yesterday, Barrett invited August Legrand, the Oliphant family, and Venetia Napier to come to the hospital and meet Rosamond. They're downstairs, in separate rooms so they can't see one another, waiting to take part in an identity parade.

"What's the matter?" Sir Gerald says, glancing at his watch.

Rosamond shrinks from the impatience in his voice. "I'm afraid." Yesterday she'd eagerly agreed to Barrett's plan, and now I'm disturbed that she's balking. She turns to me and asks, "What if I don't recognize any of those people?"

During our short acquaintance she's come to trust me, I think. "If you do, you can be reunited with your family."

Her gloved hands flutter, touching the bandages on her face. "I saw my pictures in the paper. I'm ashamed that people have seen me like that. I can't face anybody else."

I'm angry at whoever showed her the pictures, ashamed that I took them. "You need to meet these people." I fear that if we don't do something to jog her memory now, during the crucial forty-eight-hour period, her amnesia will become permanent. And I don't want to delay while Venetia Napier anxiously waits to learn whether Rosamond is her mother. "Even if you don't recognize them, one of them may recognize you."

"Well, all right," she says reluctantly.

"Good." Sir Gerald says to Dr. Enoch, "Take off the bandages."

"No! Please!" Rosamond covers them with both hands. "I'm so ugly." Tears thicken her voice. "I'm sorry, I don't think I can do this."

After much persuasion, she agrees to a compromise. The day room contains, in addition to chairs, tables, and other furniture, a folding screen made of bamboo and woven wicker. Hugh and Mick place the screen in front of Rosamond, so that she can peer through the gaps between the wicker strands but she'll be invisible to people on the other side.

"Will you stay with me, Sarah?" she says.

"Of course." I pull up a chair beside her.

"We'll bring in the first one," Mick says. He and Hugh leave the room.

Rosamond and I wait behind the screen. She twists her gloved hands in her lap. My heart begins to race. August Legrand charges into the room ahead of Hugh and Mick. Dressed in a gray suit with a turquoise ascot and magenta-and-turquoise floral waistcoat, he carries a huge bouquet of yellow roses, a black artist's portfolio, and a small, flat rectangular box wrapped in silver paper and tied with a pink ribbon. His handsome Roman face is flushed. His eager smile fades as he sees no one in the room except Barrett, Sir Gerald, and Dr. Enoch.

"Where is she?"

Barrett points at the screen.

Irritation flashes in Mr. Legrand's pale eyes. "I thought you said I could see her."

"This is how she wants it," Barrett says.

Rosamond and I peer through the wicker at Mr. Legrand. He squints, trying to glimpse her. I picture him choking her and slashing her face.

"Jenny?" Mr. Legrand says. "It is I, August—your husband."

"Am I married?" Rosamond asks me.

Mr. Legrand gasps. "That is Jenny!" Exultant, he turns to Barrett. "I recognize her voice!"

Rosamond's hand flies up to cover her mouth. I turn away from her so that she won't see my dismay.

"Are you sure?" Barrett says, his manner carefully bland.

"Yes! Jenny, *ma cherie*, speak to me!"

"I don't know you," Rosamond says, timid but definite.

Cautious relief seeps through my fear.

"What?" Mr. Legrand stares, taken aback. "But of course, you have been through such an ordeal. You are confused."

"I'm sorry," she murmurs.

"Look what I've brought you, Jenny." He holds up the yellow roses. "Your favorites. At our wedding, you wore them in your hair. Don't you remember?"

"No. I'm sorry."

"And the chocolates you love." Mr. Legrand thrusts the gift box and bouquet at Barrett. "Could you give them to her?"

Barrett brings them to Rosamond. She holds them gingerly, as if they'll bite.

"They're the same kind we bought on our honeymoon in Paris, at that little *boutique de bonbons*," Mr. Legrand says.

Rosamond squirms in her wheelchair. "I don't remember."

"Taste one," Mr. Legrand urges.

She fumbles to open the box. As she reaches for one of the sculpted confections topped with candied violet petals, I put my hand on hers to stop her. A familiar taste might bring back her memory, but I haven't forgotten that someone she knew before her coma could be the person who attacked her. It could be August

Legrand; and the chocolates, poisoned. I put the box and bouquet on the floor.

"Jenny, look at this." Mr. Legrand opens his portfolio and takes out a painting. It depicts a beautiful blonde woman seated on a Greek pedestal, swathed in translucent white drapery. Her heavy-lidded eyes, her parted lips, and her unnaturally rosy cheeks spell seduction. She's the woman in the photograph that Mr. Legrand brought to the police station.

"Do you remember posing for me?" Mr. Legrand says. "It was a cold day, and I wanted to stop painting so you could warm up by the fire, but you insisted that we continue. You were so dedicated to my work. My muse. My love!"

Rosamond puts her hands against her bandaged cheeks. "Oh God." Her body trembles so hard, the wheelchair rattles.

"What's wrong?" I dread to hear that the painting has shocked her into remembering that she's Jenny Legrand.

She bursts into sobs.

"Jenny, I'm sorry if I upset you." Legrand returns the painting to the portfolio and says to Barrett, "Let me go to her. If I can just hold her and look into her eyes, she'll know me." He stalks toward the screen.

Rosamond draws her knees up to her chest and wraps her arms around them, as if to escape him by making herself smaller. Barrett grabs Mr. Legrand, who curses in French. Sir Gerald's two body-guards, stationed outside the door, rush in and drag Mr. Legrand away.

"Jenny, this is not the last you have seen of me! No one can keep us apart. I love you, and I will not rest until we are together again!" His yells fade down the hall.

"He's gone," I tell Rosamond. "You're safe."

She uncurls herself and wheezes, her body convulsing with her effort to catch her breath. Dr. Enoch brings her a cup of water. She sips, then whispers, "I'm sorry. I don't mean to be so much trouble. That painting—was it me? Is that how I looked before?" Tears clog her throat. "Was I that beautiful?"

I draw no comfort from my relief that Rosamond didn't recognize herself as Jenny Legrand. She's suffering from the knowledge that her face is far from beautiful now and the cuts will leave permanent scars.

"That poor man. I could see how much he loves his wife and wants her back." In the midst of her despair, she's capable of compassion for the man who frightened her and rubbed her nose in the loss of her looks. "I feel so sorry for him."

"Should we tell the other people to come back tomorrow?" I say, albeit reluctantly.

"No," she says, wan but brave. "It wouldn't be fair to make them wait."

When Hugh and Mick bring Frances, Faith, and Mrs. Oliphant, I hear the commotion of a crowd in the hall. People must have heard about the identity parade and come to learn the result. The three women sail into the room like an armada, the mother again decked in ostentatious mourning garb, the daughters in gaudy print frocks. Frances is in the lead, the flagship. Mrs. Oliphant huffs after her while Faith trails them, lugging a maroon leather suitcase. They don't seem surprised by the screen; my friends must have forewarned them. They hold their tiny chins high and look down their noses with haughty disapproval. They sit in chairs placed in front of the screen, Frances between her mother and sister. Rosamond leans forward to peer at them. The bandages hide her expression, but her body is rigid with apprehension.

"Peggy?" says Frances.

Her tone reminds me of the one I've heard from patrol constables at night when they hear a sinister noise in an alley and call, "Who goes there?" I can't tell whether Frances is afraid that Rosamond is Peggy or that she's not.

Rosamond shakes her head at me; either she doesn't recognize the women or isn't sure whether she does.

Frances raises her voice. "Can you hear me?"

"They didn't say she was deaf." Faith giggles. "We brought you some clothes." She points to the suitcase beside her. "Do you want to put them on?"

"Hush, dear," Mrs. Oliphant says. "Peggy, if that's you in there, you could at least deign to speak to us." Rosamond leans back from her unfriendly gaze. "We came all the way from Wandsworth to see you, and the trip was most tiresome."

Gone is the loving concern that the Oliphants expressed toward the missing Peggy when Barrett interviewed them. I think they dislike her so much that they can't act pleasant to the woman they think might be her, a victim of a brutal attack. If Rosamond is Peggy, there won't be a happy family reunion.

Rosamond clears her throat and says, "Thank you for coming."

The Oliphants gasp, sit up straighter, and crane their necks toward her, like geese that see the farmer's wife bringing food. Mrs. Oliphant says, "Is that Peggy?"

"If it is, there's something wrong with her voice," Faith says. She and her mother look to Frances.

Now Frances brings to my mind a constable deciding whether to enter the dark alley in which a criminal may be lurking. Instead of stating an opinion, she asks Rosamond, "Why don't you show yourself?"

Rosamond raises, then drops her hands in a helpless gesture.

"If we can't see you, how are we supposed to know if you're Peggy?" Faith says.

Frances raises her hand to silence her sister. "Do *you* recognize *us*?"

"I—I don't think so," Rosamond says.

Doubt puckers Faith's brow. "She *could* be Peggy."

"There's another way to settle this." Frances says to Rosamond, "What did you name the stray kitten you found last year?"

Rosamond jerks in surprise, like a schoolgirl unexpectedly called on in class. "I don't remember a kitten."

"What day is your father's birthday?"

"I don't know."

"Who is the patient in room number seven?" Frances says.

"Here at the hospital?" Rosamond doesn't know the Oliphants own a convalescent home. We've told her nothing about the people who've laid claim to her. "Why, I don't know."

"Well," Frances says, "either the amnesia has erased those memories, or she's not Peggy."

Rosamond's shoulders slump with defeat. I have the strange feeling that I don't know what just happened. Why should she be unhappy to fail Frances's test? Did she want to be Peggy Oliphant because she thinks an unpleasant family is better than none?

Frances looks perturbed, like the constable after he's entered the alley, found it empty, and realized that the criminal he seeks has gone elsewhere. She and Mrs. Oliphant exchange a glance whose meaning I can't read.

"I think she is Peggy, and she doesn't really have amnesia," Faith blurts. "I think she's just pretending."

Everyone on the other side of the screen stares at Faith in consternation. Rosamond inhales sharply. I'm offended by Faith's accusation, for I've seen nothing to indicate that Rosamond's amnesia isn't genuine.

"Why would I pretend?" Rosamond sounds puzzled, hurt.

"So you won't have to come home and do your work," Faith says. "So you can lollygag in the hospital while people take care of you."

Rosamond turns to me, as if I'm the one to whom she must answer. "I wouldn't."

I smile and pat her hand to tell her that I agree. But although Mick, Hugh, and Dr. Enoch nod as if they believe her, I see inklings of suspicion on Barrett's and Sir Gerald's faces.

"Peggy, there's no use hiding," Mrs. Oliphant says, swayed by her younger daughter's certainty. "We know it's you."

Faith snickers with glee at the apple of discord she's tossed into the scene. "Yes, Peggy, the game's over." She opens her suitcase and pulls out a blue cotton frock that's as outdated and shabby as the one Peggy wore in the family photograph. "Get dressed. You've had your fun; it's time to go home."

"Faith," Frances says in a warning tone.

"Here." With an impudent grin, Faith tosses the dress at Rosamond. It hits the flimsy wicker screen, which teeters toward us. Rosamond gasps and recoils. I steady the screen.

"Faith! That's enough." Frances stands, grabs Faith by the arm, and yanks her up from her chair. "We're leaving."

"Ouch! Not yet!"

Frances bows to the men, then sails out the door, pulling Faith with her. Faith's expression is stormy, but Mrs. Oliphant meekly follows her elder daughter. The crowd outside barrages them with questions as I try to understand why Frances, who doesn't strike me as a woman to back away from a challenge, would decamp so abruptly. Barrett and the other men look as puzzled as I am. I turn to see how Rosamond is reacting.

She's slumped sideways in her wheelchair, motionless, her chin resting against her shoulder, her eyes closed within the mask of bandages.

Alarm stabs me. I touch her wrist. "Rosamond?" Her flesh is cold, limp, and still. In the past I've had occasion to touch the dead, and the sensation is unforgettable. "Dr. Enoch!"

CHAPTER 15

Dr. Enoch rushes behind the screen. Hugh, Mick, Barrett, and Sir Gerald hover in the background while he feels Rosamond's pulse and holds a small mirror by her nostrils. "She's breathing. Her pulse is strong and steady."

Even as I exhale a cautious sigh of relief, he taps her shoulder, calls her name, and she doesn't respond. Mick voices the fear that grips me. "Is she in a coma again?"

"Please, God, no," Hugh says.

Sir Gerald says to Dr. Enoch, "Can you bring her around?"

Dr. Enoch takes a vial of smelling salts from his pocket. We all watch, I praying silently, as he waves the vial near Rosamond's nose.

She jerks, coughs, then flails her arms and legs and screams, "No! Get away!"

Dr. Enoch stumbles backward. I step in to soothe her, and her hands hit my chest.

"Don't hurt me! Please!" Her eyes are wide open, crazed with terror.

I wonder who she thinks I am, if she's reliving the attack. "It's me—Sarah. Don't be afraid. You're safe in the hospital."

Her agitations quiet as she recognizes me. "Sarah. What happened?" She's breathless and shaking, as if just awakened from a nightmare.

"You fainted." I say reluctantly, "I think we'd better postpone the rest of the identity parade." Venetia will have to wait, but that's better than jeopardizing Rosamond's fragile health.

"No, I want to finish now," Rosamond says. "I'll be all right."

"It's too big a risk," Dr. Enoch says.

"I've come this far already, and I can't bear not knowing who I am." Quivering with desperation, she says, "Sarah, please!"

I appeal to Dr. Enoch. "How about after she rests for fifteen minutes?"

He considers, then nods. "Fifteen minutes."

Leaving Rosamond in his care, I go downstairs to explain the delay to Venetia. I find her seated in an office, at someone's desk. Today she wears a neat dark-blue frock, and her auburn hair is tightly plaited into two braids. She stands, and so does the older woman with her. Venetia introduces us. "Miss Bain, this is my aunt, Miss Caroline Napier."

Caroline Napier is dressed in a long-sleeved white blouse, umber pleated skirt, and black jacket. The simple clothes suit her tall, slim, boyish figure. She looks to be in her late thirties, and she's attractive, although not pretty, with a long neck, square face, and protuberant brown eyes. Her brown, fluffy hair is twisted up in a knot under her black straw hat.

"It's a pleasure to meet you, Miss Bain." Her voice is fluttery, old for her age. She shakes my hand; hers is clammy. After I explain that Rosamond fainted and needs a little time to recover, Caroline says, "I must apologize for my niece. If I had known she was going to the police station yesterday, I never would have let her out of the house."

I look at Venetia. "I thought you said you had permission."

She hangs her head. "I lied."

"You said you were going to play with the children down the street," Caroline says.

"I'm sorry, Aunt Caro. It was naughty of me."

"Now I know why you ran away from me—you didn't want me to bring you home," I say. "That would have required explaining to your aunt."

"I'm sorry, Miss Bain," Venetia says with a hint of a smile at her own cleverness. I have to admire her even though I dislike being tricked.

"It wasn't just naughty—you could have been run over or kidnapped—or worse." Caroline strokes Venetia's hair and says with fond exasperation, "What am I going to do with you?"

"I'll try to be good." Venetia turns to me. "May I see my mother now?"

"Venetia . . ." Caroline rubs her temples as if her niece's antics have given her a headache. "This woman is not your mother. Miss Bain, I'm sorry Venetia has put you and the police to so much trouble, but I suppose we must humor the child."

Rebellion brews in Venetia's remarkable violet eyes. "I knew you would think she's not Mother. That's why I didn't tell you I wanted to go to the police station. You wouldn't have taken me, because you think Mother is in Egypt. But she must have come back."

As a child, I was convinced that my father would return. Even after my mother told me he was dead, a part of me still believed him alive. That part of me turned out to be right.

"Why didn't she tell us she was coming?" Weary patience inflects Caroline's tone.

"Maybe she wanted it to be a surprise. For my birthday." Venetia tells me, "My birthday is the twenty-eighth of July."

I remember hoping my father would be back in time for my eleventh birthday. I waited up all night. If Rosamond isn't Maude, then Venetia will be crushed.

"Miss Bain, may I speak to you alone?" Caroline says. We go outside the room to the hall, and she lowers her voice. "I can understand why Venetia wants to believe this woman is Maude. She misses her mother terribly. Did she tell you that her father died in an accident?" I nod. "When she found out that Maude had gone back to Egypt, she cried for days."

"Her mother left without saying goodbye?"

"Venetia would have wanted to go too, but she ran a little wild in Egypt, and Maude decided it would be better to keep her here. If Venetia had known she was being left behind, she'd have thrown a tantrum. So Maude sneaked off when Venetia wasn't home."

I'm so angry on Venetia's behalf that I forget courtesy. "After she lost her father, her mother abandoned her?" I'm also angry with my own mother, who'd meant to join Lucas in America and leave me behind. "How could Maude be so cruel?"

"Shh!" Caroline glances toward the office, where Venetia is waiting for us. "Maude had good reasons, and she'd been through a lot. After my brother—her husband—died, she fell ill. That's why she and Venetia came back to England—the climate in Egypt is bad for sick people. I nursed her, and she recovered, thank God." Caroline pats the cameo brooch at her throat. "Then she needed to finish the book she'd been writing, which meant she had to watch the opening of the tomb that my brother was excavating when he was killed. She had to earn a living for herself and Venetia."

"She still shouldn't have left like that." My mother, too, would have had excuses for leaving me—I was grown up; I could fend for myself. Or perhaps she wouldn't have bothered with excuses and instead simply disappeared, just like my father did. "Why are you so sure that Maude is in Egypt?"

"According to her letters, she is." Caroline pulls an envelope from her pocketbook and offers it to me. "This is her most recent. It came three weeks ago."

It's made of thin, lightweight paper, as is the letter inside, and plastered with foreign stamps, the postmarks smeared. The address—to Venetia in St. John's Wood—and the return address—an unpronounceable street and town in Egypt—are penned in blue ink. The handwriting is neat but cramped. I read the message, which describes the weather, the scenery, and the natives. It's signed "Mother." I think of my mother's letters to Lucas Zehnpfennig. Maude Napier sent no similar declarations of love to Venetia.

"You see that she wrote nothing about coming back to England," Caroline says.

Caroline Napier is a sensible adult, and I should believe her rather than Venetia, a wayward, fanciful youngster. But some instinct in me always told me that my father was alive. Perhaps a similar instinct in Venetia is telling her that her mother is here in London.

"There's one way to find out who's right." I walk to the office, beckon Venetia, and escort her and Caroline upstairs.

Barrett, Mick, Hugh, Sir Gerald, and Dr. Enoch are waiting. I can't see Rosamond through the screen, can't tell what she's feeling as Venetia hesitantly walks toward her. Hands clasped behind her back, Venetia looks younger, her precocious, confident maturity gone. Her lower lip trembles. Caroline pauses near the door, her fingers so tightly enlaced that the knuckles are white, her expression guarded and sad. Venetia stops within six feet of the screen. Her huge violet eyes brim with hope and fear.

"Mother? It's me—Venetia?" Her small, thin voice rises as she silently begs the woman she can't see to recognize her.

My muscles tighten while my heart pounds a quickening rhythm. The atmosphere in the room seems to swell, as if holding its breath.

Venetia reaches out her hand—slowly, like a student who anticipates the painful smack of a teacher's ruler.

Rosamond whispers, "Oh God," and then *"Venetia!"* The choked cry vibrates with excitement and joy. "My little girl!"

My heart soars. *Sleeping Beauty is Maude Napier!* August Legrand and the Oliphants have no claim on her. My wish for her, and for Venetia, has miraculously come true.

Venetia freezes with her hand outstretched; her eyes light up, and wonder parts her lips; she resembles a child saint during a vision of the Virgin Mary. Hugh, Mick, Barrett, Dr. Enoch, and Sir Gerald smile. I hear clumsy movements behind the screen as Rosamond climbs out of her wheelchair. The screen falls toward us. It crashes to the floor with Rosamond atop it, on her hands and knees.

Venetia backs away, staring at Rosamond's bandaged face. Caroline utters a cry of alarm. They look as if they're seeing a ghost. The men rush forward to help Rosamond. The fall must have hurt, but she doesn't seem to feel the pain as she crawls toward Venetia. "I remember you! My dearest love, don't you remember me?" Her hoarse voice swells with pleading. She holds out her hand to the little girl.

A rapid series of emotions play across Venetia's face. Shock gives way to fear, then uncertainty. The men stand back; Caroline twists her cameo brooch while her eyes bulge in her whitened face. My heart is a battering ram inside my chest.

The light returns to Venetia's eyes. "Mother!" She moves toward Rosamond with the stiff restraint of child who's been told not to run. Rosamond opens her arms to Venetia. Venetia falls to her knees on the wicker screen, and Rosamond enfolds her in a tight embrace. Venetia clumsily returns the embrace, as if she's afraid of hurting her mother—or of discovering that this moment is only a dream and she's holding empty air. Both of them sob, their heads pressed together, their bodies shuddering.

"You came back," Venetia cries. You did, you did!"

I'll have to think of Rosamond as Maude Napier from now on. A burst of joy makes me giddy. My own eyes fill with tears.

Dr. Enoch nods in approval. Mick and Sir Gerald beam. Hugh wipes his eyes. Barrett has a smile on his lips, a pensive crease across his brow.

Caroline Napier says, "Maude." Her voice sounds strange, hushed. Color seeps back into her complexion; her hand releases her brooch and falls to her side. Her eyes shine feverishly bright. "It really is you."

★   ★   ★

"A toast to a fairy tale with a happy ending." Sir Gerald raises his glass of champagne.

He's treating my friends and me to dinner at the Savoy, the magnificent new hotel on the Strand. Our table on the glass-enclosed terrace commands a spectacular view of the river. Lights sparkle from candles on the tables, from the electric chandeliers, and from the Victoria Embankment and the Waterloo Bridge. An orchestra plays while waiters in evening dress carry wine bottles in silver buckets, and trays covered with silver domes, to wealthy, fashionably dressed diners.

"Here, here!" As we drink, the bubbles tickle my throat, and I laugh. This is the finest establishment in which I've ever dined, and tonight Sir Gerald is a genial host while we celebrate.

Before we left Maude at the hospital, where she'll stay a few more days to recover her strength, we said goodbye to her, Venetia and Caroline.

"How can I ever thank you?" she said.

"Seeing you reunited with your daughter is thanks enough," I said.

"Sarah will interview you for the *Daily World* as soon as you're well enough," Sir Gerald said.

Now we dine on quail consommé, sole with lobster chunks, lamb with herbs, potato soufflé, and vegetables in lemon–butter sauce. The delectable meal is seasoned with our satisfaction in a job well done. Between courses, Sir Gerald goes off to speak with acquaintances at other tables, and Hugh entertains Mick by pointing out famous people he recognizes. Barrett stares out the window.

"You're awfully quiet," I say. "What's wrong?"

"Doesn't it seem too convenient that Sleeping Beauty turned out to be Maude Napier?"

"No. Why do you say that?"

"It's as if we gave her three apples to choose from, and she picked the one that didn't look rotten," Barrett says. "When Faith accused her of faking, I started to wonder."

I leap to defend Maude and my belief in her. "And you think she latched onto Venetia for her own selfish purposes? She's not like that."

Barrett's manner is gentle as he challenges me. "How do you know what she's like? You've spent only a few hours with her, and she was unconscious most of that time."

"My instincts tell me."

"I have instincts too," Barrett reminds me, "and in my eleven years on the police force, I've seen criminals who look as innocent as angels."

The fact that his experience trumps mine makes me even more stubborn. "I've seen evil often enough to recognize it when I meet it again. She's not evil."

"I didn't say she was. But what if she knows who she is, and she doesn't want to go back where she came from?"

"Are you accusing a crime victim of committing fraud?" The very idea distresses me.

"No. I just I think it's possible that she remembers more than she's saying." Barrett adds, "Dr. Enoch said permanent amnesia is rare. Her memory could have started coming back since yesterday."

"I think she would have told us."

"Why would she? She doesn't know us any better than we know her. Why trust us?"

I sip my champagne to quell my uneasiness. Is the connection between her and me only my foolish delusion? Is she deceiving me? "I watched her when she saw August Legrand and the Oliphants. I could swear she didn't recognize them."

"August Legrand seemed pretty sure he recognized her voice."

The champagne has lost its effervescence. "Maybe *he* was faking."

Barrett picks up his fork, skewers a morsel on his plate, and sets it down untasted. "Why would he lay claim to a perfect stranger?"

"Maybe he's fooled himself into believing she's his wife even though she isn't."

"Maybe."

My thoughts home in on a disturbing, unavoidable realization. "You still think she's Jenny Legrand."

"Instincts die hard," Barrett says.

"You're right about that," I retort. "If you'd seen her when she saw Mr. Legrand—and the Oliphants—you'd agree with me that she didn't know them from Adam."

"How could you tell, with her face covered by bandages?"

That gives me pause. I'd interpreted her emotions via her body movements and the tone of her voice, but with her face invisible, I could have missed crucial signs that she was putting on an act. To counter Barrett's argument, I seize on the ammunition that his mention of the bandages has lent me.

"She can't hide behind the bandages forever. They'll have to come off when her face is healed. It won't stay disfigured beyond recognition. She has to know that if she's not Maude Napier, she won't be able to fool Venetia and Caroline. She must be Maude."

Barrett responds with a grim smile. "It's going to be interesting to see what happens when the bandages come off."

Sir Gerald returns to the table in time for dessert—a confection of sponge cake, caramel sauce, chocolate shavings, and meringue, topped with flaming rum. After we exclaim in admiration and begin to eat, Sir Gerald says, "Our work's not finished. Half of the mystery is still unsolved—we still don't know who attacked Sleeping Beauty. The *Daily World* needs to be first with the whole story."

"Finding out that she's Maude Napier should help us, and you too, Barrett," Hugh says.

"Right," Barrett says.

But I can tell he's thinking that our assumption that she's Maude could be a big push in the wrong direction. Even though I think his suspicions are off the mark, they've dimmed my pleasure in the celebration, and there's strife between us that the champagne can't wash away.

CHAPTER 16

It's Sunday morning, and Hugh and Mick are at home sleeping off last night's overindulgence. I'm standing outside the Chelsea Old Church, skimming the front-page story of the *Daily World*.

"Sleeping Beauty Wakes!" proclaims the headline. The illustration shows a woman with a bandaged face embracing a tearful little girl. The article praises "ace Detective Sergeant Barrett and our own Lord Hugh Staunton, Mick O'Reilly, and Sarah Bain" for reuniting Maude Napier with her daughter. The story below is titled "Face-Slasher Still at Large," and describes the similarities to the Ripper case.

I fold the newspaper and look at the church. Situated at the end of Cheyne Walk, it has arched windows set in ivy-covered walls, and a tall, square nave. Parishioners stream in through the door. Across the Walk is the river. A warm wind stirs up whitecaps on the water and shreds the fog and smoke clouds. Intermittent sunlight shines on the distant Albert Bridge. I watch the crowds of churchgoers and spot the person for whom I'm lying in wait.

Sally's mother is walking toward me with two other women. I call, "Mrs. Albert."

She stops as if I've thrown a snake at her feet. "What are you doing here?"

"I knew that if I went to the house you wouldn't see me."

"I've nothing to say to you." She flounces toward the church.

I fall into step with her. "How about introducing me to your friends?"

Sally has told me that Mrs. Albert has never breathed a word about her husband's past, or about me, to any of her acquaintances. She's too ashamed, too afraid of what they would think. Now, as her friends eye me with curiosity, Mrs. Albert says to them, "You go in. Save my seat."

We cross the street to the riverfront promenade and stand under a tree; the wind off the river ruffles our skirts. "You've got two minutes. And then, if you don't go away—" Mrs. Albert points at a police constable who stands some fifty paces down the promenade. "I'm going to scream and tell him you're trying to rob me. And you don't want any more trouble with the police, do you? Especially Inspector Reid."

"Inspector Reid might like to know about this." I reach in my pocketbook, bring out her letter to Lucas Zehnpfennig, and hold it up for her to see as I read: "'Dear Mr. Zehnpfennig, Whoever you are, stop writing to my husband. How many times do I have to say it? Leave him alone!'"

As she recognizes her words and signature, her face turns white. She snatches at the letter.

I tuck it back in my pocketbook. "What do you know about Lucas?"

Her eyes glitter like a trapped cat's. "Nothing."

"Lucas wrote to my father more than once, and you read his letters. What did they say?"

"I—I don't remember. It was a long time ago."

I'm suddenly fed up with amnesia, real or fake. "All right. I'll show this to Inspector Reid." I put the letter in my pocketbook. "I'll let him get the truth out of you."

She chokes, and her eyes pop as if I've wrung her throat. "You wouldn't."

"Just wait and see." I wouldn't deliver Sally's mother into Reid's cruel hands, but Mrs. Albert thinks I'm a chip off the block of her evil husband, the murderer.

Fuming with hatred and rage, she says, "The first letter came in 1877. It was from Chicago, in America. I didn't know that George knew anyone there. I thought it must be someone from before I met him. I was curious, so I opened it."

My heartbeat quickens; I feel on the threshold of a portal to the secrets of the past. "What did it say?"

"That man, Lucas, said he was in trouble. He asked George to send money."

"Is that all?"

Mrs. Albert nods.

"What about the other letters?"

"The same things. They never said who Lucas was or how he was related to George."

She knows even less than I do. The portal has led to a solid wall.

"I didn't want to know. I didn't want George's past to interfere with our life." Her eyes shine with remembered fear that his past was a threat to her family. "So I watched the post for more letters. I took them before George could see them, and I burned them. I wrote to Lucas, to make him stop writing."

I feel ashamed because I've been hounding Sally's mother for naught. I'm about to apologize when she bursts out, "Why do you care? How can Lucas have had anything to do with George's disappearance? He was in America."

"There was another letter after the ones you burned. I thought Sally would have told you. It came right before your husband disappeared."

"*What?* No."

"Sally gave it to our father. He read it." As Mrs. Albert gapes at me in shock, I tell her what else Sally obviously has kept from her. "Lucas wasn't in America when he posted that letter. He'd come to England. He was staying near Liverpool Street station."

The stony, hostile mask that her face usually wears in my presence melts into a shambles of misery. "I thought George left Sally and me because he didn't want us anymore." She seems less comforted by the fact that she was wrong than horrified by the realization that he'd had motives she can't imagine. "If I'd talked to him about the letters—" Her throat convulses with a sob of fury at her own mistake. "Maybe he wouldn't have left. Oh God!"

She turns and hastens down the promenade, away from the church, limping like a crippled woman.

Even as I pity her, my shoulders sag with despair. It's as if I've torn the veil off a hidden mother only to find nothing underneath.

CHAPTER 17

Two weeks after the identity parade, at eight o'clock in the evening, I'm carrying my camera equipment down Whitechapel High Street, on my way home from a crime scene. Now that we've put a name to Sleeping Beauty, and there haven't been any other incidents of face slashing, Sir Gerald prefers us to chase new stories rather than hunt the person who attacked Maude Napier. That's a crime without a corpse—milk toast in the dog-eat-dog newspaper business. I have the discomfort of a job half done, but I also have my living to earn, and therefore Sir Gerald to please.

June has given way to an unusually warm, humid July. There's been little rain, and the sun glares through a haze of smoke, steam, and chemical fumes. Horses and carriages kick up dust clouds tainted with manure. Food that's fresh in the market in the morning spoils by noon unless it's kept on ice blocks, whose price rises with the temperature. The streets reek of garbage and cesspools, the air in the trains and omnibuses of body odor, and there's no escape from the river's heavy, fetid stench. The doors and windows of the public houses are wide open to admit any breeze. People who live above the shops have dragged chairs outside, to escape the worse heat within. London is like a cauldron simmering with troubles, feuds, and frustrations. Firemen spray water from the tank on their wagon onto a mob of children who gleefully splash and scream. I'm damp with perspiration, panting for a breath of cool, fresh air.

"If it isn't my favorite photographer," Barrett says, falling into step beside me and relieving me of my heavy camera case.

"Thank you," I say, glad to see him for the first time since the dinner at the Savoy. We've been busy with work. As we smile at each other, I feel the warm tingle of desire. I blush because I know he wants to kiss me, and I wish he would, but the street is hardly an appropriate place.

"Are you investigating a case?" I say.

"Yeah, another one. The murder of a tramp." Barrett looks tired, his eyes bloodshot, damp patches in the armpits of his uniform. "Reid keeps piling them on."

"Where's Constable Porter?"

"Investigating my other cases. We have to split up, or we'll never get them all solved."

I haven't forgotten that Porter tried to dismiss Venetia Napier when she came to report that Sleeping Beauty was her mother, and I wonder what other mistakes he'll make. For the sake of Barrett's morale, I say, "It's good that there are two of you."

"It would be better if there were two of me." Barrett's wry tone says that he too has misgivings about Porter. "Where are Hugh and Mick?"

"At the *Daily World*, developing the photographs from our last crime scene. Hugh is writing up the story. He's had to do that a lot lately. They're short on reporters."

"You shouldn't be working by yourself."

"It was just a stone's throw from my house." But we both know that Whitechapel is dangerous, even with Jack the Ripper gone.

We walk down Angel Alley, a narrow passage between dingy brick lodging houses. An uncomfortable silence engulfs us. Each of us wants to know if the other has learned anything new about the attack on Maude Napier, but we don't want to resume our argument about whether she really is Maude.

"Anything new on your father?" Barrett says, introducing a safer topic.

I tell him about my confrontation with Mrs. Albert. "I haven't seen or heard from Sally. Her mother must be keeping a close watch on her." Our search for our father is more unfinished business.

I unlock my back door, which faces onto Angel Alley. Lights shine in the upstairs windows. When Barrett and I enter my studio, I pick up the mail that lies on the floor by the front door. Upstairs, Fitzmorris greets us.

"Dinner's in the kitchen," he says. "Hugh and Mick aren't back yet. I'm going to the theater."

"Have a good time," I say.

Barrett and I raise our eyebrows at each other and smile as we listen to Fitzmorris clatter down the stairs. We wait for the front door to close, then we race upstairs to my attic bedroom. It's sweltering hot, but we don't care. I don't open the window; I'd rather do without fresh air than let noises reach my neighbors. We madly kiss and fondle, too impatient to undress; we may not have much time. When Barrett tries to pull me onto the bed, I back toward the wall. One of my favorite ways to make love is reenacting what happened the first time we kissed, almost two years ago, when we were more enemies than friends. Standing with my back pressed against the wall, I tear at Barrett's trousers while he thrusts at me and pushes up my skirts. We laugh at our clumsy haste, moan with excitement.

Barrett pauses, gasping. "Is it safe?"

I want him so badly that I can't remember what time of the month it is, and I don't care. "Yes."

When we made love for the first time, we crossed a line that can't be uncrossed. We lost all restraint over our desire, and whenever we couple, I risk getting with child. We need to marry soon, but our wedding date seems far in the future.

Barrett lifts my legs around his waist. Then I hear the bell on the front door jangle, and the sound of Hugh's and Mick's voices drifts up from the studio. "Damn!" Barrett says.

We frantically arrange our clothing, smooth our hair, and race downstairs. When my friends arrive, Barrett is seated at the kitchen table, and I'm uncovering the pans that Fitzmorris left on the stove.

"We were just about to eat dinner." I hope my friends won't notice my flushed face. "Are you hungry?"

"I could eat a horse," Mick says.

He and Hugh join Barrett at the table. If they know what we've been doing, they're too tactful to let on.

"Barrett," Hugh says, "one of the reporters said he saw you at the Victoria docks the other day. What were you up to?"

A moment passes before Barrett says, "I've been making the rounds of the steamship company offices, asking if they've a record of Maude Napier traveling from Egypt to London during the month before the eighteenth of June."

I'm about to set a teacup on the table, and my hand pauses in midair. "You didn't tell me you were going to do that."

Barrett meets my gaze. "I was afraid you'd be upset."

"Why shouldn't I be? You're trying to prove that Sleeping Beauty isn't Maude."

"I'm trying to tie up a loose end. Don't you think it would be good to know for sure that Maude Napier did come back from Egypt and really is the woman who's claiming to be Venetia's mother?"

I thump the teacup down on the table. "I am sure. I think you just don't want to be wrong."

We glare at each other. Unsatisfied sexual desire is making us both edgy, and I don't want to be wrong either. I would hate to think myself instrumental in giving Venetia an impostor in place of her mother. If some man with bandages on his face pretended to be my father, how would I feel? How devastating if the bandages came off to reveal a stranger.

"Oops," Hugh says, his hand covering his mouth. "Sorry to bring up a sensitive topic."

"So did Maude come back from Egypt?" Mick says.

Hugh tries to shush him. Barrett says, "She's not on the passenger lists."

My job has put me in a position to jeopardize a little girl's welfare. "Have you inquired about all the ships at all the companies?"

"Just the British ones," Barrett says.

"Maude could have traveled on a foreign ship," I point out.

"I'll get onto those when I have time."

"Well, just make sure you have all the facts before you try to tear Maude and Venetia apart." I'm uncomfortably aware that I made up my mind about Maude before I had all the facts. My wish to reunite a child with her parent is no excuse.

Barrett holds up his hands. "Sarah, I don't want to quarrel with you. But if she is an imposter, then we need to separate them as soon as possible."

"You think she's committing fraud!"

"I didn't say she's doing it deliberately," Barrett says with strained patience. "She could have brain damage and be confused about who she is."

Realizing that he's raised good points only puts me more on the defensive. "Venetia has accepted her as Maude."

"Venetia could be playing make-believe and fooling herself."

Young as she is, Venetia doesn't strike me as a fool. "Caroline has accepted her too. Surely you don't think *she's* playing make-believe?"

Barrett frowns, unable to explain away that evidence in Maude's favor. We fall silent, each unpersuaded by the other, but neither of us as sure of ourselves as we would like to be.

Hugh clears his throat. "At the risk of blundering into sensitive territory again, I have to say, Barrett, wouldn't you rather let things lie than pick at loose ends? Officially, you've solved the mystery of Sleeping Beauty's identity. It's a gold star on your record."

Barrett's jaw stiffens. "I have to find out the truth even if it means the case gets unsolved, and the gold star turns into a black mark."

I admire his integrity, even though I wish the case would remain solved. Hugh sighs. "And here I was, enjoying not seeing nasty newspaper stories about myself."

"Took the words right outta my mouth," Mick says.

Our notoriety has faded; the rival papers have stopped running articles about our unsavory backgrounds. But if the Sleeping Beauty investigation is reopened, the limelight could scorch us again. Hugh's relationship with Tristan is already in peril, and more bad publicity will only lower Mick's stock with Catherine. Although I don't like to admit that my friends and I have a professional as well as a personal stake in Sleeping Beauty being Maude Napier, that's true as well.

"After praising us in the *Daily World*, Sir Gerald wouldn't like admitting we were wrong about Sleeping Beauty," I say.

"He'd dump us like hot potatoes," Mick says.

We're silent, our gazes averted from Barrett as I fetch silverware. Out of the corner of my eye, I see Barrett put his hands on the table as if he's about to rise and take his leave rather than break bread with us. I'm sorry that we're at odds and that my friends are all siding against Barrett, but I'm not going to back down.

Mick, seeking a diversion, wanders into the parlor and picks up the mail that I left on the table. "Hey, here's a letter for you. It's from Maude."

We all stare at the envelope as though it's Pandora's box. "Go on, read it to us," Hugh says.

"'Dear Miss Bain, Lord Hugh, and Mr. O'Reilly,'" I read aloud, "'I've been discharged from the hospital, and I'm at home with Venetia and Caroline. Would it please you to come and visit us on Saturday, 12 July, at 2:00 p.m.? We should be so happy if you would accept our hospitality until Sunday afternoon. While you're here, I can give you the interview that I promised Sir Gerald. Yours sincerely, Maude Napier.'"

My first reaction is delight that Maude and Venetia want to pursue a friendship with us. My second is that here's my chance to prove that Sleeping Beauty really is Maude, and I haven't colluded in a terrible mistake.

"Here's a chance to settle the question of her identity," Barrett says.

I examine the invitation. The words are shakily printed, like a child's; they bear no resemblance to those in the letter from Maude that Caroline Napier showed me at the police station. It seems that Dr. Enoch accurately predicted that Maude's injury would affect her handwriting.

"Um," Hugh says. "Tristan asked me to meet him that night."

Mick and I exchange glances, aware of how important that meeting is to Hugh. "It's all right," Mick says. "Sarah and I can go by ourselves."

"I don't like the idea of your staying overnight at that house," Barrett says to me.

"Why not?"

"If Sleeping Beauty really is Maude, then someone in or near the Napier house could be her attacker. You and Mick could be putting yourselves in danger."

"It can't be Venetia or Caroline," I say. "They didn't even know Maude had come back to England."

"They seems pretty harmless, if you ask me," Mick chimes in.

Barrett shakes his head. "I still don't like it. Can't you check things out, do the interview, and leave the same day?"

"I've protected Sarah before," Mick says. "I can do it again."

"We'll be fine," I say.

With a sigh and a shrug, Barrett says, "I guess I can't stop you."

Hugh speaks with forced cheerfulness. "I'll go. Tristan will probably stand me up again anyway. I might do better by playing hard to get."

"Thanks." Barrett looks far from completely relieved. "Sarah, when you get there, keep an open mind, will you, please? And be careful."

CHAPTER 18

St. John's Wood is seven miles and a world removed from Whitechapel. Because it's distant from the factories and the river, the haze in the sky is thinner; the stench is faint. A cab from the train station carries Hugh, Mick, and me along Grove End Road, where tall trees provide welcome shade from the sun's glare. Nannies stroll, pushing perambulators; footmen in livery ride on private carriages. Iron fences atop low stone walls guard opulent mansions. We unload our baggage and my photography equipment outside number seventeen, the Napier family home. Built of red brick, it's a sizable combination of an Italian palazzo and an Arabian Nights fantasy. A glittering silver dome caps a round turret, and carved stone balconies grace Moorish windows shaped like keyholes. Surrounded by tall trees, with glossy green ivy leaves covering the walls and fence, the mansion seems a palace fit for the Sleeping Beauty of legend.

"Venetia's aunt must be stinking rich," Mick says.

Unlike the gate in the fairy tale, this gate is open. We carry our bags across a garden paved with flagstones and landscaped with cypress trees. A white portico shelters a dark, carved wooden door. The knocker is a polished brass Medusa head. Through the open windows, I hear piano music—a dissonant melody repeated with slight variations, as if a novice is picking out a tune, making mistakes.

Venetia throws open the door. "They're here!" She dances in circles around us, the skirts of her yellow frock whirling. "I'm so happy to see you!" Today she seems more a child, less the hoyden who threw rocks at the police station.

"Where is your mother?" I'm eager to see Maude, whose face must be nearly healed by now. I've brought the photographs of Jenny Legrand and Peggy Oliphant to compare with her and prove that she's neither of those women.

"She's coming." Venetia helps us carry our baggage into the house.

The foyer resembles an illustration I once saw of a Roman villa. Sunlight streams through a skylight, glimmers on water that fills a rectangular pool sunk in a blue and white mosaic floor. On the walls, painted white trompe l'oeil pilasters divide a frescoed mural of men and women dressed in togas, playing musical instruments. The mural's surface is chipped, the colors faded; it looks like a genuine antique. Beyond a black iron staircase that leads to the upper galleries, French doors provide a view onto a terrace.

"Welcome!" Maude calls in her hoarse voice as she glides down the stairs. Her face is still bandaged, her hair covered with a loose, frilled white cap. The ruffles on the sleeves of her aqua, chartreuse, and violet floral dress lap over the white gloves on her hands.

So much for my simple plan to confirm her identity.

The piano music ceases. Caroline Napier emerges from a doorway. Her white shirtsleeves are rolled up, and her hair is twisted around a pencil. Breathless, she clutches her cameo brooch as she greets us.

"Your house is beautiful," I say.

"Thank you." She gives us a fleeting, nervous smile.

"Was that you practicing the piano?" Hugh says.

"Yes. Well, I'll let you settle in while I see about dinner."

Her hasty retreat makes it obvious that she's uncomfortable having us here. Venetia says, "Aunt Caro's not used to guests. Mother and I will show you to your rooms." Carrying my flash lamp, she climbs the stairs to the second-floor gallery.

We follow with the rest of our baggage. Maude opens a door. "Sarah, this is your room."

Small and cozy, the room is decorated like a Gypsy caravan. Tapestries hang on the walls. The chairs, bureau, cupboard, and washstand are painted in different bright colors, with gilded trim. Curtains made of strings of multicolored beads surround a bed covered with a velvet patchwork quilt. The beads clack in the breeze from the open window, which overlooks a leafy, sunlit back garden.

"It's lovely," I say as I set my baggage on the Persian carpet. I try to think of a polite way to ask Maude why her face is still bandaged.

"I'm glad you like it," Maude says. "And I'm so glad you came." She seems cool despite the heat, the bandages, and the gloves, and a faint scent of jasmine cologne freshens the air around her. "I'm hoping we can get to know each other and become real friends."

"I hope so too." I'm flattered and touched despite my uneasiness.

"Miss Bain, come and see Mick and Lord Hugh's room," Venetia calls.

I don't want to ask questions in front of her. Maude and I follow her across the hall. This room has wallpaper woven from dried grass, a black-and-white-striped zebra rug on the floor; the posts on the two beds are made of elephant tusks. Carved wooden masks, furniture upholstered with animal hides, and painted baskets complete the decor.

"Ain't this somethin'?" Mick says. "I feel like I'm in Africa."

Venetia has paid little attention to Mick, but now I see her take a closer look at him and notice that he's a handsome older boy. Suddenly shy, she says, "I'll show you the rest of the house, if you like."

We all take a tour of the many rooms. Other houses furnished in such various styles might look like cluttered hodgepodges, but here everything fits harmoniously together. Caroline Napier possesses a talent for design, along with her great wealth. In the most remarkable room, dim gas lamps shaped like torches illuminate statues on pedestals—the broken front half of a sphinx; rigid, stylized human figures; and a black stone cat wearing gold earrings. Against the wall stands a wooden sarcophagus. The face of the deceased person it once contained is barely discernible in paint flecks on its ancient surface. These must be treasures that Venetia's father unearthed in Egypt.

Venetia opens the sarcophagus and says to Mick, "You can get inside if you like."

"No, thanks," Mick says, giving it a wide berth. "What're these?" He points to shelves of stone vessels whose stoppers are carved bird and monkey heads.

"Canopic jars. The ancient Egyptians took out the brains from dead people through their noses and put them in these jars."

"You're having me on."

"No, it's true. Father said so." Venetia leads us to a glass case that contains smaller artifacts—jewelry, figurines, hieroglyphics on stone fragments. "Sometimes the diggers miss things. Alim and I used to search the tunnels and piles of dirt and empty graves. We found that scarab." She points to a blue carved beetle with long wings.

"Who's Alim?" Mick says.

"My friend. I sold a scarab like that one to a collector. I was wearing native clothes, and I'd rubbed dirt on my face, and I spoke Arabic. He thought I was an Egyptian boy."

"Good for you." Mick sounds surprised, impressed.

Venetia smiles demurely.

"Dinner is at six," Maude says. "Would you like to have lemonade in the garden?"

"Yes." I remember that I'm here on assignment for the *Daily World*. "The light is good for photography. Do you mind if I take your picture?"

Maude touches her bandages, as if to reassure herself that she's covered. "I don't mind."

Hugh says, "I'll see if Miss Napier needs any help in the kitchen," and departs.

He's useless at domestic work; he means to do some sleuthing. Mick helps me carry my camera equipment to the terrace. Beyond it, vines trail from a pergola that shelters the steps that lead down to the garden. The sun shines on an expansive green lawn with a gazebo at the center. Gravel paths wind around trees that cast cool shadows. I glimpse white marble statues draped with ivy, and, at the far end of the lawn, outbuildings—a coach house and stables. It's quiet except for the cooing of pigeons and the distant rattle of carriages. Dead branches protrude from trees, fallen leaves speckle the grass, and the roses in the flowerbeds have run wild. The garden is like the one at the enchanted castle where Sleeping Beauty and her household lie dreaming under a magic spell.

"Let's try in the gazebo," I say.

There I seat Maude on the bench built around the inside of the gazebo. I notice that the gazebo looks new, with fresh black paint on the railings. A maid brings the pitcher of lemonade with glasses. As I mount my camera on its tripod, I say, "We might as well start the interview." It will give me an excuse to ask questions.

"Yes, of course." Maude sounds uncertain.

"Would you like to play a game?" Venetia asks Mick.

"That's a good idea," Maude says, and I wonder if she doesn't want Venetia to hear the interview.

Mick looks disgruntled to be sent off to play, as if he's a child himself. Then I see him realize that this is his opportunity to do some investigating. "Yeah, sure." He follows Venetia to the coach house.

I duck under the black drape and center Maude in the viewfinder. She's as inscrutable as in her hidden mother photograph. "How does it feel to have amnesia?"

"Frightening," Maude says. "It's as if I woke up in a foreign country, where I don't know anyone. Why, I don't even know where to buy a loaf of bread—or where to get the money for it.

Caroline has been a big help with practical things like banks and solicitors and shopping. Without her, I would be completely lost."

The fear and confusion in her voice seem genuine. If Barrett could hear her, he wouldn't think she was faking. "What else is frightening about losing your memory?"

"That people know more about me than I know about myself. And that strangers think I'm someone I'm not. If Venetia hadn't been brave enough to come to the police station, I might have believed those other people when they said I was Jenny Legrand or Peggy Oliphant, just because I wanted to be *somebody*, not just a nameless person who didn't belong anywhere."

With her bandaged face, covered hair, and gloved hands, she looks like an effigy of a woman. I snap the shutter and say, "It must be terrible."

"But I'm thankful to be alive."

I emerge from under the black drape to see Venetia and Mick racing around the garden. Armed with bayonets attached to rifles, they dart behind trees, waging a mock battle. Venetia's gun emits a loud bang and a puff of smoke. Mick shouts, Venetia laughs, and I almost drop the negative plate I'm removing from my camera.

"Good heavens, they'll kill each other," I say.

Maude laughs. "The guns are just toys. They don't shoot bullets."

Loading another plate, I say, "Is your memory coming back?"

"Yes, but in fragments." Maude pauses for a spate of gunfire. "Like reflections on a lake, when the waves break them up. Gradually, the water is getting smoother, so the fragments come together, and the gaps between them are smaller."

That seems a vivid description drawn from the actual experience of someone who has amnesia. I change negative plates and take photographs from different angles and distances. "What exactly do you remember?"

"My strongest memories are of Venetia. When she was born, I fell in love with her immediately. I think I recognized her because

I had carried her inside me. My body remembered her even when my mind was confused."

The love she expresses toward Venetia seems more genuine than would seem possible if she were an impostor. And I've discovered nothing to indicate that either Jenny Legrand or Peggy Oliphant is brilliant at acting.

"What have you forgotten?" I say.

Maude sighs. "Oh, so much! Caroline told me that I'm an authoress, but I don't remember my own books. I'm thankful that I can read and that I can write simple things like the letter I sent you. But as for books—well, I don't remember enough of what I saw in Egypt or how I put such long stories together."

How devastated I would feel if I forgot the skills I need to practice photography.

"And I don't remember my husband. It's as if he never existed."

The very idea of losing my memory of Barrett is heart-wrenching.

"I must have been sad when he died," Maude says, "but I feel nothing about it except sorrow for Venetia, who's lost her father."

"She has you," I say. "She seems happy."

"In some ways, she's lost me too. There's so much of our life that I've forgotten. But she's helping me remember. She tells me about things that happened."

"Venetia is a very intelligent, special little girl," I say.

"Yes." Affection softens Maude's voice. "When I look at her, what happened to me doesn't seem all bad. I'm just so thankful we're together."

I can't believe she's a gold digger taking advantage of the little girl, but I have a troubling issue to broach. "I was surprised to see that your face is still bandaged. Isn't it healing properly?"

"Oh, it is. The stitches will be ready to come out soon, and I can take the bandages off anytime. But I'd rather keep them on."

"Why?" A bad feeling seeps through me as I adjust the focus on my camera.

"Because of Venetia. One thing I've remembered is a time when Venetia was seven. We were in Cairo, and we saw the lepers begging in the marketplace. Their faces and hands were disfigured. Venetia was terrified. I don't want her to see my face and hands and remember the lepers." Maude bows her head. "I don't want her to be afraid of me."

That's good reason for the bandages, and the incident is so specific that an impostor couldn't have known about it or made it up. I'm moved by her wish not to seem disfigured, ugly, and terrifying to her daughter. I can't wait to tell Barrett that he's misjudged Maude.

"I got you!" Venetia is standing over Mick, who's sprawled on his back on the grass, her bayonet pointed at his chest. "You're dead!"

Mick groans dramatically. "You win."

★ ★ ★

I spend the rest of the afternoon in my room, writing up Maude's interview and my observations of her and the house. I'm freshening up for dinner when there's a knock at my door. "Come in."

It's Venetia, pensive and serious. "Can I ask you something?"

On my guard, wondering if she thinks I'm suspicious of Maude, I say, "Yes."

I sit in a chair by the window, Venetia on a patchwork velvet footstool.

"Is it wrong to be happy that something bad happened?" she says.

Relieved yet puzzled by her question, I say, "What do you mean?"

"Mother was hurt terribly. She could have died. But . . ." Venetia pauses, eyes downcast. "I like her better now."

"Oh? Why?"

"She's ever so much nicer than before. When we were in Egypt, she spent all her time writing her books. If I went into her tent, she told me to leave her alone, that she was busy." Venetia's face looks small and pinched with the pain of rejection. Maybe she ran wild with the local children because her mother neglected her. "But now she wants to be with me." Venetia smiles. "She reads to me, and we play games together, and she's never too busy to talk."

The "before" Maude sounds like my own mother—aloof, preoccupied. An impostor who didn't know how Maude had treated Venetia might act like a doting, affectionate mother in an attempt to fool the girl. My bad feeling returns, like a stomachache after I thought I was over it.

"Why is she different now?" Venetia says.

I mustn't upset her with the idea that her mother is different because she isn't her mother, and there are other possible reasons. "Well, she's not writing at present, so she's not busy. And sometimes when people's heads are injured, it changes their personalities."

"Oh. I see." Venetia lifts anxious eyes to me. "Do you think I'm bad for being happy she's changed?"

I try to answer as I would if Maude's identity weren't an issue. "No. It's natural to be happy when people are nice to you. You needn't feel ashamed or guilty."

"But I do feel guilty. Because . . ." She lowers her gaze again. "Because there are things I'm glad she's forgotten."

"What things?"

"Before she went back to Egypt, we had a big fight. She wanted to send me away to school. She said I needed to learn how to behave properly and get an education. But I knew it was because she didn't want me around."

I remember when my mother told me that she'd found a boarding school that would take me free of charge. How unwanted I'd felt, and how coldly she'd treated me when I came home on holidays. I wasn't Lucas Zehnpfennig, her favorite, beloved, absent son.

"I told her I didn't want to go. She just said she had writing to do, and she went to her room. I ran after her. When she tried to shut the door, I hit her and kicked her and screamed. She fell down. Her mouth was bleeding." Venetia is the picture of woe. "I didn't mean to hurt her. I just didn't want her to send me away."

My sick feeling worsens. I've seen Venetia play rough, and now she's confessed to a violent act against her mother. If Sleeping Beauty really is Maude, is Venetia responsible for the cuts on her face, and her coma?

"But now she's forgotten the fight. I told her I was sorry, and she didn't know what I was talking about. I'm glad she has amnesia." Venetia's lip trembles. "Because when I asked her if she was going to send me away to school she said no, of course not, and she hugged me. I was so happy."

She'd gotten her wish because of a woman's lost memory and close brush with death. But supposing Venetia did attack Maude, how did Maude wind up unconscious and naked in Shadwell? Venetia is more resourceful than other children, but I can't picture her managing that feat.

Eyes round and haunted, Venetia says, "What if she remembers what I did? What if she changes back to the way she was, and she doesn't want me?"

I can't help imagining how I would have felt if my mother had turned into the loving, attentive one I yearned for, and then reverted to her original, cold self. "I don't think she's going to change." I only hope I'm right about that—and Maude's identity. "You mustn't worry."

A relieved sigh gusts from Venetia, and she smiles. "Thank you, Miss Bain. I feel so much better."

After she leaves, I go downstairs. A knock at the front door startles me. Looking through the peephole, I see Barrett. He's in ordinary clothes, not his uniform. Too surprised to wait for my hostess or a servant to open the door, I do it myself. He removes his hat and smiles at me.

"What are you doing here?" I say.

CHAPTER 19

"It's my night off," Barrett says. "I came to see you."

"You don't take nights off." I know he usually works late.

Barrett looks past me, into the house. "Aren't you going to invite me in?"

I step back, but with a stern look. "You're curious about Maude."

"I want to make sure you're safe." He gives me a quick, furtive kiss before he enters the foyer and looks around. "This is like walking into ancient Rome. So—what've you found out?"

"Maude's memory is coming back." I explain why she's keeping her face bandaged and tell him the story about the Egyptian lepers.

"That's pretty convincing." It's taken the wind out of his hunch that Maude is really Jenny Legrand.

I'm debating with myself whether to mention what Venetia just told me, when Hugh calls, "Sarah, is that Barrett? Why don't you bring him in here?"

I take Barrett to the dining room. It's decorated in medieval style, with exposed beams on the ceiling and fake candles in the gas chandelier. Maude, Venetia, Caroline, and my friends are gathered there. Golden sunlight brightens the antique leaded-glass windows.

"Detective Barrett, how nice to see you," Maude says in a friendly tone.

"Can he stay for dinner, Aunt Caro?" Venetia says.

"Of course. Please do," Caroline says without enthusiasm.

We sit in the heavy carved chairs around a trestle table set with floral china and a vase of roses. Dinner is a tasty summer picnic of cold ham, bread, cheese, salad, strawberry tarts, and lemonade, served by the maid. Everyone eats with relish, except Caroline. Ill at ease, she rearranges the scant food on her plate. Barrett watches Maude. She nibbles carefully, so as not to get food on the bandages around her mouth.

"If the weather's fine tomorrow, we could all go to the zoo in Regent's Park," Hugh says.

Venetia bounces in her chair and asks Maude, "Can we?"

Maude hesitates, then says to Hugh, "I would be happy for Venetia to go, but I'm not ready to leave the house."

I suppose she would be self-conscious about going out in public.

"I understand," Hugh says with quick sympathy.

"I know I'll have to go out eventually," Maude says. She must be thinking that when the bandages come off, her scarred face will draw stares of curiosity, pity, and repugnance. "I can't stay here forever." She turns to Caroline. "I don't want to impose on your hospitality."

Caroline gives her an affectionate smile. "Dear Maude, you and Venetia are welcome to stay as long as you like."

"Will you go back to Egypt?" Barrett says.

"Perhaps." Maude sounds sad, as if she realizes that since she's lost her husband, and unless she regains her ability to write books, there's no point in returning to Egypt. "I'm not ready to make decisions about the future." She smoothes Venetia's tousled curls. "I'm enjoying living one day at a time."

"Have you gotten in touch with your other relatives?" Barrett says.

"I've been told that my parents and grandparents died years ago, and I don't have brothers or sisters. Except for Caroline and Venetia, I'm quite alone in the world."

"What about aunts, uncles, or cousins?" Barrett says.

Maude looks to Caroline, who says, "You never mentioned any."

I frown at Barrett. It's obvious to me, if no one else, that he's fishing for witnesses who can verify Maude's identity.

Barrett ignores my disapproval. "Old friends, then?"

Caroline shakes her head. Maude says, "I think that because I spent so little time in England, I've lost touch with everyone I knew here. I must have friends in Egypt, but I don't remember them."

"How about if I put advertisements in the newspapers, asking your friends and relatives to come forward?" Hugh says.

Maude's gloved hands tighten on her knife and fork. "You're very kind. But perhaps my memory will come back, and you needn't go to the trouble."

After dinner, when the others retire to the parlor, I hold Barrett back with a touch of my hand on his arm. "If you don't stop it, I'll have to ask you to leave."

"Stop what?" he says, all innocence.

"Quizzing Maude."

"I'm not quizzing her, I'm making conversation."

I glare at him and stalk out of the room. He follows me to the parlor. Below a stone frieze of warriors and chariots that looks as if it came from a Greek temple, bright Dutch still-life paintings hang on walls painted a muted rose color. A rose and green floral Chinese rug covers the floor on which divans, armchairs, and tables from different countries and periods stand. A cool, refreshing breeze wafts through the open windows as twilight falls and crickets chirp outside. Hugh taps the keys on the grand piano.

"Miss Napier, how about a song for us to sing?"

Caroline hesitates, then says in the polite manner of a dutiful hostess, "Of course." She sits at the piano and plays—not the discordant music I heard the first time, but old ballads. Mick, Hugh, and Barrett stand beside her and sing. They have good voices, as does Venetia. Maude's voice is uncertain but sweet as my friends teach her the lyrics. Because I can't carry a tune, I silently move my lips. After three songs, Barrett slips out of the room with an apologetic glance, as if to answer the call of nature. He's gone a long time. I head out to look for him, and when there's no sign of him on the main floor, I tiptoe up the stairs. The second floor is vacant. In the third-floor passage, I hear movements in one room. I quietly step in, smell Maude's jasmine scent, and find Barrett rummaging through an armoire.

"What do you think you're doing?" I say.

He yelps and spins around to face me.

"Of all the nerve! Snooping in Maude's room while you're her guest!"

His expression wavers between guilt and defiance. "It's better than if I ignored my doubts about whether she's really Maude."

I'm furious at him, ashamed of his rude behavior, but I can't help asking, "Did you find anything?"

"All her clothes and things look new, as if they were purchased after she went to the hospital." Barrett gestures around the room.

It contains a bed with bamboo posts, draped with sheer white mosquito netting. Most of the furniture is carved teak, and straw rugs partially cover the dark, polished floor. It's like a hotel room in a colonial outpost in the tropics, occupied by a tidy guest who travels light. There's no feminine clutter of strewn clothing, toiletries, or jewelry. The dressing table is made of wood carved to imitate bamboo, with a rectangular mirror and matching chair. The hand mirror lying on the table has a white ivory back to match the hairbrush and comb that are laid precisely on either side of it, like silverware flanking a dinner plate. They look new.

Barrett opens the roll-top desk to reveal pencils, fountain pens, and blank stationery. "No manuscripts. Pretty unusual for an authoress, don't you think?"

"Maybe she took all her things to Egypt with her and left them there when she came back." That sounds improbable even to me. "Or she had them with her and they were stolen by whoever attacked her."

"Or she destroyed them because they could prove she's not Maude," Barrett says. "Clothes that don't fit her, papers with hand-writing that doesn't match hers. Photographs."

"That's not enough evidence that she's an impostor," I say despite my growing uneasiness. I don't want to think about the childish, printed words in her invitation and the possibility that she deliberately disguised her handwriting.

"There's more." Barrett moves to the wicker nightstand and picks up a book. It's bound in crimson leather, with an illustration of a woman seated in a canopied boat on a blue river amid reeds and water lotuses. The gold lettering reads, "A Journey Along the Nile by Maude Napier." He hands the book to me. "Read the page with corner folded down."

I open to the page, near the middle of the book. A passage underlined with pencil reads:

The Cairo marketplace, called a *souk*, is a rich banquet for the senses. Merchants beckon us to purchase their carved figurines, pottery vessels, and gold jewelry. Snake-charmers play their flutes to entice cobras from baskets. But not all the sights are pleasant. Many of the beggars are lepers. That vile, age-old scourge has transformed them into monsters with rotted skin, blind eyes, raw, gaping holes for noses and fingerless hands. When the lepers accosted us, begging for coins, my daughter was terrified. She had nightmares for weeks afterward.

It's the incident that Maude described to me. The food in my stomach feels like a stone as Barrett voices the question in my mind: "Did she remember it, or did she know about it because she read it?"

"So the story is in the book—that doesn't mean she's faking memories. Let's give Maude a chance to speak for herself."

"I want to question her at the police station. Where she can't hide behind Venetia or Caroline." Barrett adds reluctantly, "Or you."

"And treat her like a criminal? Based on this flimsy evidence?" I hurl the book onto the table.

"The evidence is a sign that we shouldn't have been so quick to accept her as Maude and ignore August Legrand when he said she was his wife."

I think of Venetia's description of the change in Maude's personality. I can't bring myself to tell Barrett. "If you take Maude to the police station, Venetia will be upset."

"If she isn't Maude, it's better for Venetia to find out now than later." Barrett points out, with irrefutable logic, "The bandages are going to have to come off eventually. What a shock for Venetia if the face underneath is a stranger's."

I haven't forgotten my own qualms about the bandages, but I say, "She must be Maude. If she's not, how can she think she'll get away with pretending she is? Her story is in all the newspapers. Wouldn't the real Maude hear about it and come forward?"

"It could take weeks for the news to reach her at the excavation site in Egypt," Barrett says. "Maybe Sleeping Beauty plans to be gone before it does—and before the bandages come off."

"Gone, where?"

Barrett shrugs. "The money from Maude's bank accounts should take her as far away as she likes."

My mind shies away from the idea. "I don't believe she's an impostor. You're making a mountain out of a molehill."

"Why would I?"

"Because you have so many cases that you can't solve. You're trying to turn this one into a crime you can."

"I wouldn't do that!" He looks wounded by my accusation, shaken by the thought that he's motivated by selfishness. "Why are you so eager to take Maude's side against mine?"

"I'm not. I just don't want this to become another instance of the police wrongly accusing an innocent person. Like in the Ripper case."

Barrett scowls. He wasn't responsible for the police's blunder, but he takes it personally. "That's a low blow." He scrutinizes me. "I'm starting to think there's something you're not telling me—something about Maude that bothers you. Is that why you're so riled up?"

He knows me too well. "I am not riled up," I say in the stiff, edgy tone used by riled-up people to claim they're not. "Although I will be if you drag Maude to the police station."

"Whether I do or not is up to me."

He's pulled rank, reminded me that he's the law, and I'm a mere newspaperwoman. As we glare at each other, the sound of laughter and music drifts up from the parlor.

"We'd better get back to the others," I say.

In the parlor, we rejoin the sing-along. Our quarrel taints the air like poisonous smoke that only we can smell, as we pretend everything is well. At ten o'clock, Maude says, "Venetia, it's past your bedtime."

"I'm not sleepy," Venetia says.

"You'd better get your shut-eye so you'll be chipper for the zoo tomorrow," Hugh says.

"All right," Venetia says. "Mick, I'll race you upstairs!"

They stampede through the house. Maude excuses herself and follows them at a sedate pace. Caroline says, "I've a few things to do in the kitchen," and makes a hasty exit.

"How about a nightcap?" Hugh says to Barrett and me, moving toward a table on which bottles, decanters, and glasses sit. "I don't think our hostesses will mind if we help ourselves."

When we're seated, glasses of brandy in hand, Hugh says in a low voice, "So what do you think, Barrett? Is she or isn't she Maude Napier?"

"I haven't made up my mind." Barrett doesn't look at me.

"I tried to pump Caroline today," Hugh says. "I'm not bragging when I say there are very few women I can't charm, but she's one of them. She deflected my subtle questions about Maude. The cook and maid were more susceptible, but no help. They're both new. They never met Maude until she came here from the hospital. And since they only work part-time and don't live in, they haven't gotten to know her very well."

"Fancy that," Barrett says.

My discomposure grows because I have to wonder if she's an impostor taking advantage of the fact that the servants can't call her bluff.

I hear a faint cough and look over to see Maude standing in the doorway.

"Venetia would like to say goodnight, Sarah." She behaves in her usual, pleasant manner; I can't tell if she overheard our discussion. "Will you come up?"

"Of course." As we mount the stairs together, I think that she seems so nice, so guileless. But I don't really know her, and I shouldn't be so quick to dismiss Barrett's suspicions.

"I want to thank you again for saving my life and reuniting me with Venetia," she says. "I can't tell you how much it means to me."

When I was the same age as Venetia, my own mother deceived me, telling me that my father was dead, concealing Ellen Casey's murder and Lucas Zehnpfennig's existence. Is this woman deceiving Venetia?

In the nursery, Venetia sits in a bed with a red-and-yellow-striped canopy like a circus tent. A mural of dancing elephants, lions jumping through hoops, and frolicking clowns covers one wall. The curtains are tasseled red velvet, like on a stage at a side-show. Much of the room is taken up by shelves crammed with books, rocks, seashells, and figurines, and chests that contain toy swords, lances, pikes, and scimitars as well as Venetia's bayonets. On a table littered with paint boxes, brushes, pencils, paper, and scissors, I see colored drawings of animals signed with her name. The drawing and handwriting both seem advanced for a child.

"Miss Bain, it's such fun having you and Lord Hugh and Mick here." Venetia looks drowsy and contented. "Mother is going to read me a story. Would you like to listen?"

Maude sits on the bed, a book in her lap. Venetia snuggles against her. Maude smiles and motions me to the chair beside the bed. My mother never read to me; she always said she was too tired. I wonder if she read to Lucas. I envy Venetia, but I can't stop wondering if this woman is Jenny Legrand or Peggy Oliphant and latched on to Venetia in order to escape her volatile husband or unpleasant stepfamily.

"Thank you, but I won't intrude on you," I say. "I'll see you in the morning."

On the stairs, Caroline Napier accosts me. "I know what you and Detective Barrett are doing." Her fluttery voice has a harsh edge, like a razor concealed in feathers.

"What?" I say, taken aback by the anger in her eyes.

"You think she's not really Maude, and you're trying to prove it."

I'm perturbed that she's accusing me of the opposite of what I want. "No, I'm not. You're mistaken."

"After all those questions you asked during your interview and he asked at dinner? Oh, spare me." Caroline is holding my satchel. She reaches into it, pulls out the photographs of Jenny Legrand and Peggy Oliphant, and thrusts them at me. "You think she's one of these other women."

"You've been snooping in my things!" I snatch the photographs and satchel, angry to have my privacy violated, chagrined because I wasn't more careful.

"Haven't you been snooping around the house?" Caroline says with an acid smile. "Isn't that why you and Detective Barrett left during the music?"

It would be wrong to put the blame on Barrett; if not for me, he wouldn't be here. "I apologize. We just want to be sure she's really Maude."

Caroline folds her arms. "I'm sure. So is Venetia. We don't need your meddling."

"How can you be sure, with her face covered?"

"Her eyes aren't covered. Neither are her lips or teeth. They're Maude's."

"Could you be mistaken?"

"I nursed Maude when she was ill. I daresay I'm more familiar with her than anyone except her late husband has ever been. An impostor wouldn't fool me for a second." She thrusts her face so close to mine that I can see the tiny red veins on her eyeballs and smell her meaty breath. "She's Maude. If you're going to persist in your ridiculous attempt to prove she isn't, then I must ask you to leave this house at once."

I recoil in alarm. I don't want my friendship with Maude nipped in the bud, and I can't leave when there's the tiniest shred of doubt about her. "If she is Maude, then you needn't feel threatened by my investigation. For Venetia's sake, you should be willing to help me confirm that the woman she thinks is her mother really is."

Caroline utters a humorless laugh. "Don't pretend you care about Venetia. All you want is a story for your newspaper. 'Sleeping Beauty Exposed as a Fraud.' That should sell enough copies to earn you a raise! I'll do whatever is necessary to protect my niece—and my sister-in-law. If you try to tear them apart, you'll be sorry."

She hastens away down the stairs. I barely have time to catch my breath before Hugh ambles up. "Everything all right?" he says.

"Fine," I lie.

"Rubbish. I noticed that you and Barrett aren't exactly love-birds tonight. What's wrong?"

I succumb to the need to unburden myself and tell Hugh about my quarrel with Barrett.

"I wish I had the luxury of squabbling over trivia with my beloved," Hugh says when I'm done.

"It's not trivia!"

"Yes, you're right," Hugh says quickly. "I'm sorry, I shouldn't have said that. It's important to figure out whether Maude really is Maude, for Venetia's sake." He adds, with less than his usual sympathy toward me, "But if you and Barrett could put yourself in my shoes, you wouldn't waste a minute of the time you could be happy together." He pats my arm and goes up to his room.

I still think my anger at Barrett is justified, but when I think about Hugh and Tristan's problems, my quarrel with Barrett does seem like a mere tiff. I go downstairs to the parlor.

Barrett is alone, sitting on the sofa, drumming his fingers on the armrest. "Sarah." His wary expression says he thinks I mean to resume our quarrel.

"I didn't want the sun to go down on our anger, and I'm sorry it already has," I say.

Barrett's face relaxes into a smile. "Same here." He holds out his hand to me.

I sit beside him. He puts his arm around me, and I lean against him, soothed by his warm closeness. Although I don't want to spoil this moment of reconciliation, I have to say, "I still don't agree with you about Maude."

"I don't agree with you either." Barrett's voice is free of animosity. "But we shouldn't let it come between us."

"You're right." I'm thankful that our love is strong enough to weather our differences, but I know that my secrecy could destroy it. I take a deep breath and confess, "There's something I haven't told you." I describe my talks with Venetia and Caroline.

Although he frowns, he keeps his arm around me. "Is that everything?"

"Yes." I'm relieved to come clean, sorry I delayed it. "You have a right to be mad at me."

"I'm not mad—well, just a little," Barrett says. "I'm more hurt because you kept another secret from me."

His hurt is a soreness in my own heart. "I'm sorry. I won't do it again." Much as it grieves me to admit, I say, "Now that I've had time to think, I realize there are suspicious things about Maude, no matter that Caroline stuck up for her. But I can't bear for somebody to be treated like a criminal when it hasn't been proven that they're guilty of anything."

"I know." Barrett holds me closer; he understands that I'm thinking of my father. "But you know I can't let things slide, close the Sleeping Beauty case, and pretend it's all happily ever after. I have to confront Maude."

I deplore the thought of her interrogated, badgered, and terrified, but I say, "Yes. It's your job. And we need to find out the truth."

"I'll tell you what. Before I take Maude to the police station, you and I will talk to her here in the morning. We'll see what she has to say. Then I'll decide whether to take the next step. How about it?"

Aware that this is the best compromise Barrett can offer, I say, "All right."

We snuggle together. The house is silent; everyone else has gone to bed. Outside, the garden is hushed except for chirping crickets and rustling trees. I lift my face to Barrett, he turns to me, and we kiss briefly, chastely. We glance at the doorway to make sure nobody is there watching. Then we kiss again, mouths open, tongues entwined, tasting each other, breathing each other's gasps. My need for him is so urgent, I don't care that we're guests in this house and any of the other people in it could walk in on us. I stand up, turn off the gas lamps, then grab Barrett's hand and pull him toward the darkest corner of the room. He doesn't ask if it's a safe time of the month, and I'm too excited to count days. We resume where we left off last time. He presses me against the wall, pulls up my skirts, and when he pulls down my knickers and discovers how wet I am, he moans.

"Shh!" Then I moan because he's caressing my breasts.

We muffle our noises with kisses while he drops his trousers. I wrap my legs around his waist, and he enters me. His every thrust raises us higher toward our pleasure until suddenly it comes, for both of us at once, so intensely that my vision goes black while our bodies shudder. We cling together, panting, enjoying our satisfaction for only a moment. Loath to be caught in such a compromising position, we disengage. Barrett pulls up his trousers, I straighten my clothes, and then we hobble to the sofa, where we collapse in warm, breathless languor.

We must have fallen asleep, because the next thing I know, I wake to the sound of a loud crash, a scream, and a thud outside. Then comes a tinkling noise, like icicles falling from a roof. As I bolt up from the sofa, Barrett says, "What was that?"

We rush out the French doors, Barrett with a poker in his hand, I with a lamp in mine. The moon floats like a white bubble in the mist that lies heavy upon the dark garden. As we move cautiously along the terrace, the lamp illuminates wrought-iron furniture, the dried leaves on the brick pavement . . . then crystalline shards of broken glass mingled with gleaming red droplets. A gulp sticks in my throat. We halt and stare at the body of a stout woman lying on her back, arms flung out, legs spread. Her black frock is patterned with mauve diamonds. A black straw bonnet trimmed with purple feathers lies near her head, from which the blood has spattered the terrace. I recognize the clothes before I recognize the face, with its weak jawline and sharp nose. Her prim mouth is open, her little eyes glazed.

"It's Frances Oliphant!"

Chapter 20

"What the hell is she doing here?" Barrett says.

It's as though fate has taken someone I thought I would never see again and dropped her on us in the most bizarre, terrible fashion.

Hugh and Mick come running out of the house. "Holy Mother of God!" Mick says. Hugh retches, turns away, and doubles over, gasping.

Frances doesn't move or make a sound. Barrett, Mick, and I look up at the house. Amid the ivy that covers the wall, a large window on the third floor glows. Jagged glass surrounds the hole that Frances made when she fell through the window. Maude, Venetia, and Caroline are standing huddled together, dark against the light in the room behind them, like images in a photographic negative.

"Is she dead?" Venetia asks in a thin, tremulous voice.

Barrett calls to them, "Don't come down here." To Hugh and Mick, he says, "Go inside and stay with them."

Mick pulls Hugh into the house. Barrett crouches beside Frances, feels her neck for a pulse. He looks up at me, and his somber expression conveys the bad news. He straightens up, shaking his head, bewildered by this turn of events.

Staring at Frances, I see other people whose violent deaths are etched into my memory. Polly Nichols, Liz Stride, Kate Eddowes—

the Ripper's victims—are only three among many. I've become hardened to these sights, but every one chips away a little more of my faith in the goodness of life. How many more deaths will come my way if I continue to work at this trade?

Barrett touches my arm. "Sarah, are you all right?"

"I'm fine." Frances's death means trouble, and there's no time for rumination. "We need to find out how this happened."

"I should notify the local police. It's their case." Barrett is as unnerved as I am, and he's fallen back on his training, observing protocol.

My old fear of the law resurges. I stall because I'm reluctant to call in strange policemen when we've a dead body in our midst. "Shouldn't we do our own investigation first?"

Barrett rakes his hand through his hair, thinks a moment, then says, "You're right. This doesn't look good for us. We'd better arm ourselves with as much information as possible."

Inside the house, we discover that the room from which Frances fell is the nursery. Venetia and Maude are sitting on the rumpled bed, hugging each other; Caroline is huddled in the chair. They're all in their dressing gowns and slippers, Maude in her white cap, bandages, and gloves. Mick gazes out the window at Frances's body.

"Looks like there was a skirmish in here before she fell." Hugh points at the overturned table, and toys and art supplies strewn across the floor.

"What happened here?" Barrett asks Venetia, Caroline, and Maude.

They shake their heads. Caroline, pale but composed, says, "We don't know. We were asleep. We came when we heard the noise."

"But this is your room, Venetia." I step inside, careful not to disturb potential evidence, keeping my distance from everyone. I feel the wetness between my legs, and I don't want anyone to smell the ripe odor of sex on me. "Didn't you see anything?"

Frightened and uncharacteristically subdued, Venetia opens her mouth to reply. Maude squeezes her shoulder and says, "She was with me, in my room. She'd had a nightmare and didn't want to be alone." Venetia nods.

"Did anyone hear anything?" Barrett says.

"Nope," Mick says.

"Nothing until smash, scream, and thud woke us up," Hugh says.

"How did Miss Oliphant get in?" Barrett asks Caroline.

"I haven't the slightest idea. Before I went to bed, I made sure the doors were locked."

"I don't think she could've climbed up the vines on the wall," Mick says.

"What was she doing here?" Barrett's gaze encompasses Maude, Venetia, and Caroline.

They all shrug. Maude says, "She must have fallen out the window by accident."

The idea that Frances came to the house for no reason, walked in through the walls, and flung herself backward out the window defies belief. Venetia presses her face against Maude's shoulder; Maude gazes at the top of Venetia's head; Caroline looks at the floor. The warm night suddenly feels cold. I can't help thinking they know more about Frances's death than they've admitted.

"I can't wait any longer to report this," Barrett says. "I'm going to the local police station."

They look up in dismay. Caroline says, "Why? Can't you do whatever needs to be done?"

"This isn't my district." Barrett, on his way out the door, pauses. "You'd better all leave this room. It could be a crime scene."

A loose fragment of glass falls to the terrace as we all contemplate the dire likelihood that Frances's death wasn't an accident.

"We should get dressed before the police come," Hugh says. "We want to look our most respectable."

"Is it all right if I take some clothes for Venetia?" Maude says.

"Yes, but don't touch anything else," Barrett says.

I remember my job, an unwelcome diversion. "I should take photographs."

"Make it fast," Barrett says, and departs.

In my room, I hurriedly wash and tidy myself. Mick helps me carry my photography equipment down to the terrace. "I can handle this," I say. "You search the house."

"For clues about what happened to Frances? Right." Mick runs off.

I race through the photographing of her body. I feel as if there's something I'm not seeing, something missing, but I haven't time to figure out what. I'm replacing my equipment in my room when Mick reappears and says, "Sarah, you gotta see this."

He leads me to the kitchen door. It's equipped with a deadbolt, which he twists to show me that it's locked. Then he yanks and pushes at the knob, jiggling the door. The bolt slips out of its slot, and the door opens.

"I think this is how Frances got in," he says, "but beats me what she wanted."

There's no time to speculate. "Can you take the negatives to the *Daily World*? Sir Gerald will want them, and we can't have them confiscated by the police."

"With the coppers on their way, I don't like to leave Venetia." Mick has become protective toward the girl.

"Hugh and I will look after her."

After Mick leaves, I go to the parlor. Maude and Venetia are sitting close together on the sofa, Caroline on the piano bench, Hugh in an armchair. Someone has made tea; the cups stand full, untouched.

"What sort of questions will the police ask us?" Venetia says to Hugh.

"They'll ask where you were when Miss Oliphant fell out the window. They'll want any information that could shed light on what happened," Hugh says.

"But we haven't any," Maude says.

"We already told Detective Barrett," Venetia says.

I steel myself to raise difficult issues. "Now is the time to think about whether you want to tell the police the same thing."

"What do you mean?" Maude says, confused.

"Listen to how your story sounds," I say. "A woman who thought you were her stepsister falls to her death from the window of your home. You were asleep, you don't know anything about it, and neither do your daughter or your sister-in-law."

"Whew, that does sound fishy," Hugh says.

"But it's true," Venetia protests. Caroline nods.

Maude appeals to me. "Don't you believe us?"

I wish I knew whether I should. "It doesn't matter what I believe. The police will decide whether they think Frances's death was an accident or a crime. And if they don't like your story, they'll make up one they like better." The police who investigated Ellen Casey's murder decided my father was guilty and let Lucas get away with it. "And it may be a story that says you or Venetia or Caroline pushed Frances out the window."

They stare at me, appalled. Hugh says, "I'm afraid Sarah is right. So if you want to reconsider—"

From the street come the rattle of a carriage and the clop of horses' hooves. We sit as though paralyzed. Then comes the knock on the front door. The police are here.

I resist the impulse to run upstairs and hide. Hugh and I walk to the foyer; Maude, Venetia, and Caroline trail behind us. When I open the door, my hand is so clammy with sweat that it's hard to turn the knob. Barrett comes in with three other men. One is a young constable in uniform, equipped with a lantern. The second is in his forties, dressed in a jacket, trousers, and derby that look expensive for a police officer. Tall and thick of build, he has a luxuriant dark mustache to match his hair, both heavily pomaded. The third is an older man carrying a black medical bag. Their footsteps are loud on the tile floor; their male scent of perspiration, shaving lotion, and tobacco smoke invades the house. My stomach clenches.

Barrett introduces the dark-mustached man as Detective Tanner, the others as Constable Jones and Dr. Wilson the police surgeon.

Detective Tanner glances at the pool and the skylight. "I've always been curious to see the inside of this place. Tonight's my lucky night."

Already I don't like him. When he sees Maude's bandages, the interest in his blue eyes sharpens. "Sleeping Beauty, in the flesh." His smile is more aggressive than friendly. "I read about you in the newspapers."

Maude backs away from him; Venetia and Caroline position themselves in front of her, as if to shield her. Tanner turns his attention to Hugh and me.

"Well, well, Lord Hugh Staunton and Miss Sarah Bain. That's a bonus." His eagerness for a high-profile case that involves celebrities in an affluent neighborhood is obvious and repellent. "Where's the body?" he asks Barrett.

"On the terrace." Barrett opens the French doors at the back of the foyer.

Detective Tanner points at the rest of us. "Make yourselves comfortable. I'll be wanting to talk to you." The distrust in his gaze says he's already thinking that Frances's death was foul play and we're suspects.

He and Dr. Wilson follow Barrett outside. The others and I sit in the parlor while Constable Jones stands guard over us. We keep silent rather than talk in his presence. The gray, misty light of dawn gradually renders the trees, pergola, and gazebo outside the French doors visible. We can't see the men, but we hear the murmur of their voices. The air is already uncomfortably warm; it's going to be another sweltering day.

Barrett joins us, looking cross, and sits beside me. "Detective Tanner told me to wait with you." Even though the case isn't his, he dislikes being shunted aside.

We listen to the commotion as Frances's body is taken away to the morgue and Tanner inspects the nursery. Maude, Venetia, and Caroline keep their gazes averted from Hugh, Barrett, and me. I wonder what they're hiding. I'm sure Tanner is searching our rooms. I think of the police threatening my father, hearing them strike him, and their voices saying the words I couldn't discern then and only deduced twenty-two years later: *You killed Ellen Casey. Admit it!*

A knock at the front door makes us all jump. "Who could that be?" Maude cries.

"I'll get it," Hugh says.

He comes back with Inspector Reid and two constables. Reid grins. "Don't look so glad to see me." Someone at the local police station must have sent him word of Frances's death.

"What are you doing here?" Barrett demands.

"I'm taking over the investigation," Reid says.

Detective Tanner hurries into the room. "You can't do that. This is my patch."

"Orders from the commissioner," Reid says. "Walk me through the scene before you leave."

Tanner sulks. Reid says to Barrett, "You're in deep trouble for letting a suspicious death happen on your watch. I'm relieving you of your cases and putting you on midnight desk duty. Get lost."

Rigid with self-control, Barrett stares Reid down. "I'm not going until you do." He must be as aghast about his demotion as I am, but he's more concerned about my safety; he doesn't want to leave me with Reid.

"Insubordination too." Malicious glee sparkles in Reid's cold eyes. "The man is digging himself in deeper every minute."

I can't let Barrett put his job in further jeopardy. "You can go. I'll be all right."

"I'll hold the fort," Hugh says.

Barrett walks out of the room, his reluctance weighting his every step. I hear him close the front door with deliberate quietness that's like a whispered threat to Reid.

Reid makes a show of dusting off his hands, then gestures to the rest of us and says to his men, "Put them in separate rooms. I'll question them after I've examined the scene."

We're all alarmed to be split up, but Maude objects first. "I'm not leaving Venetia alone." She puts her arms around the girl. "I'm her mother."

"There're folks who would disagree with that." Reid's remark is my first hint that he too, and perhaps many others, have doubts about her identity.

"Don't make him angry, Mother," Venetia pleads. "I'll be fine by myself."

Reid smiles a patronizing smile at Venetia. "A wise child."

Furtive glances pass between Maude, Venetia, and Caroline. Hugh says, "I'm staying with Sarah."

"I can arrest you both and question you in Newgate," Reid says.

Hugh and I let Reid's men march us upstairs and lock us in our rooms. I don't know where they've put the others. I'm glad Mick is absent. I pace the floor, listening to the noise as Reid examines the nursery and searches the house. I look out the window and see the ring of broken glass that surrounds the bloodstained bricks where Frances's body had lain. What are the others telling Reid, and when will my turn come? If I hadn't accepted the job at the *Daily World*, I wouldn't be here, and Barrett wouldn't be in trouble. If I quit today, nothing like this need ever happen to us again.

The door opens, and Reid comes in. He looks cheerful—not a good sign. I stand stiffly, containing my emotions.

"Here you are, in the thick of yet another crime," he says. "You and your friends are like flies drawn to shit."

Braced by my hatred and anger toward him, I focus on the bit of news he's given me. "Frances Oliphant's death was murder?"

"I'm treating it as such." He rattles the bead curtain around the bed. "Nice room. Looks like a Gypsy caravan. What, no crystal ball?"

"Sorry," I say, trying to deduce his intentions.

"That's all right. I don't need a crystal ball to predict that there's trouble ahead for someone in this house."

I'm certain he's going to use the case as a weapon against my friends and me, but my immediate concern isn't for us. "What have you done to Maude, Venetia, and Caroline?"

"Don't worry about them. They've been cooperating with my inquiries."

As I wonder if they followed my advice and changed their story, Reid says, "I understand that you went upstairs to the top floor not long before Miss Oliphant fell."

"I didn't!" A buzzing like a swarm of hornets vibrates through me. "Who told you that?"

"Information related to police business is confidential," Reid says with pompous spite. "But I can bend the rules and tell you that you were heard talking, and another woman's voice was heard answering you."

The hornets of anxiety buzz louder as I wonder if Reid accused Maude, Venetia, and Caroline, and they protected themselves by saying that I had let Frances in the house and taken her to the nursery. Did they deliberately implicate me in her death?

"How could anyone have heard?" I say. "Everyone was asleep."

"Not everyone," Reid says.

I wouldn't put it past him to lie. "When Frances fell out the window, I was in the parlor with Detective Sergeant Barrett."

My alibi provokes an odd, pleased smile from Reid. "Oh? What were you doing?"

"Talking." My face flames as I think of what else we did.

"I'll see what Barrett has to say."

Barrett and I share the same alibi, and Reid obviously thinks we would lie to protect each other. "We didn't kill Frances Oliphant. Why would we?"

"You tell me, Miss Bain. Maybe she didn't like the way the Sleeping Beauty case turned out. Maybe she still thought the woman was her stepsister. But you and Barrett and your gang were riding high after solving the case. You couldn't let Frances cock things up for you, so push literally came to shove."

Contempt gets the upper hand over my fear. "You're inventing stories because you've no evidence to prove how or why Frances died. You'd better watch out—you're going to railroad an innocent person and end up in trouble yourself. Like you did in the Ripper case."

Reid flinches because I've poked his sorest spot. "Innocent, you?" He snorts. "Don't make me laugh."

The air between us seethes with my guilty knowledge of everything I've done outside the law and his suspicions about me.

In an abrupt change of mood, his cheerfulness returns, with a sly edge. "What were Maude, Venetia, and Caroline up to last night? Any reason I should take what they say with a grain of salt?" He adds, "Tit for tat."

He's giving me a chance to incriminate them as they may have incriminated me. Although I'm certain they're hiding something, I say, "I don't know."

Reid tilts his head, studies me, and says, "What are they to you?" as if he can't understand why I wouldn't sell someone out to protect myself when given the chance.

"They're people who were kind enough to welcome me into their home." If Reid knew how much I've come to care about Maude and Venetia, he would show them no mercy. Because I care about them, I'm not going to throw them to Reid before I figure out what they're hiding. I don't want them under his suspicion unless they really did implicate me in Frances's death.

"You may want to reconsider your story." Reid's words are an ominous echo of my warning to them and Caroline. "For now, you and your friends will pack your bags and leave. Butt out of this investigation, or I'll have you arrested." He raises his eyebrows, smiles, and holds up his finger, as if a bright idea has just occurred to him. "Or maybe I should arrest your sister, Sally, instead."

CHAPTER 21

Icouldn't ask Maude, Venetia, and Caroline what they told Inspector Reid because he refused to let me see them. He told me that he would have a police guard stationed at the house around the clock, and one of his constables stood at the door to make sure Hugh and I left.

The temperature is rising, and by the time we've hauled our baggage outside, loaded it on top of a cab, and climbed in, we're soaked with perspiration. "Do you think one of them is a murderess?" I say as we wipe our faces on our handkerchiefs.

"Perish the thought," Hugh says.

"I don't like leaving them alone with Inspector Reid."

"Considering what happened to their last uninvited visitor, Reid had better watch out."

Even though exhausted, hungry, and scared, we laugh at Hugh's joke. Then Hugh says, "Reid threatened to have the vice squadron work me over again. He said he could bring my 'not so holy father' to share the fun. I'm afraid he knows about Tristan."

I shouldn't be surprised that Reid would go after Hugh's nearest and dearest as well as mine, but the breath puffs out of me, and I fall back against the seat. "How could he know?"

"Reid could have read that item in the newspaper, but he also has eyes and ears all over London," Hugh says darkly. "Witness how fast he turned up after Frances's death. He's hot for any ammunition to use against us."

At St. John's Wood station, we find Barrett standing near the ticket booth. He smiles with relief. "Thought you'd been arrested."

I'm so glad to see him that the day suddenly doesn't seem as bad. "Not quite." I tell him about my conversation with Reid.

"Reid did me a favor," Barrett says with a wry smile. "I don't go on desk duty until midnight. That means I have time to investigate Frances's death. And if it was murder, solve the case before Reid botches it."

"Count me in," I say.

"Don't forget me," Hugh says.

We've all weighed the dangers against the possibility of Reid sending an innocent person—likeliest, myself—to the gallows.

"Now that the crime scene and the suspects are off limits, what shall we do?" Hugh says.

My impulse is to protect Hugh. "You can take our baggage home. Then go to Fleet Street and tell Sir Gerald what's happened. Ask if he can pull any strings to help us." That should keep Hugh safe for the time being. "And tell Tristan and Mick what's happened."

"Right. Where are you two going?"

"To Wandsworth," Barrett says. "This is our chance to get a step ahead of Reid."

★   ★   ★

Situated on the opposite side of the river from London proper, Wandsworth is famous for its prison, which is nowhere in sight when Barrett and I arrive at a neighborhood of hilly, tree-lined streets between the town commons and the waterfront. The mansions have an air of solid, well-maintained respectability, if not elegance. The Oliphant Convalescent Home is an immense, Tudor-style brick structure, identified by its name on an unobtrusive brass plaque on the gatepost. Fetid haze from the river shrouds the half-timbered gables that crown two wings on each side of a main entrance set behind a covered porch. Stone walls that support banks of tall, thick hedges and shrubs isolate the mansion from the road. The place has a forbidding appearance that the lights within the mullioned windows don't relieve. As we head up the path to the entrance, men clad in black wheel a covered body on a stretcher out a side door, load it into a hearse, and drive away.

"I suppose that even in a fancy place like this, not all the patients recover," Barrett says, and then, "Hey, what are you doing?" as I head toward the side door. "Shouldn't we go in the main entrance and ask for Mrs. Oliphant and her daughter?"

"I want a look around, and after we tell them about Frances, they're not likely to give us a tour."

"And I thought Mick was the breaking-and-entering ring-leader of your pack," Barrett grumbles.

He follows me through the door, into a vacant passage with a stone floor and dingy plaster walls. A blare of raised voices, pots and pans banging, machinery rattling, and water splashing issues from the kitchen, scullery, and laundry. Another door leads us to a flight of stairs that we ascend to the main floor. Open archways along the corridor reveal parlors occupied by people dressed for bed, some in wheelchairs, tended by nurses. Before anyone spots us, we duck back into the stairwell. The passage on the upper floor has dark green carpet, rows of closed doors, and cream-and-beige-striped wallpaper. Stiflingly warm, it smells of urine and disinfectant.

Barrett whispers, "What do you expect to learn—"

Voices and heavy footsteps approach from around the corner. One voice is a woman's, plummy and irate and familiar. "There's a spot on the carpet. Clean it off."

"Yes, Mrs. Oliphant," says a second woman, presumably a maid.

I try the knob of the nearest door. It's not locked. We hurry into the room, which is fortunately unoccupied. Dirty sheets are wadded on the bed; medicine bottles clutter the dresser top; and a foul odor nauseates me. Seeking escape, I notice French doors behind the sheer curtains. We hurry outside to a balcony terrace and breathe fresher air that's laced with coal smoke and laundry-room steam. Below us, a garden slopes down to a line of plane trees, through which I glimpse the roofs of houses lower on the hill. In the distance, wharves and factories line the riverfront, and an iron bridge extends toward London proper, which is hidden in brown haze. Lounge chairs stand along the terrace. Two are occupied by old men wearing pajamas.

"Look, we have visitors," says one of the men, his leg in a cast.

"A pretty lady, at that." The other wears a wool muffler and helmet, both fit for the North Pole. He smiles and doffs his helmet at me.

"What pretty lady would come to see your ugly mug?" his companion jokes. "They probably wandered into the wrong room. But why don't you pull up chairs and join us?"

"Thank you. We can't stay long," I say.

Introductions follow. The man in the cast is Arthur Gaskell; his neighbor is Julian Winkworth.

"How did you break your leg?" Barrett asks Mr. Gaskell.

"Fell off the ladder in my library, reaching for *Vanity Fair*."

"Clumsy oaf," Mr. Winkworth says.

"At least *I* didn't catch pneumonia by bird-watching on Dartmoor in the freezing cold," Mr. Gaskell retorts.

"Enough about us." Mr. Winkworth asks Barrett and me, "Whom are you here to visit?"

"I think you two are just the people we want." Instinct tells me not to mention Frances's death. If I do, they'll keep us busy answering questions for which we haven't time. "I'm a reporter from the *Daily World*, and I'm working with Detective Barrett to investigate a case. Have you heard about Sleeping Beauty, the woman who was found unconscious by the river?"

"Oh lord, yes," Mr. Winkworth says. "Mrs. Oliphant and Frances and Faith—the ladies who own this home—thought she might be Peggy." Unaware that we know them, he explains, "Peggy is Mrs. Oliphant's stepdaughter. Her father was the late doctor who founded the home. She disappeared a few weeks ago."

"Now, that was an uproar to beat the band," Mr. Gaskell says. "Miss Frances had the whole house searched from attic to cellar. She called in the police."

"Do you think Sleeping Beauty is Peggy?" I say, afraid to hear the answer. Perhaps I'm seconds away from learning that she's impersonating Maude Napier.

"Well, no, because we can't figure out why Peggy would have gone to Shadwell," Mr. Winkworth says. "It's ten miles or more, on the other side of the river. Peggy never goes that far from home."

Barrett and I exchange glances. I'm glad for this clue that Sleeping Beauty really is Maude, but I can tell that he hasn't dismissed his hunch that she's Jenny Legrand.

"Maybe she didn't go on her own," Barrett says. "Maybe someone kidnapped her."

Mr. Gaskell chuckles. "I doubt there are many kidnappers lurking about Wandsworth Common."

"One is all it would take," Barrett says, "and a girl who's not right in her head would be a vulnerable target."

The old men squint at us. "Why do you think Peggy's not right in her head?" Mr. Winkworth says.

"Mrs. Oliphant and her daughters told the police so," I say.

"Bosh," Mr. Gaskell says. "Peggy is perfectly normal."

"And a good girl too," Mr. Winkworth says. "Always kind and sweet and helpful."

"Why would her stepmother and stepsisters lie?" I say.

"They don't like Peggy," Mr. Winkworth says. "They're always saying bad things about her. If anything goes wrong, she gets the blame. They're jealous because she's pretty and they're not. Haven't you ever heard the story of Cinderella?"

It appears that my notion about the relationship between Peggy and her stepfamily is accurate. I can't see that said relationship bears upon Frances's murder, but perhaps we can solve another mystery. "What do you think happened to Peggy?"

The men share a conspiratorial glance. Mr. Gaskell says, "We've a theory about that."

A movement in the room that Barrett and I came from diverts my attention. A woman wheels in a cart with a big canvas sack suspended within its metal frame. She takes the wadded sheets from the bed, dumps them in the sack, and sweeps the medicine bottles from the dresser on top of them. It takes me a moment to recognize Faith Oliphant—she's wearing a plain gray dress and white head kerchief. Any minute, she'll sense me watching her and look outside.

I touch Barrett's arm, point at Faith. He says to the men, "Thank you for your time. We have to go now. Is there another way out of here?"

They point down the terrace. We hurry to a stairway that leads to the garden, descend, and walk around the house to the main entrance. In the foyer, a porter greets us. When I ask to see Mrs. Oliphant and Miss Faith Oliphant, he asks for our names. Barrett, although not in uniform, introduces himself as Detective Sergeant. The porter rushes off to tell the Oliphants, and when he returns, ushers us to a hot, musty room. It contains a desk and chair, and glass-fronted cabinets filled with ledgers, at one end. A moss-green carpet covers the floor, and brocade curtains frame the windows. At the other end, in front of the hearth, two armchairs with violet and green floral upholstery face across a low table toward a matching sofa. A painted portrait of Dr. Oliphant shows a younger, healthier version of the man I saw in the family photograph.

Mrs. Oliphant and Faith rush into the room, their faces pinched with anxiety. "Detective!" Faith says. "Is this about Frances?"

Mrs. Oliphant clasps her bosom with one hand, extends the other to us. "Where is she? Tell me she's all right." She sees our somber expressions; her face turns white; her legs crumple. Faith helps her to the sofa, where she collapses.

"I knew it!" Faith wails. "When she didn't come home, I knew something terrible must have happened." But her eyes gleam with excitement.

In a grave, solicitous manner that policemen must be trained to use at times like this, Barrett says, "Miss Oliphant, you'd better sit down too."

Faith perches beside her mother while Barrett and I sit in the armchairs. "She's dead, isn't she?" Faith says, avid as a theatergoer when the curtain rises.

"No!" Mrs. Oliphant cries.

"I'm very sorry," Barrett says.

Mrs. Oliphant bursts into sobs. "It can't be! Frances! My dear child!" Body heaving, she leans against Faith.

Faith puts her arm around her mother. I feel awkward being present at their time of loss, but Faith looks torn between grief and ghoulish curiosity as she says, "How did she die?"

"She fell out a window," Barrett says.

"Where is she?" Mrs. Oliphant demands.

"Her body was taken to the mortuary."

"I want to see her!"

"You can't until the autopsy is finished. I'm sorry," Barrett says.

"An autopsy? Why?" Faith says. "Didn't you say she fell? Wasn't it an accident?"

"The autopsy will help to determine whether it was foul play."

Mrs. Oliphant regards him with wet, horror-stricken eyes. "Do you mean somebody pushed Frances? Oh God!" She breaks into a fresh, melodramatic spate of weeping.

"We won't know until our investigation is finished." Barrett doesn't let on that he and I aren't part of the official investigation.

Faith leans forward, as if hungry for more bad news. "Where did it happen?"

"In St. John's Wood," Barrett says, "at the house where Maude, Venetia, and Caroline Napier live."

The women's weak jawlines sag with surprise. "Whatever was she doing there?" Faith says.

"So you didn't know she went?" I say.

"She just said she had an errand," Mrs. Oliphant says between sobs. "It was strange for her to go out so late at night, and when I asked what errand, she told me to mind my own business."

Even as I lose hope of unraveling the events that led up to Frances's death, Faith says, "*I* think Frances still thought Sleeping Beauty might be Peggy, and she wanted to know for sure."

It's a plausible explanation, but Barrett says, "How would she have known where Sleeping Beauty lives?"

Both women shake their heads.

"If it is Peggy in that house, she must be laughing at us while she lazes around eating bonbons." Spite edges Faith's voice. "She doesn't have to work, like she would here."

"So Frances might have gone to confront Sleeping Beauty," Barrett says. "What did she intend to do if she discovered that Sleeping Beauty really is Peggy?"

"Make her admit it," Mrs. Oliphant says. "Make her come home."

"Since Peggy's been gone, I've had to do all her chores," Faith whines. "It's not fair."

Barrett and I frown at each other as we glimpse a possible reason for Frances's death. Maybe he's as wrong to think Sleeping Beauty is Jenny Legrand as I am to believe she's Maude Napier. If she's Peggy Oliphant, how far might she have gone to prevent Frances from marching her home to resume her position as slave of all work?

I'm afraid to ask, but I say, "Has Peggy ever been violent?"

"Oh my, yes," Mrs. Oliphant says. "She once threw a mop at me, after I told her to scrub the floor again because she hadn't gotten it clean enough."

"She slapped me in the face because I called her a lazy slut," Faith says. "She didn't dare hit Frances, but she would spill hot soup in her lap at dinner and claim it was an accident."

I dislike these women, and they could be lying, but I can't ignore the possibility that the Peggy they know isn't the sweet, gentle girl the patients described. Barrett frowns and my heart sinks as we imagine what could have happened last night.

"Did Peggy push Frances out the window?" Mrs. Oliphant's voice is hushed, fearful.

"That's one possibility," Barrett says.

I wonder whether Sleeping Beauty not only deceived me about her identity but about what happened last night. Is she a murderess as well as a fraud? Have I been so gullible?

"If she really is Peggy, how does she think she'll get away with pretending to be Maude Napier?" I say. "She can't keep the bandages on her face forever."

Mrs. Oliphant snorts with contempt. "Peggy doesn't think. I told you she's not right in the head."

I don't want to cause trouble for the patients, so instead of saying they disagree with the Oliphants about Peggy's nature, I say, "Yes, you did. Can you be more specific than you were last time?"

"She has moods," Mrs. Oliphant says. "On good days, she seems perfectly normal. On bad days, she acts like a hellion. She thinks people are out to get her, and she throws tantrums like a child. All we can do is give her pills that my dear late husband prescribed, and lock her up until she falls asleep. When she wakes up, she's all right. I think she has one of those newfangled mental conditions."

"Oh pooh," Faith says. "Peggy's only problem is that she thinks she deserves special treatment because she's Dr. Oliphant's little girl. He spoiled her rotten. And she's not stupid. I promise, if she's impersonating that woman, she has a plan for when it's time for the bandages to come off. But the little girl and the aunt must be stupid if she's managed to trick them for this long."

I don't think Venetia and Caroline are stupid, and why would they deliberately accept an impostor as Maude? I remember how vigorously Caroline defended Maude, but I also remember Venetia saying Maude's personality had changed. Last night's events aren't the only mystery in that house. The musty air in this room turns suffocating, and although my chair is comfortable, I can't sit still. My legs twitch with my urge to run away from the idea that what I thought was a joyous mother–daughter reunion is really a masquerade that's led to the murder of one stepsister by another.

"If you dislike Peggy so much, then why do you want her back?" Barrett says. "Why would Frances break into a stranger's house to bring her home instead of hiring someone else to do her work?"

"When my dear late husband was on his deathbed, we promised him that we would take care of Peggy," Mrs. Oliphant says, clasping her hands together in prayer and lifting her eyes skyward.

"Why are you asking all these questions about Peggy?" Faith says. "Aren't you here because of Frances?"

"Frances's death isn't the only case I'm investigating," Barrett says. "There's also the brutal attack on Sleeping Beauty."

Offense turns Mrs. Oliphant's homely features homelier. "You think my daughters and I were responsible? That we tried to kill Peggy and slashed her face?"

"Did you?" Barrett says.

Faith utters an incredulous laugh. "Of course not. The very idea is absurd!"

"Then where were you and your mother and sister on the night of Wednesday the eighteenth of June?" I say.

"We had dinner together. Then we sat in the parlor. Mother and Frances played cards. I read a book. Then we went to bed. We were home all night. That's our habit. We never laid a finger on Peggy— never even saw her. She'd been missing for more than a week."

"Sarah," Barrett says, "we have to go."

He points at the window. I see Inspector Reid and his two constables walking up the path toward the house.

CHAPTER 22

After our train trip from Wandsworth, Barrett and I hurry through the crowds on Fleet Street as if the hounds of hell are breathing fire down our necks. Mrs. Oliphant and Faith will surely tell Reid that we spoke to them. One step ahead of him isn't enough.

In the *Daily World* building, we find Hugh and Mick in the engraving studio on the second floor, watching an artist convert one of my photographs of Frances Oliphant's body into an etched copper plate for the illustration in the newspaper.

"Just in the nick of time," Hugh says. "Sir Gerald wants to see you."

"He's already sent down twice, askin' if you were in," Mick says.

"Only me?" I say, anticipating more trouble.

Hugh gives me a sympathetic look. "Only you."

I persuade Barrett to go home to the police barracks and sleep before his midnight duty. Although my legs quake with fatigue and I'm in a hurry, I delay my talk with Sir Gerald by climbing the stairs to the top floor instead of riding in the elevator. He's seated at his desk, writing. I'm uneasy when alone with him, and it's not just because he's powerful enough to destroy me. In the absence of other people, the residue of that night on Hampstead Heath is stronger and darker; I can almost smell the blood on his hands, and it reminds me of the blood on mine.

"Frances Oliphant's murder could be a big story," he says as he rises from his chair. "Because of its connection with Sleeping Beauty." His tone is even, without animosity, but I'm on my guard. He wouldn't summon me just to state the obvious.

"The problem is, you and your friends are in the middle of it. And by tonight, the word will be all over town." He hands me a newspaper page. "This is a proof for the *Chronicle*'s evening edition. Theirs won't be the only one like it hitting the streets in a few hours."

The proof is fresh; I can smell the ink. His spies at other papers let him know what the competition is printing. The headline for the bottom half of the page proclaims, "Witnesses or Killers?" Below are photographs of Hugh, Mick, and me. The story states that Frances Oliphant fell to her death from a window at the home of Maude Napier, better known as "Sleeping Beauty," and names everyone who was present, including Barrett. My heart sinks as I read, "It's not the first time Sarah Bain, Lord Hugh Staunton, and Mick O'Reilly have been mixed up in a murder. Did Miss Oliphant fall by accident, or did she have help from them?"

Sir Gerald fixes a penetrating stare on me. "Did she have help from you?"

"No!" I sound defensive and guilty, even though I'm innocent. "We didn't kill her. Neither did Detective Sergeant Barrett."

"I believe you," Sir Gerald says, "but not everybody will." He takes the page from me, crumples it, and tosses it in the trash. "That's bound to stir up suspicion, and after that fiasco with the hangman case, I can't afford to have my people be suspected of murder."

Because of the fiasco, the *Daily World*'s sales had dropped, and the Mariner Bank had lost customers and investors. Never mind that my friends and I solved the murder and delivered the killer to justice; with all his power, Sir Gerald is still vulnerable to public opinion, and his implication is clear: if Frances's death was murder, and my friends and I become official suspects, we're fired.

"Tell me you're working on getting to the bottom of this," he says.

"We are." We have to clear our names, never mind save our jobs. "Even though Inspector Reid threatened to arrest us if we interfere with his investigation, we're conducting our own."

I see a glint of respect in Sir Gerald's eyes; he likes that we're brave enough to defy the police. "What've you found out?"

No matter that it's only been some nine hours since Frances died; he expects results. "If Frances was murdered, then Caroline, Venetia, and . . . Rosamond are suspects." I revert to her temporary name because I'm uncomfortable calling her *Maude* when I'm less certain about her identity than ever. "None of them has an alibi." I hate to incriminate them while I'm not sure they incriminated me. When I describe Barrett's and my visit to the Oliphant Convalescent Home, I hesitate before I say, "If Frances believed that Peggy is pretending to be Maude, it explains why she went to the Napier house. And if she was right, then Peggy might have pushed her out the window rather than be exposed as a fraud and dragged home."

Sir Gerald rubs his chin. "Do you think she is a fraud?" He seems poised between the hope of a sensational story for the *Daily World* and displeasure because he, along with his reporters, might have been duped.

I'm not ready to admit my doubts out loud. "I'm reserving judgment until I investigate further." I don't mention that I think Rosamond, Venetia, and Caroline are hiding something. Nor do I want three people who could be innocent to become fodder for the *Daily World*.

"All right. Keep digging." Sir Gerald seems suddenly distracted. "One more thing before you go, Miss Bain. I need to talk to you about Hugh and Tristan."

I'm surprised that the conversation has turned personal, which it rarely does. Plus their relationship is a taboo subject with Sir Gerald, who doesn't like it rubbed in his face.

"Do you know what Tristan gets up to when he stays out all night?" he says.

"No."

"I was hoping Hugh had found out and told you."

"Hugh is as much in the dark as you are."

Sir Gerald paces behind his desk like a watchdog on a short chain. "One thing I'm sure of—my son's in trouble. And there've been rumors circulating about him and Hugh."

Those rumors must have reached Inspector Reid's ears.

"I can't have Tristan raked over the coals. God knows what it would do to him. So I'm going to ask a favor of you. Convince Hugh to break it off."

"I can't do that." Even if I had the gall to meddle in their intimate affairs, Hugh wouldn't jilt the love of his life.

The rare, pleading expression on Sir Gerald's face tells me that if there's anything he loves more than his businesses and money, it's his son. "If Hugh cares about Tristan, and you care about Hugh, then at least try."

★   ★   ★

Minutes later, Hugh and Mick and I are in the train, and I've filled them in on my conversation with the Oliphants. Now we're debating the merits of the new plan I just proposed.

"I don't quite understand why we're investigating Sleeping Beauty's identity instead of Frances's death." Hugh is bleary-eyed from our wakeful night.

"I have a hunch they're connected," I say.

"Yeah, solve one, solve the other," Mick says, yawning so wide his jaw cracks.

"Well, I'm all for hunches and killing two birds with one stone," Hugh says. "And I'll bet Inspector Reid won't be looking for us where we're going."

I haven't told Hugh what Sir Gerald said. If he and Tristan part ways, maybe they'll both be better off in the long run, but I wouldn't expect him to believe it any more than I believe I would be better off without Barrett. Whether Barrett would be better off without me is a different question. I think of all the problems that my job and our relationship have caused him. Now he's mixed up in a death that looks to be murder, and he's been relegated to the most tedious job in the police force. He doesn't hold it against me, but I hold it against myself. Should I quit my job before anything else happens to him? I'm glad to put off big decisions, and my talk with Hugh, until after I've proven that my friends and I weren't involved in Frances's death.

"Supposin' Frances was pushed," Mick says. "Who do you think done it?"

"Even if Sleeping Beauty is lying about her identity, she's a sweet, gentle soul," Hugh says. "I can't picture her shoving anyone out a window."

"Venetia's a different kettle of fish," Mick says. "I can picture her going at somebody the way she went at me with that bayonet."

Everything in me rebels against the idea that the beautiful, brave, clever little girl took Frances's life. "Don't forget Caroline."

"If the butler didn't do it, then of course it was the spinster aunt," Hugh says.

"Frances was trespassin'," Mick says. "Maybe one of them caught her, there was a skirmish, and she went out the window by accident."

"I'd love a heart-to-heart with Venetia, Maude, and Caroline," Hugh says, "but I'm not keen to run the gauntlet past Inspector Reid's watchdogs."

We exit the train at Holland Park station and take a cab to a street of large stucco houses set close together, built in Italian style. All white, in pristine condition, adorned with identical bay windows, marble balustrades, and decorative gables, they're like perfect teeth set in the city's dirty face.

"Barrett thinks Rosamond is Jenny Legrand," I say. "It's time to find out if he's right."

As we approach August Legrand's house, the glossy black-painted door opens, and a woman steps out, carrying two big carpetbags. She drops the bags on the porch and turns to lock the door.

"Excuse me," I call, "we're looking for Mr. Legrand."

She's breathless, her rosy face moist with sweat; her straw hat sits crookedly atop her dark hair, as if she'd dressed in a hurry. "He's not home." She starts to pick up her bags.

Hugh smiles, introduces us by name, but doesn't say we're reporters or why we want to see Mr. Legrand. "And you are . . .?"

I've seen his looks stop women in their tracks, and this woman pauses despite her haste. "Anne Cartwright."

"A pleasure to meet you, Mrs. Cartwright. Are you a relative of Mr. Legrand?"

"It's Miss." She's about my age, but shorter and heavier, with round features. "I'm his housekeeper. Or, rather, I was. I'm quitting. If you'll excuse me . . ."

"You're quitting without giving notice and leaving while Mr. Legrand is out?" I say.

Miss Cartwright bursts into tears. Mick looks as disconcerted as I am, but Hugh is among the few men who aren't uneasy when a woman cries. He gives her his handkerchief, pats her shoulder, and says, "There, there."

She sniffles and wipes her face. "Thank you."

Mick and I watch Hugh work his magic. "Why don't we go inside, and you can tell me all about it," he says.

"But I'm not supposed to let anyone in without permission from Mr. Legrand."

"Where is he?" Hugh says.

"At his club in town."

"When will he be back?"

"In time for dinner tonight."

"We'll be long gone by then. He'll never know we were here."

Miss Cartwright wilts under Hugh's smiling persuasion. "Well, all right."

In the foyer, a painting of the same style as Mr. Legrand's portrait of Jenny hangs on the wall. It shows a banquet scene of handsome men and beautiful women in Roman robes, with a view of
the sea between Doric columns. Awash in pink rose petals, they
look as if they're drinking and toasting in a bubble bath. Anatomy,
architecture, and the still life of food and crockery on the table
are accurately rendered, but the pastel colors are too sweet for
my taste, the pink-fleshed naked limbs and moist red mouths too
flagrantly erotic. Every woman has Jenny's face, and all the men
bear an ugly resemblance to Mr. Legrand. I wonder if he chose this
subject matter because he looks like he belongs in ancient Rome
and can use himself as a model.

"Does anybody else live or work here?" Hugh asks Miss Cartwright as she leads us to the parlor.

More of Mr. Legrand's paintings dominate this room as well.
Furnishings are sparse and unobtrusive, as if not to draw the eye
away from his young couples flirting by fountains, women cavort-
ing in a pool, and a Bacchanalia in which dancers and pipers wear
grape leaf wreaths on their heads.

"Mr. Legrand took his valet with him," Miss Cartwright says.
"The maid left yesterday, and it's the cook's night off." She starts
crying again. "Oh God."

"Shall I make some tea?" I want an excuse to snoop around
the house.

"A capital idea," Hugh says. "Mick, why don't you help?"

While we're gone, he'll soften up Miss Cartwright. She doesn't
look unhappy to be left alone with him, but we haven't much time
to look for clues that Rosamond is Jenny Legrand. We hurry to
the kitchen. Mick builds up the coal fire in the stove while I fill
the kettle.

"I'll take the downstairs," he whispers. "You take the upstairs."

I tiptoe up the backstairs to the top floor, which is Mr. Legrand's
studio. Enormous windows face north over the back garden. A
canvas covered with a sheet stands on an easel. Furnishings include

a platform for models, Roman-style furniture and props, and cup-
boards filled with robes, sandals, and wigs. My heart sinks as I realize the house is too big to search thoroughly in a short time, and
if Mr. Legrand inflicted Sleeping Beauty's wounds, he wouldn't
leave a bloodstained knife or clothes in his studio, where models
or art collectors might see it. But clues that connect Jenny Legrand
with Rosamond might be found in Jenny's room.

I hurry downstairs to the second floor. The first two bed-
rooms I enter are unused—empty of personal items, the mat-
tresses bare under the bedspreads. I can almost hear the minutes
ticking away. The next door leads me to a room that's all white
linens and lace curtains, gold-framed mirrors and delicate French
furniture, a lady's boudoir. The painting on the wall opposite
the bed is another bath scene, this one featuring both men and
women, their nude bodies visible under the transparent water.
The thought that the painting is an aphrodisiac for Mr. and Mrs.
Legrand embarrasses me.

Whose privacy am I violating—Rosamond's, or that of a complete stranger whose fate is unknown?

Everything in the room is clean and tidy. I open the armoire
and riffle through beautiful silk, satin, and fine wool and cotton
frocks. They seem the right size for Rosamond, and they're all
perfectly ironed, all hung facing left. On the dressing table lie a
silver hairbrush, comb, and oval hand mirror set. A sense of recognition strikes me, although I know I've never seen them before. It's
not the objects themselves I recognize, but their arrangement—the
brush and comb laid precisely on either side of the mirror, like
silverware flanking a dinner plate.

It's the same arrangement I saw in Maude's bedroom.

A loud, high-pitched noise makes me jump. It's the teakettle
whistling. I race downstairs to the kitchen. When I return to the
parlor with the tea tray, Mick is there. He shakes his head, to tell
me he didn't find anything useful. Mrs. Cartwright, solemn and
calmer, is sitting on the divan beside Hugh.

"I've told her who we are and why we're here," Hugh says. "She's agreed to talk to us about Mr. and Mrs. Legrand."

I can hardly be glad she's cooperating, I'm so rattled by my discovery. Maybe lots of women place their comb, hairbrush, and mirror in that same configuration, I think as I serve the tea. But I don't, and neither did my mother. I wish I knew some other women well enough to be familiar with their habits.

"You won't put my name in the paper?" Miss Cartwright says nervously.

"No. You'll be an anonymous source," Hugh says.

She bites her lip, then blurts, "I started working here three months ago. I should've quit as soon as I heard the talk."

We lean toward her, our interest piqued. Hugh says, "What talk?"

"About the other two Missus Legrands. The first drowned in the bathtub. The second took too much laudanum."

I know that many people use a tincture of opium as a pain reliever and sleeping potion. So August Legrand had been married twice before Jenny, and both previous wives had met bad ends.

"They were called accidents, but they were really suicides," Miss Cartwright says.

"How do you know?" My mind leaps to the other possibility—murder. Was Jenny meant to be the third in the series of unnatural deaths? I smell the stench of the riverbank where Sleeping Beauty had lain in a coma.

"Nell Gordon—she works next door—she told me." Miss Cartwright puts her fingers to her lips. "Please don't put her name in the paper. I don't want her getting in trouble."

"We won't," Hugh says. "You have my word."

"Her husband's a copper. She said he was called to the house both times. He said his bosses covered up the suicides and told him to keep quiet."

With her slashed face, Sleeping Beauty couldn't have been passed off as a suicide. Does that mean she's not Jenny Legrand?

"I don't put stock in gossip, and Mr. Legrand is an important, respectable gentleman," Miss Cartwright says. "It wasn't until later that I got scared."

"Scared? Why?" Hugh says.

"He has a terrible temper. When the maid didn't clean all the tarnish off the silver, he screamed and cursed at her. He said it was my fault, and I thought he was going to kill us both. He fired her and told me to hire a new maid and to make sure she did better, or he would let me go too. Nell said he's had nine housekeepers before me, and they all quit."

I had witnessed his temper at the police station and the hospital. "How does Mr. Legrand treat his current wife?"

"He tells her what to wear, how to dress her hair, and before they go out together, he inspects every inch of her, like she's a mannequin in a shop. Whenever he's around, she trembles like a leaf, and her eyes get as big as saucers. She's scared of what he'll do to her if she puts a foot wrong."

The image of the comb, mirror, and brush in Maude's room burns as if on fire in my memory. "Did she put a foot wrong?"

"Nobody can be perfect always." Miss Cartwright lowers her voice as if the absent Mr. Legrand can hear her. "I've not seen her since June second."

That's more than two weeks before Sleeping Beauty was found. But Mr. Legrand had said his wife had disappeared only two *days* before he read about Sleeping Beauty in the *Daily World*. Had Jenny actually been missing for longer?

"Where did she go?" I say.

"I couldn't ask Mr. Legrand straight out. He doesn't like being questioned. But I'd never known her to go anywhere without him. She didn't have friends, as far as I could tell—she never had visitors and never got any letters."

Was Jenny Legrand a willing recluse, or was she friendless because of conditions imposed by her husband? Is she now hiding from him, behind the guise of Maude Napier?

"I think I know where she was." Miss Cartwright points at the floor.

"The cellar?" Hugh says. "What's down there?"

"I've never seen. He keeps the door locked. I don't have a key."

"How did you know Mrs. Legrand was down there?" I say. "Did you hear something?"

"Not a peep. The walls must be thick. But I saw Mr. Legrand carry trays of food downstairs when he didn't know I was watching."

At the police station, Mr. Legrand had neglected to tell Barrett that he'd been keeping his wife locked in the cellar.

"One morning, he accused me of opening the cellar door. I reminded him that I don't have the key, but he wouldn't listen, and he flew into a rage. She must have gotten out by herself, somehow, at night while he was asleep. He went off to look for her. And the next day, when I put the newspaper on the breakfast table, I saw the story about Sleeping Beauty. When Mr. Legrand read it, he cursed and ran out of the house. He must have thought she was Mrs. Legrand."

I feel a plunging sensation, as if I've been thrown into deep water with a rock tied to my ankle. Sleeping Beauty seems more likely to be the runaway Jenny Legrand from Holland Park than Maude Napier, secretly returned from Egypt. At this point, I hardly know what to call her.

Miss Cartwright moans in distress. "I saw the picture of that poor woman. I'm afraid Mr. Legrand hurt Mrs. Legrand while she was locked in the cellar."

"You should tell this to the police," Hugh says.

Miss Cartwright gasps. "I can't talk to the police! If Mr. Legrand were to find out, he would come after me." She jumps to her feet. "I have to go. So do you."

Imposing on her any further wouldn't be fair. We let her shoo us toward the door, and as Hugh and Mick carry her bags to the street, she hails a passing cab. They've loaded the bags and helped her into the cab, when she wails, "Oh no, I forgot to lock the door."

"I'll do it," I say. "Give me the key, and I'll drop it in the mail slot afterward."

She hands it over. We stand by the gate until the cab disappears around a corner. "Quick thinking, Sarah," Mick says as we hurry into the house.

The door to the cellar is in a passage off the kitchen. It's solid wood, the lock modern and sturdy. Mick tries one of his picklocks after another. "This is the toughest I ever seen."

That's when I hear the front door opening. We freeze, sucking air through our teeth. Mr. Legrand is home early. We listen to him call, "Miss Cartwright?" He sounds as if he realizes that something isn't as it should be. His quick footsteps head straight toward us.

"Take cover!" Mick whispers.

Panicking, with no time to confer, we flee in separate directions.

"Who's there?" calls Mr. Legrand.

I find the back door, but I can't leave without my friends. As I hesitate, Mr. Legrand rushes upon me. His eyes bulge with disbelief, recognition, and anger. "How did you get into my house?" He grabs my shoulders and shakes me. "Why are you here?"

As I struggle, kick, and scream, Hugh and Mick come running. They seize Mr. Legrand and pull him away from me. Mr. Legrand turns on them. Hugh says to Mick and me, "I'll hold him off. Go!"

Even as I resist abandoning Hugh, Mick drags me through the house, out the front door, and down the steps. A moment later, Mr. Legrand hurls Hugh after us. Hugh stumbles, waves his arms in an attempt to balance himself, flies through the air, and lands face down on the path, at our feet. Mick and I help Hugh up, and we run down the street without looking to see if Mr. Legrand is following. We don't stop until we're in the underground station. By a stroke of luck, the train we want is at the platform. We jump aboard.

"That was too close a call," Hugh says as we drop, panting, onto the seat.

"Your chin is bleeding." I dab it with my handkerchief.

"Thanks. I hope Mr. Legrand doesn't report us to the police," Hugh says.

"Nah, he won't," Mick says. "He were afraid we seen somethin' he don't want seen."

"The question is, what?" Hugh says.

A thought disturbs me. "I've wondered where Mr. Legrand might fit into the fairy tale scheme of things. We've got Sleeping Beauty and Cinderella. Maybe he's Bluebeard."

"Well, he does have things in common with the Bluebeard of legend. A rich man, a forbidden chamber, and dead former wives." Hugh ticks them off on his fingers.

"The heroine of the tale is Bluebeard's latest wife," I say. "She sneaks into the chamber and discovers the blood-drenched corpses of her predecessors." I never realized how dark fairy tales are until coming upon their real-life analogies.

"Yeah, maybe Jenny found out that her husband killed his other wives," Mick says.

"That cellar would have been a convenient, private place to torture her and slash her face," Hugh says.

I'm alarmed to see my friends also coming around to Barrett's point of view that Rosamond is Jenny Legrand. I can't deny the logic of their arguments.

"Sarah, did you find anything when you searched the house?" Hugh says.

I'm not ready to mention the comb, hairbrush, and mirror, lest my friends attach too much significance to them. "Nothing," I say.

★ ★ ★

Home at last, we find Fitzmorris in the parlor, reading a newspaper. He says, "Thank God you're safe," and holds up the newspaper—not the one Sir Gerald showed me, but one that contains a story about Frances's death, our photographs, and the headline, "Killer Reporters?"

I collapse into a chair, too exhausted and overwhelmed to cope with more troubles.

"The rival papers must be dancing for joy at their new opportunity to ruin us," Hugh says.

"Sally came over," Fitzmorris tells me. "She saw the story, and she was worried about you. She had to go home before her mother noticed she'd sneaked out. She said to tell you that she'd confronted her mother about the letter, and they had a big fight, but there's nothing else to report. She said you would know what she meant."

The confrontation apparently had produced no new clues about our father. Mrs. Albert is truly a dead end, and Sally either has run out of ideas or can't get away to pursue the search.

"Has Inspector Reid been here?" Mick asks Fitzmorris.

"No, but a constable brought this letter." Fitzmorris points to an envelope on the table.

Mick opens it, removes a sheet of white stationery embossed with a seal, and reads, "'Miss Sarah Bain, Lord Hugh Staunton, and Mr. Mick O'Reilly, you are summoned to the inquest for Frances Oliphant, on the fourteenth of July, two o'clock p.m., at the Buffalo's Head Public House, eighty-four Marylebone Road.'"

Dread wraps its cold tentacles around my heart. "That's tomorrow." Tomorrow will come the official ruling on whether Frances's death was murder, and whether I'm officially the prime suspect.

CHAPTER 23

Marylebone Road is wide, clean, and lined with imposing buildings. Trees shade the broad sidewalks along which Hugh, Mick, and I pass by shops whose goods are more expensive than I could ever afford. Heat waves shimmer up from the pavement. Omnibuses roll through the haze to discharge sightseers outside Madame Tussaud's huge wax museum. I wish I were going there instead of the inquest.

"I hope we don't have to testify," I say.

Since my school days, I've been terrified of speaking in front of a group. I prayed not to be called on in class, and speech days kept me in agony for weeks in advance. My head aches from hunger and fatigue; after receiving the summons, I was too anxious to sleep or eat. Now I have more to fear than just a bad mark.

"The last time I spoke to an audience was a toast at my cousin's wedding three years ago," Hugh says. "If I managed that after half a bottle of champagne, we can handle this."

I force myself to smile at his attempt to comfort me. Mick is uncharacteristically somber, dressed in a new suit whose sleeves and pants are already too short. He's pomaded his hair, but a few stubborn strands of his cowlick have sprung up. We're all afraid of being implicated in Frances Oliphant's death.

The Buffalo's Head Public House is one in a row of buildings with brick walls the color of dried blood, their windows and doors set in white stone arches. The taproom is crowded with well-dressed ladies and gentlemen who chatter excitedly. Murder must be rare in this affluent neighborhood; the inquest, a novelty. We join the rush up the stairs. In the hot, stuffy assembly room, Dr. Wilson the police surgeon and other officials seat themselves at a table beside a lectern. A constable motions us to the first row of chairs provided for the audience. I sit with my knees pressed together, my arms clamped to my sides. Barrett comes in with Constable Porter and sits next to me. I want to clutch his hand, like a lifeline, but I can't in this public place. The other audience seats fill quickly. People stand at the back of the room; women fan themselves. The air is already rank with body odor. The twelve jurymen take the chairs placed along the wall. Next to arrive are Mrs. Oliphant and Faith, clad in black mourning dress. As the constable seats them at the end of our row, they give us baleful stares through the black veils on their hats.

"Sarah Bain!" calls a man's voice.

I turn, and the white light from a flash lamp explodes in my face. Barrett yells, "Hey!" and jumps up to accost the photographer.

"Please don't make a scene." I tug his sleeve, pull him back into his seat, and bow my head so my hat hides my face. I hear people murmur our names, and Hugh's and Mick's; I sense fingers pointing at us.

"I thought Inspector Reid would be here," Barrett says. "He's not."

"Neither are Maude, Caroline, and Venetia," Mick says.

An official pounds a gavel and introduces himself as Mr. Hardwick, the coroner. To quell the churn in my stomach, I pretend I'm photographing him. I focus my attention on his gray beard and droopy eyelids. But the buzzing hornets of anxiety in my mind drown out everything he says until he calls Dr. Wilson to the lectern. I thank Heaven that if I must testify, at least I'm not first.

Dr. Wilson says that on the thirteenth of July, he answered a summons to the Napier house, and then relates what he found there.

"Please describe your examination of the body," Mr. Hardwick says.

Here come the facts that will determine the course of events. Dr. Wilson says, "The body belonged to a white female, between twenty-five and thirty years of age. She had an injury to the back of her head, incurred during a fall from a window. The autopsy revealed a fractured skull, which was the cause of death."

This is nothing we didn't know. I relax a little.

"When I removed her clothes, I discovered bruises on her arms, chest, and shins. The fall does not account for those injuries."

A murmur sweeps through the audience. Barrett tenses beside me.

"In my expert opinion, she was beaten with a heavy stick, club, or other such weapon during a struggle that occurred before she fell," Dr. Wilson says. "Her death wasn't accidental; it was murder—the result of a violent attack."

The audience exclaims. As my fears become reality and the churning in my stomach begins again, Mick whispers, "Look who just showed up."

At the door stands Inspector Reid. "Pardon the interruption, Mr. Hardwick. May I have your permission to call a witness?"

"Who could it be?" I whisper to Barrett and Hugh.

They shrug. The coroner, who seems just as bewildered as we are, says, "Very well."

"I call Miss Margaret Oliphant." With a theatrical gesture, Reid extends his arm toward the woman who walks into the room.

Mrs. Oliphant and Faith exclaim, *"Peggy?"*

Reid has found her! Stunned, my companions and I behold the woman who had lost the attention of the press and the public after Sleeping Beauty was identified. Now, amid excited buzzing from the audience, Peggy is claiming her place in the spotlight. She has the same pretty features as in her family photograph, but instead of the shabby, outdated frock, she wears a smart new pale green one, patterned with yellow daisies. Her blond hair is sleekly knotted under her gray straw hat. Although she resembles Maude in height and coloring, she seems plumper, with robust health. Her innocent blue eyes look everywhere except at her stepmother and stepsister, who glare at her while whispering furiously to each other. Why are they upset by her reappearance? She seems to be in league with Reid, but for what purpose?

Reid positions Peggy behind the lectern. "May I be allowed to question the witness?" he asks the coroner.

Mr. Hardwick gestures, turning the show over to Reid. I can't begin to imagine what we're going to hear. As Reid takes an empty chair at the table, he doesn't look at me—or my companions, but he can't have missed noticing us. He addresses Peggy: "State your name."

"Margaret Alice Oliphant." She has a sweet, demure manner. Her voice is low, husky, her accent similar to Rosamond's—well bred, but not posh. I can see why the Oliphants could have mistaken Rosamond's voice, hoarse from the injury to her throat, for Peggy's.

"What is your relationship to Mrs. Esther Oliphant and Miss Faith Oliphant?"

"They're my stepmother and stepsister."

"Are they here? Can you point them out?"

Peggy points, and they shrink from her gaze, as if from a witch casting a bad spell.

"Are you aware that after you left home, your stepfamily reported you missing?" Reid says.

"Yes, you told me."

I wonder when and how in the world he found her. But of course we never looked for her, except at the beginning; we had other fish to fry. Now I fear that was a mistake.

"Where have you been?"

"At the Black Horse Public House Inn, Canning Town."

With the sly, anticipatory air of a magician who's about to pull a rabbit out of a hat, Reid says, "Are you living alone there?"

"No." A smile blooms on Peggy's face; her eyes sparkle; her cheeks blush pink as roses. "With my husband."

My companions and I lean back in our seats, jaws dropped. Mrs. Oliphant and Faith lurch forward and blurt the question on our minds: *"You got married?"*

"There he is!" Peggy points toward the back of the room.

A hubbub ensues as people turn and crane their necks toward the young man who stands up from his chair. He has cropped blond curls and a ruddy, frank, handsome face, and he's as nicely dressed as Peggy, in gray cotton trousers, jacket, striped shirt, and blue tie. He beams and waves at Peggy. I envision him wearing a golden crown. He's Prince Charming to her Cinderella. The audience bursts into applause.

"It's Timmy Hicks, the butcher's son." Mrs. Oliphant's manner combines horror and indignation. "The nerve of him!"

Faith grimaces in disgust at Peggy. "Sneaking around, running away to elope. What a common little slag."

"You're just jealous." Peggy's smile turns cruel; the color in her cheeks darkens to angry red. "Because you're so ugly and mean that nobody wants to marry you."

The audience erupts into laughter. Faith stammers with inarticulate rage. Mrs. Oliphant says to Peggy's husband, "Your father's shop won't get another penny of my business!"

Reid grins, pleased with the stir he's created. Mr. Hardwick bangs his gavel, shouting, "Order! Order!"

Memory stabs me. I say to Barrett, "The patients at the convalescent home were about to tell us something before Faith almost caught us. I think they knew Peggy had a suitor and suspected she'd eloped."

"I think you're right," Barrett says.

The room quiets. Reid says to Peggy, "Why did you and Mr. Hicks elope?"

Peggy casts a baleful glance at her stepfamily. "Because *they* wouldn't have let me marry him. They wanted to keep me as their slave, doing chores day and night and dressed in rags while they wore expensive clothes. But, ha-ha!" Her breath quickens; her eyes twitch and spark. "I'm married, and we've got jobs on a ship that's going to America. It leaves tomorrow. I'm never coming back. So there!" She sticks out her tongue at Mrs. Oliphant and Faith.

After displaying the sweet demeanor that the patients at the convalescent home praised, she's changed into the tempestuous, childish girl that her stepfamily described. I turn to see her husband gape; he obviously didn't know that his Cinderella has two personalities.

"This is all very interesting," Mr. Hardwick says to Reid, "but what has it to do with the death of Frances Oliphant?"

"We're getting to that." Reid says to Peggy, "Tell us the other reason you ran away."

Mrs. Oliphant sits up straight, as if jabbed in her bottom with a tack. "Peggy, dear! I'm sorry we were cruel to you. Can you find it in your heart to forgive us?"

"Yes, let us make it up to you," Faith pleads.

"What are they afraid she's going to say?" I whisper to Barrett. He shakes his head, as mystified as I am.

Peggy regards them with impish scorn. "It's too late for that. I'm going to make you pay for the way you treated me."

Mrs. Oliphant and Faith wail, "No!" and "Please, don't!"

Peggy announces to the room, "They've been killing their patients."

The audience clamors; fresh shock appears on the faces of the coroner and jurymen. Mick, Hugh, and Barrett shake their heads, dumbfounded. Another sudden memory pops my eyes wide.

"That's a lie!" Faith says.

"I was afraid they would be caught and *I* would get in trouble too," Peggy says. "I wanted to be far away by the time anyone found out."

"She's making it up." Mrs. Oliphant wheezes, fanning herself with a black-edged handkerchief. "She's always making things up."

I whisper to Barrett, "Remember the hearse we saw at the convalescent home? Someone had just died. It must have been the patient in the room that Faith was cleaning out."

Realization dawns on Barrett's face. "She was getting rid of evidence of murder."

"That's a serious allegation, Miss Oliphant," Mr. Hardwick says. "Why should we believe it?"

"I heard them say that the convalescent home was about to go bankrupt," Peggy says. "Frances got the idea to take out burial insurance policies on the patients. They killed the patients and collected the money."

"That's absurd," Mrs. Oliphant says.

"We don't kill the patients," Faith says. "They die because they're ill."

But their guilt is evident in their haste to make excuses, the terror on their faces.

Flushed with triumph, Peggy points at Faith. "I saw you and Frances sprinkling rat poison in their food."

"Shut up!" Faith screams.

"I've investigated the eleven deaths that took place at the home during the past year," Reid says. "All those patients died of sudden gastric illness. All had large burial insurance policies that named the Oliphants as the beneficiaries."

"It's not a crime to take out burial insurance policies," Mrs. Oliphant cries in desperation.

"I've ordered the bodies exhumed," Reid says. "They'll be tested for arsenic."

"Well, I'll be gobsmacked," Mick says.

"My sentiments exactly," Hugh says.

Mine too. Now I understand the Oliphants' behavior at the identity parade; I know why Frances had tried to prevent her mother and sister from offending Rosamond—if Rosamond had been Peggy, she could have spited them by telling the police about their crimes. The Sleeping Beauty case is the tip of an iceberg, with multiple murders in the submerged part. August Legrand's wives aren't the only possible victims.

"Frances thought that Maude Napier woman was me," Peggy says. "She went to kill me, so that I couldn't tell on her and Faith and their mother. But—ha-ha—she's the one who ended up dead!"

"Don't believe her," Faith begs Mr. Hardwick. "She's crazy!"

The coroner pounds his gavel, trying to quell the noise from the audience. Reid says, "Mrs. Esther Oliphant and Miss Faith Oliphant, you're under arrest for conspiracy and murder."

Constables advance toward the women. Mrs. Oliphant cries, "Don't touch me!"

Peggy giggles and singsongs, "You're going to be hanged, you're going to be hanged."

Faith throws herself across the lectern at Peggy, shouting, "You bitch!"

The lectern unbalances and knocks Peggy over. She crashes to the floor with Faith and the lectern on top of her. The constables haul Mrs. Oliphant to her feet, she swoons, and they stagger under her limp, dead weight. Faith and Peggy scream as they kick, hit, and claw each other. Prince Charming rushes to save his bride.

"I rule that the death of Frances Oliphant was murder by person or persons unknown," the coroner shouts over the noise. "The inquest is adjourned until further notice."

"We're not finished," Reid says, hot with indignation. "You have to call the other witnesses to testify."

The coroner glares. "If you wanted me to follow procedure, you shouldn't have turned my inquest into a circus."

"I had to establish Frances Oliphant's reason for going to the Napier house," Reid protests. "Now I can introduce suspects—" He gestures toward my companions and me.

"You'll have to wait until the inquest reconvenes." The coroner bangs his gavel again. "The jury is dismissed."

People in the audience surge forward to see what's happening. Constables push them, yelling, "Everybody out!" while photographers jostle for the best camera angles.

Hugh grabs my arm. "Saved by the circus. Let's go."

As he and Mick pull me toward the door, I resist because I see Barrett accosting Reid, demanding, "How did you find Peggy?"

"I reviewed the tips in the Sleeping Beauty case, and I found one that you ignored," Reid says. "Timmy Hicks told his brother that he and Peggy were planning to elope. The brother ratted on the two lovebirds."

Barrett frowns in confusion. "I didn't ignore any tips. I checked them all out." He asks Constable Porter, "Did you know about that one?"

"Nope, guv." But there's a dirty gleam in Porter's eyes.

"You did know! You told Inspector Reid instead of me. *Why?*"

Porter drops his pretense of innocence as he and Reid exchange grins. "You're getting too big for your britches. You need to be taken down a notch." Porter savors his revenge on Barrett for being promoted above him, for chastising him after he brushed off Venetia when she told him that Sleeping Beauty was her mother.

"I thought you were my friend." Barrett looks as much wounded as angry.

Porter's grin broadens. "Think again."

Barrett points at the gloating Reid. "What did he promise you for selling me out?"

"Your job," Porter says.

Barrett regards him with pity and contempt. "You fool. He just used you to do me dirty."

Anger darkens Porter's face. "Watch who you're callin' a fool."

Someone in the crowd jostles Barrett, who bumps into Porter. Suddenly they're fighting, throwing vicious punches. They stumble into the front row of chairs and go down. I rush to Barrett's aid, but I can't get past the constables trying to break up the scuffle and the photographers snapping pictures. Hugh and Mick dive into the fray. They come out dragging a wild-eyed, disheveled Barrett. His mouth is bleeding.

"Let's go!" Mick shouts at me.

We flee the room in a barrage of flashes exploding and reporters yelling, "Miss Bain! How come you missed finding Peggy Oliphant?" "How does it feel to be knocked off your high horse?" "Lord Hugh, is it true that you're having an affair with Sir Gerald Mariner's son, Tristan? Is he a sodomite like you?"

CHAPTER 24

"I'm all right. Don't fuss." Barrett is lying on the chaise longue at my house while I clean his split, bloodied lip with a cloth dipped in spirits. He pushes my hand away.

"Constable Porter is worse off than you," Mick says. He and Hugh recline on the sofa while Fitzmorris sets a plate of ham sandwiches on the table and pours tea. "I think you busted his nose."

Barrett laughs without humor. "*He* probably still has his job."

Nobody replies; nobody wants to acknowledge that Barrett could be fired for beating up a fellow policeman. Mick devours a sandwich, but nobody else is hungry. Hugh broods, and I know what he's thinking: Now that his connection with Tristan has been mentioned in public, it's only a matter of time before a scandal explodes.

Barrett stands up, and I say, "Where are you going?"

"To the station, to face the music."

"Why not stay here and wait until things cool down?"

"Reid and Porter aren't going to cool down anytime soon. The longer I wait, the worse it'll be." Barrett nods goodbye to Hugh and Mick and walks out of the room.

I follow him downstairs. At the door he kisses me tenderly, but he's distant, his attention focused on the troubles ahead. Once he's outside, he disappears into the crowds on Whitechapel High Street. Resisting the urge to run after him, I go back upstairs to find Mick and Hugh glumly silent. Often in the past, their high spirits and bright ideas have lifted me out of despair. Now it's up to me to raise our morale, guide us toward action.

"Inspector Reid did us a favor," I say.

Hugh responds with an incredulous stare. "What favor? He's had his lackeys watching you and Sally; they must have been watching Tristan and me too. No doubt they're behind the rumors about us."

I should have known that Reid has been plotting my friends' downfall as well as mine. "I mean his finding Peggy Oliphant."

"So he found her." Mick is surly, infected by Hugh's grim outlook. "Why's that good?"

"Reid has narrowed down the possible identities for Sleeping Beauty," I say. "She's not Peggy; she's either Maude Napier or Jenny Legrand."

"Who cares?" Hugh says. "The game's changed, Sarah. We're not playing 'Name the Mystery Woman' anymore. We're murder suspects, and we should be thinking about how to get ourselves off the hook."

"Yeah," Mick says. "We need to find out who done it. And it coulda been Sleeping Beauty, whoever she is."

I hate to think she not only deceived me but murdered Frances Oliphant and is now framing me. "Yes, we need to solve the murder and exonerate ourselves, but we can't just let the issue of her identity slide."

"The issue of her identity is muddying the waters," Hugh says.

"*I* think it's key to solving Frances's murder," I say.

"Sarah, you know I like hunches, but this time I think you're a mile wide of the bull's-eye." Impatience overrides Hugh's usual considerate tact.

Mick squirms; he doesn't like taking sides in arguments between Hugh and me, but he says, "We oughtta be treatin' this case like we would if there weren't no question about who's who. Maude, Caroline, and Venetia are suspects. We should do what we would normally do—investigate 'em and dig up dirt."

"Amen," Hugh says.

"You're right." I hide the turmoil that rises in me like the river in the wake of a steamship. "We should proceed as if this were any other case." Exonerating ourselves hinges on pinning Frances's murder on someone else, and if it's the woman whose life I saved, or Venetia, the child I want to protect, then so be it. I could choose to put their safety ahead of my own, but not ahead of my friends'. And of course, one of them—or Caroline—has to be guilty.

"So, who do you want to start with?" Mick says.

★   ★   ★

The morning after the inquest, I stroll along Bond Street in the West End, among the elegantly attired ladies and gentlemen who frequent London's most expensive, prestigious shops. I linger at the jewelers' windows, admiring gold necklaces, rings, and bracelets that sparkle with diamonds. I smile to think that if Hugh and Mick were here, they might suggest that burglary would be more lucrative than newspaper work—and safer too.

Yesterday I convinced them that in order to speed our inquiries, we should split up instead of sticking together. Then, exhausted from a wakeful night spent dreading the inquest, I fell into bed and slept as if under a spell by the same witch who enchanted Sleeping Beauty. Mick has gone to St. John's Wood to see what he can learn about Venetia from the neighbors. Hugh has gone to the Royal Academy of Music, where Caroline once studied. He'd said that when he tried to pump her for information, that was among the few items she'd let out. And I, refreshed and newly optimistic, mean to investigate Maude Napier and Jenny Legrand.

It has occurred to me that I know nothing about them aside from their public roles as an author of books about Egypt and the wife of a successful artist. Those roles are like the veils in hidden mother photographs—they conceal as much as they reveal. It's time to look beneath the veils, to fill in the gap in my store of information. Within that gap, I feel certain, lie clues regarding

Frances Oliphant's murder. And I begin to see that investigating Sleeping Beauty as a murder suspect and determining her true identity aren't mutually exclusive.

I stop outside Dowdeswell and Dowdeswell's Art Gallery, located in an austere, dun-colored brick building. Its only ornaments are the white pilasters flanking the front door and the red geraniums in the flower boxes. The window displays a large, dark painting of a man in an underground pit or tunnel. Dressed in black robes, he stands with his back to the viewer, barely visible in the shadows, his head lifted and his arms raised toward sunlight that streams through a crack in the earth high above him. Green grasses and spring flowers frame a patch of puffy white clouds in a blue sky. A sign next to the painting reads "New Works by August Legrand." It's a strange departure from his frothy pastel scenes of Roman decadence.

Inside, the long gallery is divided in sections by swags of dark green drapery. Down the center are round settees upholstered in gold velvet. Light from the gas chandeliers gleams on the gilded picture frames. I smell expensive perfume and shaving lotion, hear genteel murmurs from people gathered by the three largest paintings. I'm glad not to see the artist himself—if he were here, he surely would throw me out. In the first painting, maidens in white robes smile as they frolic in a sunlit meadow, picking flowers. The one at the center has Jenny's face and blond hair. Behind them, a black chariot pulled by black horses erupts from a crack in the ground. The dark-robed man drives the chariot toward the oblivious maidens. His face is August Legrand's. The artist has illustrated the Roman myth of Pluto and Proserpine. The second painting shows Pluto holding the terrified Proserpine clasped against him while the chariot hurtles them down to the underworld. In the third, Proserpine sits weeping on a black marble throne, amid flames, smoke, and tortured souls. Pluto kneels at her feet and offers her the pomegranate whose seeds she will eat, dooming herself to spend six months of every year with him in hell.

Loud hammering and raised voices draw my attention to the back of the gallery. I move in that direction. Men on ladders pound nails into the walls, and boys lug framed paintings in through the back door—they're hanging a new exhibit. Amid the bustle, two men stand arguing. One is stout and gray-haired, dressed in a tail-coat, striped trousers, and spats.

"No! You cannot show this," he says.

The other is in his twenties, tall and slim, handsome with coppery hair. His white shirt and gray trousers look cheap, ready-made. He holds a large painting. "But it's my best work."

"Mr. Legrand will not allow us to display or sell pictures of Mrs. Legrand that were created by anyone except himself."

"The hell with August Legrand! He doesn't have a monopoly on her face."

Now I look at his painting and see a naked woman who reclines in the woods, in the company of two fully dressed gentlemen. A picnic basket overflows with loaves of bread, cheeses, bottles of wine, and fruits. The woman is Jenny. She smiles at the viewer as the men converse. The painting is mischievous as well as erotic, and disconcertingly realistic.

"Mr. Legrand is our most important artist," the older man says. "We respect his wishes. So either you take that painting away, or I cancel your show."

The artist huffs and stalks out the back door. I hurry after him. He's slouched against the wall in the alley, the rejected picture beside him. When he sees me, he scowls. "Yes, what?"

"I'm sorry to bother you, but I couldn't help overhearing the argument." And he must be acquainted with Jenny Legrand.

"Legrand is such a big man, everybody has to kiss his—sorry." The artist has an educated accent as well as good manners. "Big men don't like competition poaching on what they think is their private territory."

A closer look at the painting is the other reason I followed him. Although the woman's face matches the photograph I saw of

Jenny, her body is fuller than that of Sleeping Beauty when I saw her naked. Either Sleeping Beauty had lost weight, or the artist took creative liberties; at any rate, the painting doesn't help me determine her identity.

"I think your work is better than Mr. Legrand's." I'm speaking the truth. It's less artificial and free of the vanity that taints Mr. Legrand's work.

"Thank you." The artist's lopsided grin lends charm to his regular features. "Miss . . .?"

"Sarah Bain. I'm a photographer and reporter for the *Daily World*."

"Ned Lyle, at your service." We shake hands. His is stained with blue paint. "Hey, I've heard of you. You're the lady who rescued Sleeping Beauty."

"Yes." I'm glad he either doesn't know I'm also a murder suspect and the daughter of one, or he's too polite to bring it up. "I'm following up on the story. You may have heard that Sleeping Beauty has been identified as a woman named Maude Napier, but at one time Jenny Legrand was a possibility."

"I did hear. I also understand that Jenny is still missing."

I glance at the picture. "How did you come to paint her?"

"I know her from art school. She wanted to be a painter, and she's talented, but it's hard for women students. The teachers look down on them, and they're not allowed in life drawing classes."

Jenny and I have something in common—she was a woman in a man's profession, as I am, and I was banned from studios at which photographers took pictures of nude models. I shudder as I think of Martha Tabram, Polly Nichols, Annie Chapman, Kate Eddowes, Liz Stride, and Mary Jane Kelly, the models I did photograph in the nude.

"She's a kind, sweet person. Everybody liked her. When I was sick, she paid my doctor bill, even though she didn't have much money. She was a model; she posed for our classes. Some of the fellows were in love with her. She lived with one or another at different times. Myself, included." Ned's face turns pink. "But I don't want you to think she's a trollop. She has a sort of innocence."

Rosamond has the same sweet, innocent air. I push that thought away as if closing the door on a gust of wind.

"She wasn't cut out to be a starving artist or the mistress of one," Ned says. "And then along came August Legrand. Swept her off her feet. He's a cold, arrogant man, but he's successful and rich, and we were glad he could support Jenny in style. She promised to invite us to her wedding and to visit us afterward, but they had a small, exclusive ceremony and went to Europe for their honeymoon. She never came around again. The next time I saw her was at the opening of Legrand's show last year. He wore her on his arm while his admirers fawned over him. She slipped away to talk to me and started to cry. When I asked what was wrong, she said it was nothing; she only missed all her friends, and she was really very happy."

The wind strengthens, and I push harder as I think of August Legrand's violent behavior. Is that what Jenny was unhappy about and didn't want to reveal? I remember Rosamond's emotional reaction to him during the identity parade. Had she recognized him as the husband she feared? My friends and I had imagined August Legrand as Bluebeard, but he painted himself as the king of hell. I wonder if his locked cellar is his underworld, and Jenny was the latest of his captive, tortured queens.

"Before Legrand came and took Jenny away to meet some other people, she told me she was going to have a baby." Ned adds, "She must have been mistaken. She and Legrand haven't any children."

I remember my nude photographs of the Ripper's victims, all of whom had been mothers. I don't remember seeing the same telltale stretch marks or sagging flesh on Rosamond when I saw her naked by the river. *Does that mean she didn't give birth to Venetia?* It's a disturbing thought that should have occurred to me before now. The winds of doubt are eroding my belief that Rosamond is Maude Napier, no matter how hard I cling to it. My intuition is telling me that Jenny Legrand is somehow crucial to solving Frances Oliphant's murder.

"Does Jenny have any family?"

"Her parents are dead. She never mentioned any other relatives."

"Would you recognize her if you saw her while her face was covered?"

Ned chuckles. "Oh yes. Any of our circle would, not just those who'd lived with her. When she posed for us, we spent hours staring at her body—pardon my crudeness."

If Rosamond is Jenny, then her self-consciousness about her bandaged face isn't the only reason for secluding herself in the Napier house. She wouldn't want to run into the artists and former lovers who could see through her disguise.

"I would hate it if anything bad has happened to Jenny," Ned says. "If you find her, tell her I said hello and not to be a stranger."

I'm afraid that I've already found her, and she pushed Frances out the window. I'm also afraid that she didn't—and that the next evidence I find will eliminate her as a suspect instead of exonerating my friends and myself.

CHAPTER 25

A cab takes me to Bloomsbury, a mile from Bond Street. Russell Square is a large area of lawn and trees with a broad path around the perimeter, shielded from the streets by a high privet hedge and iron railings. In and out through the gates pass women pushing babies in prams, children running with hoops, and old men walking dogs. Tired and hungry, I buy a late lunch at a stall on the roadside. I sit on a bench and listen to birds singing and fountains tinkling inside the square while I consume a sausage roll, a currant cake, and lemonade and pretend I'm one of the holiday-makers. There's no holiday for a murder suspect.

Around the square are large terraced houses, solid and neat behind black iron fences. Their plain brick Georgian structures have uniform rows of windows and little ornamentation except white-painted fronts and colored doors on the ground floor. I reach in my satchel and bring out the copy of *A Journey Along the Nile* that I stole from the Napier house because I thought it might come in handy. I can never again scold Mick for theft without the pot calling the kettle black. I turn to the page on which the publisher is named: The Egypt Society, 57 Russell Square. Located on the south side of the square, the building is distinguished by geometric-patterned grilles over the lower halves of its upper windows and a frieze of Egyptian heads above the entrance. Someone there must know Maude Napier. When I walk up the steps to the door, I see a sign posted inside the glass pane: "Open to the public Monday, Wednesday, and Friday and by appointment." It's Tuesday. When I knock, there's no answer.

Tomorrow may be too late.

Looking up at the windows, I see no signs of life. When I turn and walk back down the steps, I notice a basement with windows set above ground level, and the window on my right is open several inches. Knowing what Mick would do, I hesitate to break the law myself, in broad daylight, but I can't think of anywhere else to seek information about Maude. I glance around the street; there's no one near at the moment. I loop the handle of my satchel over my arm and lift my skirts above my knees. I hold onto the railing beside the steps, put my left leg over it, then my right. My skirt snags. Freeing the cloth with one hand while holding on with the other, I lose my grip. I fall four feet, twist my ankle as my shoes hit the narrow stone pavement outside the window, and crumple in a heap. I sit for a moment, gasping, my heart thudding. I look up at the fence that runs along the sidewalk, afraid I'll see a policeman looking down at me.

There's no one in view. I push the window fully open, sit on the sill, and drop inside to a dim cellar filled with crates and bundles. I grope my way up a staircase to a gallery where framed photographs, drawings, and maps hang on walls painted white. Glass display cases and carved stone heads on pedestals stand on the dark, polished wood floor. I examine the photographs, and one catches my attention. Near piles of dirt and broken statuary, a little girl of six or seven years, in a light-colored frock, pinafore, and bonnet, sits smiling in a wheelbarrow. I recognize Venetia from her fierce eyebrows. The men grouped around her are all dark, turbaned Egyptians, except one. He wears the same loose white tunic and trousers as the others, but he's English, with fair skin, a pith helmet on his head, and his eyes squinted against the bright sun. A card beside the photograph reads, "Dr. Cyril Napier with his daughter, Venetia, in Abu Simbel, 1887." I search the other photographs. None contain Maude Napier.

The ceiling creaks above me.

I freeze, listening to footsteps on the upper floor. Drawn to them like a hungry mouse to a baited trap, I tiptoe up the stairs. In a passage, light shines and scuffing, clattering noises issue from the only open door. I peek into a room that's furnished like a laboratory, with a sink, glass cabinets of instruments, and a microscope and other scientific equipment. A man in striped shirtsleeves, white apron, white head kerchief, gloves, and thick goggles stands behind a long table. A cloth mask conceals the lower half of his face. On the table, ragged strips of brown, dirty fabric tangle around brown bones covered with leathery, shrunken skin. At one end, the skull is an ugly death's head, its eyes sunken, nose eroded, and mouth stretched in a rictus of agony. At the other, feet resemble petrified talons. The man uses forceps to peel the fabric away from the hollow ribcage. Dust that smells of decay hits me at the same moment as the terrible thought that he must be dissecting a corpse stolen from a graveyard and I'm breathing human remains. I choke and clap my hand over my nose and mouth to stifle the sound—too late.

The man starts, drops his forceps, and looks up. His eyes, magnified by the goggles, blaze with anger. "Who are you?" he demands, his voice muffled by his mask. Before I can explain myself, he seizes a yardstick from the table and charges at me, yelling, "Get out!"

Peddling backward in alarm, I say, "Wait."

"If you want a mummy, go to Egypt and dig up your own!" He swings the yardstick.

I duck, and the yardstick whistles over my head and smacks the wall of the passage in which he has me cornered. "I'm not a thief. I just want to talk."

"Talk fast." He brandishes his weapon, glaring through his goggles.

I scramble to recover my wits. "It's about Maude Napier— Dr. Napier's wife. And the woman known as Sleeping Beauty."

The man lowers the yardstick, removes his goggles, and pushes his mask below his chin, exposing an angular face with gray whisker stubble on tanned skin almost as leathery as the mummy's. "I thought Sleeping Beauty and Maude Napier were the same person. That's what it said in the newspapers." His voice is cultured but gravelly, as if he's breathed too much debris while digging in Egyptian tombs. His intelligent gray eyes regard me with suspicion. "What's your business with them?"

Relieved because I've captured his interest and he's not going to attack me again, I say, "I'm Sarah Bain, the photographer who rescued Sleeping Beauty. I think she may not be Maude, but an impostor."

"Nathaniel Trevelyan." He removes his gloves and shakes my hand. "Why do you think so?" he says in the manner of a scientist who asks questions before believing allegations.

"There are similarities between her and a woman named Jenny Legrand, who went missing the night she was found unconscious by the river. And Jenny's husband is certain that Jenny is Sleeping Beauty, posing as Maude Napier."

"Whether or not she is, how does it justify breaking into this building?"

"I didn't break in. The basement window is open."

Amusement crinkles Mr. Trevelyan's eyes. "Tell that to the police when I report you. Which I will if you don't explain yourself to my satisfaction."

I hurry to say, "I'm looking for people who know Maude, who can help us make certain whether the woman who's living in her house, with her daughter and sister-in-law, really is Maude."

"It seems to me that her family would know."

His patience and my time are running out fast. "I brought Sleeping Beauty and Maude's family together. If there's been a mistake, I need to make it right."

Although sympathetic now, Mr. Trevelyan says, "I'm afraid I can't help you."

"You aren't acquainted with Maude?" I say, discouraged by the thought that I broke the law and violated courtesy for nothing.

"Acquainted, yes. I met her when I worked with Dr. Napier at excavations in Egypt. But I can't say I knew her at all."

"Maybe if you were to call on her, and you got a close look at her . . .?"

Mr. Trevelyan shakes his head. "I never got a close look at her in Egypt. She seemed to be a very shy, reclusive woman. She spent most of her time in her tent. When she came out, she wore a hat with a veil to protect her skin from the sun. Many Englishwomen do. The Egyptian sun is fierce." He touches his own leathery face.

It sounds as if Maude Napier hid herself in real life as well as in her photograph. "Perhaps you could identify her by her voice?"

"I don't recall ever hearing it. We certainly never had a conversation."

I'm ready to admit that I've reached another dead end, when Mr. Trevelyan says, "I can't believe Caroline Napier would be fooled by an impostor. She's much too astute."

I think so too. Is it possible that she knowingly and deliberately accepted a stranger in place of her sister-in-law? Why would she? Maybe Maude Napier and Jenny Legrand aren't the only people who merit investigating.

"How well do you know Caroline Napier?" I ask Mr. Trevelyan.

His face reddens under his tan; nostalgic regret tinges his smile. "I haven't seen her in years, but we were once, shall we say, more than friends."

I shouldn't be surprised that Caroline had had a lover—she's not unattractive—but she seems so self-possessed, so entrenched in her spinsterish ways. And I can't picture her with Mr. Trevelyan, whom I only now notice is quite handsome, with the air of an adventurer.

"I asked her to marry me," he says, "but she was dedicated to her music. She couldn't give it up to go traipsing round Egypt with me. I'm lucky to have found a wife who's quite keen."

"Her music?" I remember Caroline plinking discordant notes on the piano and playing songs for guests to sing. Could she really prefer that to marriage, travel, and adventure? "I didn't know she was serious about it."

"She had ambitions to become a professional musician, and I believe she's had some success." Mr. Trevelyan says, "Now, I really must get back to my work. I'll see you out."

★   ★   ★

In Whitechapel High Street, people are lined up to buy blocks of ice from a horse-drawn cart. Water dripping from the cart turns the dust on the road into mud. The heat seems nowhere near breaking. Angry voices emanate from a public house; tempers are short. I wonder how much time I have left to determine Rosamond's true identity and solve Frances's murder. I wonder what Hugh and Mick have learned and what's going on with Barrett. I hope they're at the house, for I can't wait to talk over my discoveries with them. My mind concocts new schemes. Perhaps we can lure Rosamond out of the Napier house to someplace where Ned Lyle, the artist, can view her, and I can force her to tell the truth about what happened the night of Frances's murder. But how to lure her out of the house? I hope my friends have some ideas.

Then I see Constable Porter some twenty paces distant, striding toward me. His nose and mouth are swollen from Barrett's punches, but he smiles malevolently. Anger whisks up in my chest, like hot ashes from banked coals.

"Get away from me." When I turn to stalk off, I bump into two other constables. Instinct tells me to run, but before I can, Porter catches up with me, and he blocks my escape. "What do you want?"

"You're under arrest for the murder of Frances Oliphant." Porter enunciates as if he relishes every word.

Even as I understand that this is another phase of Reid's campaign against me, the constables grab me, take my satchel, and lock cold metal handcuffs around my wrists.

"Help!" I cry.

People passing on the street look and keep going. To them I must seem just another criminal nabbed by the police, business as usual. The constables bundle me into a large carriage that's parked on the roadside. Painted dark green, with barred windows, it's a Black Maria—a police omnibus for transporting prisoners. How I regret going off on my own, without Hugh and Mick. Porter and his men were lying in wait to ambush me, and I'm caught in the scenario that I once envisioned for Sally—snatched off the street without warning.

"Let me go!" I scream and writhe. I don't care if resisting arrest is added to the charges against me. If I'm tried for murder, a jury could convict me despite the fact that I'm innocent, and I'll be sentenced to death. Escaping now is my best chance of staying alive.

The constables shove me onto a bench built along the wall. As one of them crouches to secure my ankles with irons chained to the floor, I kick him in the jaw. The other holds me down, and I club his head with my manacled hands. He yells and slaps me hard across my face. Both men exit the omnibus, and Porter climbs in and sits on the bench across from me. The door slams shut, and the omnibus speeds down the street.

"You can't do this. I'm innocent!"

Porter bares stained teeth in a grin. "You might as well relax and enjoy the time you have left before you meet the rope-maker's daughter."

Immobilized, sweating from exertion and fear, I say between gasps, "Tell Inspector Reid not to hold his breath waiting for an invitation to my hanging. There's no evidence to convict me."

"Oh, we've evidence now, all right." Porter reaches in his pocket, brings out three small photographs, and sets one on my lap. It shows a woman's pocketbook. "This belonged to Frances Oliphant."

I recognize the beaded bag with the silver chain handle. Now I know why I felt something was missing from the scene of her death when I photographed it. In the confusion of the moment, I didn't think of her pocketbook, without which she surely wouldn't have traveled all the way from Wandsworth to St. John's Wood.

"We found it in the Napier house." Porter speaks slowly, sonorously, the better to enjoy his revelation. "In the room that looks like a Gypsy wagon."

I balk at the direction this is heading. "I didn't put it there."

"It was behind the bed. You thought we wouldn't find it, didn't you?" Porter smiles with the pride of a man who's proven himself underestimated. "And look."

He takes the photo and gives me another. This one shows what appear to be the contents of the pocketbook—a pillbox, a handkerchief with embroidered initials FWO, coins, key ring, comb, silver compact, and a folded paper. Porter points to the paper, removes the photo, and replaces it with the third photo. It shows a letter that reads,

Dear Miss Oliphant,

Come to number seventeen Grove End Road at two o'clock tomorrow morning, and you will learn something to your advantage.

Yours,
Sarah Bain

A sense of disorientation comes upon me, as when I'm on the verge of sleep and a dream encroaches before I drop off. "I didn't write that." But it's my handwriting, with tall ascenders and full loops, some letters joined and others unconnected.

"I suppose you're going to say it was forged." Porter speaks with pitying disdain.

"It was!" I'm scrambling to think how and by whom.

"Well, here's how Inspector Reid and I see it. Frances Oliphant came to the house because you invited her. You took her upstairs and pushed her out the window."

"I didn't! Inspector Reid forged that letter." He must have obtained samples of my handwriting, perhaps from the dustbin in the alley outside my home. "He planted it in my room."

Then I remember Caroline holding my satchel, which always contains notes about assignments for the *Daily World* and old shopping lists. She or Rosamond could have seen them, imitated my handwriting, and planted the pocketbook with the note in my room. It couldn't have been Venetia . . . Then I recall the captioned drawings in the nursery, unusually skillful for a ten-year-old.

"Save it for the jury." Porter calls to the driver to stop, then opens the door and jumps out of the omnibus.

"Wait! Where am I being taken? What's going to happen to me?"

Porter's smile says he's delighted to pay Barrett back at my expense. "You'll find out soon enough." The door slams.

During the journey, I lose track of time, distance, and turns. Soon the neighborhoods I see through the window are unfamiliar. The haze is so thick that I can't use the sun to determine whether I'm heading east or west, north or south. I wonder if this desolation is what my father felt when he disappeared, leaving his entire life behind. It seems like hours before the Black Maria stops, the door opens, and Porter reappears. He unchains my ankles. My feet are numb.

"Please let me go," I say, although I hate to throw myself on his mercy. "I've never done anything to hurt you."

Porter grabs my arm; his fingers dig painfully into my flesh. He jumps down to the ground, dragging me with him.

My feet are an agony of pins and needles. When I land, I stumble and start to fall. Porter pulls me up, almost jerking my arm from its socket. I kick him in the calf. "Don't do Reid's dirty work for him. The first time you cross him, he'll turn on you, the same as he did Barrett."

"Thanks for your concern. Kick me again, and I'll give you two black eyes. That'll look good in your newspaper pictures."

We're in a street of drab brick buildings that could be anywhere in London. Twilight is descending; mist thickens and dampens the haze. A gas lamp burns over the plain door through which Porter drags me. A police officer is seated at a desk, other constables loitering nearby. Porter says, "Here's a prisoner for you, courtesy of Inspector Reid at H Division."

The officer walks to a corner that's enclosed with bars, like a cage, and opens its iron gate. Porter unlocks my handcuffs and shoves me in. The room is warm, but my sweat turns cold, and I shiver as I stand helpless in the cage. The officer asks Porter for my name and address, records it on a long sheet of paper, and says, "What's the charge against her?"

"Murder," Porter says.

"This is a mistake," I say. "I've been wrongly accused."

"Stand against the wall," the officer commands me.

There's a ruler painted on the wall, and as I obey, I say, "I'm a photographer for the *Daily World*. I work for Sir Gerald Mariner. Tell him I'm here, and he'll clear things up." I'm being pushed into the bottomless dark chute of the law, and if there's anyone who can rescue me, it's Sir Gerald.

The officer records my height and other observations about me. "Possessions?" Porter hands over my satchel. The officer examines it, writes an inventory of the contents, then says to Porter, "We'll take her from here."

"Bye-bye." Porter's mocking voice follows me as a constable marches me to a dim passage lined with cells whose heavily bolted doors have small grates set at eye level. Voices, moans, and laughter come from women inside the cells. The air smells of urine and bleach. I've had nightmares about scenes like this one.

The constable stops me at a door and unlocks it. I say, "If you take a message to Sir Gerald, he'll pay you a hundred pounds." I doubt he will, but I'll say anything to avoid falling farther down the chute.

"It's against the law to bribe a police officer."

"Can you do me a favor, then? Tell DS Barrett at Whitechapel police station that I'm—"

The constable pushes me into the cell and locks the door.

CHAPTER 26

I look around the cell. There's no window and no furniture except benches built along three walls. Two women lie on the benches, their eyes gleaming in the dim light from the grate. They sit up and stare at me like caged animals at an interloper that's been thrown among them to fight over scraps of food.

"That's a nice hat," says one of the women. She thrusts out her hand. "Gimme it."

This is a test that will determine how I'll be treated for as long as we're locked up together. My anger at Porter and Reid spills over onto my cellmate as I take her measure. She's taller and heavier than I, with mean, piggy eyes and no front teeth. She smells of liquor and body odor. I look around for something to use as a weapon and see nothing but a bucket under the bench—the latrine.

"Oh, leave her alone, Millie," the other woman says. She's slender, in her twenties, fair and pretty, dressed in a neat striped frock. She looks and sounds too ladylike to be in jail.

Defiant, then sullen, Millie flops back down on the bench. My new friend pats the bench next to herself.

"Thank you." Sitting down seems an admission of surrender to my circumstances, but I'm so shaky that my legs won't hold me up.

"I'm Alison."

"Sarah."

"This your first time here?"

When I nod, Alison says, "Thought so. You look scared to death. Don't worry—I'll look after you."

Her kindness makes me feel worse. She's no substitute for my friends, and she can't help me because she's in the same wrecked boat as I. "Where are we?"

"Marylebone police station."

Reid has sent me to the district where Frances was murdered. I suppose I should be thankful I'm not in Newgate again. "What's going to happen?"

"We'll be taken to police court tomorrow."

"Tomorrow?" I'm appalled. "We have to stay here all night?"

Alison shrugs. "You might as well get comfortable."

I soothe myself with the thought that the wait will give Barrett, Mick, and Hugh time to realize I'm missing and locate me. "What happens in court?"

"The magistrate will decide whether we'll be let go, charged a fine, or put on trial." Alison says, "What're you in for?"

Noises from the other cells quiet; the occupants are eavesdropping. "Murder." I suppose it was inevitable that fate would catch up with me. I'm only surprised that the crime for which I was arrested isn't the one I actually committed.

"Murder!" Alison seems as much impressed as horrified. So do the other prisoners, judging from their exclamations. "I never would've guessed. You don't look the sort."

Millie eyes me with new respect. "Who'd you bump off?"

"Her name was Frances Oliphant, but I didn't kill her," I say. "Somebody else pushed her out a window."

Alison cocks her head, skeptical. "What did she do to you?"

"Nothing." I'm disturbed because these strangers take it for granted that I'm guilty, and what chance that a jury will believe I'm innocent? "I've been framed."

That provokes much jeering and laughter. Millie says, "Yeah, right. Welcome to the club."

★　★　★

Startled by banging on the door, I bolt upright on the hard bench where I fell asleep. A man's voice yells, "Rise and shine!"

My cellmates sit up, yawning. I hear stirring from the other prisoners and tinkling sounds as they use the buckets. I have to go so badly that I forsake modesty and take my turn after Alison and Millie are done. I tidy myself as best I can without comb or washing facilities. A constable doles out breakfast—three slices of buttered bread and a cup of coffee for each of us. We eat with dirty hands. I'm ravenous.

Then we're herded outside, some twenty women blinking in the foggy daylight, to several Black Marias. I have my first clear look at Alison. Fine wrinkles crease the skin around her gray eyes; she's older than I thought. The white linen cuffs and collar on her frock are frayed and discolored; she seems a tart pretending to be a lady. After a short, bumpy ride, we disembark in a courtyard surrounded by high walls with barred windows. Vans from other prisons are discharging passengers—men and women, young and old, from all ranks of society. Fashionably dressed swells nursing hangovers rub elbows with ragged streetwalkers. There must be a hundred of us. Constables march the women in through one door, the men through another. I find myself in a white-tiled room that has a bench built around the walls. High partitions divide the bench into sections that seat two people and prevent communication with other prisoners. Alison and I sit together. The constables rove, keeping order; everyone is subdued, quiet.

"What happens next?" I whisper.

"We go to court when our names are called," Alison whispers back. "The magistrate hears the minor charges first. You'll have to wait awhile."

"I forgot to ask, what are you in for?"

"Pickpocketing in Regent's Park Zoo."

Soon, Alison is called. She whispers, "Good luck," and she's gone.

The hours simultaneously drag and go too fast. I alternate between wanting the suspense ended and praying for enough time for my friends to come. At noon, lunch is served—bread, butter, and coffee again. I try to eat, but the food sticks in my throat, and the rancid coffee won't wash it down. Prisoner after prisoner goes off to court; the room empties. At four thirty, my name is called. Escorted by a constable, I walk on quaky legs into the courtroom. To calm my pounding heart, I resort to my old trick of focusing on my surroundings, pretending I'm a camera. The room is plain, its only decoration the royal coat of arms above the bench where the magistrate sits. A clerk at a desk below the bench leafs through documents. Reporters with notebooks and pencils lounge in a pew. The hot air, gray with tobacco smoke, also stinks of mildew and perspiration. Behind a wooden barrier waits a noisy crowd—relatives and friends of the accused, and curiosity seekers. The constable leads me to the dock—a platform enclosed by rails. As I stand there, humiliatingly exposed to all eyes, I search the crowd.

My friends aren't there. Disappointment threatens to force tears through the barrier of my self-control. This might have been my last chance to see them as well as theirs to rescue me. A black-robed usher escorts Inspector Reid to the witness box. His cold gaze, bright with suppressed elation, meets mine. He's got me where he wants me—on the road to the gallows. The magistrate bangs his gavel, and the room quiets. He's so short that only his head and shoulders are visible; a beaky nose, hooded eyes behind spectacles, and a bald head with a roll of fat around his neck give him the look of a tortoise.

"State your name," he orders me. His voice is crusty, brisk.

My terror of speaking in public grips me. Every face in the room seems to radiate cruel eagerness to see me blunder. My lips move, soundlessly.

"Speak up."

I manage to say in a hoarse whisper, "Sarah Bain."

"You are charged with the murder of Miss Frances Oliphant." The magistrate turns to Inspector Reid. "On what evidence?"

"Miss Bain was present at the house at the time of the murder," Reid says. "Witnesses observed her accompanying the victim to the room from which the victim fell out the window. The victim had in her possession a letter from Miss Bain that lured her to the house. It's reasonable to deduce that it was Miss Bain who pushed Frances Oliphant to her death."

Witnesses? I'm alarmed to think that Rosamond, Venetia, and Caroline—all three, not just one of them—have framed me. Or did Reid fabricate the evidence and bully them into lying? The way he states it, wherever it came from, it makes my guilt sound certain.

"Furthermore, Miss Bain is a violent woman," Reid says. "She has physically attacked me on multiple occasions, and while resisting arrest, she wounded three officers."

I picture him pounding the final nail into my coffin.

"What have you to say in your defense?" the magistrate asks me.

This is going too fast, with no witnesses to refute Reid's testimony or vouch for my character. As my heart thuds, my stomach roils, and panic blurs my vision, I grip the rail for support. "I—I—"

"We don't have all day," the magistrate says.

"I'm innocent! I have an alibi—Detective Sergeant Barrett was with me." I frantically scan the audience in the futile hope that my need for him will conjure him out of thin air. There's no one to save me but myself. Desperation revives my power of speech. "I didn't see Frances Oliphant that night until after she fell out the window. I didn't write the letter—it was forged. I'm being framed!"

"Save it for Old Bailey," the magistrate says. "I'm remanding you to Newgate Prison to await your trial."

"Wait," I plead as the constable opens the gate of the dock to remove me.

The magistrate pounds his gavel. "Next charge."

He's bent on speedily moving prisoners in and out of his court. How else could he get through a hundred in a day? Reid smiles at me with pure, evil delight. I feel myself on an unchangeable course toward hanging, with no hope for mercy from a judge or jury. Fate has caught up with me in a manner I never expected.

A commotion disturbs the crowd at the back of the room. Barrett, Mick, and Hugh jostle their way up to the barrier. "Your Worship," Barrett calls, "please allow us to testify on behalf of Miss Bain."

They found me! I'm so glad to see them, I let the tears flood my eyes, and I clutch the rail so that I don't crumple to the floor in relief.

Reid chuckles. "Sorry, you're a minute late and a penny short."

As my mouth opens to wail in protest, the magistrate says, "I'll allow them."

"Hey, you can't reverse your decision!" Reid's mirth turns to alarm.

"This is my court, young man. I'll do as I please," the magistrate retorts. "Step down from the witness box."

As Reid sullenly obeys and Barrett enters the witness box and states his name, I thank God for the stubbornness of old men.

"Miss Bain is innocent," Barrett says, his voice clear and earnest. "I know because—" For the first time he looks directly at me, his expression at once loving and defiant. "Because it was I who killed Frances Oliphant." His finger jabs his chest. "*I'm* guilty."

The audience clamors; the reporters sit up straight and begin scribbling notes. I stare in horror, clutch my throat as I comprehend what Barrett is up to. He knows Reid's influence is strong, and an alibi from my lover won't save me. He's bartering his life for mine.

"No!" I cry.

"This is most interesting," the magistrate says, as if glad for a novelty to enliven his dull routine.

"He's lying," Reid says, hovering below the bench, his face a picture of indignation.

"It's the truth," Barrett says.

"DS Barrett didn't do it," Mick calls from behind the barrier. "*I* pushed her."

"Shut up!" Reid yells.

"No, *I'm* the culprit," Hugh says. "I gave Miss Oliphant the heave-ho."

They're all throwing themselves to the wolves to save me. My heart swells with love for them, but I would rather die than have them suffer in my stead. "I confess," I say, my voice loud, clear, and bold now. "I murdered Frances Oliphant."

"So you want to change your statement?" the magistrate says.

I raise my voice over the hubbub of the audience. "Yes. I'm guilty."

"No, I am," my friends chorus.

"Don't listen to them, Your Worship!" Reid says. "They're trying to trick you into letting Miss Bain off."

"It seems to me that the charge against Miss Bain was premature." The magistrate's tone is frosty with disapproval toward Reid. "Here we have three confessions from three witnesses that you either failed to discover or intentionally hid from this court. I am dismissing the charge against Miss Bain, pending further—and by that I mean less slipshod—investigation of the case by the police."

He pounds his gavel. "Next charge."

★ ★ ★

In slow, bureaucratic fashion, I'm released, given back my satchel, and shown the door. Mick, Hugh, and Barrett are waiting outside the courthouse, triumphant smiles on their faces. Tearful with gratitude, furious at their recklessness, I say, "That was a stupid thing to do!"

"You're welcome," Barrett says.

"Then we're all stupid. You tried to put your neck in the noose for us after we confessed," Hugh points out.

"How did you find me?"

"Hugh and Mick came to the police station while I was on desk duty last night," Barrett says. "They said you hadn't come home and they'd looked for you in the places you'd told them you were going and everywhere between, and couldn't find you. I still have friends in the department. One of them told me he'd heard that Porter had taken you to the Marylebone station jail." Barrett adds with bitter rancor, "I should have known what Reid was plotting."

"Don't kick yourself," Hugh says. "All's well."

He and Mick turn their backs to give Barrett and me privacy; they shield us from the stares of passersby. I fall into Barrett's embrace. He holds me while I shudder at the thought that, had things gone differently, we might never have touched again.

"I smell," I whisper.

"You smell wonderful," Barrett whispers against my hair.

My last sight of him might have been at Old Bailey as I stood in the dock during my trial.

When we reluctantly separate, Hugh says, "Now we have another chance to solve the murder as well as figure out who Sleeping Beauty is and who's trying to frame you, Sarah. How about a drink to celebrate?"

"Don't celebrate yet."

We turn to see Inspector Reid standing by the courthouse door with Constable Porter. I'd expected them to be furious about my release, but they look like wolves who've devoured the lamb.

"You played right into my hands," Reid says, fairly licking his lips. "With your confessions, I can get a warrant to arrest all four of you for murder and conspiracy. I'll have you back in police court by tomorrow. The magistrate who's sitting then is a good friend of mine."

"You better have that drink," Porter says. "It could be your last."

Chapter 27

On the train ride home, our mood is as dark as the car when it rumbles between the gaslights in the tunnel. "I'm sorry," I say to Barrett seated beside me and Mick and Hugh across the aisle. "I've gotten you all in trouble."

"It ain't your fault," Mick says. "If Reid hadn't gone after you, it woulda been one of us, and we'd all be in this same fix anyway."

"Look on the bright side, Sarah," Hugh says cheerfully. "Remember when we saw the execution shed at Newgate Prison? The gallows has places for three nooses. We could ask to squeeze in a fourth, so we can all swing together."

I don't scold Hugh for his bad joke, and neither do Barrett or Mick. It might be the last bad joke we hear from him. We burst into the helpless, uncontrollable, manic laughter of the doomed.

"But seriously," Hugh says, "we have until tomorrow to solve the murder and clear our names." After a second, jeering bout of laughter, he says, "Let's get to work. Sarah, what did you find out before you were arrested?"

I describe my encounters with the archaeologist and artist, and my schemes. Barrett says, "Forget luring Maude out. Word around the station says Inspector Reid's got her and Venetia and Caroline practically under house arrest."

I'm about to break my silence about the hairbrush, comb, and mirror, when Hugh sidetracks me. "I can't say I had better luck investigating Caroline," he says, "although I did speak with her former teacher at the Royal Academy of Music. She's much more accomplished than I'd realized. She had a full scholarship, and she went on to study composing in Vienna. She even wrote a symphony, which is rare for a woman. She had a wealthy patron—a Baron von something or other. She performed concerts at his estate and the best theaters. She's not just one of the many spinsters who dabble in music."

The discordant notes I heard her play take on a new significance: she'd been composing, not making mistakes. But it doesn't get us any closer to the truth about Sleeping Beauty or the murder.

"Even if I could picture a woman like that shoving someone out a window, I can't imagine why Caroline would have wanted to kill Frances Oliphant," Hugh says.

"And if she knows Maude ain't Maude, why wouldn't she say so?" Mick says.

"Venetia is a different story," Hugh says. "Go on, Mick—tell Sarah."

"I hung around St. John's Wood high street and chatted up some kids. They said their mas won't let 'em play with Venetia because she's a bad girl. One time, she got 'em to sneak out of their houses at night and go to Regent's Park and pretend they were explorers huntin' for hidden treasure. They ran across some bloke who tried to kidnap 'em. Venetia hit him with her walking stick until he was knocked out. The kids ran home cryin'."

That doesn't sound out of character for Venetia. Although she probably saved those children from harm, I'm disturbed to learn that she committed violence that was much more serious than her confessed attack on her mother. We argue about who we think Rosamond is and who we think is responsible for Frances's death, until the train pulls into Whitechapel station at 7:40. Hugh and Mick support Barrett's unwavering conviction that she's Jenny, and all three of them think the impostor must be the murderess too. When they see my dismay, they fall silent; after my ordeal, they don't want to upset me. As we walk toward home through the swampy, smelly mélange of smoke and fog, all I want is supper, a bath, and sleep before whatever happens next.

"Who's that?" Mick points to a woman in a neat gray frock, jacket, and black straw bonnet, looking in the window of the studio.

I halt in my tracks and stare at the one person I never thought would darken my doorway. "It's Sally's mother." I hurry forward, calling, "Mrs. Albert?"

She turns to me as if we're in a duel and she's about to draw her pistol. "Miss Bain. May I have a word with you?" Her glance at my friends conveys a disapproval that puts me off introducing them. "In private?"

Hugh opens the door for us. "Have at it."

I feel as if I'm letting in a bad fairy who will put a curse on my home, but I'm curious about what Mrs. Albert has to say. She goes in with straight-backed dignity, like a royal ambassador crossing enemy lines to negotiate a treaty. I don't think it's a peace treaty. While Hugh, Mick, and Barrett go upstairs, Mrs. Albert stands in my studio, gazing at my camera equipment, props, and display of photographs.

"You've a nice place. Too bad the neighborhood isn't very good. You'll never get the best kind of customer." There's envy under her cold, critical tone. She sighs. "But it's your own. I see why Sally likes coming here."

"Why did you come?"

"First, you have to promise you won't tell Sally that I was here or what I said."

A conspiracy of silence with her is akin to a deal with the devil. "Why don't you want her to know?"

"Just promise." Mrs. Albert takes a step toward the door.

I hope that if I break the deal, it won't have irreparable bad consequences. "I promise."

Her mouth quivers, she averts her gaze, and says in a barely audible whisper, "I think I know where your father is."

My heart thumps as if she's punched me in the chest. *"What?"* Although I'd suspected her of keeping secrets, I never expected this definitive confession. "Where?"

"In Brighton. Number one-forty-six King's Road Arches." Mrs. Albert's face bunches as if she's about to cry.

I memorize the address before demanding, "How do you know?"

"He wrote a letter. To Sally. It said"—she gulps—"he was sorry for abandoning her and asked her to forgive him. He said that if she would come to see him, he would explain everything."

There's no breath in my lungs. I've always scoffed at the idea that it's possible to die of shock, but maybe one can. I sip air until the feeling of suffocation passes. "Sally doesn't know?"

Mrs. Albert shakes her head. "She never saw the letter. I burned it."

"When was this?"

"July of eighty-seven."

I've rarely struck anyone who hadn't struck me first. I grit my teeth, clench my fists, and swallow the hot bile of my fury at Mrs. Albert. For three years she's known Benjamin Bain's location. I'm even more outraged on Sally's behalf than my own. She could have spared Sally three years of wondering what had become of him, why he'd left.

"Why are you telling me now?"

Mrs. Albert draws back from my temper, but she smiles with her usual nastiness. "You shouldn't look a gift horse in the mouth." Her smile stretches into a grimace of guilt. "I know how much Sally misses him. I can't live with the secret anymore. It's like having a cancer that's eating away at my insides."

I think of my mother, dead of cancer that perhaps had been nourished by the secrets she'd harbored. "How can you expect me not to tell Sally?"

"You can tell her." Mrs. Albert's expression turns woeful. "Just please don't say who you heard it from. She would never forgive me."

I want to retort that Sally has a right to be as angry as I am, and Mrs. Albert doesn't deserve forgiveness. But Sally loves her mother, who's her only family besides me. "How am I supposed to explain how I found out?"

Mrs. Albert dismisses my concern with an impatient wave of her hand. "You're so clever, you'll think of something." She moves toward the door and pauses. "When you see him, tell him . . ." Her anger, hostility, and guardedness desert her like ashes blown away by a storm. For a moment I see the naked pain of a deserted wife who still loves her husband. Then she makes a clutching gesture, as if at her pride, and she pieces her face together in a semblance of her normal hard, bitter expression.

"Tell him I'm sick of trying to explain his actions to Sally, and now it's his turn."

★　★　★

Upstairs, I find Hugh gazing out the parlor window. Mick and Barrett jump up from the sofa when they see me. Before I can tell them what Mrs. Albert said, Hugh exclaims, "Tristan?" Disbelief mingles with the joy in his voice.

We all peer at the street below. A cab is parked outside our house; Tristan Mariner has just stepped out. He lifts his bruised, somber face and meets Hugh's questioning gaze. Then he leans in through the cab's open door, and a woman inside begins screaming. As he struggles with her, I glimpse her thin white hands pushing at him, a bare leg flailing. Hugh runs down the stairs, with the rest of us close at his heels. As we burst out the front door, Tristan drags the woman from the cab.

"I changed my mind. I don't want to tup you, no matter how much you pay me. I want to go home." She falls on her hands and knees on the pavement, shrieking, "Help! Help!"

She's dressed in a crimson frock made of rich satin, speckled with tiny beads that glitter like ruby crystals in the light from the street lamp. Her hair is a snarl of black ringlets. I smell her odor of liquor, cheap perfume, and stale makeup. As she crawls away, Tristan grabs her around her waist. He hauls her upright.

"Tristan, who the devil is that?" Hugh says. "What are you doing?"

Mick, Barrett, and I are dumbfounded. Hugh's lover, the former priest, has apparently picked up a drunken prostitute against her will.

"Let me go, you son of a bitch!" The woman kicks backward at Tristan while he holds her against him, encircled in his arms. "Help! I'm being kidnapped!"

People on the street stare. Tristan pants as she tries to pry his arms loose, and he staggers to avoid her kicks. "I read in the newspaper that you're looking for a woman in a red dress," he says. "I thought this might be her."

I remember the ratcatcher at Mark Lane station describing the woman he'd seen the night Sleeping Beauty was found. *"Fancy,"* he'd called her dress; *"with little shiny beads all over."* I'm stunned, and not only because Tristan, of all people, has brought us a woman in clothing that fits the description. The dress looks familiar, although I don't recall where I've seen it before. It's puzzling because I should be able to place such a unique, obviously expensive garment.

"Bastard!" the woman yells. She's much smaller and slimmer than Tristan, and he lifts her off the ground. She kicks the air, squirms, and claws like a cat.

"Where on earth did you find her?" Barrett says.

"At the Salvation Army shelter in Hanbury Street," Tristan says. "I've been working there nights. Doing whatever needs to be done. Serving meals. Breaking up fights."

The cuts on his face have healed into scabs, the bruises darkened. The skin around his left eye is spectacularly purple and green. I see how relieved Hugh is to learn how Tristan came by these injuries.

"But she can't be Sleeping Beauty," I say. Whoever Sleeping Beauty is, she's ensconced at the Napier house. The Salvation Army shelter isn't far from Shadwell, and this could be the same woman in the red dress, but she now seems irrelevant to the case, a distraction.

"I know." Tristan turns to Hugh, a hopeful plea in his eyes. "But I thought I should bring her anyway." He speaks as if she's an apology gift for his behavior.

While Hugh stands open-mouthed and speechless, the woman throws back her head and yowls. Now I see her delicate, pretty features, her angry eyes that are as sharp, hot, and glittery as fresh cinders. I feel a dizzy, disoriented sensation, as if a whirlwind had rearranged time and geography and brought me together with someone who belongs in the past, in a distant locale.

"Rose?" I say.

She starts at the sound of her name and turns her attention on me. Her red gown has a ruffle around its high neckline, but when I last saw her, she was wearing a low-cut yellow frock.

"You know her?" Barrett says.

"Yes," I say. "She was in the crowd that gathered around Sleeping Beauty on the riverbank."

"Hey, I know you too." Rose stops fighting Tristan to stare at Hugh, Mick, and me. "You're them photographers." Her eyes flare with suspicion. "Are you in on this with him?"

"We're friends, that's all," I say.

"What do you want with me?"

"To talk." I want to make sense of things about that night that never made sense, and determine whether they bear upon Sleeping Beauty's identity and Frances Oliphant's murder.

"Yeah, I've heard that before." Rose's voice drips scorn.

"Come in for five minutes," I say, "then we'll send you home in the cab."

"Hah! It'll cost you more than that."

I also want a longer look at her dress, so I can figure out where I've seen it before. I scoop coins from my satchel and drop them into her palm. Mick opens the door, and with a cautious glance at us, she enters.

Tristan hunches his shoulders, as if to hide from the watching crowd. "I'd better go."

"Wait," Hugh says. "Please."

Barrett, Mick, and I leave them alone together and join Rose in the studio. I light the gas lamps, and she looks at my camera. "You want to take dirty pictures of me? Is that what this is about?"

"No." I'll never go down that road again. "What a pretty dress."

She simpers and twirls; the crimson skirt fans out; the beads sparkle. "Ta."

"Were you wearing it that night?"

Rose falters to a stop. "Uh . . ."

Now I'm sure she's hiding something. "Where did you get it?"

"What—you think it's too fine for the likes of me?"

"Too expensive, certainly."

"Why're you so interested in the bleedin' dress?"

Mick points at Rose. "What're them stains?"

Brownish patches discolor the fabric of the bodice, sleeves, and ruffles. They're faint, as if scrubbed with soap and water. "Blood," I say, disturbed by an inkling that my theories about what happened to Sleeping Beauty that night are all wrong, and reality lies somewhere in the wilderness of Rose's evasions.

Alarmed, Rose backs away from me. I advance on her. "Where did you get the dress?"

She turns to bolt out the door, but Barrett stands in front of it. Her eyes flash; she snarls like a cornered fox. "I didn't steal it!"

"Tell me where it came from, and we'll let you go."

"It weren't exactly stealin'. I thought she were dead. I figured she didn't need it no more."

Mick and I look at each other, astonished as comprehension dawns. "You mean, you took it off Sleeping Beauty?" I say.

"Yeah." Rose hangs her head in shame, then says defiantly, "I didn't know she were alive 'til you said so."

"Sleeping Beauty was the lady in the red dress!" Mick says.

I'm flabbergasted and adrift in confusion; this news is a piece of a puzzle whose entirety I still can't see.

"Am I in trouble?" Rose says.

"If you tell me what happened, I'll make sure you won't be." It's a promise I may have to break.

Rose glances at Barrett, as if calculating whether she could fight her way past him and out the door. He shakes his finger in warning. She sighs and says, "I was on the terrace behind the pub when I seen her comin' down the steps."

My friends and I had taken it as a fact that Rose's girlfriend and the Indian man had been first to discover Sleeping Beauty, because they had thought they were, and nobody at the scene had contradicted them. Our erroneous assumption had hindered our investigation at the onset.

"She trips and falls ass over teakettle to the bottom. I run over and see that her face is all bloody, like it'd been carved up with a knife. I ask, 'Are you all right?' She don't answer. When I touch her, she don't move. That's why I thought she were dead."

Our theory that she'd been transported to and dumped by the river while unconscious was wrong too.

"Her dress were more beautiful than anything I ever had," Rose says with childish envy. "I thought, it's my lucky night. I stripped it off her. Took her hat and petticoats and corset and everything else too—why not? She didn't need 'em. After I was done, I felt sorry for her, lyin' there stark naked and carved up. I thought it would be kinder to let the river take her, so I started dragging her over."

I remember the long scuff marks in the mud. I think Rose also wanted to cover up her own theft.

"Before I could get her in the water, I heard people comin'. I ran away and left her on the bank. I hid her clothes underneath the pub, and I stayed there until they found her and started yelling and everyone came to see what'd happened. I pretended I'd been inside all along and was as shocked as they were. After the police left, I took her clothes home."

I'm appalled. "You didn't think you should show them to the police?"

"And get arrested for stealing? Are you daft?"

"The dress could have helped them identify her," I say, disgusted. She's as selfish as Mrs. Albert, keeping secrets that she had no right to keep.

"Yeah, well, she were identified soon enough anyway. I heard she's some rich bitch. She probably has hundreds of dresses. She can afford to lose one." Rose caresses the crimson silk. "I never had anything so beautiful."

I've touched my cameras in the same loving fashion, and I can understand her possessiveness, but I reach out my hand and say, "Give it to me."

Rose clutches her sleeves. "No!"

"Why do we need it?" Mick says.

"It's evidence." I say to Rose, "I'll give you something else to wear." I open the costume wardrobe and take out a floral calico dress. "Here, put this on."

"The hell I will!"

"Then you're under arrest," Barrett says, "for theft and for obstructing a police investigation. You'll serve at least a year in the workhouse."

Rose glares at me, rips off the dress, throws it on the floor. She seems not to care that Mick and Barrett are seeing her in her undergarments. She snatches the calico from me, puts it on, and stalks out of the studio, calling over her shoulder, "Fuck you, bitch!"

I'm holding the red dress, trying to jog my memory, when Hugh comes in, his manner tense from whatever happened between him and Tristan. After I tell him what happened here in the studio, he says, "That's one mystery solved. But how does it tell us who Sleeping Beauty is or who killed Frances Oliphant?" He takes the dress from me, holds it under the gas lamp, and tilts it back and forth so the beads flash tiny, reflected white lights.

I stare at them as I feel that dizzy sensation again and my heart leaps. I rush to the office at the back of the studio, rummage in the desk drawer, pull out a photograph, and run back to Barrett, Mick, and Hugh. "Look!"

We study the photograph of August and Jenny Legrand. Barrett says, "That's an identical dress, only black."

"It's the same dress," I say. "Red comes out black in photographs." I touch the white specks on Jenny's dress in the print. "I thought these were from defects on the negative plate. They're the beads reflecting the light from the flash lamp."

"Gorblimey!" Mick says. "Sleeping Beauty *is* Jenny Legrand."

Barrett and I look at each other. I silently apologize for brushing aside his doubts, for valuing my own instincts over his. There's a gleam of satisfaction in his eyes, and a smile tugs his mouth, but he does me the favor of not saying, "I told you so."

CHAPTER 28

At eleven o'clock, Grove End Road is deserted except for the cab in which Hugh, Mick, Barrett, and I ride past dark, silent mansions. A cool breeze blows in through the cab's open windows. The branches of the trees rustle, creak, and sway in the light of the street lamps, casting moving shadows. Clouds gather above the haze of smoke while distant thunder rumbles. The weather is finally breaking. The night seems alive with our reckless, driven mood, and despite fatigue and nerves, my mind is clear, my thoughts focused as if through a prism toward a confrontation that now feels destined.

I don't think Jenny ever had amnesia. I'm sure she deliberately deceived everyone—everyone except her husband and Barrett. Whatever August Legrand did to her, she shouldn't have saved herself at the expense of other, innocent people, and the fact that she played me for a fool is the least of her sins. If she hadn't ensconced herself in the Napier house, Frances Oliphant wouldn't have died there, and my friends and I wouldn't be facing a murder charge. Whether or not Jenny is guilty of the murder and framed me, Frances and we aren't her only victims. Venetia will suffer the most when Jenny's fraud is revealed, and I must be the messenger who delivers the crushing blow, who sets matters straight tonight.

Barrett calls to the driver to stop down the street from the Napier house. After we climb out, Hugh pulls his pistol from inside his boot. Our first task is to get past the guard that Inspector Reid stationed outside the Napier house. We march down the road like soldiers toward a battle. The wind gusts, cooling my sweat-damp skin; electricity in the air lifts strands of hair off my brow. I spare a moment to think of my father in Brighton, to hope that after tonight there will be time to go to him. Then I put him out of my mind as the house comes into view.

The cypress trees in the front garden stand stiff and vertical, unmoved by the wind. A flash of lightning reflects on the silver dome on the turret. The house is unnaturally quiet and still. The only hints of life are the lamp burning inside the white portico and bright gaps between the curtains in the Moorish windows. The place seems under the spell that put the princess and her household to sleep for a hundred years. Hugh raises the gun with which he means to threaten the constable and force him away from the house so the rest of us can confront Jenny. My heart pounds as I silently pray that the constable will go without resisting, without violence. My thoughts leap ahead to telling Jenny that her masquerade is at an end, venting my anger, and forcing her to reveal what happened the night Frances died. I tremble with fearful anticipation. God forbid it was Venetia who pushed Frances out the window.

The gate is open, as if the hundred years are up; it creaks as it swings in the wind. We halt, look up the path toward the house, and see no one guarding the door. We exchange glances of relief. Either the constable deserted his post, or Inspector Reid decided a guard wasn't necessary because he thought we would be under arrest by now. I start forward, but Hugh motions me to wait while he goes first. Mick, Barrett, and I watch as he steals up the path, gun brandished. He reaches the steps and glances to his right, then his left, into the garden. He jumps as if a firecracker had exploded under his feet. He turns, mouthing silent, frantic words, and beck-ons us. We hurry to him and look where he's pointing.

Beneath the cypress trees, a police constable lies on his side, his face turned against the flagstones. I cover my mouth to stifle an exclamation.

Hugh groans, and Mick shushes him. Barrett crouches, examines the man, and feels his neck. When he rises, his own face is blanched with shock. "He's dead. Strangled." Barrett gulps, then says, "He must have bitten his tongue—there's blood on his mouth. It's still wet."

Whatever happened to the constable happened not long ago. Astonished by this unexpected development, we glance around, toward the empty street, the shifting shadows. His killer could be out there. Then our gazes move to the carved wooden door. The brass Medusa head knocker stares at us from beneath its crown of writhing snakes. The air seems charged with my sudden, alarming certainty that the danger is inside—not outside—the house. *What's become of Jenny, Venetia, and Caroline?* I don't wait to discuss plans for action or consider my own safety. I seize the knocker, and even as Barrett says, "Don't, Sarah," I pound on the door.

No one answers. Fearful for the inhabitants, yet still spoiling for the confrontation I came for, I shout, "Jenny!" It feels strange but satisfying to call her by her real name. "I know you're in there." If I must break Venetia's heart, at least I'll have the pleasure of telling Jenny what a selfish, despicable liar she is. And although I can't picture her strangling the constable, I suspect that she was involved in his death. "Open up!"

I hammer so loudly that the pounding echoes like thunder through the night. My anger is so powerful, I feel as if I could break the door down. After several minutes, there's no response. The windows are closed, and I can't hear a sound from within the house.

"Maybe they're asleep," Mick says.

Nobody suggests the other, terrible possibility—that they've fallen victim to whoever killed the constable. "Nobody could sleep through that noise," I say. "I think Jenny knows why we're here, and she's hiding." I'm hot with exertion and temper because she thinks she can evade the consequences of her actions.

"I'll go around back and have a look," Barrett says.

He moves past the shrubbery along the front of the house and disappears into the darkness. A minute later, I hear the lock rattle. I brace myself to meet whatever awaits us in the house, and I gather my breath to unloose the full force of my rage at Jenny, the fraud. The door opens a scant six inches. The face that appears belongs to Caroline Napier. Her eyes bulge with fright; long hanks of hair have come loose from the knot atop her head. I smell her rank odor of anxiety-induced sweat.

"What do you want?" Her voice is a breathy whisper, the flutter more pronounced.

I'm at a momentary loss for words; somehow, I hadn't expected anyone but Jenny to answer the door. "To see . . . Maude." I stumble over the name by which Caroline knows her, the name that doesn't belong to her.

"Not so loud! You already must have awakened the neighbors." Her own voice rises; she lowers it. "You can't see Maude. She's . . . not here."

I think she's lying, protecting the woman she either believes or is pretending to believe is Maude. "Let us in."

"Go away!" Caroline starts to close the door.

Mick and I push on it. Caroline pushes back. Her disheveled appearance and frantic struggle to keep us out trigger my instincts. An ominous feeling eclipses my anger.

"Where is Maude? Where is Venetia?"

"They—they went on a holiday."

But "Maude" didn't want to leave the house. It wasn't because of her bandaged face; she was afraid of running into someone who would recognize her as Jenny Legrand. Something is badly wrong. I'm not angry enough to let her fend for herself, and I won't leave Venetia in danger.

"Venetia!" I call. Only echoes of my voice reply.

"The constable who was guarding you has just been murdered," Hugh says to Caroline. "How did it happen?"

"What?" Caroline stares blankly; her gaze darts to the gun in his hand.

I can't tell whether she already knew about the murder or this is the first she's heard of it. She wrings her hands, her pale face shiny with sweat and her eyes unblinking with panic. The tail of her white blouse hangs outside the waist of her black skirt. Her sleeves have red smears on the cuffs. My heart thumps as I begin to realize that her music isn't the only thing I didn't understand about Caroline. Sleeping Beauty wasn't the only person I misjudged.

"What have you done with them?" I demand.

Her mouth twitches. She looks over her shoulder. Now I hear thumps and muffled cries. Mick, Hugh, and I throw our weight against the door. Caroline shrieks as she gives way. "Please, no!" Her voice is raw with desperation.

We barge into the foyer. Low flames burn in the frosted-glass sconces on the walls. Beyond the rectangular pool and the iron staircase, a man dressed in a beige suit and green paisley waistcoat lies on the floor. His ankles are bound with the end of a white cord that secures his wrists together behind his back. He screams through the flowered tea towel stuffed in his mouth. Blood from a wound on his left temple has drenched his cap of light brown hair, his white shirt collar, and the blue mosaic floor under his head.

"August Legrand!" I thought I'd already seen everything tonight, but I lean against the banister while I absorb this new shock.

Writhing, he thumps his boots against the floor. His pale eyes are wild with terror, his nostrils flaring; he reminds me of a photograph I once saw—a fallen statue of a leaping horse, in some Roman ruin.

"What the blazes is he doin' here?" Mick says.

"He broke in. I hit him with the poker." Caroline points. The iron shaft lies near Mr. Legrand, its end wetly dark. "I tied him up so he couldn't run away. I was just about to fetch the police."

That doesn't make sense. If she's telling the truth, why did she want to keep us out? Why not be glad that help has arrived?

Mr. Legrand grunts, trying to speak. Mick reaches down and pulls the gag out of his mouth. A protest bursts from Caroline. "No!"

"Thank God you're here!" Mr. Legrand gasps with relief. "She was going to kill me."

"Don't listen to him," Caroline says. "He came to kill Maude."

"I certainly did not. She is Jenny, my wife. I came to take her home."

I remember Mr. Legrand's words to her at the identity parade: *"No one can keep us apart. I love you, and I will not rest until we are together again!"*

"Did you kill the constable outside?" Hugh says, aiming the gun down at Mr. Legrand.

"I didn't mean to. I wanted to come in, and he tried to stop me." Mr. Legrand wrenches at his bonds. "Please don't shoot me."

My mind reels at the news that even if Mr. Legrand didn't kill his wives, he's still a murderer.

"There's the knife he brought to kill Maude." Caroline points to the floor under the mural of Romans playing musical instruments. There lies a folding pocket knife, its long, sharp steel blade angled out of its black enamel sheath.

I'm not ready to believe her; I don't trust her. Mr. Legrand says, "She was not going to fetch the police. I woke up more than an hour ago, and I have been lying here while she paced the floor and muttered to herself, 'He won't live to tell. I won't be blamed.'"

Caroline's face falls, as though she's disturbed to learn that she'd been observed while she'd thought he was unconscious.

"Tell what?" I say.

"I do not know," Mr. Legrand says, "but she repeated over and over, 'My lucky break. Two birds with one stone.'"

"I never said those things!" Caroline cries. "Don't you see he's delirious?"

"I heard you," Legrand says, urgent with his need to be believed. "You said, 'No one will know what happened. They'll be gone. I can stop this charade. I'll be free.'"

"Shut up!" Caroline picks up the poker and swings it at Mr. Legrand.

Mick grabs and restrains her. I think Caroline has gone mad, and the words Mr. Legrand heard her say are clues to intentions that she doesn't want revealed.

"Get out! All of you!" Caroline shrills.

"Not until we get to the bottom of this," Hugh says.

With a high-pitched yelp, Caroline breaks away from Mick and runs out of the room.

"Hell!" Mick takes off after her.

"We need to find Jenny and Venetia," I say to Hugh. I'm growing ever more concerned about their safety; I fear that Mr. Legrand isn't the only person Caroline has hurt.

"Please don't leave me alone," Mr. Legrand begs. "She will come back and kill me!"

"You go," Hugh says to me. "I'll stay with him."

I run through the house, searching. They're not on the main floor. The air is hot, stale, and smells of cooked food; all the windows are closed. On the second floor, I find empty rooms. Then, from the third floor, I hear faint cries of "Help, help!" The door to Maude's room is closed; banging erupts from within. I knock.

"Venetia?" I call.

"Sarah!" Jenny says, relief in her voice.

"We're locked in," Venetia says. "Let us out!"

Caroline must have locked them in, and why unless she meant to harm them? There's no key in the keyhole. I push against the door. Solid wood, with a strong lock and hinges, it doesn't budge. I can't ask either Hugh or Mick to help and leave the other to deal with both Caroline and Mr. Legrand.

"Detective Barrett is outside," I say. "I'll fetch him."

Not wanting to stray far from them while Caroline is running amok, I go into the room next door, open the window, and call Barrett. He immediately appears in the garden below. "Caroline has locked Venetia and Maude in Maude's room," I call. "She's gone mad. Help me get them out. The front door is open. Bring something to break their door down."

"That won't be necessary." Barrett hurries away into the darkness and returns dragging a ladder. "The gardener's been pruning trees."

"Venetia, open your window," I say.

I hear cranking, scraping sounds as she obeys, the thump as Barrett leans the ladder against the house, and footsteps as Mick chases Caroline. I run down the backstairs and out to the garden. The temperature has dropped and the wind quickened during the short time I've been inside. Trees sway, falling leaves twirl, and the scent of roses wafts. I join Barrett and Venetia at the foot of the ladder while Jenny climbs down. She moves gracefully, like the artist's model she once was. Her pale nightdress, rippling in the wind, resembles the Roman robe that she wears in her husband's paintings. As she alights, vengefulness enflames me.

This is the last moment she'll exist as Maude Napier. Whatever else happens tonight, I shall hold her accountable for her deception.

"Thank you so much for rescuing us," she says to Barrett and me.

"Where's Aunt Caro?" Venetia says. "What's she done?"

I say to Jenny, "Your husband is here."

Her eyes blink with confusion behind the mask of gauze bandages. "Who?"

"August Legrand. You remember him—don't you, Jenny?"

"Oh God." She covers her mouth with her gloved hand.

Venetia looks puzzled. I feel terrible doing this in front of her, but I tell myself it's like cutting off a gangrenous limb—the quicker, the better. "You're not her mother. You're Jenny Legrand."

"No. You're wrong." Jenny's voice rises in frantic protest.

That she's trying to deny her fraud is intolerable. "We found the dress you were wearing the night you disappeared from your husband's house. We know who stole it from you while you were unconscious. We have a photograph of you wearing it."

She whimpers; her hands clutch the bandages as if they're armor she can't bear to lose.

"You may as well take those off." Barrett sounds uncertain; she's not the usual kind of criminal he unmasks. "There's no use hiding behind them any longer."

"Mother?" Venetia's voice quavers.

Jenny drops her hands and then doesn't move; she seems turned to stone. The necessary action is up to me. I reach out, as if to remove the veil from a hidden mother, and peel the bandages from her face, forcing myself to tame my anger and be gentle so as not to hurt her. I let the bandages fall to the ground, where they swirl in the wind; they look like living skin shed by a snake. Strip by strip, her face becomes visible. The swelling around the red scars and black stitches has gone down, the bruises faded. Her delicate features are indisputably Jenny Legrand's. Her blue eyes overflow with tears of misery. My disappointment is so grievous that I realize I'd been hoping I was wrong and she really was Maude. Venetia begins to cry. I feel stirrings of pity for Jenny as well as for the little girl she deceived. In spite of myself, I think her affection for Venetia is real.

"You never had amnesia, did you, Jenny?" I say.

"I did at first."

"When did you remember who you were?" Barrett says.

She wipes her eyes with her glove. "Before the identity parade."

Pity doesn't quell my indignation. "Which means that when you saw Venetia, you knew she wasn't your daughter."

Her body heaves with sobs as she whispers, "Venetia, I'm so sorry."

"It's all right. I knew from the beginning you weren't my mother." Venetia flings herself into Jenny's embrace. "But I don't care!"

CHAPTER 29

My mind and body have withstood so many shocks tonight that it's numb to this one; I can only remember that I'd originally thought Venetia was too smart to be fooled by an impostor, and now I see I was correct. Barrett widens his eyes at me, puffs his cheeks, and blows out his breath.

Jenny holds Venetia at arm's length to stare at her in bewilderment. "You knew right away? How?"

Venetia buries her face against Jenny's bosom. "You smell different from my mother."

"I thought you didn't know until the night Frances Oliphant died!"

Now is the time for the truth about the murder. "What happened?" I say.

"I was in the nursery, reading to Venetia," Jenny says. "We fell asleep with the lamp on. I woke up when Frances came in and started tearing at my bandages. She said, 'The game is over, Peggy.' She thought I was her stepsister. I tried to stop her, but it was too late." She sighs with regret. "The bandages were off. Venetia was awake. She saw my face."

"I didn't mean to do it." Venetia's earnest gaze begs Barrett and me to understand. "I was just trying to protect my mother."

I taste cold, poisonous dread. "What did you do?"

"She didn't do anything," Jenny hastens to say. "I'm the one who killed Frances."

"No, Mother, I won't let you take the blame for me." Venetia stands in front of Jenny and faces me. "Mother told me to get you and Mick and Lord Hugh. But then Frances said to her, 'You're not Peggy, but you're also not Maude Napier. I recognize you from the picture in the newspaper. You're Jenny Legrand, the artist's wife.' She smiled, and she looked so mean. 'Wait until I tell the police. They'll put you in jail for fraud. You'll never see that child again.'

"I couldn't let her tell. I jumped out of bed and grabbed my croquet mallet. I said, 'Promise not to tell, or I'll kill you!' and I swung it at her. I just wanted to scare her. But when she ducked, she tripped on the rug and stumbled, and I hit her arm. She said, 'You little bitch, you ought to be locked up too.' I hit her again and again because I didn't want her to take my mother away, and I didn't want to go to jail. She started fighting back. She threw things and overturned the table on me. When I fell down, she grabbed the mallet."

Jenny interrupts. "She was so angry, I thought she would kill Venetia. I pushed her away from Venetia, and she crashed against the window." Jenny puts her hands over her ears, squeezes her eyes shut, and clenches her teeth, as if she hears the shattering glass and the thud of Frances's body on the terrace.

"We didn't mean for her to die!" Venetia's hand flutters at her chest. "Cross my heart!"

Barrett and I look at each other in consternation. The truth about Frances's death is less straightforward than we would like—a mixture of premeditation and impulse, accident and intention. We can't be wholly certain of anyone's motives. Did Frances come to kill Peggy? Did Jenny and Venetia try to silence Frances to protect their secret? In the heat of the moment, did any of them know? Hindsight is like a warped camera lens.

"What are you going to do?" Jenny says as she and Venetia cling to each other.

Barrett shakes his head, as much at sea as I am.

"I didn't mean to impersonate Maude for this long," Jenny says. "I was only planning to stay here until I figured out where to go. I couldn't go back to my husband." The terror in her eyes suggests that he's guilty of all the sins for which I suspect him. "I meant to sneak away one night. But I always wanted a child, and I couldn't have one."

I remember Ned Lyle mentioning the baby Jenny had been expecting, which was never born.

"When I saw Venetia for the first time, it seemed as if a miracle had happened, and I'd been given this beautiful, special little girl." Caressing Venetia's hair, Jenny smiles a tearful smile. "I fell in love with her. That's why I stayed."

Venetia hugs Jenny. "I love you better than my real mother. You're nicer to me than she ever was." She entreats Barrett and me, "Please don't tell anyone she's not my real mother. Please don't take her away!"

We shake our heads. There's a world of reasons why we can't leave things be. The most important is Maude Napier, who must be in Egypt after all, and who's bound to return someday and discover that an impostor has taken her place.

"We'll discuss this later," Barrett tells Jenny and Venetia. "We've a more immediate problem now."

I'm glad he's put off our decision. Even though Jenny and Venetia aren't kin, and their relationship is born of a fraud, I think they share more love than my mother and I ever did.

A loud bang explodes within the house. We all start. Night birds wing up from the trees. Before the echoes fade, Barrett says, "That was a gunshot!"

He runs along the terrace; I hurry after him. "Stay there!" he shouts to Jenny and Venetia.

We burst through the French doors, and the sulfur smell of gunpowder hits us. Smoke hazes the foyer, where Caroline stands holding a small silver pistol in both hands, trained on Hugh and

Mick. Their hands are raised, their faces frozen in expressions of panic. On the floor at her feet lies Hugh's gun. She must have run away to fetch her pistol and returned before Mick caught up with her. She took Hugh by surprise, fired first, and made him throw down his weapon. The light is brighter because her bullet shattered one of the sconces. Fragments litter the floor. August Legrand is lying where we left him, still bound. His face wet with blood and tears, he calls to Barrett and me, "Help! She's going to kill us all!"

Caroline swings the pistol around to aim at us. "Don't come any closer!" Her voice flutters; the gun trembles in her hands; her eyes jitter like rattled marbles.

Barrett pushes me behind him, shielding me with his body, and speaks in the calm manner he learned for taming panicky, dangerous criminals. "It's all right, Miss Napier. Drop the gun and we'll talk."

She reaches in her skirt pocket, brings forth a key, and tosses it on the floor. "Get Venetia and Maude."

A second later, Venetia and Jenny come panting up behind me. Venetia cries, "Aunt Caro, what are you doing?"

"Get out of the house," I urge them. "Run away, now."

"Everyone stay where you are, or I'll shoot!" Caroline screams.

Barrett, Jenny, Venetia, and I all stand immobile. Mick says to Venetia, "It's gonna be all right." She can't take her bewildered gaze off Caroline. Hugh looks at his gun, as if wondering whether he can grab it before Caroline shoots. Caroline kicks his gun into the pool, where it splashes and sinks. Jenny and August Legrand's attention is all for each other.

"Jenny, *ma cherie.*" Threatening rebuke hushes Mr. Legrand's voice. His pale eyes feast on her damaged face. "You should have known that you could not escape me forever."

Jenny trembles; her eyes glitter with tears.

"Mother, who is he?" Venetia says.

"Tell her, Jenny. Tell everyone that you are my wife and not that woman you have been impersonating."

Jenny's throat spasms as if she's swallowing guilt as well as panic. There's no surprise on Caroline's tense white face.

Venetia tugs Jenny's hand. "Why are you so afraid of him? What did he do to you?"

"Jenny." The menace in Mr. Legrand's voice intensifies.

Even while Jenny flings up her arm as if to ward off a blow, a reflex born of habit, she speaks up bravely. "I went into the cellar. I saw the paintings of your other wives. I know what you did to them. And when you caught me, you locked me in there and did the same things to me." She touches her neck, once bruised from his choking her, and the scars on her face. "You painted me while I suffered."

"Shut up!" Mr. Legrand contorts his body, trying to free himself.

"That night, you made me put on the red dress. You told me it was the same dress that the others wore before you killed them."

Their deaths weren't suicides. The gossip that his housekeeper had heard was true, and Mr. Legrand is Bluebeard indeed.

Jenny turns to me. "One night, he forgot to lock the door. I ran away. At the station, I got on the first train that came. That's all I remember until I woke up in the hospital." Her remorseful gaze pleads for my understanding. "I'm sorry I lied to you after you saved my life. But I knew that if I went back to him, he would kill me. The day of the identity parade, I decided I would pretend to remember that I was Peggy Oliphant or Maude Napier—whosever family I liked better. Just so I could have someone else's life instead of my own."

Now I understand why, after seeing the Oliphants, she'd been so upset that she fainted. She was afraid that the new family she chose would be no refuge.

"And when I saw Venetia—well, I've told you the rest," Jenny says. "Can you forgive me?"

"Yes." I can. She did what was necessary to survive; so have I, albeit in different circumstances. But forgiving doesn't mean condoning her fraud or excusing the consequences.

"Caroline, I'm sorry I deceived you too and abused your hospitality," Jenny says. "If I hadn't become so fond of you and Venetia, I'd have been gone long ago."

A caustic laugh bursts from Caroline. "Don't flatter yourself. You didn't deceive me. The minute I saw you at the identity parade, I knew you weren't Maude." She smirks at the surprise on everyone's faces.

Mr. Trevelyan had said she was too smart to be fooled. I'd thought so too, and we were both right. Now I remember her strange reaction when she "recognized" Maude. "If you knew, why did you play along with her?" I ask. "Why not say she was pretending, and Venetia was mistaken?"

Caroline's eyes jitter faster, as if trying to follow her own rapid thoughts. "It was to my advantage." She says to Mick, "Get the knife." When he doesn't move, she points the gun at me and says, "Or I'll shoot Miss Bain."

My hands fly up of their own volition. Jenny wasn't the only person engaged in a masquerade. Caroline had hidden behind the guise of a gentle spinster, a devoted aunt and sister-in-law. She must have hired new servants who wouldn't know that Maude wasn't Maude. Now her guise has disintegrated, and I see a maniacal stranger whose intentions I can't fathom. The little black hole at the end of the pistol is a glimpse of the oblivion that she could blast me into. I calm my fear by thinking that as long as she's aiming at me, she can't shoot anyone else.

Mick picks up the knife. Caroline glances at Mr. Legrand and says, "Cut him loose."

Jenny gasps. "No!"

"Listen, Miss Napier," Hugh says, "why don't we put the weapons aside and start over with a nice, civilized chat over a cup of tea?"

"Do it!" Caroline orders Mick.

Mick reluctantly slices the ropes that bind Mr. Legrand's wrists and ankles. Mr. Legrand flexes his cramped muscles, groans, and staggers to his feet. He never once takes his smoldering gaze off Jenny. As she backs away from him, Caroline says, "Stay still."

My life depends on everyone following her orders. I trust Hugh, Mick, and Barrett, but not the others. And Caroline hasn't promised to let us go unharmed, whatever we do.

"Give Mr. Legrand the knife," Caroline says.

"Why—" The gun pointed at me chokes off my voice.

Mick frowns, hesitates, then holds the knife flat on his palm and offers it to Mr. Legrand.

Although his pale eyes narrow in suspicion, Mr. Legrand snatches the knife.

"You wanted to kill your wife," Caroline says. "Go ahead."

Everybody joins in my exclamation of shock and protest. Venetia thrusts herself between Jenny and Mr. Legrand. "I won't let you!" When Mick tries to pull her away, she fights him. "Let me go!"

Mr. Legrand flips the knife's blade open with a deadly click, seeming astonished and elated to be granted his wish in a way he never imagined.

"I'll see that she's punished for impersonating Maude," Barrett tells Caroline. "There's no need to take justice into your own hands."

Caroline emits a nervous giggle that turns into a bray of contempt. "You think justice is what this is about? You're a fool."

"He ain't gonna get away with it," Mick declares. "Neither are you."

"Not with five witnesses," Hugh says.

Caroline speaks in a mechanical tone, like a schoolgirl reciting a lesson she's memorized. "Mr. Legrand killed the police constable. He broke into the house and killed Maude, then Venetia. When Miss Bain, Lord Hugh, and Mr. O'Reilly tried to stop him, he killed them too. I got Father's gun, but I was too late to do anything but shoot Mr. Legrand."

"He won't live to tell. I won't be blamed." The mutterings that Mr. Legrand heard from Caroline begin to make sense, and my mind balks at the scenario she's concocted, into which she worked

my comrades and me after our unexpected arrival. I ask her one of my many questions. "Why would you have him kill Venetia? I thought you loved her."

"Venetia is in the way. With her gone, I can write my music, go abroad, and do whatever else I like."

"If you don't want to take care of her, then hire a governess," I say. "Abandon her, but for God's sake, let her live."

"I haven't the money." Caroline sounds as practical as though we're discussing household budgets. "Writing, performing, and teaching music doesn't pay enough to live on, at least not for women. I need to sell the house."

"Why not just sell it and, hi, ho for the seven seas?" Hugh says.

Caroline regards him as if his question is stupid. "Because the house isn't mine. Father left it and the rest of his estate to Cyril— my brother. When Cyril died, Maude and Venetia inherited everything."

If I dared move my raised hands, I would clap them over my head. Hugh voices my thoughts. "We assumed you were the wealthy owner of the mansion. Just goes to show how wrong assumptions can be."

There's another layer to Caroline's disguise, a veil under a veil; this night seems a chain of revelations with no end in sight.

"I'm just the caretaker," Caroline says bitterly. "For that I get to live in this house, on a stingy allowance. But if Maude and Venetia die, I inherit the house and the money. I'll be free."

That explains why she didn't give my friends and me a warm welcome when we came to visit—she was afraid we would tumble to the truth about her status and her scheme to eliminate Maude and Venetia. If I can persuade her that it won't work, maybe I can save us all.

"There's one problem with your plan," I say, and point at Jenny. "Remember, she's not Maude."

"It doesn't matter. Everybody except the people in this room thinks she is."

And now, with a sudden shock, I see how and why I came to be arrested for Frances's murder. "It was you who told Inspector Reid that you heard me with Frances that night. You forged the letter from me and planted it in her pocketbook. You were afraid 'Maude' would be arrested for the murder, and the police would discover who she really is. That would have ruined your plan."

"Bravo." Caroline smiles sardonically, then glances at Mr. Legrand: "Kill Venetia first. Then your wife."

Venetia screams. Jenny wraps her in a protective embrace.

"This is an outrage!" It seems that even a multiple murderer has scruples; Mr. Legrand doesn't want to kill an innocent child. Then he says haughtily, "If you are going to kill me, then kill me, but I will not cooperate with your scheme to blame all these deaths on me. I have my reputation to protect. You will have to kill the others yourself."

I see the first twitch of uncertainty on Caroline's face.

Barrett hurries to press our advantage. "When the real Maude hears what happened, she'll come back from Egypt. The house belongs to her. Do you think you can kill her too?"

Caroline's face relaxes, as if she's sidestepped quicksand and reached firmer ground. "I don't need to kill her. I already did."

Chapter 30

"Holy Mother of God," Mick whispers.

I stagger as my shock collides with disbelief. Groans emanate from Hugh and Barrett.

"But I saw the letter from Maude, from Egypt." And then I understand.

"I forged her letters too," Caroline says smugly. "I traced her manuscripts."

Mr. Legrand and the Oliphants aren't the only ones with murders to their names. And I thought I'd reunited Sleeping Beauty with the best family of the three possibilities.

Jenny covers Venetia's ears, but Venetia pushes Jenny's hands away. "No, I want to hear."

"Maude was going to send Venetia away to school and sell the house," Caroline says. "She had a lover—a woman author she met in Egypt. They were planning to travel the world together. After I nursed her back to health, the ungrateful wretch was going to throw me out on the street with nothing!"

She hid her lover like my mother hid Lucas Zehnpfennig; and she, like my mother, had put her daughter second behind the person who meant more to her. "How did you know?"

"When I went through Maude's things, I found letters from the woman. I had a bit of worry over her. What if she turned up someday looking for Maude? Then I forged a letter from Maude, saying she was breaking it off, staying in England, and thought it best that they didn't see each other again." Caroline smiles at her own cleverness.

If only I had encouraged Barrett to pursue his inquiries regarding Maude, he might have discovered that she'd never returned to Egypt, never left England. Now he asks Caroline, "How did you kill her?"

"I put monkshood in her medicine. It grows in the garden. While she had convulsions and gasped for breath, she begged me to call the physician. But I couldn't, because he might figure out what I'd done. I waited hours for her to die, and she just wouldn't. I hadn't given her enough monkshood. Then she accused me of poisoning her. I couldn't let her live to tell. So I strangled her." Caroline's teeth and free hand clench as if with the remembered effort of throttling Maude.

Venetia has been listening with a fierce scowl on her face. "You killed my mother."

Caroline regards her with neither pity nor remorse. "It was when you went on holiday with the neighbors."

"And when I came home, you said she'd gone back to Egypt!"

"Where is Maude?" Hugh asks Caroline.

"I put her body down an old well in the garden." She couldn't notify the authorities that Maude had died and let them find the telltale bruises around her neck. "Later, I had the well filled in and the gazebo built over it."

I had photographed Jenny in that gazebo. Maude was buried below us, and we were oblivious to the fact. Venetia's instinct had been right—Maude *was* in London.

"Now I don't have to keep pretending she's alive." Caroline speaks with relief rather than guilt. "I don't have to pretend I believe *she's* Maude." She points at Jenny.

I can stop this charade.

"But with Maude's body hidden, and nobody aware that she was dead, how did you think you were going to inherit the house?" Hugh says.

"I was going to wait a few years, then report Maude missing. Nobody would find any trace of her. I packed up all her things and threw them in the river. She'd have been declared dead. Now I don't need to wait."

"If Maude were declared dead, the house would belong to Venetia." I feel sick to my stomach because I see the rest of Caroline's cold-blooded scheme.

"Venetia would have fallen down the stairs or drowned in the bath." Caroline sounds as matter-of-fact as if she's predicting the weather. "Terrible, but accidents do happen to children."

Venetia cries, "You pretended she left me without saying goodbye!"

"That was bloody cruel," Mick says.

Caroline shrugs, all her feigned affection for Venetia gone. "She was going to leave you anyway. And knowing what a selfish, neglectful mother she was, I can promise you'd never have seen her again."

"You tricked me with those letters."

Venetia's anguish touches on my own. My father left me without saying goodbye; my mother tricked me. But I'm better off than Venetia because neither of my parents was murdered, and the one I long for is still alive.

"You were happier to think she was writing to you than you would have been if there weren't any letters," Caroline says.

"I loved you." Venetia's eyes are bright with tears. "I thought you loved me. I thought you loved my mother."

"You're standing between me and everything I love," Caroline says in the same cold, matter-of-fact tone. "So was she. Mr. Legrand has given me a chance to get rid of you both."

"My lucky break. Two birds with one stone. I'll be free."

"You're mean. I hate you!" Venetia charges at Caroline, fists raised.

"No, don't!" I shout.

Mick lunges and grabs Venetia. They slam into Caroline, who screams as they knock her to the floor. Venetia explodes in a frenzy of punching, kicking, and shrieking.

"Venetia!" Jenny hurries to join the scuffle.

Mick, caught between Venetia and Caroline, tries to push Venetia away while Caroline flails. "Somebody, get her gun!"

I stomp on Caroline's wrist. She shrieks but doesn't let go of the gun. In the same moment that I see it's pointed at me, there's a loud bang. Sparks fly from the muzzle, I hear shouts of alarm through a haze of pungent smoke, and I feel a thud against my right shoulder.

I've been shot.

Even as I realize it, I can't believe it. My surprise overwhelms physical sensation, and it doesn't hurt. I feel only warm wetness flowing down my arm and see the black-rimmed hole in my gray dress, the cloth darkening with blood.

Venetia, Mick, and Jenny spring away from Caroline as if hurled by the gunshot. Mr. Legrand, knife in hand, lunges at Jenny. Barrett cries, "Sarah!" and rushes to me.

Now a throbbing pain begins, like an alien creature hatching inside my flesh. It has teeth; it gnaws. Suddenly, my weight is too much for my legs to bear. They crumple, and Barrett catches me, eases me to the floor. Hugh tackles Mr. Legrand. They go down together with a crash. Venetia grabs Jenny by the hand, and they flee out the front door as Hugh and Mr. Legrand fight for possession of the knife.

Barrett examines my wound. The gentle touch of his fingers feels like blades stabbing me, and I moan. "The bullet's lodged inside you. You're lucky Caroline's gun is small with not much power." He's trying to sound calm, but I sense his panic.

"I'm all right," I say while my mind screams with the fear that I'm going to die.

Caroline, wild-eyed and gasping, scrambles to her feet. She aims the gun in one direction then another, as if she can't decide whom to shoot next. Mick picks up the poker from the floor and throws it at her. She dodges and it shatters a windowpane in the French doors. When she aims the gun at Mick, he ducks behind the staircase. Mr. Legrand breaks away from Hugh. Then Caroline runs after Jenny and Venetia. So does Mr. Legrand, no doubt to capture Jenny and take her to some private place where he can do with her what he will.

"Stop them!" I urge Barrett.

Hugh and Mick give chase. Barrett lifts me, carries me into the parlor, and lays me on a sofa. He kneels beside me and presses his hand against the wound.

"Don't!" It feels like a hot iron clamped over the pain that throbs and gnaws more savagely.

"I'm sorry. I have to stop the bleeding."

Panic makes my heart beat fast and hard, pumping more life-blood out of me. I hear running footsteps outside, and I seize Barrett's wrist. "Go help Hugh and Mick." My fate is sealed; either I'm going to die or I'm not, but they still have a chance to stop Caroline and Mr. Legrand, rescue Venetia and Jenny, and survive. "Please!"

Barrett's eyes fill with grief-stricken realization: This could be my last wish—for him to save my friends—and he doesn't want to leave me, but he can't refuse me. He takes his hand off the wound, presses mine against it, and says, "Keep pressing. I'll be back soon to take you to the hospital. You'll be fine, I promise." He kisses me hard, perhaps for the last time. His gaze locks with mine as if it could anchor me to the world of the living. "When this is over, we're going to get married. We won't let anything stop us."

I nod even as our marriage recedes into a future I'll never see. When he's gone, I lie rigid, straining my ears for sounds outside. I can't hear anything except my own labored breaths and the tick of a clock. I think of my father and all my lost opportunities to find him. Now I'll never see him again. I'll never see Sally again. As my physical strength deserts me, passionate emotions swell to fill the void. I can't bear to languish while my friends are in danger and two killers are on the loose, and I experience an urgency that's even stronger than my need to help them. I sit up. Despite the faintness that stipples my vision with black spots, I swing my legs over the side of the sofa. The fear that Caroline will kill everyone else and come back for me isn't the reason I rise shakily to my feet. My hand, still pressed against my wound, is drenched with blood, and the throbbing in my shoulder sends waves of agony down my arm, but I stagger to the open front door. A yearning such as I've never felt before propels me outside.

It's loneliness for the company of those I love, the fervent wish not to die alone.

The front walk and garden are deserted. I hobble to the gate. The wind is blowing so fiercely, it almost knocks me down. Thunder booms louder, closer. The pools of light under the street lamps teem with moving shadows—from the trees above or from human movement? The night is filled with noise made by rustling foliage, wind chimes tinkling, and debris scattering. Then I hear footsteps pound the earth behind the house. Mr. Legrand must have chased Jenny and Venetia into the back garden. I tiptoe around the house, guided by the lights from the windows. On the terrace, empty chairs stand. Vines hanging from the pergola wave like tentacles. Blood seeps down my sleeve and onto my hand, which is ice-cold. I'm afraid that if I try to move it, I'll discover it's paralyzed. It dangles like the wax hand on a mannequin as I stagger down the steps to the lawn. Within the dark shrubbery, an indistinct figure emerges.

Caroline?

I leap backward, causing a bolt of pain that drops me to my knees. Stifling a moan, I realize the figure is only a statue. I struggle to my feet. The whole right side of my body is weak, heavy, and I list toward it as I start down the gravel path. I hear footsteps crunching on dried leaves, but I can't tell from which direction. No one speaks. Venetia and Jenny don't want to betray their whereabouts to Caroline and Mr. Legrand, who in turn don't want Mick, Hugh, or Barrett to catch them. My friends keep quiet, lest they provoke an attack from Mr. Legrand or gunfire from

Caroline. It's a silent game of hide-and-seek, with life or death the consequences. I join in despite my animal fear that Mr. Legrand and Caroline can smell the blood on me.

The air grows colder as the storm approaches, and the bleeding drains warmth from my body. The light from the house diminishes as I venture deeper into the garden. I lurch from tree to tree, pausing to hide behind each while I rest. The throbs of pain in my shoulder coalesce into a single, relentless ache that makes it harder to move after I stop. My breaths are too loud; I can't control them. The gazebo looms like a skeletal haunted house. I collapse beside it and hear footsteps coming toward me. I think they belong to Barrett. I want so much for it to be him that I forsake caution and crawl in their direction.

Mr. Legrand materializes out of the shadows that distort him into an ogre. He raises his head, as if to sniff his prey. His eyes, and the blade of the knife in his hand, shine with reflections of the dim light. I dive back into the shadow of the gazebo and wait, heart pounding, clammy with sweat and blood. My mind, addled by fear and pain, conjures up a vision of Maude Napier curled under the gazebo, her flesh worm-eaten. Mr. Legrand steals past me and vanishes into the shrubbery. Even as I exhale with relief, I feel my strength seeping away. Blood leaks between the fingers of my hand pressed against my wound. As I wonder if there's a back way out of the garden and everyone except myself has left the premises, I hear whispering.

"Where are they? What am I going to do? Oh God." It's Caroline. Buffeted by the wind, she falters between the trees like a lame ghost.

I stagger after her. If I can take her by surprise, knock her down, and seize the gun, that will leave only Mr. Legrand for my friends to capture. But my eyes play tricks—I see two, then three Carolines. I limp after the one I think is real and find myself alone in the rose garden. The sweet perfume makes me dizzier. The thunder, the roar of blood in my ears, and the quickening tempo of my pulse are like a magic incantation that urges me to lie down among the roses and let death come.

A muffled squeal startles me into alertness. I trudge for what seems like miles to the darkest part of the garden, by the outbuildings.

"No!" The voice, shrill with horror, is Jenny's.

Human figures are grouped by the coach house; I can't tell how many. Running footsteps pelt the ground. A sudden, brilliant light chases away the darkness. Squinting into it, I see a double image of Barrett holding a lantern that he must have brought from the house. The images blend into one as he sees me and his eyes flare with alarm. Hugh and Mick come running up behind him. The scene illuminated by the lantern captures our attention. Mr. Legrand is clasping Venetia against him with his left hand over her mouth while his right hand holds the knife to her throat. Her feet kick helplessly above the ground. Her eyes roll as she strains away from the blade and squeals.

"Please don't hurt her!" Jenny cries.

Sweat trickles down Mr. Legrand's face, over his bared teeth. In the moments since I last saw him, he's shed the trappings of civilization and become Bluebeard, the beast drooling over his prey.

"Let the girl go," Barrett says. "You said you wouldn't kill her. Be a man of your word."

Mr. Legrand ignores Barrett, fixes his crazed stare on his wife. "Jenny." His voice is a growl.

"It's me you want." Sobbing, Jenny says, "Take me instead."

"It wasn't supposed to turn out this way." His growl turns mournful. "When I first laid eyes on you, I thought you were my goddess, my salvation."

I recall the paintings at his house, in which every woman is Jenny.

"You were so beautiful. So good, so kind. I hoped your love would exorcise the devil that possesses me. I thought you could drive the darkness out of my life and let in the light."

My mind swims in the dark ocean between this world and the next. Notions surface and submerge like luminous dolphins, with unnatural clarity. Mr. Legrand's paintings of Pluto and Proserpine take on a new meaning. Pluto kidnapped Proserpine not out of lust or greed but a desire for redemption. Mr. Legrand wanted Jenny for the same reason. The events that led up to tonight stem from a story that had begun long before he met her, long before it turned into "Sleeping Beauty."

"It can still be that way." Jenny reaches her trembling, gloved hand toward him. "I love you. Let me help you."

"It's too late. The devil is too strong. He lured you down to the cellar and showed you my terrible paintings of my other wives." The anguish in his tone evokes scenes of cruelty, torture, and suffering. "I couldn't resist when he bade me to treat you as I did them. Jenny, I am sorry."

"I forgive you. Let Venetia go. Come to me." Desperate, Jenny opens her arms wide. She's bargaining her life to save the child of the woman she impersonated. She loves Venetia that much.

"Mr. Legrand," Barrett says, "it's not too late to save yourself. You haven't hurt anybody here yet, and there's no proof that you killed your wives. Just drop the knife and walk away."

"Let me walk away with Jenny, or the girl dies."

"I can't let him kill her!" Jenny cries. "I'll go with him."

"If you go with him, he'll kill you," I say. The mere effort of speaking makes the pain worse. "You know too much." Every word drains more of my strength. "He can't let you live."

He'll always fear that she'll reveal that he tortured her, slashed her face, and killed his other wives. Even if the law never punishes him because it's her word against his and he's an important man, a scandal could ruin the reputation he values.

"As long as Venetia is safe, I don't care." Jenny is a truer mother than Maude Napier, than my own mother. "August?" She beckons him with a smile that renders her scarred, stitched face beautiful, heartbreaking.

With a groan like a wounded animal, he shoves Venetia away from him. She stumbles like the maidens in his painting who fled when Proserpine was kidnapped. He lunges at Jenny and clasps her to him in the same pose as Pluto when he carried Proserpine down to hell in his chariot. He clutches the knife instead of the reins.

Jenny screams, "Run, Venetia!"

"Mother!" Venetia flings herself toward Jenny, but Mick restrains her.

Mr. Legrand caresses Jenny, mauling her with his free hand. "Jenny," he murmurs. His mouth slavers at her neck while she holds herself rigid and weeps. "My Jenny!" He lets loose a stream of endearments, curses, and incoherent laments in French and English.

"August. I love you." Jenny's voice breaks as she sobs. "I always will, no matter what. I'm yours forever."

Now he's sobbing too. She takes his tear-drenched face between her gloved hands and presses her lips to his. He moans, his body convulses, and he gulps as if trying to drink the goodness from her soul.

Forgetting my anger at her deception, I stagger toward them in the vain hope of rescuing Jenny. Weakness overcomes me. My legs totter. I start to fall.

"Sarah!" Barrett catches me, holds my shoulders as we sink onto the grass. I feel the first raindrops pelt my cheeks, or maybe he's crying and they're his tears.

Mr. Legrand detaches his mouth from Jenny's. Panting, he stares at her face; he touches it with tenderness rather than the lust for possession or murder. His pale eyes darken and his complexion flushes, as though her kiss has replaced the human blood that his devil had stolen.

"Jenny." His voice belongs to a man wakened from enchantment. The knife dangles in his hand. He and Jenny smile at each other—she with relief, he with gratitude.

We're in a different story now, I think. She's not Sleeping Beauty anymore; this is the final scene from "Beauty and the

Beast." I hear Barrett call my name, see Hugh and Mick run to me. They look terrified for me, but I'm happy because I'll die surrounded by those I love.

Now Caroline appears at the edge of my vision. I don't know how long she's been close by, watching and listening and trying to make up her mind what to do. All bedraggled hair and wild, bulging eyes, her gun flourished like a magic wand, she's a witch come to cast her ultimate evil spell. *"Kill her!"* she shrieks at Mr. Legrand.

I hear Venetia and Jenny scream. Mr. Legrand releases Jenny and charges toward Caroline. She fires. As the bullet hits his chest, he falters but doesn't stop. She cries out, firing again. Blood spurts from his thigh, and he stumbles as he forges onward. Again, again, and again. His body jerks. Propelled by sheer will, he raises the knife.

The pistol clicks, its chamber empty. Caroline lowers her hand and lets the pistol drop. She stands immobile and stares at Mr. Legrand as if he's as immortal as the Roman king of hell and she's the one bewitched.

He slashes her throat.

CHAPTER 31

I set up my camera on the first-class deck of the *Britannia*, a gigantic steamship that towers above the crowds on the Royal Victoria Dock. The warm, sunny day resounds with ship whistles blasting, a band playing lively music on fiddles and horns, and the rattle of carts and carriages laden with cargo. Passengers on board and people on shore call and wave to one another. At the railing, Barrett, Mick, and Hugh are gathered with Jenny, Venetia, and Sir Gerald for a group portrait. They converse and laugh, their spirits high, as I peer at them through the viewfinder. Jenny wears a blue-and-gray-striped frock and a blue hat with a black veil. Her face has healed well, and with the aid of the veil, she looks normal and quite pretty. Venetia is in a sailor suit and cap, holding binoculars. In the background, other ships are lined up along the dock, flags waving atop the masts, tall funnels belching smoke. I wipe soot off the lens of my camera, breathe the smells of tar, spices, and the high summer reek of the river.

Sally, beside me, says, "Sarah, this is marvelous! I've never been on a ship before, and I'm so happy to be here with you and everybody else."

I smile at her. "You're part of the team now."

Sally scribbles in her notebook, recording descriptions of the scene. "I still can't believe Sir Gerald hired me."

Three weeks have passed since that night at the Napier house, and my friends and I are, for the moment, back in favor with Sir Gerald.

I'd put in a word for Sally, and he'd given her a test assignment—an interview with me, in which I gave a highly edited account of the events that led to August Legrand's and Caroline Napier's deaths. He published it, and now she's the *Daily World*'s new ladies' features writer. It turns out that reportage, not fiction, is her forte—but there's considerable overlap between the two categories.

"Look this way and hold still," I call to the group. They turn toward me, smiles on their faces. I take several photographs. When I'm finished, everyone cheers.

"Thank you all for coming to see us off," Jenny says.

"We wouldn't dream of letting you two set sail without a bon voyage party," Hugh says.

"We couldn't let you get away without a picture for the *Daily World*," Sir Gerald says.

"How do you feel about going to America?" Sally asks Jenny and Venetia.

"I'm excited but a little nervous," Jenny says.

"Don't worry, Mother," Venetia says. "I know how to manage in foreign countries. I'll take good care of you."

A waiter brings us glasses of champagne. Sir Gerald raises his. "A toast to new beginnings."

As we drink, I relive the events of that night. My memory was hazy because of my injury, but later my friends filled in the details for me. Right after August Legrand killed Caroline Napier, we heard a shrill, alarming whistle: The police were coming; they must have heard the gunshots. We had little time to make serious decisions. Hugh and Mick led Venetia and Jenny into the parlor while Barrett carried me. Jenny said, "I think we should tell the truth about everything that's happened. I want to confess that I've been impersonating Maude. My husband and Caroline are dead because of me, and it's only right that I bear the consequences."

"You mustn't!" Aghast, Venetia clung to Jenny and begged us, "Please don't tell anyone that she isn't my real mother. She's all I have!"

Hugh wiped tears from his eyes. "You've convinced me." I knew he was thinking of his own parents, whom he'd lost when they disowned him.

"If we tell, will Venetia have to go to an orphanage?" Mick looked dismayed, as if recalling the strict discipline, bad food, and bleak conditions at the orphanage where he'd lived.

"She'll probably be appointed a guardian and go to a boarding school until she's eighteen," Hugh said.

"I say we let 'em stay together," Mick declared.

"We're the only people who know Jenny isn't Maude," Hugh said. "Caroline and Mr. Legrand can't blab."

"I have to report Maude's murder," Barrett said.

That was the most serious but not the only reason against colluding in a fraud.

"He's right," Jenny told Venetia. "We can't just let your mother stay buried under the gazebo."

"Caroline's been punished," Mick said. "That oughta be good enough."

"But Maude deserves a proper funeral," Jenny said.

"Mother, listen to Mick and Hugh," Venetia urged. "They're right."

"I have to tell the police that my husband killed his previous wives. Their families deserve to know that they didn't commit suicide."

"He's been punished too," Hugh says, "and a big scandal won't help their families."

Then came a heavy knock at the door and shouts from outside: "Police! Open up!"

"Sarah, what do you think we should do?" Mick said.

Mine was the deciding vote. With no more leisure to vacillate, I did what my heart said was right. How many laws we've broken, I hate to imagine, and I've more secrets to add to my cache.

Now Barrett moves close to me and says in a low voice, "Are you feeling all right?"

After I was shot, I spent a week in the hospital, where I had an operation to remove the bullet from my shoulder, and Dr. Enoch gave me intravenous fluids to remedy the blood loss. I'm still sore and weak, and I can't lift anything heavy, but I've regained full use of my hand.

"I'm fine," I say. "Just thinking."

He nods with a wry smile; the same thoughts and secrets can never be far from his own mind.

"Sir Gerald, we want to thank you for all you've done for us," Jenny says.

"My pleasure," Sir Gerald says.

I suspect that paying for their luxury accommodations on shipboard and in American hotels isn't all he's done. That night, when the police came, Barrett told them that August Legrand had killed the constable and broken into the house, and he himself, our friends, and I had arrived in time to see Mr. Legrand attacking Jenny outside while Caroline threatened to shoot him. Mr. Legrand had turned on Caroline. Before he cut her throat, she fired the gun, shooting me by accident and mortally wounding him. The rest of us corroborated Barrett's story. It's the one that Sally wrote up in my interview for the *Daily World*. Sally knows the truth. There are secrets I keep from her, but the events of that night aren't among them. How much Sir Gerald knows, or has guessed, is another matter. He never challenged our story, and we weren't told what was said during a private talk he had with Jenny and Venetia the next day. When we all testified at the inquest, the coroner accepted the story without question, ruling that Mr. Legrand had murdered Caroline and she'd shot him in self-defense. In addition, the official cause of Frances Oliphant's death has been changed from murder to death by misadventure. My friends and I think Sir Gerald twisted some arms in high places.

Now we all smile at Sir Gerald, thankful that we're no longer murder suspects, but uneasy because he'll expect something from us in return someday. He didn't get where he is by excusing debts.

Sir Gerald smiles at Jenny. "I thought you and your daughter could use a change of scenery."

I also suspect he knows she's not Maude Napier. In America, she's less likely to run into anyone who knows her than in England. I think Jenny and Venetia's plight touched his hard heart. As far as the police and the public are concerned, Jenny Legrand is still a missing person. I only wish Ned Lyle and her other friends could know she's safe.

"The *Daily World*'s readers will be interested to know what your plans are for the future," Sally says to Jenny. She's getting over her shyness. Her job has done wonders for her self-confidence.

"I'm going to be an explorer when I grow up," Venetia says. "I'm going to travel all over the world and discover all sorts of marvelous things."

Everybody laughs, but I can picture her doing exactly that. Jenny smiles at her with affectionate pride and says, "Our plans aren't definite. If we like America, we may settle there."

In America, she can make a fresh start. She's told me that Sir Gerald's bank is handling her and Venetia's financial affairs and the sale of the house. The proceeds, plus the money from Venetia's parents' estate, should be enough to support them for the rest of their lives.

Sally claps her hands. "Can I have your attention? Sarah and Detective Sergeant Barrett have some good news."

My cheeks warm with self-consciousness. Barrett smiles, clears his throat, and says, "We're getting married on September ninth."

The others cheer and applaud. Mick says, "That's less than a month away."

We set the earliest date compatible with making arrangements for our wedding, in the hope that by racing full steam ahead we can mow down any obstacles. Those include the fact that we don't know where we're going to live. At least the top police brass have reinstated Barrett to his detective sergeant duties. They also fired Constable Porter for insubordination and reprimanded Inspector

Reid for letting his personal feud with me affect his professional judgment and trying to railroad me to the gallows based on false evidence. No doubt Reid and Porter are plotting revenge, but Barrett and I won't let them stop us from keeping the pledge we made to each other the night we thought I was going to die.

"It's about time you two tied the knot." Hugh raises his champagne glass. "A toast to the happy couple."

As I drink, I feel as if I'm taking a running leap off a cliff, leaving my fears and doubts behind.

"We'll cover the wedding in the *Daily World*," Sir Gerald says.

I smile through my dismay. After all Sir Gerald has done for us, it would be ungracious to tell him I don't want publicity.

"How about if I take your picture?" Mick says.

Barrett and I stand by the railing, and Mick positions himself behind my camera. I feel uncomfortable on this side of it. As he snaps the shutter, I can envision the photograph—Barrett beaming proudly; me concealing a guilty conscience under a stiff expression. I haven't told anyone that I know my father's whereabouts. I need time to get used to the idea, and I had to recover from my injury before traveling to Brighton. Excuses. Fear is the real reason. Soon I'll tell Barrett, Sally, and our friends. But my old habit of secrecy lingers, and I remain as much a hidden woman as the mothers in the old photographs.

The ship's whistle blows. Deckhands yell, "All ashore that's going ashore!"

"We'd better disembark or we'll find ourselves in New York next week," Hugh says.

Jenny hurries over to me with Venetia. "Sarah, before you go, we want to thank you again."

They understand that I made their fresh start possible, that I could have taken Barrett's side, chosen to tell the police everything that happened that night, and persuaded Hugh and Mick to go along with me. I could have revealed her identity, for the sake of justice. But I went against my moral duty as well as the law. Jenny and Venetia are parent and child in spirit although not blood, their reunion as real as if they were destined to be together.

I am the last person to tear them apart.

Barrett was right to believe that Sleeping Beauty was Jenny Legrand, but I was right too. Sleeping Beauty is Maude Napier, now and forever.

I'm at peace with my job, for it gave me the opportunity to create happiness as well as feed the public's appetite for morbid thrills.

"Good luck." As I shake hands with Jenny, I think of her fingers clasping mine while she was unconscious, and I'm sad to see her go. Under other circumstances, we could have been friends. "Write and let me know how you're doing."

"If I write to you, will you write to me?" Venetia says to Mick.

He gives her a fond smile. "Sure."

They shake hands, and Venetia looks up at him with big, solemn eyes. Then she stands on tiptoe and kisses him quickly on his cheek. He blinks at her in surprise. Her violet eyes glow, her cheeks blush; she looks mischievous, daring, and suddenly years older.

As we walk down the gangway with our companions, Mick looks over his shoulder at Venetia waving to him. "She's somethin', ain't she?" he says in the tone of a man who's been startled from a sound sleep.

I'm not the only one who's seen the Venetia of the future. Even if Mick isn't over Catherine Price, he's woken up to the fact that there are other girls in the world. Perhaps Venetia and Jenny aren't the only ones destined to be together.

On the dock, Hugh stops and frowns at a queue of people waiting to board the ship behind the *Britannia*. There, near the head of the queue, is Tristan Mariner. I know Hugh hasn't seen him since the night he brought Rose to our house. Hugh hurries toward him, calling, "Tristan? What are you doing here?"

The rest of us follow. Tristan sees Hugh and Sir Gerald, and the dismay in his eyes says that running into them is the last thing he wanted.

"Where do you think you're going?" Sir Gerald demands.

"To Switzerland."

"What for?" Hugh looks flabbergasted.

Tristan swallows hard, as if choking down misery. "I need some time away. To think."

Anger darkens Sir Gerald's face. "If you think you can take a holiday from the bank whenever you want—

"It's not a holiday. I'm quitting the bank."

While Sir Gerald stares, speechless, Tristan says to Hugh, "I'm going to a retreat for men who've left the priesthood."

Hugh shakes his head, bewildered and hurt. "When were you planning to tell me?"

Tristan glances up at the ship. It's obvious that he'd planned to tell his father and Hugh after he was in Switzerland. "I didn't know how to. I didn't want to hurt you." From the hunted, haunted expression on his face, I think that if he could disappear into thin air, like my father did, he would. It may be uncharitable of me, but I also think he wanted to avoid recriminations as well as causing pain to Hugh and Sir Gerald.

"You can't do this." Sir Gerald speaks in a loud voice, this man whose mere whisper or gesture compels legions of men to do his bidding.

The queue moves toward the gangway, Tristan with it. "I must, Father."

I notice how thin Tristan is, how his clothes hang on him, how the bruises have faded to reveal the sickly pallor of his skin. I can believe he'll die unless he sorts himself out and comes to terms with the choices he's made. I see the same disturbing knowledge dawn in Hugh's and Sir Gerald's stricken eyes.

"I forbid you." Although Sir Gerald looks to his bodyguards, as if he would order them to keep Tristan from boarding the ship, the wind has gone out of his authority.

"When will you be back?" Hugh says.

A long, yearning look passes between him and Tristan. I can feel the heat of their desire, the anguish of their love. Tristan says, "I don't know."

"Well, then." Hugh grasps for his usual lighthearted manner; he smiles, although his eyes shine with tears. "Can I—your father and I—at least see you aboard?"

"I—no, it would be better if you didn't." Tristan's voice is hoarse with emotion. He reaches the front of the line, hands his ticket to the attendant. As he and a porter with his luggage walk up the gangway, he doesn't look backward.

Mick claps Hugh's shoulder. "Let's get drunk someplace."

"No, you and Barrett take Sarah and Sally home. I'll stay awhile."

Sir Gerald waves his bodyguards toward his carriage, which is parked on the dock. He and Hugh stand together, silently gazing at up Tristan's ship. As I imagine them waiting until it sails and disappears from sight, I'm sad because not all stories have happy endings.

There's another story left to finish.

EPILOGUE

Rain and wind blast me as I walk the deserted promenade in Brighton. On this cold, gray day, the summer guests at the hotels by the ocean are sheltered indoors. The English Channel is rippled with whitecaps. Waves dash the beach, which is devoid of human life . . . except for one man. A dark cap covers his head, and a mackintosh flaps around his legs. Contemplating the stormy seascape, he makes a viewfinder with his hands and looks through it at the ironwork pier where seagulls soar above the pavilion.

I remember seeing my father do this many times.

My heart gives a mighty leap.

Then I'm running down the steps to the beach, across the sand. The years fall away from me, and I'm a child again. "Papa!"

He doesn't hear; the sound of the wind, waves, and shrieking gulls absorbs my voice. I breathlessly stagger up to him, and my footsteps crunch to a halt on broken seashells. He turns. His red, wind-burned face is partially obscured by white whiskers, and a lifetime of peering through a camera lens has narrowed and etched deep lines around his eyes. He nods to me with the polite, quizzical expression of a man accosted by a stranger. Then he blinks, and his eyes widen with recognition, disbelief, and shock.

"Sarah?" His voice is rough with age but heart-wrenchingly familiar.

The spell of the past is broken, the evil that kept us apart vanquished. He reaches toward me. His tearful eyes mirror the joy I feel, and I extend my hand to meet his. Then his drops, and so does mine. Twenty-two years of absence, a gulf wider than the English Channel, separates us.

"How did you find me?"

It's a long story that I'm too shaken up to tell coherently. "Why didn't you let me know you were alive?"

His bushy white eyebrows knit in confusion. "I wrote to you many times. Your mother wrote back and said you wanted nothing to do with me."

"It's not true! All I ever wanted was to see you again!"

My father looks as appalled as I am. "Do you mean she didn't give you my letters?"

"She said you were killed in a riot."

"Oh dear God." My father moans. "She said she told you that I murdered Ellen Casey."

Astounded by this new instance of my mother's deceitfulness, I say, "But she didn't! I found out about the murder on my own, not long ago. Why did she lie?"

My father rubs his mouth. His hand trembles—his hand that was so steady when he taught me to use a camera. "To punish me."

"But why? You're innocent. Lucas Zehnpfennig murdered Ellen Casey."

My father staggers; his eyes go blank. "How do you know of Lucas?"

"Sally told me about the letter you received from him."

The redness drains from my father's cheeks. "You've met Sally."

He seems so distressed by the news that I'm glad I decided not to let her know about him until after I'd seen him. "We know that Lucas was my mother's illegitimate son, and we know about the little girls he violated. Sally will be so happy to hear that I've found you."

"No!" He flings up his hands. "Don't tell her. Forget you saw me, and never come back!"

"Why?" All these years I've harbored the fear that if I found him, he would reject me. Now my eyes sting, and it's not because of the wind. "Don't you want me—or Sally?"

"All I ever wanted was to be with you again! My Sarah! How I've missed you!" His arms spread to embrace me, but when I step forward, he violently waves me off. "I can never be with you or Sally— not after what I've done." The wind gusts; the ocean roars louder, the waves hurling spray at us. My father shouts, "Lucas didn't kill Ellen."

I was so happy to think I've identified the culprit if not found proof that my father is innocent, and now he's telling me I'm wrong. Such grief pains my heart that I clutch my chest.

My father turns away. "You were never supposed to know . . ."

"Know what?" I need to hear it all, no matter how much it hurts. "Tell me!"

He shakes his head, then sinks to his knees on the sand. I crouch near him. The sea and wind and gulls hush, as though all of nature is listening. "That day I was taking photographs of Ellen. I went downstairs to the darkroom to develop them. I left Ellen in the kitchen with Mary—your mother. Then I heard Ellen screaming. By the time I got there, she'd stopped. She was lying half-naked on the floor, not moving. Mary and Lucas were with her. I asked, 'What have you done?' They didn't answer, but it was obvious—Lucas's trousers were open, and there were red bruises around Ellen's neck. She was dead."

The horror of that moment fills my father's eyes. In this moment I feel only confusion because so far his story roughly corresponds to the scenario I'd imagined.

"I thought Lucas had strangled her. I said I was going to the police. But then Mary said, 'I had to stop her screaming.'"

The wind howls; waves crash. *"My mother* killed Ellen?" I fall backward and sit on the sand.

"Lucas said to me, 'If you turn me in, you'll have to turn her in too.' He was so smug, so mocking! But he was right. I couldn't do it."

"Instead, you ran away. And my mother let the police think *you* killed Ellen!" I'd thought my anger at my mother had already reached its peak, but now it's a flaming inferno, for here is the ultimate secret she'd kept from me. "She sacrificed you to save herself and Lucas!"

My father rushes to say, "It wasn't like that. Just listen. Mary said, 'Sarah will be back from school soon.' We couldn't let you find out what had happened. I sent Lucas home to his lodgings, and I carried Ellen to the cellar and put her in a trunk."

I have no recollection of that day; it must have seemed like any other. While I was eating supper and washing the dishes, Ellen lay dead beneath the floor!

"Late that night, Lucas and I sneaked the trunk out of the house, and . . ."

He falls silent, as if he can't bear to admit that while I was asleep, he and the half-brother I didn't know existed were disposing of the girl my mother had strangled. If had to choose which parent should be blamed for the murder, I'd choose my mother, the true criminal. "You shouldn't have protected them. You should have told the police and let them face the consequences!"

My father looks surprised by the suggestion. "Mary was my wife. I loved her; I always tried to protect her. But that's not the only reason I didn't tell. It was to protect *you*." As I frown in disbelief, my father says, "I was an accomplice. I covered up the murder. If I'd told the police the truth, your mother and I both would have been hanged."

I want to protest, but I think he's right.

"You'd have become an orphan, Sarah. Your mother was estranged from her family, and I'm an orphan myself. I grew up in a children's home, a terrible place, and I didn't want the same for you. So I made a bargain with Mary: I would run away and let the police think I killed Ellen—but only if Lucas came with me. I wasn't going to leave you with her while he was still in the picture."

I remember the day Lucas came to our house. My father had found him holding me on his lap and fondling me.

"Mary begged me to let Lucas stay, but he was afraid of the police, so he agreed to go with me even though there was no love lost between us. Mary made me promise to look after him. We went to America. I thought we could make a fresh start there, and if I kept an eye on Lucas, he would behave himself." My father says sadly, "You asked why your mother wanted to punish me. It was because I took away her son. She told you I was dead. She took away my daughter."

Thinking about my mother is unbearable. "Why did you come back to England?"

My father's hand sketches a motion that asks for my patience. "When we reached New York, Lucas sneaked out of our lodgings while I was asleep." Crumpled on the sand, my father looks like a marooned sailor. "I searched for him for years, moving from city to city. But America is vast, and I couldn't find him, and I had to give up. I was homesick, and I thought enough time had passed— the police wouldn't be looking for me anymore—so I came back to England. Not long afterward, I met and married Sally's mother. I didn't hear from Lucas again until his letter came."

There are so many questions my father hasn't answered. His story is like a photographic print that hasn't been in the developing solution long enough for the fine details to emerge.

"Lucas said he was in London. He'd been working for a rich man in Chicago, and he'd raped the man's daughter. The police were after him, and he'd had to leave the country. He asked me for money, and he reminded me that I'd promised Mary I would look after him!" My father is clearly outraged that Lucas had called in the debt after destroying our family. "He asked me to meet him at Liverpool Street station. I knew that if I didn't do it, he would come to my house, and I didn't want him near Sally. So I went.

"He was the same as he was after Ellen died—not ashamed of what he'd done to this other girl, smug because he'd gotten away with it. He was never going to change." My father speaks more slowly, as if dragging the words through a mire of reluctance. "We were walking across the bridge over the train tracks. I pushed Lucas off it. A train ran him over."

I feel my face distort into a grotesque visage of the shock that floods me. It's as if I've gulped salt water into my lungs.

The accident in which Lucas died was no accident.

My father killed Lucas!

I thrash in an attempt to stand up and escape the drowning sensation. I'm Sleeping Beauty, awakened not by a kiss, but by a terrible truth.

My father watches me mournfully. "You're disgusted. I don't blame you."

What I'm really feeling is blindsided, astonished. *My father wasn't responsible for Ellen Casey's death, but he is guilty of murder.*

"But I'm not sorry I killed Lucas. He'll never hurt anyone else." His voice is sad yet resolute. "That's why I never went back to Sally and her mother. Sarah, that's why you must forget you found me. Because there's blood on my hands."

He holds up his chapped, trembling hands, as if Lucas's blood is visible. I stare, breathless, while I absorb the fact that I'm not the only member of my family to deliver a criminal to illegal justice.

He pushes himself up from the sand and trudges away. Once again he's leaving me, and this time I'll lose him forever, unless . . .

I lumber to my knees, run to him, and grasp his blood-tainted hands in my own. "Father. Listen." I tell him the story that few people outside my circle of friends know, about the events leading up to, during, and after my hunt for Jack the Ripper. The distant and near past mix like photographic chemicals to produce a startling picture.

Two outlaws swapping confessions on a cold, windy beach isn't the reunion I dreamed of having with my father.

His eyes show bewilderment and surprise, dismay and shock, and finally horror. His hands are as coldly inanimate as stone.

When I'm finished, he doesn't immediately speak, and I wait in an agony of suspense.

Sometimes a pot will call the kettle blacker.

Then my father exhales, and his hands clasp mine. "Sarah, I'm sorry. There's something in me that made me do what I did. I must have passed it on to you."

But if there's such a thing as bad blood that renders one capable of murder, then my mother had it too. *"A chip off the old block,"* Mrs. Albert had called me. Neither she nor I knew that it was both blocks.

"We're both on the wrong side of the law," I say. "There's no reason not to be there together."

He frowns as though he can't believe this turn of events, then breathes as though a weight has lifted off him. "I suppose you're right. But Sally—"

"Sally will understand."

We look down at our joined hands. My father says, "My only regret is that I abandoned my daughters. Can you ever trust me again?"

I remember those awful weeks after he disappeared, the lonely years when I thought he was dead. But I shan't dwell on the past while I'm where I've waited twenty-four years to be—with my father. The ocean wind chills me to the bone, but I breathe it in huge gulps that expand my lungs. I glory in the miracle that I'm here, alive, feeling the cold and the joy, the anger and sorrow, and everything else I'm feeling. I smile at my father.

He smiles, his eyes brimming with love that warms me for the moment before trepidation clouds them. "I'm still wanted by the police, Sarah. I'll be a fugitive for the rest of my life."

Everything has changed, and nothing has changed. I've solved the mystery of my family's past, but the two people who could exonerate my father are both dead. Still, I shan't let that tragic fact spoil our reunion.

"Never mind that now," I say. "We've so much else to talk about."

We stand side by side, gazing out to sea, as if waiting to take a photograph of the future that has yet to appear on the horizon, that we must face bravely when the time comes.